Lucy Ellis has four loves in life: books, expensive lingerie, vintage films and big, gorgeous men who have to duck going through doorways. Weaving aspects of them into her fiction is the best part of being a romance writer. Lucy lives in a small cottage in the foothills outside Melbourne.

New York Times and *USA Today* bestselling author **Barbara Dunlop** has written more than fifty novels for Mills & Boon, including the acclaimed *Gambling Men* series for Mills & Boon Desire. Her sexy, light-hearted stories regularly hit bestsellers lists. Barbara is a four-time finalist for the Romance Writers of America's RITA® award.

Niobia Bryant is the award-winning and national bestselling author of more than forty works of romance and commercial mainstream fiction. Twice she has won the RT Reviewer's Choice Best Book Award for African American/Multicultural Romance. Her books have appeared in *Ebony*, *Essence*, *The New York Post*, *The Star-Ledger*, *The Dallas Morning News* and many other national publications. One of her bestselling books was adapted to film.

Confessions

Confessions of the Billionaire

LUCY ELLIS

BARBARA DUNLOP

NIOBIA BRYANT

MIX
Paper from
responsible sources
FSC   FSC® C007454

This book is produced from independently certified FSC™ paper
to ensure responsible forest management.

For more information visit www.harpercollins.co.uk/green

Printed and bound in Spain using 100% Renewable electricity at
CPI Book Print Barcelona

MILLS & BOON

First Published in Great Britain 2022
By Mills & Boon, an imprint of HarperCollins*Publishers*
1 London Bridge Street, London, SE1 9GF

www.harpercollins.co.uk

HarperCollins*Publishers*
1st Floor, Watermarque Building,
Ringsend Road, Dublin 4, Ireland

CONFESSIONS OF THE BILLIONAIRE © 2022
Harlequin Enterprises ULC

Redemption of a Ruthless Billionaire © 2018 Lucy Ellis
The Illegitimate Billionaire © 2018 Barbara Dunlop
A Billionaire Affair © 2018 Niobia Bryant

ISBN: 978-0-263-30573-9

REDEMPTION OF
A RUTHLESS
BILLIONAIRE

LUCY ELLIS

To the memory of my dear dad—Robert 'Jim' Giblett—who didn't get to see this one finished after many hours on the phone listening to me making up these stories, laughing in the right places and telling me I could do it when I thought I couldn't.

Life isn't the same without you, Dad.

You were everything to me.

Your Lucy/Kareena

CHAPTER ONE

'I'VE FOUND YOU a girl,' was the unexpected news his grandfather greeted Nik Voronov with cheerfully. 'She's local, so you'll have to come down.'

The key words, Nik suspected, were, *You'll have to come down.*

His conscience pricked. He hadn't set out ten years ago, when he'd founded his company, to work twelve-hour days and seven-day weeks, but he did. He had the world on his shoulders, and his grandfather more of late on his conscience, and balancing the two was hard.

Nik lowered his head as a gust of wind buffeted him on the approach to the complex of site buildings where he had an office.

Around him was the site where his company, Voroncor, were sinking down exploratory equipment and mining kimberlite deposits from the rich Siberian earth. Work went on all year round, and because it was January everything was white except in patches where the ashy black earth showed through.

At least the wind had died down and he could see what he was looking at. Three years' hard work to pull this reserve into the Voroncor fold.

'Is that right, Deda?'

'Her name is Sybella and she has everything a man could want. She cooks and cleans and she's wonderful with children!'

The triumvirate of qualities guaranteed to ensure a man a good life, according to his seventy-nine-year-old grandfather.

Nik was well aware he could remind the old man he had

a chef on the payroll, cleaning staff for all four of his international residences and no children to speak of. Moreover, no woman in the twenty-first century would view cooking, cleaning and raising children her sole responsibility.

But he'd be wasting his breath and it wasn't the point.

Tactfully he rolled out the line he'd been using since his grandfather became actively interested in his personal life, which had—not mysteriously—coincided with the loss of his own wife, Nik's adored grandmother.

'When and if I do meet the right woman, you'll be the first to know, Deda.'

His grandfather harrumphed. 'I've seen you on the Internet with that model.'

The Internet? The last time they'd spoken the old man was using the tablet he'd got him as a tea tray.

But he knew who his grandfather was referring to.

Voroncor's sister company Voroncor Holdings had bought out a retail corporation and Nik found himself in possession of some premium retail brands, including the fashion house Spanish model/actress and 'it' girl Marla Mendez was currently spruiking for.

The lady had pursued him around the world seeking his investment in her personal project, a lingerie line, not exactly his field but he had a personal reason for stumping up the funds that had nothing to do with Ms Mendez herself. A few photographs of them together at events had been enough for the tabloids to seize on the idea they were personally involved. He saw no reason to set his grandfather straight.

'That woman is not right for you, Nikolka. There is something hard about her. She would not be good with little children.'

Nik considered reminding his grandfather he had no children, but he suspected that was Deda's point.

'Sybella works with children,' his grandfather added helpfully.

No surprises there.

'I think you should come and see her at work. I think you would be impressed, *moy mal'chik*.'

There was a long pause as Nik shouldered his way down the corridor and into his office, signalling for a coffee as he passed one of his admin assistants.

'Did you hear me, Nikolka?'

'I'm here, Deda. How did you meet her?'

Nik began pulling off his gloves, idly glancing at the information he'd asked for on the screen of a laptop another assistant silently opened in front of him.

'She lives down the lane from the Hall, in the village. She's a tenant. I believe she pays you rent.'

Vaguely Nik remembered some old English custom of the squire having first rights to local virgins. He held fire on mentioning it to his grandfather.

When he'd bought Edbury Hall a year ago he'd flown over in a helicopter. The village below had been merely a small sea of roofs swallowed up by the encroaching forest. His attention had been on the magnificent Elizabethan 'E', its outbuildings and the undulating pastureland around it.

His lawyer had done the groundwork and put everything in place. The purchase was a good investment, and it currently housed his grandfather while he was in the UK undergoing tests and treatment for a variety of complaints set off by his diabetes.

Nik hadn't paid much attention to a lane, or the village, or the fact he had tenants. His admin dealt with that.

'What are you doing consorting with the tenants? That's not your problem, Deda. You're supposed to be relaxing.'

'Sybella comes to the house to keep me company and help me out with a few secretarial things.'

'You have staff for that.'

'I prefer Sybella. She is genuine.'

'She sounds great,' Nik said mildly enough, making a mental note to ask a few questions of the house staff. He didn't want his grandfather's kindly nature being taken advantage of.

'We have a busload of children from all over the county once a month, up to thirty at a time, and Sybella is unflappable.'

'Unflappable, good to know.' Nik indicated he had what he needed. Then his head shot up. 'Busloads of—what? Hang on, Deda, where is this?'

'At the Hall. The children who come to see the house.'

Nik stopped finding this amusing. 'Why are busloads of children coming to the house?' But he already knew.

'The Heritage Trust show them around,' Deda said cheerfully.

The Heritage Trust. The local historic buildings preservation group, who had kept the Hall open to the public since the nineteen seventies.

His purchase a year ago had shut all commercial activities at the Hall down. There had been a picket at the end of the drive for a week in protest until he'd called in the police.

'This is not what we agreed, Deda.'

'I know what you're about to say,' his grandfather blustered, 'but I changed my mind. Besides, no final decision was made.'

'No, we talked about it when you moved in and we decided to leave the matter in my hands.'

'And now it's in Sybella's,' his grandfather said smugly. Sybella.

Nik couldn't help picturing one of the matronly women who had picketed the drive, in her husband's oversized hunting jacket and wellington boots, face like the back of a shovel, shouting about British heritage and marching a troop of equally appalling kids through his grandfather's home. When she wasn't going through Deda's papers and possibly siphoning his bank account.

This was not what he wanted to hear. He had a new pipe starting up in Archangelsk, which would keep him in the north for much of this year. Business was expanding and he needed to be on site.

But now he had a new problem: a white elephant of a property sitting up in the English Cotswolds he'd been ignoring for too long, currently housing his grandfather and apparently the local historical group.

Nik didn't have time for this, but he knew he was going to have to make time.

'And what does this *Sybella* have to do with the Heritage Trust when she's not cooking and cleaning and herding children?' he asked tightly.

His grandfather chuckled and delivered the coup de grâce. 'She runs it.'

CHAPTER TWO

THE PRESIDENT OF the local branch of the Heritage Trust stood up, removed her glasses and announced somewhat dolefully to the committee members assembled that a legal document had been lodged this morning at the trust's London office suspending any further activity of the trust in the Hall.

'Does that mean we can't use the empty gatehouse as a visitors' centre?' Mrs Merrywether wanted to know. 'Because Sybella said we could.'

A dozen grey heads turned and Sybella found herself sinking a little lower in her chair, because she had indeed waved a letter around last month claiming they had the right.

But dodging responsibility wasn't her way.

'I can't understand why this has happened,' she told the meeting, feeling very guilty and responsible for the confusion that had gripped the room. 'I'll look into it and sort it out. I promise.'

Seated beside her Mr Williams, the retired local accountant, patted her arm. 'We know you will, Sybella, we trust your judgement. You haven't led us wrong once.'

There was a hum of agreement, which only made Sybella feel worse as she packed up her notes and made her usual early departure.

She had worked hard for twelve months to make Edbury Hall a place of life and activity for its new incumbent, Mr Voronov, and continue to earn its keep for the village. While this house might personally remind her of some grim stage set for a horror film starring Christopher

Lee, the Hall also brought in its share of the tourist trade and kept the local shops turning over.

If this all collapsed it would affect everybody. And she would be responsible.

Rugging herself up in the boot room for her dash home, Sybella fished her phone out of her jeans back pocket and rang her sister-in-law.

Meg lived in a jaunty little semi-detached house on a busy road in Oxford, where she taught art to people with no real aptitude for painting and belly danced at a local Egyptian restaurant. She took off and travelled at the drop of a hat. Her life was possibly the one Sybella would have gravitated towards if life in all its infinite twists of fate hadn't set her on another course, with much more responsibility and less room to move. Sybella considered Meg her best friend.

'It's the letters. I should have known,' she groaned after a brief rundown on tonight's meeting. 'Nobody writes letters any more.'

'Unless you're a lonely seventy-nine-year-old man rattling around in a big empty house, trying to fill it with people,' said Meg.

Sybella sighed. Every time something new occurred at the Hall Mr Voronov gave the same advice.

Just write to my grandson and let him know. I'm sure there will be no problems.'

So she had. She'd written just as she'd been writing every month for the past year detailing events at Edbury Hall.

Because she'd been too damn timid to face him on the phone.

She'd let her native shyness trip her up—again—and this was the tip, Sybella suspected, of a huge iceberg that was going to take her little ship out. She said as much, leaving out the bit about being a timid mouse. Meg didn't cut you slack for being a mouse.

'My ship, Meg. My ship of fools, me being the captain!'

Meg was silent and Sybella already knew what was coming.

'You know what this is a result of? That weird life you lead in the village.'

'Please, Meg, not now.' Sybella shouldered her way out of the boot room. The corridor was dark and faintly menacing, although she suspected anyone coming across her would probably run the other way. She was wearing her Climb and Ski gear that was packed with a substance that was supposed to keep you warm and dry in the Arctic. It wasn't particularly flattering to a woman's figure and it also inhibited natural movement. She was aware she currently resembled a yeti.

Meg was persistent. 'You hang around with all those oldies…'

'You know why I volunteer with the Heritage Trust. It's going to get me a job in the end.'

Sybella made her way to the servants' entrance, from which she could slip unnoticed out of the house, cross the courtyard and disappear through a space in the hedge that led to the lane that wound down the hill to the top of her road.

'Really? You've been doing unpaid work for them for over a year. When does it pay off for you?'

'It's work experience in my field. Do you know how difficult it is to get a job with just a degree?'

'I don't know why you won't move down to Oxford with me. It's bristling with opportunities.'

'Your parents are here,' she said firmly. She was always firm when it came to her daughter's well-being. 'And I'm not removing Fleur from her home.'

'It's a two-hour drive. They can see her on weekends.'

'Who is going to look after her while I'm at work? Think of the practicalities, Meg.' God knew she had to. If she hadn't been so busy juggling all the balls life had thrown at her she might have thought through those practicalities with a little more precision at the Hall.

'Fair enough,' conceded Meg. 'But you've put a lot of eggs in that house of horrors basket.'

'Yes, because I have a growing daughter who has her roots in this village—a village with no other job opportunities in my chosen field. I've tried Stansfield Castle, Belfort Castle and Lark House. None are interested in someone with lots of education but no on-the-ground experience. Without Edbury Hall, Meg, I'm stuck!'

'So in the meantime you're writing letters to a man you're never going to meet. Should I ask about your love life?'

'What has my love life got to do with the letters?'

'I think if you had a boyfriend you wouldn't have all this extra time to sit around writing letters and sealing envelopes. You'd be like the rest of us and use freaking email.'

'It wasn't extra time. It was extra *effort*. Besides, I do use email. And I'm not looking for a romantic relationship, Meg Parminter.'

'I don't know why not. My brother's been gone six years. You can't keep hiding away in Mouldering Manor with those oldies, Syb. Seize the day!'

Given her days were quite long, what with her part-time archivist job at the town hall, her volunteer work with the Heritage Trust and sole responsibility for her home-schooled five-year-old daughter, Sybella wasn't quite sure which part of the day she wasn't seizing.

Besides, the idea of taking off her clothes in front of a man after six years of not having to endure that specific kind of embarrassment with Simon was not an encouraging one.

'You know that film you love, *The Ghost and Mrs. Muir*?' Meg asked. 'Do you remember at the end when her daughter comes home all grown up with the fiancé? One day that will be Fleur, feeling guilty because she's got a life and you haven't!'

'I will have a life,' Sybella shot back, confident at least on this point. 'I'll be in the midst of a brilliant career as a curator and very fulfilled in my life's ambition, thank you very much.'

'Okay, maybe that analogy doesn't work in the twenty-first century,' Meg grudgingly allowed. 'But are you really going to wait another twenty years before you pull the "take a detour" sign down off your bed?'

Sybella pushed open the heavy wooden door and made her way outside. She blew out a breath and watched it take shape in the air.

Blast, it was cold.

'It's not a priority for me, Meg.'

'Well, it should be!'

Sybella looked around to make sure no one was lurking in the bushes to overhear this.

'I really don't want to discuss my sex life, or lack of. I'm just not interested,' she said firmly. 'There, I've said it. Not. Interested. In. Sex. I am, however, very interested in what I'm going to say to Mr Voronov's grandson when he prosecutes us!'

Which was when she noticed a pricey-looking off-road vehicle coming up the drive, followed by another and another.

Mr Voronov hadn't mentioned guests. She was familiar with his schedule, given she came and gave him a hand with a few things he refused to entrust to the personal assistant his grandson had engaged for him.

She told Meg she'd call her tomorrow and stowed her phone, pulled the ski mask down over her chin to repel the cold and headed out across the drive to see what they wanted.

Nik parked in the courtyard, slammed the door behind him and crunched through the snow to open the boot and retrieve his overnight bag.

He'd never seen England's little tourist Mecca from this vantage point. Driving in, he thought it looked very much as if he'd stumbled onto the film set of the dramatisation of an Agatha Christie novel. Or maybe it was a recreation of Shakespeare's youth because if he wasn't mistaken, as the road had opened out into the town square, there had been a maypole.

Sticking up like a needle without a thread.

Everything else was under a ton of snow and ice.

He glanced up at the looming walls of Edbury Hall, with its multifaceted windows and grey stone. Snow drifts had made clumps of the carefully tended hedges and topiary.

It was a picture postcard of Ye Olde England.

No wonder those crackpots and loonies from Edbury's branch of the Heritage Trust were bombarding his offices in London every time something got raised or lowered on the property.

He sensed rather than heard movement coming up behind him.

Good. Someone around this place was doing their job.

'Here.' He bundled the luggage at the rugged-up figure hovering at his shoulder. Then he slammed the back of the vehicle closed and hit the lock device on his keys.

He turned around to find the help was staggering under its weight. Which didn't last long because the next thing he knew the guy was lying flat on his back in the snow.

He waited. The man wasn't getting up. He did, however, stick a gloved hand in the air and wave it around. He also made a noise that sounded like a cat being drowned in a barrel. Nik liked animals; he didn't much like incompetence in people.

Which was when he noticed the black ski mask under the hood of the guy's coat and Nik lost his easy stance, because in Russia personal security was often a matter of life and death, and right now instinct was telling him this guy was not one of the people he had authorised to work for his grandfather.

He grabbed the interloper by the scruff of his coat and heaved him to his feet.

Sybella tried to cry out but her voice box was currently lodged somewhere in the snow after the impact of hitting the ground.

She found herself being lifted by the scruff of her neck until she was almost hanging, her parka cutting up under her arms, the toes of her new boots scrambling for purchase.

'Give me your name and your reason for being out here.'

Her assailant had a deep, growly baritone that corresponded with his size. His rich Russian accent meant he probably had something to do with the current owner of this property. Given his size and strength he was possibly a bodyguard.

He was also clearly a bear.

'Imya?' he barked out when she didn't immediately respond.

'There's been a mistake,' Sybella gasped through the fine wool barrier formed by the ski mask over her mouth.

'What are you, journalist, protester, what?' He gave her another shake. 'I'm losing patience.'

'Put me down,' she pleaded. 'I don't understand what's happening.'

But even to her ears her plea was muffled into incoherence by all the wool and the wind.

Nevertheless, he dropped her and she landed heavily on the soles of her boots. Before she could react he whipped back the hood of her parka and gathered up a handful of her ski mask, yanking on her hair in the process. The ski mask came away and with it her long heavy flaxen curls. Freed, they began whipping around her face in the frigid wind.

His arms dropped to his sides.

'You're a woman,' he said in English as if this was entirely improbable. His voice was deep and firm and weirdly—given the circumstances—reassuring.

Sybella pushed the wildly flapping hair from her eyes and, finally able to be understood, choked out a little desperately, 'I was the last time I looked!'

He stepped in front of her, and if she didn't suspect a little brain damage from all the pushing and shoving, she'd think it was to shield her from the wind and elements.

'Did I hurt you?' he demanded, his head bent to hers.

'N-no.' Scared the life out of her, but she was in one piece.

At least she no longer felt in danger of ending up on her bottom again. She was also staring, because you didn't see men like this every day in Edbury.

He was a good head taller than her and she couldn't see around his shoulders and up close he had slightly slanted grey eyes, thick golden lashes, high flat cheekbones and a strong jaw stubbled in gold. He was gorgeous. His mouth was wide and firm and she found her attention constantly returning to it.

'What are you doing out here?' he demanded.

She could have asked him the same question.

Trying to gather her wits, Sybella took her time checking the seams on the arms of her parka. They appeared intact. Seams, that was. Apparently the fabric could withstand being dangled by a bear, but not the ingress of water. She was soaked through.

And cold.

'I asked you a question,' he repeated. He really was very rude.

'Minding my own business,' she said pointedly, making a show of brushing the snow off her cords to cover the fact her hands were shaking.

'Never show them you're rattled' was one of the few useful lessons a draconian English public boarding school education had taught her. Also, 'be the one asking the questions'—it made you look as if you knew what you were doing.

'Maybe the better question is what are you doing here?' Pity her voice shook a bit.

'I own this house.'

Her head shot up. 'No, you don't. Mr Voronov does.'

'I am Voronov,' he said. 'Nikolai Aleksandrovich Voronov. You are talking about my grandfather.'

Sybella's knees turned to jelly and a funny buzzing sound began to ring in her ears.

'Kolya?' she said a little faintly.

His eyes narrowed and Sybella felt as if she'd been knocked over in the snow for the second time tonight. Somehow, some way, she'd got this all wrong.

He looked her up and down.

'Who did you say you were?'

CHAPTER THREE

IN TROUBLE, THAT was who she was.

'I asked you a question,' he repeated.

Yes, he had, and he expected an answer, she interpreted from the way he just stood there, arms folded, on closer inspection less like a bear and more like some angry Norse god.

'Speak,' he commanded.

She literally jumped but then her training kicked in. She handled tour groups of small children regularly and knew one had to establish rules and boundaries if chaos wasn't to ensue.

'I think you need to calm down,' she said shakily, aware her heart was beating so fast she should probably take her own advice.

He took out his phone.

'Wh-what are you doing?'

'Ringing the police.'

Oh, that wasn't good.

Sybella didn't think, she just made a snatch for his phone. It wasn't the cleverest thing she could have done, but once the area's constabulary were involved this would be around the village in a flash. Her parents-in-law already thought she wasn't handling her life to their satisfaction. It would be another reason why she and Fleur should move in with them.

He held the phone just out of her reach, which was easy for him, given he appeared to be a god stepped down from Asgard. Sybella wouldn't have been surprised if he'd grabbed a stake of lightning while he was at it. Only he was looking down at her as if she were a puppy with muddy paws that had suddenly decided to jump on him.

It was beyond frustrating.

'Please,' she tried again, 'this is just a misunderstanding.'

'*Nyet*, this is trespass. I want you off my property.'

Sybella shook her head in disbelief. 'Are you going to let me explain?'

'*Nyet*.'

She stepped up to him and laid her hand on his forearm. 'Please, you have to listen. I'm not a trespasser.'

He frowned.

'I've never trespassed in my life. Not knowingly.'

Which was when the committee members of the Heritage Trust appeared out of the side entrance of Edbury Hall, humming like a hive of wasps.

Sybella's heart began to beat so fast she seriously thought she might pass out.

'Who in the hell are they?' he demanded, because clearly nothing was getting past this guy.

'The Heritage Trust committee,' she croaked. This was a disaster! She had to go and warn them.

Turning quickly, she didn't notice the bag at her feet until her boot caught on it and Sybella found herself for the second time tonight arms extended, launched head first for the snow.

Strong hands caught her around the waist and literally lifted her, this time bringing her into contact with his big, hard body. Instinctively she wrapped her arms around his neck. It was the wrong move. Sensation zipped through her body like an electrical charge and it dipped right between her legs.

Sybella panicked and tried to pull away but he had her held tight.

'Stop wriggling,' he ordered gruffly and she stopped. Mainly because her face was dangerously close to his and a part of her was finding the physical contact thrilling.

'Can you—just—look, stop holding me!' She was mumbling this into his bare neck, because apparently he thought hugging her to him was a good idea.

It wasn't. Even with the layers of fabric between them she'd been a man-free zone for so long it was like landing on planet Mars and discovering there wasn't enough gravity to hold you down. Worse, he smelt awfully good, manly in a way she had forgotten, and, combined with his warm solidity, she was beginning to enjoy all the contact.

Not interested in sex? She'd clearly sent a message out into the universe and the sneaky gods had sent down one of their own to make a liar of her.

'Please,' she begged, turning her face to meet his eyes, which was a mistake because he was looking back at her and they were dangerously close.

She could see how thick his golden eyelashes were, and his eyes had seemingly soaked up the colours around them like the Northern Lights she'd seen on a documentary about the Arctic. She could have sworn a moment ago they were icy grey.

Her panicked breath caught and everything telescoped down to his amazing eyes before his gaze swooped to her mouth. He looked as if he was going to kiss her or was that just her idea?

Panic renewed, Sybella began to thrash about in earnest. 'Please let me go before this all gets out of hand!'

On the contrary, Nik was confident he had it all in hand.

He would deal with the small tide of humanity edging towards them, and then he would find out why there appeared to be no security at all in operation at his grandfather's home.

But first he needed to deal with what he had in his arms, the problem being he wasn't sure what that was. He'd turned his head to find something other than what he'd first imagined. She had a vivid face, eyes that seemed to be searching his and the kind of sensuous full mouth that gave men creative thoughts. She also smelt of flowers, which was distracting him. He set her down in the snow.

'Do not move,' he told her.

He went around to the cab of the SUV and turned on the headlights to high beam, capturing the dozen rugged-up intruders like a spotlight on a stage.

'I'm Nikolai Aleksandrovich Voronov,' he said in a deep voice that didn't need to be raised. On its own it carried across the front façade of the house and possibly beyond. 'If you're not off the estate in the next two minutes, I'll have you all arrested for trespass.'

He didn't wait to see what they would do. He knew what they would do. Scatter and run.

Nik hoisted his bag over his shoulder and gave his attention to the unhappy girl, standing there encased in what looked like cladding. In the dark she no longer looked like the sensual siren he'd imagined a moment ago and was back to being the abominable snowman.

'You can go with your friends,' he said with a curt nod, before turning his back on her.

Sleet was falling more heavily as he approached the house.

He used the side entrance lit by lamp posts that glowed through the snowy gloom like something out of *The Lion, The Witch and The Wardrobe*, a book his Anglophile grandfather had given to him when he was a boy. No wonder the old man loved the place. Nik saw only an investment and right now a heavy oak door he pushed open with his shoulder.

He was aware he'd been followed, alerted by his companion's crunching footsteps over the stones and her hitching breath, because clearly the woman was out of shape with all that extra weight she was carrying.

He waited for Rapunzel because he wasn't in the habit of closing doors in women's faces. Another glance reinforced what he already knew. She was tall, abetted by a pair of what looked like hiking boots, and the parka and trousers gave her a square look not identifiable as female in the dark.

'What do you want?'

She had planted herself just inside the threshold.

'To explain.'

'I'm not interested.'

She stepped towards him, clearly reluctant, the light falling full on her.

She was wearing the ski mask now as a beanie, most of her astonishing hair caught up inside it. She had full cheeks pink from the cold and her hazel eyes he'd already established were bright, but it was her lush pink mouth that drew the eye.

'Actually, about that…you probably do want to talk to me.'

Nik had it on the tip of his tongue to tell her while she looked like a Christmas angel he wouldn't be changing his mind.

Instead he gave her a moment to clarify.

'I work here.'

She was staff? Why in hell hadn't she said so?

'I'm Sybella,' she said. 'Sybella Parminter.'

Nik took a moment to reconcile the girl standing in front of him with the woman with the wellington boots and the face like a shovel. He'd underestimated his grandfather. The old man had rigged a honey trap.

Nik crossed the floor to her in a few strides and, before she could react, reached behind her head and yanked off the ski mask.

Her hair tumbled out.

'What are you doing?' she demanded, lifting her bemittened hands to her head in a protective gesture, as if he might start pulling at her hair again.

It was exactly as it had looked in the snow, heavy and flaxen blonde almost all the way down to her waist. The electric light made it shimmer, or maybe he was just tired and even ordinary women were beginning to look like goddesses.

That fast a picture took shape of a golden angel ministering to his grandfather and putting ideas in his head about English heritage and great-grandchildren while she eyed the title deeds to the house.

'You can't just manhandle me,' she said, pushing back her hair self-consciously and eyeing him as if he were a wolf about to leap at her. He also saw the feminine awareness kindling in her eyes and knew exactly how he was going to handle this.

'Call me Nik.'

'Nik,' she said warily, taking a big step back. 'Well, I would like the opportunity to explain. If I could come back tomorrow?'

'I think you will stay where you are.'

'But you just told me to go.'

'Glad you're keeping up.'

She blinked.

'What were you doing outside?'

Sybella didn't know whether to run for her life or stand her ground. His pulling and pushing, not to mention the way he'd looked at her hair as if it were some kind of man snare, had left her unnerved. But she had people relying on her. She couldn't let them down.

'The Heritage Trust meet here on Thursday nights. I'm secretary. Assistant secretary.' She took a breath. Honesty was the best policy. 'I'm the only one who can do shorthand. We don't use a recording device.'

'You don't run it?'

'Well, no.'

He was shrugging out of his coat, looking around the entrance hall as if expecting minions to appear and help him. 'So you don't run it, you're the secretary. How long has this been going on?' he asked.

'A little under a year. Mr Voronov was kind enough—'

'For you to take advantage.'

'No, that's not—'

Sybella promptly lost her train of thought as the tailored wool slid down his arms and she discovered what had felt so solid outside when she'd been holding onto him. An expensive-looking charcoal sweater clung to broad shoulders and a long, hard, lean waist, apparently packed with bricks. Narrow muscled hips and long powerful legs filled out his dark jeans. By the time she reached his big, got-to-be-size-fifteen hand-tooled boots the tour had effectively rendered Sybella slightly dazzled and a whole lot mute.

She realised she'd just checked him out.

It was either her silence or the raptness of her regard that had him look up from shaking out his coat and give her that once-over thing men did, the subtle up and down assessment as to whether or not he'd consider sleeping with her...and Sybella had the humiliating thought he'd caught her staring and assumed she was doing the same thing.

Which she was. Unintentionally. Not because she was considering sleeping with him. Goodness, no. She hadn't *meant* to ogle him. It had just happened. But he didn't know that.

What made it worse was the Climb and Ski gear had currently turned her perfectly nice woman's body into a flotation device and the likelihood of him finding anything attractive about her was zilch.

'Care to tell me what you were really doing jumping out at me in the dark?' His eyes held a new awareness now that she'd pretty much flagged she found him attractive.

Sybella could feel her cheeks hot as coals. He made her feel like a teenage girl with a boy she liked. It was ridiculous at her advanced age of twenty-eight.

'I didn't jump out at you. You threw luggage at me!' He had moved across to the open boot-room door to hang up his coat. Sybella followed him, a tiny tug boat to his tanker.

'I expected to be greeted by staff,' he said.

She guessed that put her in her place. Sybella surreptitiously admired his rear, which like the rest of him appeared to be pure muscle, which was when he just tossed the grenade in.

'I also thought you were a man.'

And there went what was left of her self-image tonight.

'Wh-what?' she bleated, like a stupid lamb for slaughter.

'I mean, obviously you're not,' he said, frowning at her as if he'd just noticed her stricken expression and was assessing what it meant.

'No,' she choked, 'not a man. Thanks.'

'It was dark and you're wearing unisex clothing.' He was hanging up his coat, drawing attention to the flex of muscles along his back.

'This isn't unisex.' Sybella looked down at her considerable padded bulk. 'It's oyster-pink.'

His expression told her he didn't make the connection.

'Pink is traditionally a female colour,' she spelt out.

He continued to look doubtful.

She huffed out a breath. 'Look, this parka was clearly marked "Women Size L" on the rack,' she insisted. Then stopped.

Had she just informed him she was size large?

Yes—yes, she had.

'It was dark,' he repeated, and the frown was back.

He closed the door behind him, crowding her back out into the corridor.

When she picked up her bruised and bloodied self-esteem from the floor, Sybella would remind herself she was tall, wearing layers and a ski mask, and he was right—it was dark. Her throat felt tight, because it wasn't *that* dark.

Sybella only felt worse when he took the main stairs with an effortless stride that left her labouring as best she could in his wake, because by now she was not only wet through, the all-weather gear was making it difficult to move freely.

It begged the question how people climbed mountains in these things when she was finding a staircase hard going.

She was a little out of breath at the top.

'You need to get a bit more exercise,' he said, stopping to look down at her. 'You're out of shape.'

Really? That was what he had to say to her? The only time she ever got to sit down was on a quiet afternoon at the records office where she worked.

'Shouldn't you be on your way up to see your grand-father?' she said instead, no longer at all keen to explain anything to him. She just wanted to go home. Preferably to a hot bath where she could enjoy a little cry.

'He'll keep.'

He'll keep? What sort of grandson was he? Well, she knew the answer to that. The absent kind. She scowled at his back. If he hadn't been absent she wouldn't be in this fix.

Sybella followed him down the Long Gallery. She regularly conducted tours of this room, pointing out the features, recounting the history of the house. She suspected Mr I-thought-you-were-a-man wouldn't be very happy if he knew.

There were six Jacobean chairs piled up in the middle of the room, awaiting a home.

'What in the hell?' he said, circling them.

She opted for a cheerful, 'Don't you love these? Your

grandfather had them brought down from storage in the attics. We haven't worked out where to put them.'

'We?' He rounded on her. 'You're interested in the contents of the house?'

As if she were some kind of criminal. Sybella found herself backing up a bit. 'No, I'm interested in the past.'

'Why?'

A little flustered by the way he was looking at her, all suspicious and hard-eyed but making her feel very much a woman despite what he'd said, she found herself struggling for an answer. 'I don't know. I just am.'

He looked unimpressed.

She had to do better. She rummaged around for something he'd believe. 'If you grew up like I did in a very modern house in a relentlessly upmarket housing estate you'd see the beauty in old things too.'

He looked skeptical.

'It was the most soulless place on this green earth. I knew from an early age there had to be something better. More meaningful.'

Sybella took a breath, realising she'd told him a little more than she had meant to.

'Why does furniture have more meaning if it's old?'

'Because old things have stories attached to them, and the furniture that's survived tends to have been made by craftsmen and women. Artists.'

'You're a romantic,' he said, again as if this were a crime.

'No, I'm practical.' She'd had to be. 'Although I guess as a child I read books about other children who lived in old houses and fantasised that might be me one day.'

'Is that so?'

Nik was tempted to ask her if she could see herself in this house.

'It's not unusual,' she said defensively. 'Lots of children have thoughts like that, and I had a good reason to.'

Nik suspected he was about to hear a sob story. He was also aware if he gave her enough rope she'd probably happily hang herself. She was nervous around him and it was making her talk.

'I'm more curious about your interest in this house,' he growled.

'No, you asked me why I was interested in the past.'

He added pedantic to overweight and possibly a con-artist.

'Old houses, miserable childhood, check.'

'I didn't say I had a miserable childhood.' She looked affronted. 'I said the house was soulless,' she said firmly. 'We were the only people who had ever lived there. Which was ironic.'

'I'll bite—why?'

She tried to fold her arms, which was rendered difficult by the bulk of her clothing. 'Because the woman who raised me was obsessed with genealogy. Her genealogy, not mine, as it turned out.'

'You were adopted?'

She nodded, for the first time looking less communicative. Her pretty face was closed up like a fist.

He'd been fifteen when he was told his father was not his father, and Nik had always looked at his life in terms of *before* and *after*.

'When did you find out?'

She looked up at him as if gauging whether to tell him. 'I was twelve. It was when my parents separated.'

'Must have been difficult.'

'Yes,' she said. 'It was more difficult when they handed me back.'

'They handed you back?'

She was radiating tension now. 'Dumped me in a very nice boarding school and left me there for six years.'

He almost laughed. *That* was her complaint?

Spoilt upper-class girl still bemoaning her school years at what—going by her elocution—was an upmarket school. He wondered what else she had to complain about. And here he was, actually feeling sorry for her.

She was good, he had to give her that.

'Have you ever considered they were giving you a good education?'

'They gave me a very good education,' she said tonelessly, looking down at her clasped hands. She probably understood her bid for sympathy was going nowhere. 'But I saw them very rarely in the term breaks and now not at all. It was as good as handing me back.'

Sybella was pleased with her command of herself and that she could talk about her adoptive parents in a forthright way. He'd asked the questions; she'd merely answered them. No external emotion needed.

Only for all her firmness on the subject she could feel the cold running like a tap inside her and she would have trouble turning it off tonight.

'That is a sad little story,' he said, something in his tone making her think he didn't quite believe her.

She suddenly felt self-conscious and slightly annoyed. 'I guess it is. I don't know why I told you all that. I'm sure it's not at all interesting to a man like yourself.'

'You'd be surprised what interests me.'

Sybella discovered she didn't have anything smart to say in answer to that. But she couldn't help running her gaze over his broad shoulders, remembering how strong and sure he'd felt holding her.

His eyes caught hers and something flared between them. 'And what exactly interests you, Miss Parminter?'

Sybella knew what interested her, and it wasn't going to happen.

She could feel her face filling up with heat.

'It's Mrs,' she stated baldly in a desperate attempt to deflect whatever he might say next. 'Mrs Parminter.'

'You're married?'

There had been a current of awareness zipping between them from the time she'd been grappling with him in the snow, only Sybella didn't know that until this very second as it was sucked back to nothingness and what was left was a tense, awkward silence.

Sybella didn't know what to say.

But he did.

'Does your husband know you're out at night running around with other men?'

CHAPTER FOUR

With too many bad memories still beating around in her head something snapped inside Sybella, enough to have her hand arcing through the air.

Fortunately his reflexes were quicker than hers and he gripped her wrist, holding her immobile.

There was a fraught silence in which all she could hear was her pulse drumming in her ears. Then he said quietly, 'That was out of line,' releasing her arm so that Sybella could slowly lower it to her side.

'It's none of my business,' he added. Which was when she realised he wasn't talking about her trying to hit him. He was apologising for what he'd said.

The fight went out of Sybella, and with it flooded in the knowledge she'd almost hit another person.

Last year Fleur had pushed over a little boy in her social group and Sybella had sat down and had the talk with her. Physically hurting someone was wrong. Whatever the provocation, she must use her words, not her fists. And here she was, mother of the year, trying to slug a perfect stranger!

She'd had provocation all right, but that wasn't an excuse.

She needed to apologise to him but Sybella found herself struggling because he'd implied something, and he hadn't taken that back. Which was very different from saying it was *none of his business*.

'Six years ago my husband kissed me and climbed into his van and drove it out to the Pentwistle Farm,' she said in a low voice, 'and on the road between the farm and the turn-off he was struck by another car coming over the rise.'

Nik was looking at her with an expression she hadn't seen before in this man.

As if he were taking her seriously.

'So no, Mr Voronov, my husband has no idea what I'm doing nowadays—but I do. I wish I hadn't tried to hit you. I can't take that back. But you don't get to say things like that to me. I don't deserve your contempt, or do you just have a problem with women in general? I suspect you do.'

Sybella had no idea where all those words had come from or her ability to say them or even if they were true. But nothing had just 'happened' here tonight. It had been building since he'd held her in his arms outside in the snow and all the sensuality latent in her body had woken up.

She resented it, and she resented him. But none of that was his fault.

'I suspect I have a problem with you, Mrs Parminter,' he said slowly. 'But I am sorry for what I said.'

'You should be.' She held his gaze. She could see her words had affected him and she could also see some grudging respect in his eyes and that gave her the grace to say, 'I'm sorry too.'

She forced the apology out, because as wrong as her actions were she couldn't yet let go of them, or the feelings that had provoked them. None of this had made her feel better; she felt worse. She wrapped arms around her waist as best she could in her ridiculous parka.

He was looking at her as if she deserved some compassion. He was wrong. She deserved a good talking-to for all the mistakes she'd made in dealing with this house.

'You're cold,' he said. 'You need to take off your wet things.'

'I don't—'

'You can dry them in front of the fire, or I can have them laundered.'

'Please don't bother.' She passed a hand over her face.

'I'm going to take them back to Climb and Ski tomorrow for a full refund.'

'Are you all right?'

She blinked, taking her hand away from her face to find him watching her as if she might keel over. 'I guess so.'

Which was when her eyes filled with tears. *Oh, blast.*

Tired, wet, in some serious trouble over her activities in this house, and yet troublingly aware of Nik Voronov as a man and her own deficiencies in that area, Sybella wanted nothing more than to wriggle out of her wet things and cast herself down in front of the fire and sleep for a hundred years.

But she didn't get the fairy-tale option. She should be practising a better apology.

There was a rattle and clatter as Gordon, who ran the household, entered from a side door, wheeling the drinks trolley.

Saved by the man with the alcohol!

A long-time bachelor, Gordon was her ally in the house, having worked here for almost thirty years under the previous owner. He gave her a guarded look of surprise but didn't say anything. He was too good at his job.

Her host meanwhile had signalled to Gordon he could deal with the drinks.

Sybella wondered if she could just slip out with the trolley. But the fire lured her and she turned away to deal with her wet things, surreptitiously sniffing and wiping at her eyes with her wrist. She stripped off her parka and then her cords, feeling self-conscious in her tights but not exposed. They were of a durable denier and thick enough to act as leggings. Frankly, it was a relief to be able to move her body freely again.

She laid out her jeans before the fire and had just straightened up when a towel dropped over her head.

She gave a start but with a gruff, 'Hold still,' her host began to vigorously but not roughly rub dry her damp hair.

After an initial protest of, 'I can do this,' she gave in, because really he was impossible to argue with.

But this was her role. For five years she'd been the caregiver. It was disconcerting to find herself the one being cared for. And as his strokes became more rhythmic Sybella found herself going quiescent, some of the tension of the crazy evening leaving her.

It had been so long since her needs were seen to by someone else. She'd forgotten it could be like this. Even when Simon had been alive he'd been so busy with his new veterinary practice in the few months they were married they had seemed only to bump into each other at night in bed, and Sybella could feel her skin suffusing with heat because another man's hands were on her, if only drying her hair. But when she looked up and clashed with his grey eyes she was shocked into feelings so raw and insistent she barely recognised them as the gentle, awkward finding their way she'd had with Simon...

'That's enough,' she said, her voice a little rough with the sudden upsurge of feeling beating around in her.

He paused but then continued to dry her even more vigorously.

'If you collapse from pneumonia in a few days' time—' he said gruffly.

'You don't want it on your conscience?'

'I don't want a lawsuit.'

Sybella snorted, she couldn't help it, and she felt rather than saw him smile.

'I'm not a lawyer,' she said, 'and I don't have the money for a lawyer.'

'What do you do,' he asked, removing the towel so that her head came back and she could see him, 'besides haunt this house?'

She didn't miss a beat. 'I could give you a list?'

A slow grudging smile curled up his mouth, taking Sybella's entire attention with it. 'Why don't you do that?'

As if he had all the time in the world to listen to her life story. As if like before she'd spill her guts.

Instead she asked, 'Why don't you visit your grandfather more often?' It was the one thing that really bothered her, and it was more important than anything to do with the open house and how much trouble she would be in.

He reached out and gently smoothed the drying ringlets back from her face.

'I would have visited earlier,' he said, 'if I'd had any idea something so beautiful was here.'

Then his gaze dropped to her mouth.

She relived that moment in the snow and realised it hadn't been her imagination. There was a very strong attraction between them.

Only she didn't do things like this.

Given the last man to kiss her existed now only in her memory of him.

She wasn't even sure what she would do if he…

His mouth covered hers. He gave her no opportunity to back out, or overthink it, he just made it happen. One hand sliding around the back of her head to cradle her, the other at the small of her back. His hand was so broad he could span her waist from behind.

In a flurry of sense impressions, Sybella had never felt so delicate, so utterly aware she was a feeling, sensate woman and, as exciting and dangerous as this was, she felt completely safe in his arms.

Where he had been so rough with her out in the snow he was now showing due care and acknowledgement of her as a female, which put to bed his remark about mistaking her for a man and engendered a fluttery feeling inside her. It bloomed high in her chest and a swirling warmth gathered down below.

He brought her in close to his body and she felt the full hard, muscular strength of him and it was enough.

She gave way, her mouth softening under his, the entire lost art of kissing returning to her with some subtle but much appreciated changes.

His tongue touched, grazed, tasted, seduced and the feel of him was so completely male and so overwhelming in the certainty of his approach Sybella took what he gave her instinctively and with an utter disregard to where this might be leading.

Until all her doubts came rushing back in and she ducked her head.

'What's wrong?' he asked gruffly.

Apart from he was a stranger, and they didn't know one another, and she suspected given her activities in his house only trouble could come from this?

'I don't know.' She did know—she was feeling a bit too much and it had been so long and she no longer had any certainty in her ability to meet him as a sexually confident woman. But had she ever?

She wasn't ready for this.

Meg would say whatever sense of herself as a desirable woman had been shoved into the back of her wardrobe in a box along with her preserved wedding bouquet and all the plans she and Simon had made for the future. But it had happened before that. It had happened when Simon had briefly dated another girl and slept with her.

It was a little disconcerting to say the least to discover, gazing up at this intense, beautiful man, she had no idea where to go from here with him. But she did know one thing. She had to let him know what was going on in his house.

'I have to tell you something,' she blurted out. 'Edbury Hall is open to the public on weekends.'

Nik didn't immediately let her go. His hand was still curled around her sweet waist gloved in soft cashmere wool that made the most of her glorious curves above and below.

He could pinpoint the moment he'd stopped thinking clearly. It was when he'd seen her bending down by the fire, the most female-looking woman. She was the proverbial hourglass, and if there was a little more sand than was standard in that glass his libido didn't make that distinction. She had ample breasts and long, shapely legs, deliciously plump around her thighs and bottom, and in his arms she'd felt like both comfort and sin.

Which explained why his brain took a little longer to catch up, because his body was happy where it was, Sybella's curves giving him a full body press.

'Why is the house open to the public?' He forced himself to set her back. 'On whose authorisation?'

'Mr Voronov senior's, and—and yours.' Sybella's voice gave out, so the 'yours' wasn't much more than a whisper.

'Mine?' he growled, any trace of the man who had begun to kiss her and rouse such passionate feelings in her evaporating like the last patch of sunshine on a cold winter's day.

'You were sent the paperwork. I didn't just go ahead only on your grandfather's say-so,' she protested.

'I received no paperwork.'

No. She gnawed on the inside of her lip. Now she would have to explain about the letters. But she didn't want to be responsible for a further breach between grandfather and grandson. Family was important.

No one understood that better than someone who for a long time didn't have any.

No, it would be better if his grandfather confessed.

And what if Nik Voronov decided to blame her anyway?

Blood was blood, and old Mr Voronov might easily side with his grandson.

Sybella knew she had nobody to blame but herself and for a spinning moment she just started babbling. 'I don't see who has been hurt by any of this. Mr Voronov is a lonely man and he enjoys having people into the house…'

'And you have taken advantage of that.'

'No!' Sybella closed her eyes and took a breath. Arguing with him wasn't going to accomplish anything. 'I understand you don't know me,' she said, keeping her voice as steady as she could, given the escalating tension, 'and you say you're worried about your grandfather—'

'I am worried about him.'

'Well, I don't see any evidence of that given you're never here!'

Oh, she should have kept that to herself. And now he was looking down at her without a shred of give in him.

'I suspect you've taken my grandfather for a ride, and, if I find out that's the case, you really don't want me for an enemy Mrs Parminter.'

It was difficult not to take a step back.

She swallowed hard. 'Do you go through life mistrusting people?'

'When it comes to my family I don't allow anything past the keeper.'

Those words took the indignant air out of her because she guarded her little family too. His grandfather had become of late an honorary member of that family and for a moment she wondered if *she'd* got it wrong. Nik Voronov might genuinely care about his grandfather. If the shoe were on the other foot she would be suspicious too.

She tried again. 'Honestly, Nik, it's not what you think.'

'I think we can probably go back to Mr Voronov.'

He was making her feel as if she'd done something wrong.

Which was when she noticed he was getting out his phone.

'Are you calling the police again?' She tried not to sound despairing because, really, what were they going to arrest her on? Impersonating a married lady? Kissing a man she'd just met?

'I'm arranging a car for you. I take it you live in the village?'

It was no more than a ten-minute walk if she took the lane, but Sybella didn't intend to argue with him about the lift.

'If this is your organisation's way of drumming up support you can let them know that honey traps went out in the nineteen seventies.'

Honey trap?

He turned away and spoke rapidly into his phone in Russian.

Sybella wondered if being shaken about like a child's toy earlier had affected her hearing. It had certainly loosened some of her native intelligence.

What did he think, she was Mata Hari kissing men for state secrets?

Oh, boy, she definitely needed to get out of here.

Cursing her own stupidity, she pulled on her damp jeans and then bent down to reattach her boots. Everything was cold and unpleasant and would chafe but there was no helping that.

'I want you back here nice and early, let's say eight o'clock for breakfast,' he said from behind her. 'You have some explaining to do, and it will be in the presence of my grandfather.'

Sybella became aware he was probably getting a really good look at her wide womanly behind at this moment.

But everything was such a shambles—what was one more humiliation?

'Eight o'clock is too early.'

'Tough. Get an alarm clock.'

She straightened up. 'For your information I'll be awake at six, but I have a great deal to organise myself. You're not the only busy person in the world, Mr Voronov.'

He looked unimpressed.

'I am running a billion-dollar business, Mrs Parminter. What's your excuse?'

A five-year-old girl, Sybella thought, eyeing him narrowly, but he looked like one of those unreconstructed dinosaurs who thought raising children happened by magic. Besides, she was not bringing her daughter into this hostile conversation.

'The fact is I'm out of here tomorrow,' he informed her. 'Let's call this your window of opportunity.'

'To do what?'

'To convince me not to involve my lawyers.'

All the fight went out of Sybella. She couldn't quite believe this was happening. But she told herself surely old Mr Voronov would clear the air tomorrow.

'Fine. I'll be here.'

To her surprise he took his wool coat and handed it to her with a less antagonistic, 'You'll need this.'

Sybella looked at her Climb and Ski jacket she'd been unable to bring herself to put back on and self-consciously drew his coat around her shoulders.

The gesture reminded her of how kind he'd been drying her hair, how he'd made her feel cared for if only for a brief time. It was enough to make her want to cry, and she hated crying. It didn't change anything.

She turned away from him, his scent surrounding her inside the coat.

She spotted the bottle of brandy and on a whim picked

it up. After the events of this evening she needed it more than he did.

He didn't say anything and when she went downstairs to climb into the waiting car she was holding it to her like a safety blanket.

Stupid really, when she didn't drink. Stupid being in this car, when it would take only ten minutes or five minutes if she'd legged it. She brought her fingertips to her mouth. It still felt a little swollen and sensitive from all the attention. Stupid, probably, to have kissed him.

CHAPTER FIVE

'MUMMY, THERE'S A GIANT standing in our garden. What do you think about that?'

Given yesterday it had been an elephant under the stairs, Sybella didn't rush to call the fire brigade or police station or even Jack the giant killer.

When she did put away the bath towels she was folding and came into her bedroom, she found her five-year-old daughter was kneeling at the dormer window in her pyjamas, her big violet-blue eyes full of innocent curiosity for a world that produced fairy-tale characters in human guise.

Joining Fleur at the glass, she obligingly looked out. Her pulse hit a thousand and she stepped back and said a silent prayer. Then she leaned forward again to get a better look.

She became aware of Fleur watching her, waiting for a cue as to how to respond to this stranger at their door. Sybella shook off her astonishment.

'That's not a giant, darling, that's a Viking god.'

He was facing their door and in a minute he'd work out the old-fashioned bell-pull was indeed the bell—but it was broken.

Then he'd probably pound on the door until he broke it down.

'Mummy will go down and speak to him. Why don't you stay here with Dodge? You know how nervous he gets around boys.'

'Because they're noisy.' Fleur picked up her toy bricks and returned to fitting pieces together. Sybella wasn't fooled. Her daughter would wait until the coast was clear and make her way to the top of the stairs and peer down through the bannisters.

Sybella wouldn't have minded that option herself. Instead she took the stairs by twos, then stopped in front of the hall mirror and checked her face was clean. Clean but her eyes were shadowed with lack of sleep.

She'd been on the Internet late last night checking up on Nik Voronov and how much damage he could possibly do her. Given he was on the *Forbes* list, probably a lot.

At least she was wearing her work clothes: a white silk blouse, a knee-length caramel-coloured suede skirt and boots. Pretty respectable. She ran a hand through her yet-to-be-braided hair and went to open the door.

Then hesitated and looked at herself in the glass again, this time undoing her top two buttons.

There, just a hint of cleavage. It had nothing to do with making herself more attractive for the man who had called her a honey trap last night. It was about her own self-confidence as a woman.

She opened the door, and her self-confidence did a wobble and promptly fell over.

He was wearing a tailored suit and tie. He might as well have been wearing a surcoat and carrying a broadsword. She knew he'd come to take prisoners.

His eyes flared over her as if he were dropping a net and Sybella instinctively dug her heels into her shoes to keep herself from being dragged in towards him.

And just like last night in the snow it was his mouth she was drawn to. The wide lower lip, the slight curve at the ends that could go either way, like Nero's thumb, up or down, and decide your fate. She'd been kissed by that mouth last night and it had definitely been going her way for a little bit. But in the end it had all been a ruse to make her look as foolish as possible.

'Enjoy the brandy?'

The brandy? She hadn't known what to do with the

bottle when she'd got home so she'd stashed it in the linen closet.

It had occurred to her that Catherine, her mother-in-law, was regularly in and out of that cupboard when she babysat Fleur.

Sybella was forever coming home to freshly changed sheets, which she appreciated even as it drove her crazy.

Hiding spirits behind the bathroom towels, Sybella, dear?

A little devil she didn't know was in her made her say, 'Yes, thank you, I drank the lot.'

'Careful,' he said, his deep voice wiping away any comparisons with her mother-in-law, 'excessive drinking is a slippery slope to all kinds of illness in later life.'

'I'll keep that in mind.'

What did he want? Why was he looking at her in that way, his eyes trained on her, cool and watchful and somehow taking her clothes off?

'So,' she said, swallowing. 'How can I help you today?'

Nik eyed the two undone buttons.

'It's nine o'clock.'

'I told you my mornings were busy.' She made a gesture with her hand, wriggling her fingers. 'Serene on the surface, duck legs churning underneath.'

Nik's attention had drifted to her hair because it seemed to have grown more abundant overnight like some Victorian-era maiden. He suddenly found himself right back where he was last night. Wanting her.

He cleared his throat. 'My grandfather tells me you take tours of the house.'

She stood a little straighter. 'The third Thursday of every month, we have school groups in. Only in the west wing.'

'You bring people into my house?'

'I don't think your grandfather considers the house

yours,' she said, her fan of lashes flickering nervously. 'Really the house belongs to everyone in Edbury in a manner of speaking. There has been a manor house on this spot since the time of the Normans—'

'Fascinating.'

'It is fascinating!' She firmed her mouth. 'Your grandfather understands we're only caretakers of a place like this. That's why he agreed to open up the estate again to the public.'

Nik tried not to notice how her blouse hugged her breasts or her skirt flared over those rounded hips. 'I am more interested in discovering exactly why my property is being treated like a theme park.'

Sybella's heart sank. If this was his attitude there was no win for her here.

Only she noticed his gaze was roaming a little too far south of her face again and she could feel her body responding, the warmth rising up into her cheeks, the backs of her knees tingling.

'I'm not a theme park either,' she said flatly.

To her surprise a streak of colour rose over his high, flat cheekbones.

'And no one is treating Edbury Hall that way,' she hastened on, wanting to put the sexual awareness behind them where it belonged. 'It's more of an educational facility.'

He folded his arms. 'Who is paying your salary?'

'No one. Everyone volunteers.'

'Right.'

'No one's ever been paid at Edbury. All takings are funnelled back into other projects in the area.'

His gaze zeroed in on her. 'You're not an employee?'

She shook her head.

'Good, that makes this less ambiguous.'

'What do you mean "ambiguous"? What's ambiguous?' Sybella didn't like the sound of that.

He looked up at the lintel above her head and over the local stone that walled her house.

'You're also my tenant,' he spelt out, cool gaze dropping to hers once more. 'The lease on the Hall includes these weavers' cottages.'

'Yes,' she said feeling hunted, 'and I've never missed a rental payment.'

'Nobody said you had. But just as a hypothetical example, how would you like it if I turned this row into a tourist attraction on the weekends?'

'They are a tourist attraction.'

'Prostit?'

'People come from all over the world to photograph our cottages. Several film crews have been on site in this street in the past four years.' She folded her arms across her chest. 'I'm beginning to think you know nothing of Edbury at all.'

'You'd be right. I own the Hall for tax purposes.'

'I'm sorry?'

'I'm required to own a certain amount of property in the UK for tax reasons.'

She stared at him as if he'd announced he'd stolen the Crown Jewels and was currently storing them in the Kremlin.

'You must be joking? You've caused all this upset in the village because you want to cheat on your tax?' Her voice had risen exponentially.

Nik shifted on his size fifteens. 'I do not engage in illegal activities, Mrs Parminter, and I would be careful about what you say to me.'

She looked taken aback and retreated a little into the safety of her doorway.

Nik expelled a deep breath. He did not bully women, but every conversation with this girl turned into a confrontation.

'I'm not interested in your financial dealings, Mr Voronov,' she said, looking persecuted, 'any more than I enjoy being doorstepped at nine o'clock in the morning. Say what you've got to say and go.'

He looked her up and down, which she clearly didn't like.

'I've said it.'

'Good.'

She took another step back into her house and began to close her door. But he hadn't finished with her yet.

'Anything more you'd care to tell me before the lawyers get involved?'

She halted and then stuck her head out again. 'What do you mean "lawyers"?'

'I seem to have an echo,' he observed.

She pinned her lips together and those hazel eyes fixed pensively on him as she stepped reluctantly outside again.

'I—I hardly think lawyers are necessary.'

'Fortunately that decision is mine.'

Awful man. Why was he so set on blaming her for everything? And why was she still finding it difficult not to drink in every last masculine inch of him?

Sybella tried to find something reasonable to say but what popped out was, 'Why are you down here bothering people?'

He leaned in a little closer.

'I told you,' he said in that fathom-deep voice. 'I am visiting my grandfather.'

Sybella could have told him right now it didn't feel that way. After the events of last night it felt as if he were visiting her! For purposes that felt entirely too hormonal on her behalf.

'Well, perhaps if you'd bothered to turn up before now you'd know what was going on here,' she threw back at him a little desperately, 'instead of stomping around like a big bully and making everyone go through lawyers.'

'Given I'm based in St Petersburg, turning up isn't that simple.'

'Is that where you live?' The question just slipped out, openly curious, and Sybella knew she'd given herself away. Her stupid interest in him.

She could feel the heat rushing into her face.

'Da,' he said, and there was a silence during which Sybella remembered how much she'd told him about her life last night. The intimacy that had created.

'Well, maybe it isn't so easy for you to get down here regularly,' she admitted reluctantly, 'but your grandfather needs family around him at this time of his life.'

His eyes iced over. 'My grandfather is well taken care of.'

'Is he? Do you know he doesn't like his nurse? He doesn't trust her.'

Nik frowned. 'He hasn't said anything to me.'

'Perhaps if you visited once in a while you could talk to the people around him who matter, not the people you're employing, and you might have a better idea of what's really going on instead of making up these stupid stories and—and picking on me!'

'And you're one of the people who matter?' he asked.

'I don't matter, but I am here. I do see what goes on.'

Nik didn't like the picture she painted, that his grandfather was unhappy, that in some way he was failing.

Only her hands had migrated to her hips again, and he was finding it difficult not to be distracted by the way her chest lifted every time she made her point and the button holding back the mystery of her cleavage strained.

'Here's what I think, Mrs Parminter. You've been using my grandfather's kindness to benefit yourself.'

'Yes, you would think that.'

Sybella glared back at him.

The truth was so much more simple and delightful than anything this man could make up in his suspicious mind.

His grandfather had forged one of those charming inter-generational friendships with her small daughter.

Sybella had watched a lonely and reserved man come to life in the company of her forthright, imaginative Fleur, and the sight of Mr Voronov's white head bent over a book with Fleur's small dark one as they read together made every Thursday afternoon a treasure.

Fleur didn't come easily to reading. She was a child who wanted to be out of doors, climbing trees, chasing cows and getting muddy. All the things possible because they lived in the country. She was, in short, very much like her late father.

Simon had always struggled with reading comprehension and he wouldn't want his daughter to go through that.

His own father shared the same difficulty.

Mr Voronov was a godsend.

Furthering her career had been the last thing on her mind.

But she wasn't telling this man any of that.

She'd told him too much in her stupid confessional last night.

It was her business. It wasn't any of his.

'Frankly, I don't care what you happen to think. I am going to continue to visit your grandfather and there's nothing you can do about it!'

Sybella's soaring moment of satisfaction was short-lived.

'Mrs Parminter, let me tell you how it's going to be.' His voice had dropped to a calm dead certainty. 'Your visits to the house are over. You are to stay away or there will be consequences. Are we clear?'

'What consequences?'

'Legal consequences.'

The colour had gone; not a scrap of it remained in her face.

Nik waited to feel satisfied by that. He didn't. But he damn well wasn't taking ultimatums from this woman. Dealing with this had already taken up too much of his valuable time.

'Listen, I didn't mean for all this to get so out of hand,' she began.

'Are we clear?' he repeated in the voice he used on mine sites.

She trembled, visibly intimidated for the first time.

Nik could see the struggle in her face and his anger evaporated in a wink.

He'd spent the night with some fairly explicit sexual fantasies about this woman, and this morning he'd learned a lot of things that didn't make him very happy with her. It wasn't a particularly good mix.

'I understand perfectly,' she said, swallowing hard, making it clear with her eyes she didn't.

Unlike the last woman throwing ultimatums at him like plates, a Spanish model who had apparently never heard the word no before, Sybella Parminter didn't really seem to understand the way this was played. If she backed down, he'd give her a break. She wasn't backing down.

It was disconcerting because he'd just discovered he didn't like her looking bewildered and upset.

For the second time. Because of him.

He stepped towards her.

'Mummy!' A small person flew out of the house and wrapped herself around Sybella's legs.

Mummy?

Six years widowed. He wasn't good with kids' ages but this one fitted the time span. Sybella was immediately scooping her up, the little girl wrapping her arms and legs around her mother like an octopus.

'This is your daughter?' he said redundantly.

'Yes.' She turned away to go into the house and the child cast a look over her mother's shoulder at him as if he were an ogre in a fairy tale. She stuck out her tongue.

Nik found himself staring at a blue door shut in his face and with the uneasy suspicion he'd made a mistake.

CHAPTER SIX

SYBELLA DROVE AS fast as she was legally able along the familiar road from Middenwold Town Hall where she worked on Fridays, back into Edbury.

In a panic from work she'd rung and let Mr Voronov know she was coming and that she was bringing the letters.

Beside her on the passenger seat was the box of letters that would clear her name.

She didn't want to be responsible for a further breach between grandfather and grandson because family was important, but she didn't see that she had much choice. She couldn't put her kindly impulses towards Mr Voronov above the risk to her future professional reputation if her activities at Edbury Hall were publicly condemned.

She switched on her hands-free phone device as Meg's name came up and her sister-in-law's excitable voice filled the car.

'I can't believe you've got one in the village!'

Sybella cursed silently. If Meg had heard about it down in Oxford, it must be all over the village.

'We lay traps and snares and catch them that way,' she responded drolly, although she was in *so much trouble* it was no longer funny.

'What'd you use?' said Meg wryly. 'A net?'

'No, the possibility of a lawsuit.' Sybella breathed in through her nose and out through her mouth and told herself she shouldn't drive and panic.

'I don't think that's your main problem. So Nik Voronov actually stepped off his boat and onto dry land.'

'Boat? What boat?'

'His billion-foot-long superyacht—all Russian oligarchs have them. They live on them.'

'Where do you get this from?'

'I have my sources. I also have other sources. According to the village grapevine, the two of you were throwing some serious sparks last night.'

Oh, yes, there had been sparks, but they had definitely fizzled. Then a new fear gripped her. 'What do you mean "the village grapevine"?'

'Syb, *everyone* knows. I've had three phone calls and Sarah was banging on Mum's back door at seven o'clock this morning wanting to know if it was true you were having sex up against a SUV in the car park at Edbury Hall last night. With *a man*.'

'Well, of course I'd be having sex with a man,' Sybella huffed impatiently, even as she recoiled from the idea her mother-in-law knew. 'Not that I was, mind, I was just… holding onto him—and Sarah's been cutting my hair for five years. She should know me better.'

'You're missing the point. To half the village this morning you're just an exhibitionist floozy—Sarah's on board with that, by the way—but everyone else thinks you're legitimately on together. They think he's your boyfriend.'

'*What?*'

'It explains why you were able to get the Hall opened again with so little fuss.'

Sybella's mouth fell open.

'Now's not the time to panic,' advised Meg. 'This guy owes you—after everything you've done for his grandfather, and now he's compromised your reputation.'

'I doubt he sees it that way,' Sybella said, gripping the steering wheel and wondering how floozy was going to translate at the pony club and how she would navigate that with Fleur. Her friends were too little, but their mothers were not.

'He's closing down the house to the public, Meg. He came over and told me this morning. He warned me off ever going near the place again.'

'He came to your *house*?'

'He was very angry with me.' Sybella took a breath and swallowed to avoid sounding as vulnerable as she felt. 'Up until then I thought I could persuade him to keep the place open, appeal to his better nature.'

'Good luck with that.' But Meg was oddly quiet for a moment and Sybella got the impression she'd given something away. 'You like him, don't you?'

'No, don't be silly. He's not my type at all. He's—he's bearish.'

'Well, remember what Goldilocks did in the original fairy tale? She jumped out of a window never to be seen again.'

By the time she reached the Hall, parked and made her way across the crunching gravel, Sybella wished she could leap out of that proverbial window. She was also praying she'd find Mr Voronov alone. What if Nik had heard the boyfriend gossip? She wouldn't be able to look him in the eye after that. Although she guessed, when it came to the court case, it would be his barrister who was asking the questions...

So much depended on Nik Voronov being reasonable. Reasonable! She was so sunk.

Sybella was shown inside and as she reached the open sitting-room door she could hear male voices. Her knees gave out a little and she wondered if she could just leave the box of letters here and run...

'She has a kid. You could have mentioned it, Deda.'

'How was I to know you would take this much interest?' Mr Voronov sounded amused, his rich accent rolling the 'r's.

Sybella ventured a little closer.

'Nor did you mention the husband.'

'She's a widow. She was barely married when the poor boy's van was hit by an oncoming car. It's a sad story.'

'One you fell for hook, line and sinker.'

Sybella stiffened.

But Mr Voronov still sounded amused. 'Your cynicism will not win her over, my boy.'

Win her over?

'I'm realistic, and you, old man, need to stay still or this is going to hurt.'

Sybella didn't know what she expected to find as she came abruptly into the room but it more than niggled that if his eldest grandson was overprotective when it came to his legal rights, it wasn't translating into the kind of care the elderly man deserved.

What confronted her wasn't an angry Nik Voronov bullying his grandfather, but the younger man hunkered down in front of his grandfather's chair, deftly applying ointment to the abscess above his ankle.

'Sybella, *moy rebenok*, this is a surprise. Come and sit down. My grandson is looking after me today.'

'So I see.' It was not a surprise; she'd rung ahead to let him know she was coming. So now she was feeling a little set up.

Only Nik looked just as taken aback as she felt.

'What are you doing here?' he growled.

'Nikolai!'

'I've brought biscuits.' She held up the tin. 'My mother-in-law made them and sends her regards.'

'You didn't whip them up yourself in between all the dusting and vacuuming?' This was from Nik, who continued to lay a gauze strip over the wound and tape it up.

Sybella couldn't help noticing he was utterly competent at the task. It didn't exactly fit her image of him as the absent grandson. Clearly he'd done this more than once.

'I would, if I whipped them up at midnight,' she said, not sure of her footing here. 'My mother-in-law doesn't work. I do.'

Nik straightened up and Sybella was reminded all over again of his physical presence and how it could fill the room. He was entirely too dominant for her peace of mind.

It would probably be better for everyone if he left the village today, and quickly.

Only she kept remembering how his hands had felt against her skin, how gentle he'd been drying her hair and later kissing her, making all the lights turn on and leaving them on.

'Nikolka, I think you should take Sybella to lunch.'

'Oh, no, that's not why I'm here.' Sybella stumbled in her haste over the words and she knew she sounded rude but it was excruciating to think Nik might feel obligated to sit through lunch with her.

'I just wanted to deliver the biscuits—' she reached into her handbag '—and these. The letters you sent me, Mr Voronov, in your grandson's name.' She put them down on his side table. 'I would appreciate it if you showed him the documentation I gave you. He might be a little kinder on all of us.'

She glanced up at Nik, who was now standing dangerously close to her. Her whole body was vibrating like a tuning fork. She had to get out of here!

'This just proves we were in a correspondence, or rather I was with your grandfather, and everything I did was above board.' She couldn't look him in the eye or she'd lose all her courage.

'What have you been saying to her, Nikolka?'

'Nothing he didn't have a right to—given he had no idea what was going on.'

She went over and crouched down, putting a hand on

Mr Voronov's arm. 'I understand why you did it, but it's caused me a deal of trouble and upset your grandson.'

The elderly man covered her hand with his own. 'You cannot blame an old man for trying.'

Sybella rather thought she could, but she wouldn't.

'You really need to sort this out with your grandson, but whatever happens with the Hall, I'll continue to bring Fleur here for stories. That won't change.'

She glanced a little furtively at Nik, who looked as if he was about to say something, and straightened up, making her way to the door. Every step felt awkward but she couldn't be in this room a moment longer with Nik Voronov looking at her like that.

Sybella was almost at her car when she heard his heavy crunching footsteps.

'Sybella, we need to clear a few things up.'

'There's nothing to clear up.' Sybella tried not to sound breathless, a little dismayed at how everything female in her sat up to pay attention. 'We don't have anything more to discuss.'

He looked down at her as if he didn't agree.

'You know everything now,' she said in a tight voice. 'I'm pretty much an open book, as you can see.'

She thrust her chin at the small cigar box he carried in his hand.

'Let me drive you back to town,' he said.

'I'm perfectly capable of looking after myself, thank you very much.'

'You haven't done a very good job so far,' he said bluntly. 'You should have spoken up for yourself earlier.'

'Right. Good to know for future reference, but, if you hadn't noticed, I was thinking of your grandfather.'

She dipped her head as a tremor ran through her and without a word Nik put his arm around her.

It wasn't an invasive gesture, he was just there, and it

felt so good she found herself with her face against his shoulder, taking a few sustaining breaths because she had to end this in a moment. She couldn't be doing this with this man.

'I meant to me,' he said quietly against her ear. 'You should have spoken up for yourself to me.'

'Why?'

'Because I like to get my own way. But I'm human, Sybella. I could have got this wrong.'

She stilled.

'Besides,' he said, 'what was I supposed to do? Let this all slide? I had to get to the bottom of it. I owe my grandfather a duty of care.'

'No, of course.' Breathing deeply, Sybella extricated herself and he let her go.

She'd seen how tender he'd been with his grandfather, the bond between them. It made her feel graceless for her critical words to him. She'd clearly understood very little. And Nik was...well, overwhelming her. Sybella allowed that thought in for the first time. She guessed it was only to be expected. He felt so solid and dependable and she was so tired of being the solid and dependable one, and, besides, he made her feel like a desirable woman.

She couldn't remember Simon ever making her feel this way. Loved, yes. Cared for. But not this pulsing, breathless awareness every time he came near her.

She gave him a quick upward look. 'I should go.'

She opened her car door. He held it while she climbed in, but the hand she extended to reach for the ignition was shaking badly.

Nik knew this was down to him. He had this out-of-character urge to reassure her. He couldn't stand it that her lips were mashed together and seeing that tremor in her hand had him wanting to put his arms around her again, but she was clearly embarrassed.

Instead he said gruffly, 'I'll drive you—that way you won't end up parked up a tree.'

To his surprise she didn't argue. She let him take the keys with another subdued 'thank you'. He walked her around to open the passenger door.

'You have amazing manners,' she said, looking a little shy now. 'I guess it's a Russian thing.'

'*Net.* It's my grandfather's thing.'

'You are close to him, aren't you?' she said when he got in the other side.

'He raised me from the age of nine.'

She was looking at him curiously as he adjusted her driving seat to accommodate his long legs. 'I didn't know that.'

He never spoke about his childhood or his relationship with Deda to anyone, but there was something about Sybella that consistently had him relaxing his guard.

'They had a summer house on the Baltic. There were cherry trees along the drive so in spring it was like a tunnel of pink and white petals, and in summer Deda would take me sailing the fjords.'

'It sounds idyllic.'

He shrugged. 'It was a haven of sorts.'

'From what?'

'Boarding school.'

'We have something in common,' she said.

'I know.' He named the elite public girls' school she'd attended and then regretted it because she went stiff as a board again. 'I did a little basic research on you this morning.'

'Research?'

'You're in my grandfather's life. I have to check you out.'

She sighed. 'I guess so. What did you find out?'

'Don't worry, I didn't have your taxes hauled over.'

'I didn't know anyone could do that. Search into someone's background that easily.'

'It's just basic facts anyone could find on your social media page.'

'I'm not on social media.'

'No.'

'Then how—?' She broke off and shook her head. 'Don't bother, you're rich, you have your ways.'

'You probably know just as much about me from the Internet.'

'I know you have a big mine in the Urals. I looked it up. It looks like a vast crater.'

'You can see it from the moon,' said Nik.

'I won't ask you if you have a problem with your ego,' she murmured, and for the first time a small smile tipped up one corner of her mouth.

'I didn't dig it all myself,' he responded, trying not to get too distracted by the sudden desire to make her smile some more, 'but, yeah, my ego is pretty healthy.'

She exhaled a soft crumpled laugh and looked away, her cheeks a little flushed.

Nik couldn't rip his eyes off her.

'Your little girl,' he coaxed, 'what's her name?'

Her expression instantly softened. 'Fleur.'

'It's a pretty name.'

'My little flower,' she said.

'How old is she?'

'Five and a half.'

'I didn't mean to scare her,' he said, the words feeling outsized, almost as if he was blundering again.

'You didn't scare her. She's just not used to raised voices.'

'Yeah, I deserve that.'

She eyed him almost shyly and again he got the impression Sybella wasn't anywhere near as tough as she pretended to be—or maybe needed to be. 'Your grandfather is teaching her to read. On Thursdays, when I'm here to take tours. Afterwards Fleur and I have tea with him.'

And he had forbidden her to come to the Hall again. He wanted to ask her why she hadn't let him know this earlier, but then he knew he hadn't given her much of a chance.

He was revisiting every hard thing he'd said to her since they'd met. He was beginning to think Sybella Parminter didn't really want anything from anyone, she was so determined to do it all herself.

'What I said about the house. I'm not here to ruin your or your daughter's relationship with my grandfather.'

She nodded, focused on some point outside the car.

'But I can't have my grandfather's home turned into…'

'A theme park, I know, I heard you.'

He had a strong urge to pull her into his arms, but that wasn't going to go down well.

'Mr Voronov talks a lot about his grandsons.' She looked over at him as if trying to read his face. 'He—he seems very proud of both of you.'

'Possibly simply relieved the two of us have managed not to break any laws or tarnish the family name,' Nik said, the brief smile he gave her almost boyish, and Sybella's heart did a stumble. 'He's not the robust man he once was. When my grandmother Baba died it was sudden and unexpected. We were all left floundering.'

Sybella suspected Nik was including himself in that floundering and her susceptible heart did more than stumble, it completely softened.

'Deda went overnight from the man who adapted to anything to how he is now, sometimes querulous and unhappy and mostly set in his ways.'

Sybella privately acknowledged the older man could be difficult, but she suspected it was because he felt managed. 'Mr Voronov has spoken to me of his wife.'

'Baba was everything to him.' And perhaps to her grandson, Sybella thought, watching a sadness weight his expression.

'Why did he come here of all places?'

'His health required visits to a clinic in London. I found myself with no choice but to accommodate his wish to not live in the city. He was in a hospital bed when he put a copy of *Country Life* in front of me and pointed out the photograph of Edbury Hall, and I hadn't been in a position to say no.'

'But you wish you had now.'

He was silent for a moment and then said quietly, 'No, things have changed since I arrived yesterday. It's not that clear-cut any more.'

Sybella told herself he wasn't referring to her but it was difficult to hold his gaze when he looked at her like that.

Nik watched the shyness she worked so hard to keep hidden soften her features, her hands working nervously in her lap.

'I don't suppose we can sit here all day,' she said, 'or is that your intention?'

Nik laughed and she appeared taken aback, as if his amusement was something slightly shocking. Was he that bad?

'Where do you want to go?'

He expected her to say back to work, but she looked out across the gravel courtyard and said, 'I've got a window of an hour before I need to pick Fleur up. Why don't we just go for a drive?'

There was a wash of colour in her cheeks again. He knew he couldn't start anything with her, but it couldn't hurt to take a drive.

'Why don't we?' he said and started the engine.

Sybella directed him to Linton Way Forest and they parked under the oaks. She got out and they walked down the overgrown walking track that famously weaved in and over the hills.

She told him about the uses the village had for the estate, and he listened.

'We have tours on Thursday afternoons. People are free to look at the west wing on weekends. The pony club use the grounds once a month for the gymkhana. That's about it so far. It doesn't impact on your grandfather's private life in the house. In fact he often appears unannounced to talk to tourists himself.'

'What I'm more interested in is the financial benefit to your little organisation.'

Sybella looked genuinely surprised.

'The Heritage Trust is a charity. Any money goes back into preservation—no one is pocketing it. We all volunteer.'

Nik reached around to massage the back of his neck and Sybella tried not to ogle his biceps. She was aware of him physically in a way that was making it difficult to concentrate on the serious matters they were discussing.

Although something had changed between them, Sybella just couldn't put her finger on what it was. He was more willing to listen and she was incredibly conscious of him physically.

'How did you come to be involved with them?'

'I have a degree and a diploma in archives management I earned part time when Fleur was younger. I needed some work experience and the Heritage Trust is all that's available in the area so I volunteered. That was three years ago.'

'That can't have been easy with a baby.'

'No.' She slanted a shy look his way, because it was nice to have that acknowledged. Encouraged, Sybella plunged into the tough stuff. 'I met your grandfather when the trust approached him about opening the house. He took an immediate dislike to our president but he was rather taken by Fleur, who was with me, and invited the two of us to tea. I do tours now on Thursdays for various schools and Fleur and I take tea with your grandfather afterwards. It's become a sort of ritual between us.'

'He talks about you a great deal.'

Sybella chewed on her lip. 'Nice things, I hope.'

'Nice being the word. He wants me to settle down with a nice girl.'

Oh, yes, she'd seen those girls on the Internet.

'The thing is, Sybella, I work hard,' he said unexpectedly.

She could have told him she worked hard too, but she guessed he and the rest of the world put more value on his work.

She watched those long lashes sweep down, the irony in his voice only making him seem more impenetrable, and Sybella could absolutely see why very beautiful, sought-after women would make an attempt at breaching all that male beauty and privilege with the aim of being the one to stick up her flag.

'I don't have time to invest in someone else's life. I date women with a corresponding world view.'

Sybella just kept nodding because she wasn't sure why he was telling her this.

'My grandfather doesn't approve,' he said dryly.

'He's very good with Fleur. I guess he wants great-grandchildren.'

Which was when it all fell neatly into place.

'Oh, no,' she said.

'Exactly. You knew nothing of this?'

'It simply didn't occur to me.'

'You do fit the criteria,' he said, with a slight smile that had Sybella's head snapping around in astonishment. 'He told me you would cook, clean and be a wonderful mother to our children,' he added.

But not Nik's criteria. Beautiful and not looking for—what did he call it—an investment? Sybella wrinkled her nose. It was a horrible term. The antithesis of an emotion.

He was talking about his grandfather's criteria.

Which she guessed were somewhat less exacting. To do with being a mum and a homebody. What would he say if she told him she'd never planned to take on any of this, it was life in its infinite surprises that had laid down those roles for her?

That she still, deep down, thought of herself as the independent individualist she had always been.

Did he really think she was angling herself at him?

'I didn't stand around in the courtyard last night waiting for you because your grandfather put me up to it!'

'Good to know.'

So that was what this romantic walk in the woods was all about.

She was being given the message he wasn't interested. He clearly thought she needed that message. Sybella's stomach hollowed out.

Probably now was a good time to sort this, when her ego was still reverberating from his direct hit and she was feeling a bit numb.

'There's just one small problem I should probably alert you to before we go our separate ways,' she said with as much dignity as she could muster. 'After the other night a lot of people in the village think you're my boyfriend.'

'Boyfriend?'

Sybella could feel herself turning pink. This was possibly one of the more embarrassing moments of her life.

'It's not what you think. I haven't rushed about telling people you are.'

'I'm not thinking that,' he said slowly.

'The other night at the Hall when you were holding me, some of the committee members got the wrong idea.'

She looked up at him, biting the inside of her lower lip. 'It will blow over, but I thought you should be made aware of it.'

Nik did his best to repress his amusement. He cleared his throat. 'People do jump to some out-there conclusions.'

'I know, crazy, right?' Sybella began to talk faster, because now they were at the more awkward bit, but she had to ask. 'There's one other thing. There aren't many opportunities in the immediate countryside for curatorial jobs, and my CV isn't exactly bursting at the seams, and if it gets out what happened with the house being open to the public on false pretences and you shutting things down, I can't see anyone ever hiring me. Ever.'

'I see.'

'Reputation matters in this business.'

'Makes sense.'

'If you could see your way clear to not pressing any legal charges—'

'Sybella, I didn't have all the information to hand. I'm not going to make your life any more difficult than it already is.'

'Oh.' She said a silent prayer. 'Thank you. You're not nearly as scary as you pretend to be, are you?'

It was his turn to look vaguely bemused.

'I don't mean to offend you,' she rushed on, 'but you can be a bit intimidating. I suppose it's because you're so big.'

'There's that,' Nik drawled, not sure if she knew how adorable she looked babbling at him as if he had feelings to hurt and she was worried about having stepped on them. 'I also have a lot of financial clout. You'd be amazed, Mrs Parminter, how the world works.'

'I suppose I would,' she said, blushing. 'I should probably get up to speed on that.'

He almost idly wound the end of one of her ringlets around his index finger before releasing it. It was a gesture implying intimacy, touching her but not quite touching her, which made her think about when they had touched, when they'd kissed.

'No, don't do that,' he said. 'Stay the way you are.'

'Too tall, too opinionated, too fat,' she blurted out.

Oh. God. Where had that come from? Because there was nothing more attractive to a man than a woman who bemoaned her looks. At least in some far-flung universe they didn't currently occupy.

To forestall any opinion he might have about her round body or her interest in him, she bowled on, 'Sorry, I don't know where that came from. I guess all those women you date don't go on about their looks because they're so gorgeous it doesn't occur to them.'

Sybella took a breath and stared in disbelief into the middle distance.

There was this awful silence. She wondered if he'd think it was odd if she just ran off at this point, screaming, into the forest.

Instead she made a swipe of her watch under her long sleeve.

'Oh, goodness, is that the time? I have to pick up Fleur from communal play. She's got a birthday party tomorrow with her little friends. She's taking fairy bread, and I still have to pick up the ingredients.'

She didn't wait for his response but started hurrying away from him, back towards the car.

'Listen to me babbling,' she threw over her shoulder. 'You don't mind me driving, do you?'

His steady tread on the gravel mocked her hasty, messy retreat. She climbed in the car and waited, clammy with horror. Although he'd told her she wasn't his type, he knew now, if he hadn't already suspected, she was besotted with him.

CHAPTER SEVEN

SYBELLA SAT CROSS-LEGGED on her sofa, looking into the inquisitive brown eyes of her daughter's house rabbit.

'I committed the cardinal sin,' she told Dodge. 'I exposed every last one of my frailties in front of Nik Voronov. I may as well have told him no one has seen my good lingerie except the wash bag in the machine in six years.'

She answered herself with a question. 'Can you get more specific there, Syb?'

'I told him I was fat and lonely and pretty much desperate.'

'Why would you do that?'

'Because he probably dates glamazons and his grandfather wants him to date me instead and he basically told me that wasn't going to happen and I sort of went…crazy.'

'Well, you do go a bit weird with a full moon.'

'I don't think it was the full moon, although given not only am I talking to a rabbit, I'm doing the voice so he answers back, it might be. And now I'm not even talking to the rabbit, I'm talking to myself. I am so screwed.'

'I wouldn't say that,' said a deep voice and Sybella almost fell off the couch.

Standing in the doorway off the hall was her Viking god.

'How did you get in?'

'You left the front door unlocked and I heard voices. I used that bell-pull. Are you aware it doesn't work?'

Sybella's cheeks felt red hot, mainly because she'd been caught making an idiot of herself. In front of the one person in the world she couldn't bear to think any worse of her.

'I'm sorry but you can't just walk in here.' She eased herself off the sofa carefully, not wanting to alarm Dodge, who was now sitting up, peering at Nik, ears aquiver.

'You even apologise to intruders into your home,' he said as if she'd revealed some secret about herself, then a look of amusement crossed his face. 'Is that rabbit for real?'

'His name is Dodge, and he's a house rabbit, there's another one around, so please keep your voice down.'

'I wouldn't want to frighten the woodland creatures,' he said, lowering his voice, looking at her in a way that made Sybella weirdly think he was including her in that. He closed the door gently behind him so that suddenly her living area felt very small.

'What are you doing here?'

'I came to say goodbye. I'm leaving in the morning.'

Sybella was hit by a punch of utter disappointment. He was leaving? 'Oh.'

He wore a T-shirt and jeans, as casual as she'd seen him, only on him it looked like one of those ads in a glossy magazine where the guy was glowering sullenly at the viewer and toting some serious machismo, and usually there was a dangerous-looking motorcycle behind him. Yes, Nik Voronov appeared to have stepped out of those pages into her living room.

And he'd come to say goodbye?

'I read your proposal about opening the gatehouse as a tourist hub for the house and estate.'

Sybella was so busy swimming in disappointment he was leaving she didn't completely take it in.

''It's a sound proposal,' he said. 'I'm willing to talk about it.'

Now? This was good, he was staying—to talk about the Hall. It was a big step in the right direction—for the Hall.

Sybella did an internal eye roll. She really needed to get herself together around him.

'The truth is I'm under a bit of pressure with the old man.'

It wasn't what she expected to hear and it wiped all the nonsense in her head. He needed her help. He actually moved a hand over the back of his neck, the age-old posture of male admission he was willing to lay down arms. That alone spoke volumes about his feelings for his grandfather.

She melted. 'You really love him, don't you?'

He shrugged. 'He's my grandfather.'

Sybella thought of her lousy, self-interested parents and then shoved them back where they belonged, over a cliff and into the ocean of people who could break your heart if you let them.

'I'd like to speak to you about him, something personal. Can I sit down?'

He didn't wait for the invitation, but lowered himself onto the armchair, catty-corner from the sofa she was now inhabiting.

He leaned forward, resting his forearms over his broad knees, fixing her with that intent grey gaze.

She'd been entertaining so many romantic fantasies about this man over the last twenty-four hours, to have him in the flesh inhabiting her small living room had the quality of one of those.

'Where's your little girl?'

'Her aunty Meg is here for the weekend so she's having a sleepover with her at my parents-in-law's house. They live on the other side of the village.'

Something flickered in his gaze and Sybella could suddenly hear her heartbeat in her ears.

'You were going to tell me something…personal about you and your grandfather?' she prompted, aware her voice had a slightly airless quality to it.

He gave her a half-smile as if acknowledging the irony

of the 'something personal' when right about now everything about him being here felt personal.

'I am,' he said. 'It begins with my parents. They were childhood sweethearts, Darya and Alex, and had been together for a long time before they had a separation of about a year, and my mother got pregnant with me. She mustn't have thought that much of the guy because she rekindled her romance with Alex and he was apparently happy to call me his son.'

Sybella didn't know what to say.

'I don't have any memories of my mother. She had a rare kidney condition and died when I was still a baby. Papa raised me alone until he remarried. They were good years or so I'm told. I lived on a lot of film sets but this is in Russia. Alex always used the same people and the crew were like family. When I was five I got a very flashy stepmother and several months later a baby brother. Sasha. I'm sure you've heard about him.'

'Your grandfather mentions him from time to time. He seems to be in the public eye quite a bit.'

'My little brother is famous for his films and his parties, not always in that order,' Nik responded, but there was real warmth in his voice, as there had been when he'd spoken to his grandfather. Sybella was beginning to feel a little foolish about all her doubts. They were clearly a strong unit.

'Sasha was four years old when our father slipped on a ledge climb in Turkey. Papa was chasing a shot for a film he was putting together. He always took risks. My brother is very much like him.'

Nik's expression conveyed this wasn't necessarily a positive thing.

'I went to live with my grandparents after Alex's death. My grandfather was a successful businessman. I don't know if he's talked to you about that part of his life.'

'No, not really. We talk about family and books mainly.'

'His favourite subjects.' Nik was scrutinising her and she couldn't blame him. She was fast becoming the vault of Voronov family secrets.

'I'm not indiscreet, Nik. I won't talk about this to anyone.'

He smiled then. 'I wouldn't be sharing this with you if I thought you would. I'm telling you all this, Sybella, because it appears my grandfather has taken quite a shine to you, and he's told me how good you've been to him, and I behaved badly last night and I don't want to leave here with you thinking the worst of me.'

'But I don't,' she began, a little too anxious to assure him her feelings had changed. 'I saw how close the two of you are this afternoon.'

'I owe him so much,' Nik said simply. 'I only knew how much when I was fifteen and needed a blood transfusion and neither of my grandparents could help out. That was when Baba and Deda sat me down and told me the true state of affairs. I wasn't their grandson.'

'But you are,' said Sybella unbidden, and then flushed. 'I'm sorry, you don't need me to tell you that.'

'It's all right.' He was smiling at her and the effect of that smile was singing all over her body. 'So you see,' he said, 'we have something in common.'

'Have you tracked him down, your biological father?' She stopped, embarrassed. 'I'm sorry, that's another very personal question. You don't have to answer that.'

'No, I haven't met him.' He shifted and Sybella could see this weighed on him. 'I have his name. I haven't done anything about it. I don't know if I ever will.' He rolled those big shoulders. 'What about you? Have you gone looking for your real parents?'

Which was a neat way of diverting the conversation. Sybella wondered if he was even conscious of how everything in his body conveyed tension when he talked about his biological father.

'According to the records office, my father is unknown and my mother was a student who gave me up for adoption,' she answered. 'We got together when I was twenty. She came to my wedding. She remembers Fleur with birthday cards, which is something. I think it's hard for her to maintain relationships with people. She seems to have had a difficult life.' She looked down at her hands.

'I'm sorry I was dismissive about your adoptive parents the other night,' he said. 'I shouldn't have said what I did.'

She looked up. 'That's all right, it's forgotten.'

Nik was gazing back at her steadily, and this intimacy created by their mutual confessions was making Sybella feel something like the first steps in a friendship was springing up between them, only none of her friends were six-feet-six-inch Russians with Cossack eyes and a way of looking at her that made her think he might like to kiss her again.

'What a pair we make,' he said in that quiet, gravelly way of his.

Sybella dropped her gaze, suddenly immensely shy.

'What I guess I'm getting around to, Sybella, is that Deda has helped me through some difficult times as a kid, Baba as well. I owe them both a great deal. I'm cognisant I may have dropped the ball with Deda recently, but I want you to know he's in safe hands and why.'

Sybella blinked rapidly because she could feel ready emotional tears surging up.

Blast those pregnancy hormones. They'd arrived six years ago and never really gone away.

'I could see how close you were earlier today.' She dabbed at her eyes. 'I'm sorry if I implied anything else. I obviously didn't have the full picture and you weren't obliged to tell me. I mean, it's not as if we know one another.'

'I'd like to get to know you better.' His Russian accent was suddenly stronger and Sybella almost slid off the sofa again.

He would? Don't be stupid. He doesn't mean it like that.

'I would too.' She tried to think of something to avert attention from her burning cheeks. 'I can offer you something to eat. I was just going to mix up a stir-fry for dinner. Would you like some?'

Nik didn't hesitate despite having just eaten a full meal with his grandfather. 'Yes, I would.'

When she leaned forward to stuff her feet into slippers, as if to completely assure the direction of the evening, her breasts moved sumptuously against her top, giving him a glorious view of how generous Mother Nature had been.

'The kitchen's this way,' she said, straightening up as if nothing extraordinary had just happened, and with a shy smile she gestured for him to follow her.

Nik followed.

His gaze dropped to the fulsome curve of her bottom beneath the soft fabric of her drawstring pants. He'd never considered himself a connoisseur of the female bottom. But right now he was seeing the benefits of a woman with some heft in her pendulum. In fact he was pretty much transfixed by that sweet wobble and sway.

In the kitchen she had a bottle of Spanish red out on the counter.

'Can you get some glasses? They're in the cabinet over there,' she instructed as she began gathering her ingredients around her.

He found a couple of wine glasses and poured. He'd drunk worse.

Presently the place began to smell delicious from whatever was heating up on the stove.

Vaguely he remembered his grandfather mentioning Sybella's cooking skills, and he had to admit there was something about Sybella that made a woman being competent in a kitchen sexy.

He didn't do domestic scenes with women. He had a chef, or he ate out. His stepmother had been allergic to anything but restaurants, and until his grandparents had swept in and given him a home he'd eaten a lot of take-out.

So deep down he associated home cooking with stability and the love of his grandparents. But he wasn't one of those guys who clung to redundant gender roles. Which made this weird because underneath all that he was still the son of generations of conservative Russian males, and he really was enjoying watching Sybella cook for him.

'So you work at the town hall?'

'Yes.' She was busily chopping up apples but she gave him her shy smile. 'I'm the assistant archivist. You can find me in the basement with all the dusty files. We're putting a lot of things on the computer system but so much of what we handle is original documentation, dating back before the English Civil War, registers of births, deaths and marriages, land holdings, town maintenance. It's all there, and we keep the originals in the library for academics and the occasional documentary film maker. I chase things up for people three days a week.'

'This interests you, doesn't it, the past?'

'I like permanence,' she said, laying down the knife. 'It comforts me to know ten generations have lived here, in this house. People have been born here and died here, been married out of this house, triumphed and suffered and dreamed within its walls. I like old things, the way they soak up the lives of the people who have lived in them and with them.'

Nik remembered what she'd told him about being adopted, about being handed back, about her adoptive parents not being in her child's life.

This was important to her for good reasons. She'd pulled a bad hand as a kid, and, looking around her house, he could see she'd made more than a home with her daughter. She'd put down roots.

'So what plans did you have for the Hall before I bought it?'

She looked up in surprise, 'How did you know—?' She broke off and shook her head. 'You've been ahead of me all along, haven't you?'

'It's not difficult to work out.'

'Well,' she said, beginning to dice again, 'apart from turning the gatehouse into a tourist hub, we were planning on having open-day picnics in the grounds, but that was under the last owner. He was an American, you understand.' She cast an almost mischievous look at him through her lashes.

'Meaning a Russian is not big-spirited enough to get out of the way of English heritage?'

'No, no,' she said, laughing, and the sound arrested him. He'd never heard her laugh. 'I meant he knows the value of a buck. Edbury could be quite profitable.'

It was the last thing he'd expected Sybella to say, and he agreed with her. He'd been thinking along the same lines, but ruled a line under it. This was his grandfather's home; he wasn't dislodging him.

'It can't be done. Deda loves it here.'

Sybella put down the knife she was using with a clatter. 'Oh, my goodness, no, you misunderstand me. This wasn't my idea, it was your grandfather's.'

'Prostit?'

Sybella bit the inside of her lip. She was beginning to look forward to the moments when he spoke his language to her.

'Mr Voronov has been looking at literature from other local stately homes. We've been talking about what could be done here. To hold onto the heritage of the Hall to pass on to future generations. I thought you could be brought on board,' she said, then lowered her gaze because she was beginning to wonder if in a minute he'd warn her off going within twenty metres of the Hall again. 'We all care desperately about keeping the place historically intact for the future. And to be honest, Nik, I think it's given your grandfather a reason to get up in the mornings.'

Nik unfolded his arms. 'Why don't you tell me about it, then, your plans?'

'Truly?' she said.

Their eyes met and hers dropped first. She began dicing a little harder.

'Naturally it would take a lot of setting up. There are bylaws, not to mention the increase in traffic using local roads. We don't want the village being overrun by tourists. We get quite enough in the summer. Not so much Brits but busloads from overseas. Everybody wants to poke around in some between-the-wars version of England with its winding lanes and thatched cottages.'

'Says the woman who lives in one.'

She smiled and Nik felt something lodge behind his breastbone. This beautiful woman, who had blinked back tears when he'd told her about his parents, and dissolved in his arms the other night and now was preparing dinner for him, was smiling at him.

Those eyes stayed locked to his and he was suddenly only aware of the hard, heated consequences of being around her for the past twenty-four hours beating against the buttons on his jeans.

'Careful.' He laid a hand on hers where she was chopping up the apple. She looked down to see she'd almost nicked her finger. 'You're not paying attention,' he chided, stroking her finger with his thumb.

'No, I'm not,' she said with a small smile, those hazel eyes flitting to his shyly but with a look of unvarnished sexual yearning before they swooped down to his mouth, giving her away so entirely all he could do was remove the knife from her hand and wait for her eyes to lift again and dance to his.

He hadn't planned to make a move on her. He'd only known he owed her an explanation and an apology and the temptation of seeing her again had been too strong.

She had lowered her lashes and he was able to study her face, the boldness of her mouth, the soft, full curve of her cheeks. She was so damn lovely.

The heat from the pot had turned her cheeks pink and curled the fair tendrils escaping from her bun around her face. The fragrance of rosemary and basil, along with the olive oil from the pan, was on her fingertips and he was imagining those fingers touching his skin.

He wanted to lift her onto the bench, lay her down among her fresh ingredients and plunder her soft pink mouth until she was his.

'So your daughter is at her sleepover?' Nik heard himself ask as if they were having a general conversation.

Sybella nodded, not trusting her voice. She knew what the question meant. Telling him there was a fifty-fifty chance she'd get a phone call from Meg at around eleven and Fleur would want to come home would probably sink things where they stood.

She could surely keep these two halves of her life separate for an evening. He would be gone tomorrow and she would go back to keeping all those balls in the air.

But she didn't want to think about tomorrow. Just thinking about everything she had on her plate would surely close down her inner sex goddess completely.

She turned away from him abruptly and went over to the hob. She fumbled with the gas as she turned off the flame under the saucepan and pan, telling herself she could have this once. With this gorgeous man. Nobody needed to know.

Besides, it wasn't anyone's business…

Her breath caught as he put a hand around her waist and turned her and then laid a finger against her cheek and eased away an errant curl.

She gazed into his heated eyes and said, 'Maybe we can skip dinner.'

CHAPTER EIGHT

SHE TOOK HIS HAND, sliding her fingers along his, and he enfolded her slighter grasp within his own and she led him out of the kitchen into the narrow hall and to the foot of the stairs.

Nik saw a moment's hesitation in her, as she laid a foot on the first step and then stopped. Which was when he picked her up. She said something ridiculous about being too heavy but he'd already mounted the stairs and she was looking at him as if no man had acted like a Neanderthal around her, when he could imagine most of the men she met probably fantasised about doing this with her. But didn't make it past that first step. Her hesitation, the way she looked at him, told him this was not a regular occurrence in her life.

Her bedroom door was directly opposite the stairs and open. The double bed didn't look big enough but as he lowered her onto it he could see there was enough room for their purpose.

'Let me do this,' she said, before he could kiss her.

She was climbing up on her knees, tugging and pulling his T-shirt up over his head.

He was surprised by her willingness to take the initiative given her nervousness, but he wasn't complaining as he finished the job for her and tossed the T-shirt over his shoulder.

'I'm going to do this,' she said and he could have told her he wasn't going to argue.

She ran her fingers down his torso, exploring the defi-nition of his muscles and tendons beneath the skin intricately converging to form that V below his taut abdomen, undoing a few of the buttons on his jeans.

Nik's breathing was already coming in snags as he watched her explore him with her fingertips. Her touch was so light, the expression on her face transfixed.

'Is this okay?'

She foraged under those loose buttons, meeting his eyes. 'Yeah, that's okay,' he said, swallowing as she slowly slid her hand over the length of him.

Nik sucked in a breath and went still, eyes lambent, the breath hissing between his teeth as she explored him with her hand.

When she was sure he definitely hadn't had enough she smiled and removed her hand and then slowly, enticingly began to move that same hand over the button fly of his jeans, opening it up.

'Are you trying to kill me, *dushka*?' he half joked, his voice hoarsened with the effort.

'That would defeat our purpose, don't you think?' Somehow that combination of her shy smile and her knowing eyes as she tugged his jeans down over his lean hips, taking his boxers with them, had the same effect as her hand on his erection.

She came over him, measuring him with her eyes, and lowered her head, her hair sliding forward to curtain her face as she licked him from base to tip.

Nik hissed and gripped the coverlet, fisting it as he fought not to disgrace himself. He was on a hair trigger; just watching her was enough to set him off.

She'd been so shy.

He really hadn't expected this…this sex goddess.

He tried to control the building reaction to her lapping, swirling pink tongue, the graze of her plump lips, and as she slid him into her mouth he knew he wasn't going to make it if she went any further and he gently disengaged her and deftly rolled her back onto the bed.

She lay there, smiling up at him as if she'd accomplished something she was proud of, as she should be, her eyes glistening, her mouth wet, her breaths coming even shorter as he slid one finger into the vee of her soft cotton top, where it dipped into the valley between her breasts.

He went to strip her shirt off but she clamped her hands over his.

'The light,' she said, blinking anxiously at him as if he might say no.

He looked up at the overhead, a vintage frilled thing that was currently lighting things up to his satisfaction.

'It's in my eyes,' she said, looking suddenly oddly flustered. 'Can we have it off?'

Only an idiot would argue with her at this point. He bounded from the bed to turn the main light off. Sybella had reached across and switched on the lamp. The room was suddenly in shadows but Sybella was bathed in a diffused caramel glow.

She looked positively feline and possibly the most sensual creature he had ever laid eyes on.

'Anything else you want doing?' he asked, coming down beside her on the bed.

He ran his hands over her hips and behind to the curve of her generous bottom still clad in satin something and into her eyes crept a touch of tension. He snuffed it out by kissing her hungrily, devouring the soft, sweet mouth he'd been dreaming about for the last twenty-four hours.

He pushed her cotton top up over her breasts, lifting her arms and arching over her as he slid the cotton free. She was wearing a simple bra embroidered with pink forget-me-nots and with her flaxen hair tumbling over her shoulders she looked like every fantasy he'd ever had.

'*Bogu*, you're beautiful,' he said, sliding one strap off her shoulder.

'Am I?'

'Gorgeous.' He tried to imbue the assertion with some of the reverence he really did feel, but it wasn't easy when all he wanted to do was fall on her like a sex-starved teenager who'd never been this close to a naked woman's body in his life.

'You're a bona fide sex goddess,' he asserted and she responded by wrapping her arms around his neck and coming up to meet him.

As their mouths fused he was no longer able to keep up this song of seduction and skill; he was just a man a little clumsy with lust.

He slid his mouth down her throat, licking over her cleavage, feeling her shiver against him in anticipation. He reached under her and released the catch of her bra and then slowly, with an intensity of purpose because frankly her breasts deserved worshipping, he peeled her pretty cups away.

He took his time to look his fill, feeling her eyes on him, her rapid, short breaths telling him she found this thrilling too. He took one taut pink nipple between his lips and licked. She gasped and bucked under him. He moved from one breast to the other, licking and sucking and moulding her, listening to her sighs and the little noises she made.

He untied the drawstring on her pants and hooked his thumbs under the sides of her satin knickers on the way down and peeled them both off, his hands actually shaking. She'd left herself as nature made her, the soft fair curls at the apex of her thighs as pretty as anything he'd ever seen.

He traced the seam of her sex with his index finger and she gave a little 'oh' as he lowered himself to kiss her there and inhale the heady scent of aroused woman. He licked her without warning and then again and she cried out and pulsed to her first orgasm, but he didn't stop, he went on and on until he wrung the last glorious ripple from her.

When he lifted his head and looked up she had her eyes half closed, her hair spread around her, the sensuality of her on full uninhibited display, and satisfaction thundered through him. She gave him a dreamy smile.

'What a little honeypot you are,' he told her and placed a kiss on her lower belly, where she was softer and she had a silvery pale tributary of zigzagging lines and some pinkish ones that hadn't faded yet, if they ever would.

Sybella watched him through her lashes. She didn't mind those tiger stripes—her baby had given her those. He traced them with his tongue and kissed her belly again, coming up over her with intent.

'Not a honey trap any more?' Her voice was smoky with satisfaction.

His grin turned rueful. 'I take it I'm not forgiven for that.'

Sybella reached for him, her hands smoothing over the warm breadth of his chest to curl over his shoulders where the muscles were bunched. She couldn't get enough of his body. 'Oh, I think you're forgiven.'

'Happy?'

She gave him a sly smile. 'Not completely.'

'I still have some work to do—what could the lady possibly want from me now?'

He settled between her thighs and Sybella had a blissful moment of being exactly where she wanted to be with exactly the right man.

He'd seen her body now in all its opulent glory and she was beginning to think just maybe the awkwardness with Simon hadn't been entirely down to her, because at no point in any of this had she wanted to be covered by a sheet. Nik was obviously, unashamedly devouring her with his eyes.

She could feel him hard and impatient, stroking himself against her. *Right there.*

Sybella shifted her pelvis to bring him to her but he was pulling away.

No, no.

'Where are you going?' she asked incredulously.

'I need to suit up.'

Sybella flopped back on the mattress, grateful one of them was using their brain.

Nik had pulled a couple of condoms out of his wallet.

She gave him a lopsided smile. 'You were confident.'

'I had hopes.'

'Hurry,' she urged.

Nik discovered his hands were shaking slightly as he rolled one on and she moved to take over.

'You really are going to kill me,' he said between his teeth.

'Well, like I said before, that would defeat our purpose.' She said it with a little smile on her face that grew as she slid her hands over his hips, coming up on her knees and then looping her arms over his shoulders.

He spread his hands around her bottom, enjoying the give of her, the softness, the sheer female voluptuousness of her body against his harder frame.

He was against her and she made a soft little noise against his throat. Nik didn't need the encouragement and drove home, the sheer size of him paralysing her senses for a moment and then his mouth was hot at her neck and he was sheathed inside her and Sybella sighed her deep-felt appreciation, turning her mouth to his as he kissed her, smothered her mouth with his, before lowering his head to suck on her breasts, leaving her gasping.

He positioned her with his big hands and thrust again

and again and when he thought he couldn't hold back she climaxed around him, the intensity of it tipping him over the edge. Conscious thought was a long time coming and when it returned to Nik they were lying in each other's arms, her eyes soft and no longer as curious as they had been when he'd first looked into them in the snow last night. She had her answer.

'Well,' she panted, her breath soft against his shoulder, 'that was…something.'

'*Da*, something.' Too fast, too urgent, just…sensational. He felt grateful, dazed and looking forward to taking that trip to heaven again.

Soon.

He stroked the hair off her face, feeling an unaccountable level of well-being he hadn't felt in years. Her skin was dewy with faint perspiration, her cheeks pink; she was fairly glowing.

His gaze moved over the rounded shapes of her sumptuous breasts and flagrant hip curved under his hand. He squeezed her softly, enjoying the flesh under his hand.

'You like looking at me,' she said, her fingers tangling in his chest hair.

'I'd be crazy if I didn't.' He touched his lips to the tip of her nose and then her eyelids and finally her temple. Nothing salacious, more in reverence for how tender she made him feel.

'I like looking at you.' She massaged her lower lip with her teeth, as if something else was on her mind. 'I always had…trouble taking my clothes off in front of Simon. I felt, I thought, I don't know, I wondered what he saw.'

He gave her a lascivious smile and she smiled back and then her eyes filled and overflowed with tears.

'Sorry,' she gasped, cupping her face with her hands, 'so silly. Don't mind me.'

She was so English. So polite in the oddest circumstances. She was a woman. She was emotional. She shouldn't be ashamed of it. It made him feel tender. So he reached for her and kissed her tears and murmured to her in Russian, which seemed to quiet her. Presently her shoulders stopped quaking and she lay still against him.

'You were very young when you got married,' he said.

She nodded against his shoulder. 'Only I didn't think I was. I felt like I'd lived a lifetime before I met Simon.' She raised her face to look at him. 'He was my first love. We met in my first year at university. But after a year he—we—decided to take a break for the summer. He was going on a dig in Athens—amateur archaeology was his hobby, we kind of had that in common—but I couldn't go with him. I needed to work, save some money, so it was a break in our relationship.'

Nik waited; he suspected he knew where this was going.

'The next term he wanted to get back together but he told me he'd had a sort of a fling with another girl. It was okay,' she hurried on, glancing at him as if daring him to condemn her precious Simon. 'We were split when it happened.'

But he could hear in her voice there had been no splitting as far as Sybella was concerned. She was loyal. He'd known her twenty-four hours but he'd seen her loyalty in action, keeping the crucial information about the letters from him to protect Deda.

'Then, you see, she was in a few of my tutorial groups so I had to spend the rest of the year seeing her several times a month. I got a little funny about it. She never said anything, I don't think we ever exchanged any more than the normal pleasantries, but she must have known.'

'Do you want me to comment or just listen?' Nik had a number of thoughts, all of them about her fool of a husband.

'Listen, I think.' She gave a soft, nervous laugh. 'I've

said all the critical things in my head and I said a few to Simon at the time. It's just, we got back together—obviously—but I knew something wasn't right. Even on my wedding day there was this niggle.'

'He was still seeing her.'

'Gosh, no, no! Simon wasn't that kind of guy at all.'

Nyet, and in Sybella's partial eyes probably never would be. Nik did his best not to take a dislike to her dead husband.

'He was very ethical. I mean, he didn't have to tell me.'

Nik wisely kept his own counsel. But the thought remained, I wouldn't have told her, I would have protected her from the knowledge. Then the next startling thought arrived: I wouldn't have gone to another woman.

Not when the girl was Sybella. She seemed to him a little traditional, the kind of woman who would expect fidelity. If the guy had loved her, he would have known that.

She eyed him, nervous once more. 'I know this will sound silly but I got a bit funny about my body. I got it into my head Simon didn't find me desirable.' She frowned a little, as if puzzling over the girl she'd been.

Now Nik officially wanted to punch her dead husband.

'You see, this other girl, she was very pretty and she was tiny, like a fairy tiny, and I'm not.'

Nik didn't know what to do with that. 'No, you're not,' he said.

She shoved him. 'You're not supposed to say that.'

He nudged up her chin to look at her, so incredibly lovely with her light-in-a-forest eyes and her pale pre-Raphaelite curls tumbling over her shoulders and those gorgeous breasts, and he knew in that moment what all men knew: they would never understand women.

'Listen, Lady Godiva, my interest in fairies ended around about the age of four. I want a woman in my bed, and I want her soft and warm and capable of giving as good as she gets—in and out of bed. Your Simon was young, yes?'

'Twenty-two when we got married.' Sybella's voice was soft and she was looking at him hopefully, as if he might say the very thing that was going to fix all this for her.

Nik wasn't so sure. He knew from personal experience how deep resentments could shoot those roots when they attached young. Rejection by your parents had to leave deep fault lines, and Sybella had just admitted hers. To him. As if he was worth her trust. But to respond in kind was something he couldn't do.

So he took hold of the surface problem and strangled the life out of it for her.

'I'd pretty much sussed it by twenty-two,' he said, meeting her eyes, 'but it can take some men a lifetime. Whatever package it comes in, Sybella, it's the woman inside who makes you notice her, who reduces you to an idiot and has you promising all kinds of things just to get her naked.'

Her mouth had fallen open slightly in the same way it had when he'd swooped her up into his arms earlier this evening and carried her up here.

Then her eyes began to kindle.

'You didn't promise me anything,' she said in a low voice.

He grinned at her. 'You should have asked, *dushka*.'

She was clearly trying not to smile.

'You're just saying that because you think it will get you laid again.'

'*Da*, there is that.'

The wounded vulnerability in her eyes had been replaced by the light he'd seen earlier.

That light was like a lighthouse beam guiding him right back to her and all that female lusciousness deep down she must know drove men mad.

'So how about it?'

And her mouth, which had become an instrument of both torture and pleasure to his body, curved up in a smile, carving that dimple deeply.

Bogu, he wanted to kiss that sweet mouth.

But she tucked her hand behind his neck again and brought his mouth down to where she wanted it, on her breasts.

Yeah, he'd died.

This was heaven.

CHAPTER NINE

SOMETHING GAVE A CRACK and the bed lurched to one side and then another crack and the headboard came away from the iron frame.

Nik sprang out of bed and, saying something in Russian, went around and checked out the situation.

'Should I get out?' she asked, not wanting to move in case it all collapsed.

'Hold still,' he grunted. 'I'll fix this.'

She gave a soft shriek as he dislodged the mattress base from the rest of the frame and Sybella found herself staring up at a ceiling that was significantly farther away than it had been a moment ago.

Nik carried the iron base in its two pieces out into the hall and leaned it up against the wall. Sybella watched him, craning her neck.

'You don't have to go, do you?' she called. 'The bed still works.'

Sybella screwed shut her eyes. *The bed still works?* Why didn't she say *I still work* and be done with it?

When Nik came back into the room he sized up the bed and then lowered the lean strength of his magnificent male body down beside her.

He shifted on the mess of twisted sheets and Sybella was suddenly very conscious of the lack of space in general, of how absurd this situation was in her small bedroom where she'd spent the last six years being nothing more than a harried working mum with no head space for what had happened here now.

No, space at the moment was definitely at a premium.

His eyes were like dark onyx in the available light from

the steadily burning lamp, and Sybella could see herself reflected in them but in a way she'd never really viewed herself before. This wanton creature who had revelled in her seduction of this powerful man, whom she'd pretty much brought to his knees—literally given a couple of the positions he'd held her in.

'I have to say, *dushka*,' he said in a gravelly voice, 'leaving is the last thing that's on my mind.'

He propped himself up, those big shoulders rising over her like cliffs, making it impossible to see over or around him, and Sybella found herself sinking under him again because this old bed, despite being a double, was really not made for two when one of them was six feet six. She enjoyed, however, that sensation of being rendered small and delicate and in thrall to him.

'You shouldn't have dragged me up here if you didn't want me to stay the night.'

'What do you mean I dragged you up here?'

'Lured me, then.' He gave her that slow, sexy smile and laid a kiss on her shoulder, her collarbone, the slope of her right breast, grazing dangerously close to her nipple. Little traitors sat up. She shivered as he brushed the underside of his unshaven jaw over one.

'You look like a wanton dairymaid—how could I resist?'

'Is that a reference to the size of my breasts?'

'Da,' he chuckled, brushing his lips over them, 'and your blonde hair and your dimples—and your roomy arse.'

'My what?' She hit his chest playfully as he slid his hands under her.

'More to get a grip on.' He laughed, doing just that. She'd never been more proud of her wide, womanly behind.

Then a thought hit her. 'I just imagined you'd be wanting to get back to your superyacht or whatever.'

He studied her. 'Superyacht?'

'Meg, my sister-in-law, has this theory that's where all the rich Russians live.'

'You've been talking about me?'

'Everyone in the village is talking about you.'

'I'm only interested in what you had to say.'

Sybella stroked his chest in seemingly idle circles. 'I said you weren't very happy with me.'

'I'm happy with you now.' He gave her bottom a squeeze.

She gave him a gentle shove.

'My yacht is about this big.' He measured it out to about an inch between his thumb and forefinger.

Sybella couldn't help it. 'Lucky for me that's only your yacht.'

'I could show it to you some time.'

'I thought you already had.' He smothered her giggle with a kiss and her blood began to hum again.

'I also have another estate in Northumbria,' he murmured against her mouth, and he named it and Sybella went a little pale.

'That's one of the finest castles in the north.'

'Too far and too cold,' he dismissed.

Sybella sat up, dislodging the sheet in her surprise. 'Then why did you buy it?'

'Tax purposes.'

'If you keep buying up my nation's history at this rate I'll end up working for you.'

'Would that be so bad?' He traced a line from her collarbone to her nipple. 'If we could keep doing this.'

Sybella's breath stuttered in her chest and not just because her breasts felt sensitive and responsive to him. Did he think they could find a way to keep doing this?

'Any more grand estates I should know about?' she asked, pulling at the sheet to cover herself again.

'No, just the two.' He kissed the exposed slope of one

breast and then the other, dislodging the covers so he could look at her while he played with them. Sybella was put in mind of a boy with a new toy.

'Real estate in London is more profitable. Russia isn't the safest place to keep all your eggs—' he spread his hands to cup either side of her breasts '—so I've got other baskets.'

Then mercifully he stopped talking about real estate and concentrated on their mutual pleasure.

When she opened her eyes hours later it was light. Nik was pulling on his shirt, and she sat up on her elbows, dragging the covers with her.

'What time is it?' She yawned.

'Almost nine.'

'I guess you should go,' she said half-heartedly.

'I should go,' he concurred.

He was looking down at her as if he still wanted her and Sybella's ego swelled a little more than it should, along with the plummeting feeling she was going to have to let him go and there didn't seem to be a clear-cut path for them, assuming he wanted one.

'When will you be back? In Edbury, I mean.'

Nik began reattaching his watch.

'I was thinking I could fly you up to London next weekend, if you could arrange someone to look after your daughter.'

Fly her up to London? She'd been thinking more along the lines of, When are you coming back to Edbury to see your grandfather? Maybe we could have dinner... Although given they'd already plunged in at the deep end dinner was always going to end here. So maybe London was the right option.

Only it sounded so illicit. And at the same time he was making plans for them, they didn't involve him stepping into her world, and she was a little taken aback by the impression he saw her daughter as an impediment.

'Fleur,' she said uncomfortably. 'Her name is Fleur.'

He smiled but he didn't say her name and a little part of Sybella curled at the edges like blight on a rose leaf.

'I guess I could come up to London. The thing is, I'm really only comfortable with Fleur staying with her aunty Meg or her grandparents, and I can't be away from her for more than a night. She's still so little…'

Sybella trailed off. He was getting out his phone. She guessed he wasn't really that interested in the logistics. It was her domestic life—not his.

He finished buttoning his shirt.

'Where's your phone?'

But he'd already spotted the chair in the corner where her soft patchwork carryall was slumped. Her phone lay on top of it.

She climbed out of bed, wrapping herself in the pale gold blanket, and drew close behind him to see what he was doing, although she had a pretty good idea and it made her warm inside.

'I'm programming in my numbers.'

His head was bent as she peered around him to watch what he was doing, a little confused about the entire procedure. It wasn't as if she had much experience with the whole casual dating thing. She'd only ever dated Simon.

'This way you'll be able to contact me if there's a problem.'

She was about to ask, *But what if there's not a problem?* when she heard it. Like a bat, she was on Fleur signal. It was a single muffled word. Then nothing for the count of one, two, three, four, five, six… And then the rattle of keys and her front door opening.

Battle stations.

She dived for her clothes on the floor, pulling up tracksuit pants and dragging a fluffy old jumper down over her head, flashing her boobs at him.

'They're back. You have to go,' she babbled, hunting around for his shoes. 'Listen, I'll head them off and get them into the kitchen and you come down and let yourself out.'

She shoved his shoes against his chest. 'Put these on and just stay there.'

Nik was caught by an unexpected wave of tenderness.

'Sybella.' He caught her arm and she gazed up at him with equal measures of annoyance and longing that had him wanting to prolong the moment. 'You are an incredible woman and you shouldn't doubt how sexy you are, or how lucky I feel after last night.'

She looked utterly transfixed, and in that moment he cursed her very young, very stupid dead husband.

Then a voice called out, 'Mummy!'

Sybella said something under her breath and he let her go.

As she came noisily down the stairs Sybella was convinced she had a scarlet 'A' painted on her forehead.

Meg was removing Fleur's coat and scarf. She looked up with a smile.

'I thought I'd bring her home and save you the drive, Syb. I have to be in Middenwold this morning anyway. Mum's having a tooth drilled and she says she can't drive herself home.'

'Mummy!' Fleur ran to hug her and be lifted. Sybella gave a little grunt. Her daughter was getting heavier by the day.

After some kisses Fleur was struggling to be put down. 'I want to show Aunty Meg my new shoes,' she complained, but Sybella had no intention of letting Fleur go up until the coast was clear.

'How about we go and put the kettle on first and make

some porridge?' She charged down the hall, making as much noise as possible. She dived for the radio and turned it up. A cheerful pop song filled the room with chants about love not hurting any more. Fleur began to bop up and down and Meg to dance with her.

By the time Fleur remembered her shoes the porridge had been eaten and at last Sybella was able to step into a shower and wash all of her extraordinary night off her glowing skin.

As she stepped out of the bathroom Meg was examining the broken bedstead Nik had arrayed at the end of the hall.

'How on earth did you do this?'

Fleur appeared with her new red shoes in either hand. 'It must have been the giant.'

A week from the day Nik had climbed out of Sybella's broken bed her name flashed up on his phone with a text.

For a moment he just rubbed his thumb lightly over the screen but purposely didn't read her words, aware of all the times this week he had called up her number only for his thumb to hover and then pass off. Indecision was not his way. He'd let the week get away from him and now he had a choice to make. If he didn't call her they could put a line under it.

He put his phone down to avoid temptation and picked up his drink.

'Problem?' His brother Sasha was watching him.

'Nichevo.'

They were sitting on the deck of his one-hundred-metre yacht, *Phantom*. The great beast was moored in the Adriatic, as it always was at this time of year, off the coast of Montenegro.

The centuries-old ramparts of the town of Budva, with limestone hills rising up behind it, was a starry backdrop of lights as the velvety evening dropped around them. The muted sound of thumping dance music heaved from the other end of the boat.

His brother, although long having given away the drugs and alcohol that had derailed him as an adolescent, seemed to need noise and activity around him. His parties on this boat were legendary. Nik had dropped in via helicopter to spend the evening comparing notes and swapping stories before he headed on to some talks and a symposium in Moscow.

'What are you doing with Deda?' Sasha asked, leaning back in his deckchair, resting his glass of fizz against his jeans-clad thigh.

Bare feet, Nik noted, the scorpion tattoo on his left ankle. His own were clad in hand-tooled moccasins stretched out in front of him. Kind of conservative, but he was kind of a conservative guy.

He eyed his phone again, wondering if she had a problem and he was ignoring it.

'When are you moving him out of that old pile?'

'I'm not.'

Sasha looked out across the water, in profile a muscle clearly leaping in his jaw. His brother liked to pretend he was chilled about everything that went down with Deda, but Nik knew better. He had missed those early years with their grandparents, forced to live with his mother abroad, and it made him diffident about interfering in the old man's life.

He saw himself as an outsider, the irony being Nik knew himself to be the one who didn't belong.

'He's happy with the public prowling around the place. To be honest it appears to have given him a second lease of life.'

'Looks like you're stuck with Mouldy Towers for the interim.'

Nik glanced again at his phone.

'What's her name?' Sasha asked, lifting his glass of fizz and ice to his lips. 'The woman whose call you don't know whether to take.'

Nik debated for a moment saying nothing. 'Her name's Sybella. She volunteers at the Hall.'

'So put it through to your office in London.'

Nik shook his head slightly. 'I slept with her.'

Sasha laughed out loud. 'Does that qualify as *droit de seigneur*?'

'*Nyet*, it means it's complicated.' Nik flashed his brother a quelling look.

'It's always complicated, man. Women as a species aren't happy unless they're raiding your head for what you're thinking at any given moment and then using it to crucify you.'

'Bad break-up with what's-her-name?'

'Just brotherly advice. I've never met a woman who didn't want full access to both your bank account and your darkest secrets.'

'Not Sybella.' Nik settled back, still nursing his phone. 'She mainly wants to keep the Hall open and for me to spend more time with Deda.'

'Oh, man, that's worse. She's already managing you.'

Nik frowned. 'It's not like that. It's complicated because she's got a daughter.'

'So? Has she got a nanny for the kid?'

'Even if she had the money for help it's not that kind of set-up. She's hands-on, home schools, community oriented. She's the whole package.' Nik shook his head slightly. 'Why am I telling you this?'

'So I'll talk you out of it. How long have you known her?'

'Forty-eight hours.'

Sasha obviously did his best to keep a straight face. 'That long?'

It had been enough time to get her life story, lose himself in the wonderland of her body for one night and find himself here on the deck of a yacht half a world away unable to stop thinking about her.

He downed his whisky.

'Why don't you stop overthinking it and show her a good time? You might find out she's more than happy to have a bit of a break from her packaged life. Is the kid's father in the picture?'

'She's a widow.'

'Then I don't see your problem. But if it bothers you that much move on. I've got a phone full of numbers I don't want. I can hook you up.'

'Really?' Nik raised a brow. 'You're farming out women now? Nice, Sasha.'

He ignored his brother, whose personal life was a car crash of beautiful girls and a man who walked away from the wreckage without a scratch, and stared meditatively at the tough glass, stainless steel and tiny circuit board he held in his hand that had revolutionised people's lives and made it hard for a guy to go to ground.

Surely he was doing the right thing keeping away?

He'd seen the photo on her bedside table, of the dark-haired, homely young man with an even younger, bright-eyed Sybella welded to his side.

That was what she needed. A man who would be there for her every day, not one who couldn't fix anyone's life.

He'd tried with his grandfather, but there was no bringing Baba back, which was all Deda really wanted, and Sasha was never going to forgive him for having the upbringing that was stolen from him.

Although Simon Parminter hadn't been there for Sybella in the end, he'd left her pregnant and with some hang-ups about her body that made Nik wish he could have set the guy straight.

Which was idiotic. If her husband was still alive Sybella wouldn't have looked twice at him.

She was that kind of woman.

Clearly her husband hadn't left her with much money either, given she was leasing the cottage.

He frowned. He could at least stop her payments. If they were seeing one another she could hardly be paying him rent.

Were they seeing each other?

Not that Sybella would accept any handouts. But he hated the idea of her struggling.

Maybe he could sort out the bed. Start with something basic.

Something solid.

Not a bed he would be occupying. Just a bed.

And under no circumstances was he delivering it himself.

He checked the text.

Can I have a yes or no on whether you're closing west wing down? Syb.

After all that, not a romantic bone in that sentence's body.

He exhaled a snort of amusement. She wasn't pining for him at all. Practical, realistic Sybella.

He texted her back.

No, dushka.

No, dushka?

Sybella stood at her kitchen sink, scowling at the message on her phone.

It had been a week since Nik had stormed into her world and made love to her so thoroughly and tenderly he'd set

the bar ridiculously high for any other intimate relationship she might have one day, far into the future, and left
her with a broken bed and a bit of a bruised heart because
she really liked him.

Then she'd sent a text.

She'd been sitting in front of an old film last night, sip-
ping on a glass of red and nibbling some comfort chocolate, when she'd worked up the nerve to text him. Not *Why
haven't you called?* but a perfectly reasonable professional
enquiry. She'd sat there while Jimmy Stewart carried a
tipsy Katharine Hepburn back to her room, trying not to
envisage Nik reading her text and saying *Sybella, who?*

Then *No, dushka* had popped up on her screen. She'd
held her breath, feeling he was suddenly in the room with
her, waiting for more. Only there was no more.

It answered her question whether she could show a pre-
booked school group through the Hall on Thursday, but
left her completely in the dark as to whether he was even
interested in seeing her again.

She shoved her phone in her back pocket and ran the tap,
frowning as her kitchen sink began to fill with dirty water.

Only it wasn't coming from the tap, it was surging back
up the drain.

That wasn't good.

Sybella removed her gloves and opened her laptop,
which was sitting on the bench where she'd been doing a
little Internet surfing earlier this morning. She'd put 'Nikolai Voronov' into the search engine and up had come a few
images of him in a suit at various glamorous functions with
equally glamorous women clinging to him, and even more
of him in hi-vis gear on mine sites. He did know how to
rock a hard hat.

Irritably she wiped the screen of Nik Voronov and
tapped the more prosaic 'blocked kitchen sink' into the
search engine. The reality of her life restored.

She began rifling through the bottom odds-and-ends drawer, pulling out the shiny spanner her father-in-law had given her for just these emergencies.

Why pay a plumber you couldn't afford when you had videos on the Internet?

Inserting herself under the sink, she focused on fitting the head of the spanner to the grip on the pipe joint.

No, she certainly wouldn't be using those numbers he'd programmed into her phone again.

Frankly she didn't need a man in her life. She was a confident, independent woman. Able to clear drains with just a spanner and a bucket.

She repositioned the bucket.

But she didn't have the upper-body strength to turn the wrench.

'Mummy! Mummy!' Fleur's high, sweet voice came floating into the kitchen.

Sybella adjusted her face into something approximating calm and stuck her head up over the bench.

'What is it, sweetheart?'

'Mummy, the giant is standing in our garden again.'

I wish.

'Is he really? What do you think he wants?'

'Come and see!' Fleur urged.

Another time Sybella would have indulged her and played the game, but the man on the screen had moved on to unclogging your bath in the next video, she still hadn't loosened the pipe grip, and she had to meet Catherine in forty minutes.

'It's very cold outside. I think you'd be warmer in your jeans.'

Fleur hitched up her skirt to reveal she was, indeed, wearing her jeans.

Sybella's tension dissolved into a big smile. 'Excellent fashion choice. Now, I need you to go upstairs and make up your backpack. Do you know what you're taking to Gran's?'

'Ebby.'

Ebby was her much sucked-upon cloth doll.

'We're making a dress for her and fixing her eyes.'

Bless Catherine. 'Pack your jumper—the green one. Do you remember which one that is?'

Fleur nodded confidently, which meant anything could end up in there.

'Off you go. I'll be up in a minute to help. Mummy needs to beat a pipe into submission.'

Sybella crawled forward, angling the wrench at a better angle. She could hear the guy on the online instructional video telling her that sometimes a simple plunger would do the job.

She knew where she wanted to stick that plunger…

'You'll break it,' said a deep voice, testosterone wrapped in velvet, that had Sybella's head snapping back and hitting the top of the sink cavity.

'Ouch!'

She crawled out, her heart pounding in an attempt to escape through her chest, and angled a look up…and up.

Oh, blast.

Fleur had been right. There *was* a giant. Only he'd migrated into her kitchen.

CHAPTER TEN

SYBELLA WAS HOLDING a spanner, dressed much as she had been when he'd come here the last time, casually but this time in jeans and a jumper.

But the spanner in her hand, the brown water in her sink, the harried expression on her face gave him the feeling he was seeing Sybella as she really was, those little duck legs she'd spoken about churning around.

He took in the mess and began shedding his jacket.

'What are you doing?'

He took the spanner out of her hand and tossed his jacket onto a chair. 'I'll fix this. You go fix yourself up.'

Sybella just stood there. Had she missed something? Some lost text where he explained why he'd made no contact for a week? Although the ground shifted under her there, because she could surely have texted him something better than a line about the Hall.

And she was so *glad* to see him.

Then she realised she was standing in front of him in an oversized jumper with the neck and head of a giraffe appliqued on its front.

Yes, she would fix herself up. Immediately.

Nik had retrieved the culprit in the pipe, a plastic figurine about an inch in diameter, had the water draining away and had put through a call to a cleaning service when he realised he wasn't alone.

He turned around. A small dark head was bobbing around the edge of the doorway.

'Hello,' he said.

The head vanished. He waited. Gradually it inched forward again and a pair of big violet-blue eyes in a sweet squarish little face presented itself. The winter-dark hair that had fallen around her face the last time he'd seen her was tied up in bunches.

She was cute as a button.

'Do you remember me?' he said, keeping absolutely still and feeling completely out of his depth. He had no problem facing down angry mining bosses but confronted with a little girl he discovered he had nothing. 'I'm Nik. I'm a friend of your mama's.'

She didn't vanish this time; instead she edged her way into the kitchen, shy as a mouse. She was dressed in a long green skirt that didn't look entirely legit and some sort of long-sleeved yellow top with an appliqued picture of a horse on it. Apparently the fashion had caught on.

Nik was struck by how little she was, and also that he was a strange man in her house. He reached for something to say that wouldn't scare her.

She beat him to it. 'You're not a real giant, are you? Because you can fit in a house.'

This was said in a piping voice with a great deal more confidence than he'd expected from her entrance.

'No, I'm not a giant,' he said slowly, trying not to smile.

'Mummy said you were an angry giant and a north god.'

A north what?

'I wasn't really angry with your mama. I got some things wrong. I'm sorry if I upset her.'

She lifted and dropped her small shoulders. 'That's okay.'

Nik remembered what he had in his hand and held it out to her. 'I think this might belong to you.'

The little girl trotted forward and put up her hand to take it. Nik didn't have much experience with kids—in his circle of friends only one had offspring and it was still a baby. He was struck by how tiny her hand was, how perfect her grubby little chewed-down nails. Her eyes were full of curiosity and liveliness and if she was shy it was leaving her fast.

She studied the figurine with the same interest she'd given to him and now seemed to forget he was there.

Nik heard the truck pull up.

He headed for the front door, yanked it open. Excellent. Edbury village might be full of crackpots and run on its own Brigadoon-style timescale, but money talked in London and one of the city's premier furnishing companies had delivered.

Which was when Nik became aware of a rabbit loping past him and out into the garden.

Hadn't Sybella referred to them as house rabbits?

He managed to corral the other one, closing the front door behind him. It took off in a flash into the sitting room.

Which was when her little girl appeared, said dramatically, 'You've done it now,' and disappeared after the fleeing rabbit. Then he heard Sybella shouting from an upstairs window.

One of the famous trucks from Newman and Sons with its distinctive gold lettering was pulled up in front of her house.

Sybella watched on in astonishment as the two men flung open the back doors of the truck.

As the pieces of a bed frame and then a mattress appeared and were carried piece by piece up her garden path she threw open the window and stuck her head out.

'I think you've got the wrong house!' she called down to them.

When the men ignored her and kept coming she leaned further out.

'Excuse me, lady of the house up here! This isn't my delivery!'

'It's the replacement for your bed.'

Sybella jumped as Nik's deep voice was suddenly right behind her in her bedroom, narrowly missing knocking her head on the window frame.

The scene of their crime.

She clutched her hand towel to her chest like a maiden in a pulp novel, her shower-damp hair hanging over her shoulders, the rest of her encased in a thick bath sheet, anchored under one arm.

'Nik.' It came out with a load of longing she'd rather he didn't hear. She swallowed, revised her plan. The plan she was trying to formulate as he stood there looking more gorgeous than she even remembered. The best she could come up with was, 'I didn't invite you up here!'

'Bit late for that.' He was looking at the bed. 'We'll get that shifted. You might want to get dressed and come down and supervise Fleur. She's trying to catch those damn rabbits. I think I let one out.'

'Oh, Lord!' Sybella dropped the towel—the hand towel, not the bath sheet—and went to hurry past him but he caught her around the waist with those big hands of his.

'One more thing,' he said as she looked up in astonishment, her body instantly melting like an ice cream in the sun under his touch, and he bent his head and kissed her.

A brief but comprehensive exploration of her mouth and then he let her go.

Sybella stuttered for a moment on her feet, not sure whether to tell him off or ask him to do it again, but that was all taken out of her hands when she heard a high-pitched cry from Fleur and she was down those stairs in a flash. Vaguely she was aware Nik wasn't far behind her.

Fleur was standing in the hall, holding Dodge in her arms, his head pushed comfortingly under her chin as Sybella had taught her.

'Mummy, Daisy got out.' She extended an accusatory

finger at the man standing behind her mother. '*He* let her out. She'll be squashed!'

Nik deftly set Sybella aside with the timely utterance, 'Go and put some clothes on,' and strode down the hall, clearly a man with a purpose.

Sybella sent Fleur into the kitchen to put Dodge in his hutch, grabbed her raincoat, shoved her feet into her galoshes and ran outside, doubting Nik was going to have much luck. She passed the two men carrying a quilted bed end. They stared at her with her bath sheet clearly visible under the semi-transparent plastic. She looked at the bed end, a little baffled by what she was supposed to do. She didn't want Nik buying her a new bed! But at the same time she was currently sleeping on a mattress on the floor and she had a frightened female rabbit to corral.

Sure enough, Daisy had hopped into the compost, long brown ears quivering.

Good girl, thought Sybella, making sure the bath sheet was secure with one arm, scooping Daisy out with the other. At least one of the females around here had some sense.

She carried her back to the kitchen and made sure the hutch was firmly latched. She could hear thumping overhead, which meant someone was in her bedroom. Just what she needed. A man-free zone since they'd arrived here six years ago and now she had them coming down the drainpipe.

She shivered in her towel and plastic raincoat. She really needed to put some clothes on!

Fleur was jumping up and down excitedly in the doorway. 'They've taken away the old mattress, Mummy!'

Sybella tried to access her own hallway but there were three men and Nik and a new mattress wrapped in plastic.

Which was when Nik came up beside her, put a hand to her waist and angled her out of the way.

'Do you think you can get dressed?' he growled.

'I'd like to. I am aware the delivery men don't know where to look.'

'I think they know exactly where to look. Go and put some clothes on.'

'I would but they're in my bedroom! Nik, listen, I can't accept this.'

'Let me do this for you,' he said for her ears only in that quiet, sexy Russian drawl of his. 'I did break it.'

She found herself a little transfixed by the sound of his voice, the look in his eyes. For a single moment she forgot the fact there were strange men in her house, she was wearing a towel under a raincoat and she had to meet Catherine in twenty minutes…

'Sybella! What on earth?'

Then she remembered, Catherine was meeting them, and it had just got worse.

'My mother-in-law,' she bleated. Then more plaintively, 'I have to get all this cleaned up.'

'I've called a cleaning service,' Nik said, observing the well-groomed older lady standing on the doorstep at the end of the hall.

Sybella blinked. 'I'm sorry?'

'Cleaners are coming. Go and dry your hair, whatever it is you need to do. I'm taking you and your daughter to lunch.'

'What about Grandma?' asked Fleur, looking up at her mother for guidance.

Sybella put a hand to her own temple. 'Catherine's spending the day with us,' she said, looking a little harassed. He could see what was coming. *Maybe this isn't a good idea.*

Nik didn't hesitate at this mere stumbling block. 'Catherine too, then.'

CHAPTER ELEVEN

'I BELIEVE YOU were seen having sexual relations with my daughter-in-law up against a car at the Hall.'

Sybella had taken Fleur off to the facilities, or 'loo' as she called it, leaving him alone with the real Mrs Parminter in the low-beamed, snug confines of The Folly Inn, a pub in Edbury with Civil War origins, according to Sybella, and an impressive wine list that spoke of Edbury's prominence on the Cotswolds tourist trail.

Nik cleared his throat. 'That didn't happen.'

The older woman lifted her wine glass with a faint smile.

'I didn't think it did. Sybella is too tightly wrapped up in the memory of my son.'

Great. He really didn't want to hear about the sainted Simon, who'd given Sybella some ridiculous but deeply felt anxieties about her body and left her with a baby, although he guessed the guy couldn't be blamed for that—he hadn't known a truck was coming for him. But he had brought her to a village with so few career prospects she'd been forced to invade his home. Although, Nik was no longer exercised over that little tweak in fate given it had brought Sybella into his life.

'I wish to God it had though,' Catherine added and tipped back the rest of her wine.

Okay, she now had his full attention.

He waited. He figured the stylish older woman was leading up to something and his input wasn't really needed.

'Why don't you take her away somewhere? Marcus and I can look after Fleur for a week, and you seem rather smitten.'

Smitten? Not a word anyone had ever used about him. He usually got ruthless bastard or ice man.

However, Catherine Parminter had just earned her lunch. Taking Sybella away somewhere—alone—had begun to look like an impossible task from the moment he'd clapped eyes on Fleur in the kitchen, and up until this moment he hadn't fancied his chances separating mother from daughter.

He caught sight of Sybella leading Fleur across the room. Male heads were turning. She looked sensational in a green jersey dress made sexy by the simple act of cinching a fabric belt around her waist. Not that she appeared to be thinking about herself and how she presented; she was obviously too busy keeping an eye on her small daughter.

'I believe I will,' he said, not paying much attention to the smug look that now settled on Catherine Parminter's face.

He stood up as Sybella approached.

'Everything takes double the time,' she said with a smile, 'but we get there eventually.'

Fleur wasn't interested in taking her seat. Nik didn't know much about kids but even he could see she was over-excited by the day's events and actively resisting her mother's attempts to get her seated back at the table.

'I might take Fleur for a ramble along the river,' said Catherine, pushing back her chair noisily. 'Why don't you finish that bottle of Merlot, Syb?'

Sybella gave her mother-in-law a look of outright surprise but Catherine was already moving her granddaughter off and there was nothing else for Sybella to do but sit down.

Nik seated himself and picked up the bottle but she shook her head.

'I don't know what's got into Catherine. She doesn't usually like it when I drink.'

'She thinks it might loosen you up.'

'Sorry—what?'

Nik decided to just put it out there.

'She wants you to get laid.'

'What do you mean?' Then her eyes widened. 'No! She didn't?'

'Apparently you're missing out.'

'I'm not! I mean, that's not true.'

'Obviously,' he drawled complacently.

She flushed and looked away, clearly flustered.

'Although it has been seven days,' he added.

'Try six years,' she said, then her eyes flew to his in dismay; she was clearly aware she'd given far too much away.

Nik was a little unsettled by the rush of male primacy he experienced at this news. She hadn't let on once in those cold blue hours of the morning when he'd been keeping her warm in that creaky, too small double bed that he was the first since her husband.

'Carino!'

Nik had his attention ripped off Sybella at this crucial moment by the too familiar rasp of what was becoming a weight around his neck.

Sybella was so startled for a moment she couldn't get past the blaring thought: *She's even more gorgeous in the flesh.*

Marla Mendez, trailed by a small entourage of equally happy, shiny people, had just upped the charisma wattage between The Folly Inn's snug walls and the spotlight was on their table. Which Marla was suddenly all over.

'Nik, darling, I have travelled into the wilds of rural England to find you. I wanted to see for myself if it was true. You have a house in the English countryside. How utterly *Russian* of you!'

Sybella watched as Nik lounged back in his chair and regarded Marla with the same cool distance he'd shown her when they'd first met. Only there was no gentlemanly rising from his chair. Even when he'd thought she was an interloper he'd held the door for her. It didn't dim Marla's wattage by even a degree.

'I absolutely want to see it. Have you stocked it with a private zoo? Aloyshia has a zoo—it's hysterical.'

'No zoo, Marla.' Nik surveyed the group of people moving over to the bar. Sybella was watching them too, and also keeping her eye on Marla, who hadn't looked at her once. He knew he had to introduce them, but something was crouched in the back of his mind, growling, warning him not to let Marla and what she represented anywhere near his time with Sybella.

The noise level from the bar shifted up a notch. Sybella flinched as one of the crowd dropped a glass and there was some laughter.

'Try and keep the noise level down,' Nik advised. 'This isn't New York. It's a family pub in a small village.'

'How quaint.' Finally Marla's dark eyes dwelt on her for a moment and Sybella realised she might be coming under the 'quaint' umbrella. Well, that was one for the books. Marla Mendez saw her as a threat.

Nik looked unimpressed. 'Why don't your people call me when you get back to New York, Marla, and we'll set something up?'

'Oh, no, you will have dinner with me, Nikolai Voronov. This is non-negotiable. I need your advice. Besides, I want you to show me this house of yours.'

Nik said something sharply in Spanish. Marla responded and then made a gesture at her that Sybella was pretty sure went along the lines of, *Lose the local...come and play with me.*

Sybella didn't know what came over her. But Nik hadn't introduced them, Ms Mendez was being very rude and Nik not much better, and frankly she wasn't going to spend another second sitting here like a gooseberry. She plonked her glass out of the way, leaned across the table, took Nik's face between her hands and kissed him. For a moment as she leaned in she saw his eyes flicker with surprise but he sure as hell kissed her back.

Then she melted back into her seat, straightened her dress and angled up her chin at Marla.

'Nik can't have dinner with you,' she said firmly, and her voice didn't wobble a bit, 'because he's having dinner with me.'

'Marla Mendez,' Nik said, amusement lacing his voice, 'this is Sybella Parminter.'

Nik's belated introduction was hardly necessary. She had all of Marla's attention now. 'Sybella,' Marla said, those dark brown eyes acknowledging her at last. 'I am staying at Lark House. Do you know it?'

'I know of it. It's an estate several miles from here,' Sybella said, looking at Nik. 'The Eastmans own it.'

'Yes, Benedict and Emma,' said Marla. 'They are having a party. You can both come, yes?' Suddenly she was beaming at Sybella as if they were friends.

'No party,' said Nik decisively.

'I'd love to go to a party at Lark House.' Sybella found herself staring down a Famous Woman who didn't have thighs and feeling amazingly good about herself. Certainty was rolling through her and with that came confidence.

There was nothing between Nik and this woman, not even a speck of sexual tension, and Sybella felt oddly freed by it. She wasn't that twenty-two-year-old bride any more, feeling as if she didn't measure up. It was as if she'd cut the cord on the spectre of the other woman who had haunted her brief marriage. Only she suspected now that other woman had been the Sybella who was sitting here now, claiming what she wanted.

She'd never felt able to assert herself with Simon for

fear of losing the place he'd made for her here in Edbury when he'd brought her home as his wife.

Whatever was between her and Nik, it wasn't about this woman thrusting herself into the middle of their intimate conversation.

She and Nik didn't have a problem. They just had an interruption to their lunch.

Phones had appeared stuck up in the air all around the pub, angled to take pictures. Sybella guessed at least as a non-celebrity she'd probably be lopped out of any shots that appeared on the Internet.

'We will have such a good time!' Marla put her hands on her hips and swivelled to face Nik. 'I will let you out of dinner, but invite me down to your yacht in Nice this year for Cannes and I will forgive you.'

'There's always an open invitation.'

As Marla retreated to her table on the far side of the room people actually got up and followed her.

Nik leaned forward, the bored look on his face during Marla's performance replaced by real concern.

'*Prohshu prahshehnyah.* I apologise, Sybella. I didn't know she'd be here.'

'Clearly. She followed you, *darling*, all the way to the wilds of Gloucestershire.'

Nik scanned her face. 'She didn't bother you?'

'No, but she's chomping at the bit to bother you. Luckily you'll let her on your yacht. Even if it is only this big.' She inched her thumb and index finger apart to show him.

Nik was observing her as if she'd turned into some species of wild animal he'd never met with before but fascinated him.

'Do you really want to go to this party?' He was looking at her mouth and Sybella, already stirred up by that kiss and her little flag-raising exercise over this man, could feel her erogenous zones jumping up to meet him.

'The Eastmans own the most beautiful stately home in the county,' she insisted. 'Of course I want to go to that party.'

He leaned forward. 'What would you like to do after the party?'

Right now her thighs were liquid and her nipples tight and she knew exactly what she wanted to do after the party and she guessed he did too.

If she were free to do it she would have dragged him into the coat room and made love to him within earshot of the entire pub. Only, she wasn't free to follow her instincts. Her mother-in-law would be back at any moment with her five-year-old daughter and that kiss was the best she could do with what she had to hand.

Instead she asked, 'What on earth do the two of you have in common?'

'Marla came to me for business advice.' Nik's thick lashes had screened his eyes and he sat back, and Sybella got the feeling he wasn't telling her the entire truth.

'You mine for minerals. She models lingerie. It must have been an interesting conversation.'

He looked almost weary for a moment and Sybella shifted forward. 'What's wrong, Nik?'

'She has a son,' he said unexpectedly, 'a few years older than Fleur, and she pretty much stocks her entourage with her family.' He frowned as if this bothered him. 'I think the two of you would probably get on well—if you could put up with the theatrics.'

'And you can't?' But her feelings softened. Single motherhood wasn't easy—for anyone.

'It's business, Sybella. She wants to design what she models and she has a very savvy designer on her payroll who happens to be her sister. I'm the money. Full stop. I'm expecting to see a tidy profit from this transaction, which interests me much more than seeing Marla socially.'

Nik knew then if he told Sybella about the other woman's impromptu striptease ending with her in his lap, even if it was a week before he drove into Edbury, it wouldn't go down well. Not after the story she'd told him about her husband and another girl.

No, Marla needed to keep her clothes on and to stay at the end of a long boardroom table and Sybella could never know the truth of just what his plans were for this small business venture. To use it and close it.

Because she was looking at him with those clear, frank green-brown eyes, and he knew she wouldn't understand.

He touched his hands to hers.

'What are you thinking, *moya krasvitsa zhenschina*?'

'I imagine being your girlfriend would involve more of this kind of thing, with other contenders for the title.'

Nik stroked the length of her thumb with his. She dropped her gaze to their joined hands.

'There are no other contenders.' He spoke softly, his voice roughened by the crackle of sexual tension in the air.

Meaning she was the one? Sybella guessed she had just declared something when she kissed him in front of, not only Marla Mendez, but the rest of The Folly Inn.

'But I told you once before, I can be an eminently shallow man.' He had lowered his voice. 'Because you do know I'm thinking about that roller-coaster ride from your delicate throat down to your slender ankles, and the place that probably thrills me most is when it reaches the lush promise of your lovely, voluptuous bottom.'

Sybella expelled a hot little breath and wondered if that coat closet idea was completely bonkers.

He put his hand under her chin and lifted it so she had to look at him.

'I flew back from Montenegro to take you to lunch because try as I might I couldn't keep away.'

That awful week of not knowing was suddenly at the forefront of her mind. 'But why did you try?'

They both heard Fleur's voice on the perimeter of their table and Nik raised a brow to signify the reason.

Fleur?

Sybella was suddenly a little confused. He'd kept away because she had responsibilities? Because she had a child?

She tried to pull herself together and look cheerful and composed for her daughter, but her head was pounding with the idea Nik found Fleur a stumbling block to their relationship.

Not that it even was a relationship. At the moment it was all very up in the air.

She tried to focus on what her daughter was saying.

'Mummy, Grandma says after tomorrow the ice rink will be closed. You promised and we never got to go!'

Ice rink? Sybella gave an internal groan. She *had* promised. She was the world's worst mother. 'We'll go next year, poppet.'

Fleur's lower lip trembled.

'Where is this ice rink?' Nik's deep voice had both Parminter girls turning their heads to look at him in surprise.

'Belfort Castle opens a rink every year from November through January,' Sybella explained. 'We missed it last year too.' She turned back to her unhappy daughter. 'Mummy is so sorry, darling.'

'Where is this castle?'

Sybella blinked. 'Half an hour west.'

Why was Nik asking all these questions? Couldn't he see it only gave Fleur more of a platform to agonise over it? But then, he knew nothing about children. He clearly didn't want to know anything about her daughter.

'We can do this now,' he said.

Fleur's quivering lip disappeared under her gapped

front teeth. She gave a tremulous little squeal. 'Mummy, Mummy, please. *Pleeeease.*'

'If your mother's agreeable,' he added, and suddenly Sybella's own platform for agonising collapsed.

He was making an effort. For her daughter.

'I think that would be lovely.' She gazed at him, feeling a lot of stuff that she'd have to shelve for the moment.

'What would be lovely?' asked Catherine as she reached the table.

'Ice-skating, Grandma!' Fleur was looking up at Nik as if he might pull a rabbit out of a hat for her. Sybella was aware she was doing much the same.

'Wonderful.' Catherine sat down, drawing Fleur up onto her knee. 'Will any of this involve Fleur spending some time with Marcus and me tonight while you take Sybella to dinner?'

'Catherine—'

'*Da*, if you would,' Nik interrupted her smoothly. 'I'm taking Sybella to a party.'

CHAPTER TWELVE

THE RINK IN FRONT of Belfort Castle glowed with fairy lights as the afternoon dwindled.

Nik parked the SUV and waited for the girls to organise themselves.

On the drive Fleur, buckled up in the back in her child's seat, chattered nonstop about various skating adventures she'd had. From the sounds of it she was the local Edbury skating queen.

'Great, so she'll be okay on the ice?' Nik queried as they approached the boardwalk where they could sit down and put on their skates.

The ice rink was swarming with couples and family groups.

'Fleur's never been skating,' said Sybella with a small smile.

'Okay, then what was the story about winning the race and her friend tripping up and breaking her wrist?'

'Fleur likes to make things up and they usually involve her friend Xanthe breaking something.' Sybella stood up, getting her balance. 'She has an active imagination. I don't discourage it.'

Fleur was dancing up to them now, wanting her mother to put her skates on.

He circled Sybella and Fleur on the rink, keeping an eye on the other skaters as Fleur continually took spills. For the first time in his life he wasn't entirely sure of his role here, but when Fleur toppled for the umpteenth time he leaned in and scooped her up before her bottom hit the ice.

She looked up at him with those big violet eyes, solemn as a church hymnal at this unexpected development, but

as he set her on her feet again she kept hold of his hands
and let him glide her along the ice. Sybella glided along
behind them, applauding Fleur's achievement at actually
staying upright, and exchanged a smile with him.

It didn't take long for Fleur to begin to flag and it was
time to take her off the ice. She greeted his suggestion they
go in search of hot chocolate happily enough.

They were standing a few yards from where Fleur was
lined up to hand over the money to the lady behind the
counter when he said without thinking it through, 'Poor
guy.'

Sybella was so busy going over what today had held
and what it might mean, she was delayed in processing
what Nik had said.

'Who?' She looked up at him, aware he'd slid his hand
around her waist while she'd been watching Fleur. 'Nik?'
She raised her eyes to his.

'Poor guy, your Simon, not getting to enjoy any of this.'
He looked into her eyes as he said it and Sybella knew
then he wasn't going to tiptoe around the memory of her
husband.

Thank God.

'But that doesn't mean you and Fleur can't enjoy it,' he
said, proving he understood a great deal more than she
was probably comfortable with.

Unaccountably a flood of hot, messy tears hit the backs
of Sybella's eyes and scalded her face before she could even
think to blink them away, and then she was tucked up in
his arms, her face, her whole body out of the elements and
safe, warm, protected.

'If it were me,' he said in a deep voice, 'I would want
this. I would want the two of you to have this. It's okay to
move forward, Sybella.'

She nodded her head resolutely against his chest, relief

making her a little light-headed. Then she tilted up her chin. 'Why are you doing all of this with us?'

He shook his head at the inanity of the question. 'Because you've let me.' Then he fitted his mouth to hers and she felt it to her toes.

When she floated back up to take in air there was a stillness about Nik that warned her something wasn't right. He was looking over her shoulder.

Sybella turned around.

Fleur was looking up at them, clutching her change.

'What are you doing to my mummy?'

Later in the early evening, as she drove her daughter round to her grandparents, Sybella acknowledged Nik had handled her immediate descent into panic mode with considerable sangfroid, keeping his hand firmly around her waist and making Fleur see it was all right for him to show her mother affection.

It wasn't as if Fleur hadn't seen her grandparents being affectionate with one another, or Aunty Meg locked in a kiss with the odd boyfriend, all of which Fleur ignored with the lofty disregard of someone who was five and a half. But it was different when it was her mother.

Sybella understood. What surprised her was Nik had understood it better. He'd also handled it better. She'd underestimated him.

Fleur had picked up on what Nik had told her—*I want to kiss your mama because she's so nice*—and when she'd seen Sybella in her frock and heels tonight she'd confided, 'I think Nik will want to kiss you again, Mummy.'

Sybella couldn't help thinking about her marriage as she drove back home.

If she'd had that time over she might not have come back to Simon, and she certainly wouldn't have married him until she'd felt secure in their relationship. She'd been so young, and maybe that was partly why she'd stayed faithful to his memory, perhaps for too long.

Simon had never not been her friend, but Nik was something more. He was her lover.

Nik's SUV was parked outside her house when she pulled up.

As she walked towards him his eyes told her everything she wanted to hear.

He reached into his pocket and produced a bracelet that slithered through his hand.

'I thought this would look well on you.'

He draped it over her wrist. The stones were small white diamonds. Sybella gave a soft gasp.

'Nik, I can't accept this. Diamonds?'

But he was trying to work the delicate silver catch with his big, blunt fingers and there was something about his lack of response and the concentration of his expression and his complete inability to finish the job that made her heart melt. This man who ran an empire was defeated by a delicate catch on a woman's bracelet. God help her, she didn't want to give it back, not when he was being so genuine.

'Here,' she said, handing him her evening bag, 'let me fix it.'

She carefully gathered both ends between the fingertips of her right hand and slid the catch closed. Then she held up her arm to inspect its beautiful drape to the top of her forearm. It was exquisite.

'You like it?' He asked as if it mattered.

'It's beautiful. I don't know what to say, Nik. No one's ever given me such an expensive gift.' She made a face. 'I shouldn't have mentioned that, should I, the cost?'

'I want you to be yourself, Sybella, and I want you to wear it, if you will.'

She stroked her bracelet and wished she had the courage to stroke his face and kiss him and take him upstairs to her new bed, but her newfound confidence of this afternoon seemed to have deserted her. Instead she took a deep breath.

'Didn't Marla say something about a party?'

Lark House was lit up like Christmas. It was also the closest stately home to Edbury Hall.

The owners were apparently happy to entertain the elusive Russian oligarch who was their nearest neighbour on such short notice.

Sybella loved this house. It had all the charm Edbury Hall did not, but, while it was open to the public for functions, it didn't require the services of the Heritage Trust. It was very much a family home, even if that family consisted of two socialites and their grown-up children and was open to weddings and functions on weekends.

All the lights were on, an assortment of cars filled the drive and were planted in odd positions under the oaks, and there were fairy lights strewn along the paths that led to the back terrace, where the party-goers were a blur of colour behind glass.

It was a freezing night and Sybella huddled in her wool coat as Nik put his arm around her and propelled her up those steps.

She hadn't felt this excited or nervous in years, but as soon as she stepped into the warm conservatory the number of people gave her a welcome feeling of anonymity. She was just one of many women in gorgeous bits of nothing. If anything she felt a little overdressed in her backless, knee-length pink silk georgette frock. But she could feel Nik's hand resting lightly above her waist, against her bare skin, and she felt a renewed surge of confidence.

Everyone wanted to talk to them, and then Nik left her alone with their hostess, Emma Eastman, a former model who had married a celebrity agent and was one of the locals who arrived on weekends and whose food bills for her guests helped keep Edbury's local food producers very happy.

'How can it be that you're local and I've never met you?' Emma asked bluntly.

Sybella considered mentioning she'd actually applied to Lark House for work experience but decided the wise course was to smile and say, 'It does seem odd.'

'Of course, we're *delighted* to get Nik here. He's so elusive. When Marla said he'd agreed to come we were over the moon.' She leaned close and said sotto voce, 'I have to say, my husband's line of work means I'm always entertaining performers, TV personalities, big egos, but Marla Mendez takes the cake. She just rang Benedict and invited herself.' Emma suddenly pulled a face. 'Oh, heck, have I spoken out of school? Do you know Marla well?'

'I don't know her at all.'

'Ah.' Emma looked around in a covert fashion. 'Well, just a word to the wise—she's not very happy with you. I suspect she thought this weekend was going to play out somewhat differently. Otherwise I doubt we would have got her here.'

Sybella didn't have to ask what Marla imagined might be different.

'You make a fabulous couple,' said Emma, clearly wanting to hear all the details.

'I don't know if couple is the right word. We've only known one another a handful of days.'

Emma's face fell. 'So you don't think you would have any sway with Nik if Benedict and I were to ask him to sponsor our Wells for Africa project? It would mean so much having his name attached, and I think it would go over well, you know, socially if he was seen to be contributing.'

Sybella felt as if she'd suddenly waded out beyond her depth. Her parents-in-law existed on the edges of the county set in the area, but she'd never paid any attention to it. She didn't like snobs—she'd been raised by two. But Emma's entire manner, even if it was a little manufactured, had something engaging underneath it. She seemed like a genuinely nice woman.

'I'm sure he's open to charitable enterprises—you only have to ask him. He's not nearly as ferocious as his reputation.'

Emma beamed at her. 'As soon as we heard he was bringing a local girl with him we knew Edbury Hall must be in safe hands.'

At dinner Nik was monopolised, but again she didn't mind, although it was a little disconcerting when the man sitting beside her slipped his business card under her plate.

'If you could get this to Mr Voronov, and let him know Forester & Bean have represented most of the established families in the area for over a century.'

Sybella politely smiled and went on with her dinner.

Nik sat opposite her, fielding questions from their host about the ecological impact of mining. Nik rolled out a convincing line about his company's determination not to log where it wasn't necessary and his refusal to use chemicals underground. Any mine was a major habitat modification and Voroncor did their best to limit biodiversity issues. But he admitted freely once a mine had gone in, the site would never be the same again.

Some of the other guests were clearly dinner table ecological warriors—rather like herself—but Nik handled them well. He explained Voroncor had posted bonds with all their sites. Once mining ceased the clean-up would not stop until they had proved the reclaimed land was once more productive.

'So you're not just digging holes in the earth and ruining habitat,' she said to Nik as he pulled her out of her chair after dinner.

'I'd be a poor excuse for a human being if I did,' he said, taking her hand. 'Mining isn't for sissies, Sybella.'

'I don't think anyone here is going to mistake you for a sissy, Nik. Do you know everyone here wants a piece of you?'

He had his other hand around her waist now and was leading her into the ballroom.

She had so many questions, but mostly what she wanted to do was be in his arms, far away from all these people.

'I do know every man here is envious of me at this moment.'

He finally held her in his arms as they drifted onto the dance floor and Sybella rested her head against his shoulder.

Envious? Probably not. But right now her heart was wide open and banging like a barn door and she was just waiting for him to come on in.

Because she could have this. Nik didn't seem to be going anywhere and she'd spent the last week pretending to herself it didn't matter if he came back.

All the silly things she'd been telling herself. None of it was true.

'I never get to do this,' she said confidingly, 'put on a beautiful dress and be admired.' She shook her head against his shoulder. 'I don't know why I'm telling you that. You're a man. You wouldn't understand.'

He stroked an invisible strand of hair from the curve of her neck. 'You've denied yourself a great deal, I think,' he said.

'Not any more.' Emboldened, she put a hand to his chest. 'Are you going to make love to me?' She framed the question she'd been longing to ask him all night.

'Is that a question?' His breath brushed her ear tip.

'Just looking for a time line.' Her skin felt hot; her words sounded so bold and sure.

'You think I brought you here to take another look at your beautiful lingerie?'

Sybella's heart skipped a beat. 'I didn't think men noticed those sorts of things.'

'I notice everything about you.'

Sybella swore she could feel his hand at her lower back through the boning of her gown. Impossible, and yet...

'I want you now,' he said against her ear. 'Is that a problem?'

Sybella moved her smooth cheek against his rough jaw. 'No, not at all.'

'But possibly not at a party,' he observed.

Sybella, a little weak with longing, couldn't at this moment see exactly why.

'Surely there's a guest room somewhere?' Then she sighed, because she would never do something like that. 'Oh, Nik, it's a long drive home.'

'It's been a long week,' he said, his mouth warm against her ear. 'I think we can withstand another half-hour in a car.'

She looked into his eyes and saw everything a woman could possibly want to make her feel like the only female in his universe.

His arm came away from her waist but he held onto her other hand and wordlessly he began to lead her across the dance floor towards the exit.

People parted ways to allow them passage. There was nothing subtle about what they were doing, leaving early, and Sybella was thrilled.

An hour later Nik didn't want to move. Sybella was draped across him. She stroked his chest, nuzzled him.

'I missed this,' she said.

'Six years,' he murmured against her sweet-smelling hair. 'It's a long time.'

'No, you.' She raised her pleasure-dazed eyes to his. 'I missed this with you.'

Nik experienced a surge of something he couldn't control. It was a wave of feeling that had him holding onto her. She didn't seem inclined to let him go either.

Every time he touched her it was like a conflagration of the senses. Every time it felt like the best thing that had ever happened to him.

Why were they denying themselves?

Then he remembered a small person who would arrive home in the morning.

He sat up, banging the back of his head on the frame of the backseat of the SUV.

Sybella winced for him and tried to sit up, but she was hampered by the space. He chuckled and she dissolved into helpless giggles. They had got as far as the Linton Way Forest when Nik had pulled the car off the road and into this clearing. It was private, but they could hear any cars going past on the road.

Nik was certain from the outside they would be invisible; the steamed up windows helped with that. Sybella, still in her dress but wondrously dishevelled, her hair falling down and the hem of her dress so high it hinted at the shadowy mystery between her thighs, gazed up at him. He, with his shirt hanging open and his trousers unbuttoned, was trying to make sense of what this woman did to him. They hadn't even made it into Edbury.

He drove them to the cottage and carried her inside. Put her in the shower and then crowded her against the splash back until the water ran cold. Then he wrapped his bigger, warmer body around hers in the new bed.

'I've got a boat moored at a place I own off the coast

of South Africa,' he said. 'Come there with me for a few days, just you and me.'

Sybella looked at him with those clear hazel eyes. He waited for her to say, *No, I won't leave my daughter* but she surprised him with a simple, 'I'd like that.'

No hesitation, no questions. Instead she asked, 'Can we do it soon?'

'I'll make the arrangements.'

She rubbed her cheek against his arm. 'I've never travelled outside the United Kingdom. Does that make me parochial?'

'No, *dushka*, just busy.' His hand stroked her damp hair and she was whisked back to that evening last week when he'd dried her hair with a towel and she'd first begun to let down her guard with him. He'd also just acknowledged how hard she worked.

There was nothing sexier.

Deep inside her a feeling Sybella had never had before began to stir.

'It's good to take a break from real life, yes?' he said, his chest rumbling against her back.

'Yes,' she sighed. Only later would she wonder if this was only that for him, a break from real life? When it felt all too real to her. But she quieted that thought because, after all, it was only a long weekend away.

CHAPTER THIRTEEN

SYBELLA CAME DOWN the stairs into the galley of the boat, her long bare legs appearing first and then her body clad in a black bikini, a diaphanous shirt unbuttoned and billowing around her. With her hair pulled back in a ponytail she looked happy and carefree and about twenty.

Lust licked along his veins, but it was mingled with something more lasting, something that went along with seeing her so light-hearted, simply enjoying herself and it had a corresponding effect on his spirit. He felt satisfied. *Da*, satisfied. He had her at last.

'Nik, who is this woman?'

It was then he noticed the magazine she was carrying and wondered which old girlfriend she'd stumbled onto, but then he saw the photograph of the eighteenth-century villa on the lake and he knew.

As she came closer she held out the magazine. 'It's got a feature on a Galina Voronov, a Russian socialite with fashion connections and a very nice villa on the shores of Lake Geneva. All very lah-de-dah. She apparently tried to sue you but that failed. You rate two lines, by the way, neither of them informative. Is she a relative?'

Nik ignored the magazine in favour of sliding one hand over her hip as he brought her in against him, the other expertly turning over pancakes in the skillet.

'Who taught you to do that?' she asked, distracted by his unexpected dexterity in the kitchen.

'Baba, my grandmother. We made *blini* all the time. She made her own jam from her orchard and I would stuff myself on them.'

They had a twenty-person staff on the forty-metre yacht

and their meals were sublime, but for their last day of four blissful days together on the boat Nik had sent their staff ashore and they were completely on their own.

He was making her breakfast. It was bliss.

'I can imagine you as a boy, always getting into trouble because you wanted everything your own way.'

'I might have wanted it but Deda made sure I was kept in check,' he said, but he was smiling as he upended the crepes onto a plate with the rest.

'What about your brother? It can't have been easy for your grandmother with two boys.'

Nik's smile vanished. 'My brother wasn't there.'

'I don't understand.'

'Sasha was living with his mother.'

'They split the two of you up?'

Nik looked grim. 'No, my stepmother split us up. At Alex's funeral she took Sasha by the hand and put him in a car and they drove away and I didn't see him again for ten years.'

Sybella was effectively silenced by that image.

'My reputation rises and falls on those blinis,' Nik said, as if he hadn't just dropped a bombshell. 'Why don't you take them out and I'll bring the coffee? Leave the magazine.'

Sybella put the old magazine down on the bench and put a hand on Nik's arm but he gave her a firm smile that didn't reach his eyes. 'Off you go,' he said.

When he reappeared with a tray, coffees and some condiments she knew he wasn't going to say any more, and it was clear this was a painful subject for him, as well it should be. She didn't want to pry, but suddenly she knew this terrible thing about his boyhood.

'I'm so sorry that happened to you, Nik,' she said as he set the tray down. 'Your grandfather would talk about you as a boy, but not Sasha. I didn't make a connection.'

'Why should you?'

Nik settled down opposite her at the table, all masculine grace in shorts and an open shirt, the brown hair on his body glinting gold after four days in the hot sun. Sybella thought she would never get tired of looking at him.

He sighed, rubbing his unshaven jaw. 'Deda and Baba both tried every legal means possible to bring Sasha home but it was like hitting a brick wall. It took Galina going into rehab for Deda to get custody.'

'Galina? The woman in the magazine, who tried to sue you?'

'The same.'

'What was it you said about rehab?'

'Alcohol. She'd run out of money and options, and Sasha was fifteen and I imagine every time she looked at him she saw how much he hated her. So Sasha came home to my grandparents. He was already six feet tall and carrying a mountain of resentment on those kid shoulders of his.'

Sybella weirdly felt a little sorry for Galina Voronov. From what Nik had said she was clearly a troubled woman, but to have your child look at you and hate you?

'How did your grandparents cope?'

'They got him a psychologist and did everything they could, but it was a rough first year. I was just out of national service and doing a science degree, living at the campus. I came home weekends but he resented me from the start, and we argued a lot. I can't blame him. I got everything that by rights should have been his.'

'What does that mean?'

She had linked her hand with his across the table top, but now that hand closed over hers and he smoothed his broad thumb against the pulse point at her wrist. How that had happened Sybella wasn't sure. It was like when they were in bed and one minute he'd be letting her have her way and the next she was exactly where he wanted her and happy to be there.

Yes, Nik was telling her a painful personal story and she was thinking about how sexually dominant he was.

'Nik? What do you mean everything that by rights should have been his?'

'He is their grandson, I'm the ring-in.'

'Nik, that's a terrible thing to say. I know you don't believe that.'

'*Net*, but I suspect Sasha did.'

He must have seen the look on her face because he squeezed her hand. 'When he was sixteen I took him with me on a geological survey in the Urals. I put him to work helping me out and we started to interact as brothers for the first time in over a decade. He was with me when I first saw the abandoned Vizhny mine and talked about putting some shareholders together and buying it up. Sasha said he wanted in, so when I finally made a bid three years later he fronted up with his life savings. It was a risk, our relationship would have imploded at that point if something had gone wrong but it didn't and it's made both of us rich men.'

Sybella got up and came around and climbed onto his lap and pressed her cheek to his rough one.

'I'm so glad you told me this.'

'It's over now,' he said, appearing more interested in how affectionate she was being than seeking comfort. He was stroking the side of her breast so she was distracted when he added quietly, 'Almost over.'

'Almost over?' She drew back and looked into his eyes quizzically.

'*Nichevo.*' He shook his head and gave her a rueful smile, the fingers of his other hand engaging with the ties holding her bikini top together.

'Stop it.' She fidgeted and began to laugh. 'I told you,

I am not walking around topless on this yacht, Nikolai Voronov.'

By the time she'd restored her modesty and been kissed the blinis were cold and the coffee was tepid and Nik had effectively changed the subject.

It was only when she took some of the plates inside that she saw him binning the magazine.

'Can I ask what the legal matter was about with your stepmother?'

He shrugged. 'It's not a secret, *dushka*. Galina was the daughter of a high-ranking Kremlin *apparatchik*. He pulled strings. She got control of our father's archive of work, films, documentaries. She owned all the rights for twenty years and, if that wasn't bad enough, she effectively locked it away so nobody could see it. He's virtually forgotten now in my country.'

'That's wicked.'

Nik stretched his arms and gave his shoulders a roll, showing off that honed physique she already knew very well. But she also got the impression he was shucking off all the tension that had gathered as their conversation had progressed.

'That's my stepmother,' he observed dryly. 'She's a classic fairy tale villain.'

'Will you ever get it back?'

He scrutinised her through those thick lashes. 'You underestimate me, Sybella. I purchased it for several million US dollars two years ago. We settled out of court. It paid for that very nice villa on Lake Geneva you were admiring.'

Sybella shook her head at the figures involved but mostly the weight Nik must have carried all those years, wanting to restore his father's reputation and unable to do so.

It wasn't just the absence of his brother that had weighted him down but the loss of his father's legacy.

'At least she's out of your lives. Is she out of your lives?'

Nik consulted his watch. 'How about we take the tender to a cove near here and I'll show you some of the sights?'

Sybella was changing into shorts and a T-shirt when she realised Nik had once again very neatly sidestepped her question for the second time.

An afternoon spent ashore, climbing to a lookout with spectacular views of the coast, concluded with a swim at dusk near the boat.

The water was warm and Sybella's legs entangled around his, her hair falling in heavy ropes over her shoulders like the mermaid he'd discovered she was, her arms looped around his neck.

Talking about his brother and his stepmother this morning had brought the two sides of his life dangerously close together.

He didn't want to think about his plans for Galina and the money she'd extorted out of him when he was with Sybella. She made it seem unimportant, and, worse, mean and small. Like a spiteful act she wouldn't recognise him as being capable of.

She bobbed in the water in front of him, holding onto him like her own personal life buoy.

'So have you met him? Your real dad?' She was gazing into his eyes as if daring him to change the subject.

Trust Sybella to be worrying over this.

'I've got a name. I know where he is.'

'And?'

'Helsinki.'

'And?'

'I still haven't done anything about it. I don't know if I ever will. I mean, he has a family, a life. I'm busy.'

He could feel her stroking the back of his neck, treating

him like Fleur or one of those damned rabbits she kept. Only he found he didn't mind because it was Sybella.

'No, you're not. You're just like all of us, a little afraid of what might happen when we let down our guard with other people.'

'Is that what I am, *dushka*?' He tried not to sound too disparaging of her well-meant words.

'You know you are.' She smiled at him as if she knew all his cynical thoughts but didn't believe one of them.

The truth was it was getting harder and harder to hold onto that cynicism when he was around Sybella. Her lashes were wet and sticking around her eyes like a doll's. She was so beautiful it hurt. Did she know how strange it was for him, letting another person into his head like this?

'I've let my guard down with you,' he said, almost as a warning, although to her or to him he wasn't sure.

Her arms tightened around him and he could hear her breathing quicken, the almost ferocious way she hung onto him as if that was all she'd wanted to hear, and it answered a need in him he hadn't known until now existed.

'How lucky you are, to at least have known one dad, and now you have a chance with another,' she said urgently. 'Don't let that chance go by, Nik.'

She meant it, and coming from Sybella with her history it had a great deal of force.

He put his mouth close to her ear. 'How lucky your Simon was, to be first in your heart.'

Sybella's grip tightened. 'He's not first in my heart any more.'

They were flying home to Heathrow in his jet from Cape Town International Airport when Sybella, comfortable in a ridiculously luxurious seat, began to giggle.

Nik, standing over her with two glasses of bubbly, raised an eyebrow.

'What's so funny?'

She looked up, smiling at him. 'One day I'll be telling this story and no one will believe me.'

'What, is it the champagne? I thought you'd appreciate it before you were back in that storybook cottage of yours hiding spirits in the airing cupboard.'

'How do you know about that?'

'Your mother-in-law at the restaurant.'

Sybella rolled her eyes.

'So this is my last taste of luxury?' she queried lightly as she accepted her glass, because suddenly they were bang, smack in the middle of making decisions.

'No, although…' He crouched down in front of her. 'How about I ask you what your plans are for the future?'

'Hugging my daughter and not letting her go for a couple of days,' Sybella admitted honestly.

'I was thinking a little more along the lines of your plans for me.'

He started to smile but he was serious too and she could feel her heart thumping like Dodge's hind legs on the kitchen floor.

She thought of her kitchen at this moment, the menagerie of animals, of Fleur running riot and leading a pack of her little friends up and down the stairs like Napoleon orchestrating his Grande Armée, and tried to picture Nik amidst it all. She failed.

'You won't fit,' she blurted out.

'*Lyubov,* I think we've already tested that out.'

Sybella couldn't help it. She snorted. 'I mean in my kitchen,' she said softly, worryingly.

'I'll build you a bigger one.'

She had a vision of her cottage writ large, squashing all the others in the row and Nik with a big hammer.

As silly as it was, it was also true. He had a way of taking over.

She knew she should be happy; instead she was beginning to panic. It was crazy.

'We'll take it a day at a time,' he told her gravely. 'There's no schedule on this.'

She snorted again. With Nik there was always a schedule. He was the busiest man she knew and she had seen the way his grandfather had jockeyed for his attention.

God knew she wouldn't be here if old Mr Voronov hadn't been driven to desperate means to get his grandson down to Edbury...

Sybella had the odd thought she didn't ever want to be in that position.

Driven to desperate means to get Nik's attention.

She just hoped he could accept she came as a package, and she still wasn't at all sure if Nik understood that.

It had been incredible. The boat, the time together. But it wasn't real life.

'One day at a time, Sybella,' he said, leaning forward until she was drowning in his eyes and all of her worried thoughts were subsumed, and then he was kissing her and nothing else seemed to matter.

They had been home for more than four weeks and Nik had spent most of that time under her thatched roof, although he was officially living at the Hall.

It was a situation that delighted his grandfather and caused no end of gossip in the village.

But Sybella didn't mind the talk, especially as she put her head around the door and watched Nik reading to Fleur. Her daughter was leaning against him on the sofa and had her thumb tucked inside her mouth and was deep inside the Wild Wood. Nik's dark velvet voice lent an exotic charm to the story Sybella knew herself off by heart from listening to his grandfather.

These Voronov men had somehow colonised her daughter's life, and for the better. Nik had made an effort to be around and was currently running his empire with a small staff and a state-of-the-art computer system he had set up at the Hall. Some evenings he could be found pacing into the night across her living room as he argued in a mixture of Russian and English via video conference with various boardrooms around the world. If Fleur wandered in he would break off to help her with some puzzle she had or answer her questions. She was a good girl and knew not to interrupt when people were on the phone, but it gave Sybella enormous satisfaction Nik didn't view her comings and goings in her own home as an interruption to his work.

After dinner, when Fleur had been put to bed and the house locked up and Nik had done his usual round of phone calls and she'd gone over the invoicing for the refurbishment of the gatehouse, they bumped into each other in the bathroom.

Nik was shaving, and she just wanted to be with him as well as wash her face.

She shimmied in between him and the basin. He grinned and she wriggled her bottom teasingly as she wrung the warm face cloth to clean off the remains of her make-up.

'Can you ever see yourself getting married again?'

The question took her off guard.

'I haven't given it much thought,' she said truthfully.

She couldn't help noticing what a good pair they made in the mirror. Because she was tall most men looked her in the eye, but Nik's height and strong frame made her curvy body shape fit him, and she saw what he'd been showing her in bed: that they were a perfect physical match.

She preened a little.

'You didn't like being married?' He drew the razor along his jaw.

'If that's a question about Simon wrapped up with a

bow, I did like being married. I guess I felt safe for the first time in my life.'

Nik stilled and met her eyes in the glass. 'You didn't feel safe before that?'

'I felt alone,' she confessed. 'For so long it was just me, and then Simon picked me up and carted me off to his life in the village with his parents and his sister, and their neighbours and friends accepted me just because I was his wife. It was an amazing time for me. And then, a few months later, he had the accident.'

Nik wrapped an arm around her. He didn't mouth any pointless platitudes.

'Can I tell you something?' she asked.

He looked down into her eyes and Sybella knew she was about to take a jump into the unknown. She hadn't told anyone this.

'I cried for Simon, of course I did, but I remember at the funeral thinking, *I'll have to leave now. I'll have to leave the village.* And somehow that felt worse, that felt like the bigger loss.'

It was an enormous admission and Sybella waited to feel guilty, only she didn't.

'Makes sense. It sounds like when you married Simon, you married the life you needed.'

'Yes, I suppose I did.' She relaxed against him, relieved he understood.

'Of course, thanks to Fleur I never did have to leave Edbury.'

Nik towelled his freshly shaven face and switched out the light.

'When did you find out you were pregnant?'

He followed her across the hallway to her room. The house was quiet but for the usual creaks and groans of age. Fleur's door at the end of the hall was ajar and Sybella could see the red glow of her nightlight.

'The day after the funeral. Meg needed a tampon on the day, and it occurred to me I'd been carrying that little box around in my purse for several weeks. So I did a chemist test and then I went to my doctor and my life changed. Again.'

She climbed into her new bed and he stretched out beside her. 'That's the thing about life—it's constantly surprising you.'

He put out the light and pulled her into his arms.

'I guess the long and the short of it is I got married young because I was alone in the world, but I'm not alone any more. I have a daughter, I have in-laws, I have a whole village.'

'And you have me,' he said, and her body began to hum as he slid his hands over her bare skin and found all the places that made her squirm and gasp and sigh.

She woke some hours later, hot and disturbed after a dream. She couldn't remember the contents, but a kind of anxiousness was knotting her chest and presently she got out of bed and quietly crept downstairs. She took her coat off the coat-rack and, wrapped up in it, stepped out of the back door and into her garden. It was the place where she did her thinking.

Spring would be here soon but it was still bitterly cold at night and she'd only stuffed her feet into her old slippers.

The sky over the Indian ocean had been so high and far-reaching. Here at home the sky was hugger mugger with the low hills, but that sense of snugness and enclosure made her feel safe.

'What are you doing out here by yourself?'

Nik wore a pair of boxer shorts, but if he was cold he didn't show it. His physical similarity to one of those more-than-life-size male sculptures the Italians liked to make in the Renaissance was all too obvious.

'I couldn't sleep.'

He didn't ask her why she'd decided to come out into the vegetable patch.

'Do you want to be by yourself?' His deep voice was pitched low.

There was something about the way he was standing there, not coming any closer, that sent a shiver hightailing down Sybella's spine.

'No, I don't. I don't want to be by myself.'

Before she could move his arms were closing around her from behind and she was washed with the feeling of security and rightness the dream had upended. She'd already begun to take this feeling for granted with Nik.

It was so dangerous. He could hurt her and she didn't know if she'd get over it.

But, Mrs Muir be damned. She couldn't go through her life wondering what might have happened if she hadn't let him in. The idea of keeping her heart locked up and on a high shelf held no appeal.

Sybella knew she'd remember this when she was old and grey and had great-grandchildren who would never believe their granny had once given her heart to a Russian billionaire and sailed the Indian Ocean in his boat, a man who had the world at his fingertips but right now wanted only her, Sybella Frances Parminter, and her wide, womanly arse. All at once she began to giggle.

'What's so funny?'

She looked up, smiling at him. 'One day I'll be telling this story about you and me and standing in a vegetable patch and no one will believe me.'

'Come inside, then.' He scooped her up and carried her back into the house and up the creaking stairs and past Fleur's room with its night light and into the corner bedroom where she had moved in alone, almost six years ago after Simon had died, and spent the first night wide awake, tearless and terrified because of the enormity of facing life alone—that was until her baby had kicked.

Fleur had kicked hard. As if to remind her being alone was no longer her fate.

It was time to stop being afraid and to accept that maybe Nik was her fate too.

Nik looked at the clock. He needed to get up but Sybella was lying partially on top of him, her mermaid hair strewn across his chest.

He eyed the low ceiling above them. If he stood up and extended his hand he could flatten his palm on that ceiling. He frowned. Damn this place was small. Built for pygmies. They needed to move.

Which was when he flipped his gaze from ceiling to woman and he grinned. He knew then he could get used to this very quickly. How in the hell had she pulled him around this far in the span of several weeks?

Only Sybella didn't give him a clue, she continued to rest her angel face in the crook of his shoulder, as if he were more restful for her than a pillow. He shared the sentiment. She was warm and her lavish curves cushioned him perfectly. They complemented one another in more ways than one.

He traced the fine skin beneath the soft arc of her pale lashes and trailed his finger down to the curve of her slightly parted lips. She grew more beautiful to him every day and stirred strong feelings in him he didn't recognise.

Smitten didn't even begin to cover it.

He cared about what she thought of him, and at the moment he had a lot to hide.

It was almost ironic when his phone lit up several minutes later and he palmed it off the bedside table, not surprised to see it was from his assistant.

Pavel worked the mad hours he did.

It was a message about an explosion in the Urals mine.

He left Sybella to sleep because he was accustomed to handling things alone, and only remembered to call her when he was in-flight and she wasn't answering.

He sent a message.

Sybella read the message.

Real life intrudes, accident at mine, no loss of life, I'll ring tonight.

For the next two days she didn't hear from him and consequently found herself up at midnight, boiling tea, standing over the sink and wondering how her bed had got to feel so lonely when he'd been sharing it for only a brief time.

Which was when it occurred to her there would probably be some information about the mine accident on the Internet.

She fired up her laptop and sure enough the screen filled with various links connected to Nik's name, but at the top with an accompanying small image was an article from an infamous British tabloid. *Marla puts raunchy moves on Russian oligarch!*

Sybella just stood there. For a moment all she could think was, *Don't look...don't look.*

But she was clicking and scrolling and, like Bluebeard's wife, once seen, she couldn't forget it.

There was an image of Marla Mendez in tiny black barely there underwear, holding a bottle of champagne. Another of Marla pouring champagne over her breasts, her virtually bared breasts, because the bra was basically there as a frame for the main event. Marla climbing onto some guy's lap. The fourth image was recognisably of Nik, in profile, sitting on a chair with Marla astride him, looking, well, looking...

It was hard to get past all the naked female flesh and *her boyfriend*, but Nik didn't seem to be touching her in any way or engaging with her.

Sybella leaned onto the bench and rested her head in her hands, utterly thrown.

It must have happened before they met.

She had no right to be angry or hurt or reproach him with it.

But, oh.

Her kitchen was dark and quiet around her, disturbed only by the ticking of the clock and one of the rabbits making scraping noises in his litter tray.

Nik phoned her first thing in the morning when she was still groggy.

'Sybella, did you see the photos?'

She sat up, rubbing her eyes still swollen from all her crying. 'Yes, last night. How is it going? Are you making any progress?'

He ignored her question about the mine.

'We were in a boardroom, she took off her clothes and I told her to put them on again. I had no idea it was being filmed.'

Sybella fell forward and touched her forehead to the mattress. *Thank you, God.*

She pitched her voice at exactly the right tone, gentle and amused. 'Nik Voronov, are you explaining yourself to me?'

There was a pause. 'Sounds like it.'

'It's fine. I understand. I didn't think anything of it.'

There was a lingering silence.

'Nik, are you there?'

'You are one incredible woman.'

She bit her lip. She'd got this right.

'I try. Now tell me about what's been going on.'

They talked for twenty minutes, he promised he'd do

his best to be back tomorrow evening to take her to dinner and then he had to go. She stepped under the shower, and if she cried a bit it was because she hadn't slept much last night and she had to take a tour today of a couple of dozen eight-year-old children, and it was stressful, and she missed him. It had nothing to do with Nik having his face pressed into Marla Mendez's breasts.

CHAPTER FOURTEEN

*Marla Mendez in Sex Shocker with
Russian Ice Man!*

SYBELLA STOOD OUTSIDE the Edbury newsagents, her whole
attention riveted to the tabloid newspaper front page pinned
up alongside other legitimate papers reporting on local and
international politics.

As far as she knew Nik was in the Urals, dealing with
some labour-hire problems on site in the wake of the explosion and had been for the last three weeks. He'd phoned
a couple of times, sent a few texts, one saying he should
be back in the UK this weekend and another asking her
to check something in person with Gordon about the roof
on the Hall.

He hadn't mentioned anything about a *sex shocker*.

'I'm sorry, Sybella,' called Leanne Davis, coming outside. 'Doug insisted we put it up…we're required to display
all the newspapers. It's not personal, sweetie.'

'No, no, of course not,' murmured Sybella, unable to
rip her attention off the image. They appeared to be coming out of a nightclub, Nik in an open-necked shirt looking
well…gorgeous, and Marla Mendez in her usual skin-tight
handkerchief.

It didn't make sense, and Sybella had to resist the urge
to buy the paper just to find out what it said.

Nik had specifically told her he had not seen Marla
Mendez socially.

'It's not true,' she called after Leanne, but it was too
late, she'd gone inside.

She found herself half an hour later in her car, parked

across from The Glue Box, the local arts and crafts supply shop that held art classes for under tens, furtively peering at the tiny screen on her phone as she read the tabloid article. It was the usual 'friend of a friend' who said they'd been close for months, that Nik had flown her from Miami, where she was currently working, to his Cape Town compound for a secret tryst. She shut it off in disgust.

Me, he had a secret tryst with me.

But the tabloids weren't interested in single mothers living in the Cotswolds and she could hardly take out a full-page ad in the local paper outing herself as the most recent guest on Nik Voronov's boat!

She had just about convinced herself, as she crossed the road and dodged up the steps of The Glue Box, that it wasn't important and she should rise above it when she was bailed up by two of the mothers, one of whom actually asked, 'Can we expect more stories to come out about your rich boyfriend and other lingerie models?'

Mortified, she somehow resisted grabbing Fleur and running. Sybella made herself speak to the art teacher and gather the information flyers amidst a gaggle of other mothers who she was sure were whispering about her. In the car Fleur showed off the picture she'd done.

'This is Jack and this is the Beanstalk, and this is Nik!'

Sybella studied the drawing, the tiny Jack, the scrawny beanstalk and Nik, taking up half the page and coloured golden as the sun, and she realised what she should have been focused on from the start. Having Nik with them, sleeping under their roof, Fleur saw Nik as an established part of her life.

Clearly a big, important golden part.

Sybella started the engine, gave Fleur a reassuring smile. 'Shall we put it on the fridge when we get home?'

'I want to give it to Nik,' Fleur said, fussing with her container of fruit pieces.

Sybella knew then this morning she'd just been embarrassed, now she had a problem.

Nik found her the next day on her hands and knees in the gatehouse with a handful of other volunteers cleaning up after the builders. There was a flutter of movement and a sudden lull in noise to alert her.

One of the women gave her a nudge and Sybella sat back on her haunches and looked around.

Nik stood in the open doorway, arms folded. King of all he surveys, Sybella thought, putting down her brush and pan and rising to her feet. Despite everything that had gone down in the last few days there was a happy girl inside her doing cartwheels because he was back.

He was back.

The problem was she kept seeing him coming out of that nightclub. How many nightclubs had he been to in the last week?

None, Sybella, because he's been on a mine site. You know that.

'Dushka.'

In a couple of strides he was lifting her as if she weighed nothing and then kissing her. In front of everyone.

Sybella pressed her face close to his shirt front as he lowered her until her feet touched the ground, embarrassed but also incredibly pleased.

'What are you doing here?' she asked.

'I could ask you the same thing.'

'The builders need to be supervised, Nik.'

'This is why I have hired professionals.'

'I know, but the committee want to help. We want to be involved.'

'Cleaning?'

'It's a start.'

He stroked her hair back out of her face. 'Who am I to come between you and a bit of builders' dust?'

For dinner Nik took her to a gorgeous little place in Middenwold she hadn't even known existed, a Tudor dwelling as intimate and charming as she could have wished. Sybella resisted raising the issue about the pictures and tried to enjoy her dinner and the atmosphere and Nik's company.

But something of her low mood must have shown through because they left early. He put an arm around her as he led her back to the car, but nothing would lift this feeling. All the pretending nothing was wrong meant something important had shifted between them.

Nik left her in the car while he went to check on one of the brake lights, which gave her time to check her phone. No messages, but she couldn't help almost compulsively looking at those images again.

The little screen filled with the logo of the same popular British online tabloid she'd seared her eyeballs with a few nights ago. Only this time as she looked at it something struck her she hadn't noticed before.

It looked like a lingerie ad.

Sybella was making faces at it when Nik yanked open his door and brought the night and the familiar scent of his faint cologne and him into the cabin of the SUV.

She breathed him in and it just hurt more.

'What's happened?'

'Nothing.' She held the screen of the phone to her chest, not wanting him to know how vulnerable he'd left her. She felt she had precious few defences remaining against him, she could at least keep this one.

'Sybella, you look like someone died.'

Her eyes flew to his and he cursed. 'Sorry, bad use of language. Is this about those photos?'

'I can't help it. People are sending them to me.' She

looked down. 'Do you remember when you told me you'd never been personally involved with Marla Mendez?'

'Sybella, nothing happened, she ambushed me. I told her to put her clothes back on and I wasn't interested.' He sounded tired, which perversely annoyed her more.

'I know all that, this isn't about me not believing you— but why did you lie to me?'

'This happened before we were together.'

He was right, of course. But, 'My friends, workmates, my family, the whole village are looking at this and I know what they're thinking.'

'Who cares what they think?'

'Not you, obviously.' It just slipped out and she stared at her hands in her lap.

'Sybella,' he said, at least sounding as if he cared, 'I don't like it any more than you do but it is what it is.'

'I don't even understand why you're investing in her company.' It was on the tip of her tongue to ask him to pull out, but she felt as if it was her old insecurities at work. A lot of people probably relied on this project going ahead.

She needed to woman up.

But she couldn't help adding, 'Is this what you like?'

'That's not what this is.'

Something in her kicked. 'I asked you a question,' she said softly.

Nik made one of those frustrated male sounds but he didn't answer her. He was smart enough to know when to keep his mouth shut.

She should have been smart enough to shut hers.

'I guess it's what most men like. Woman in next to nothing writhing around on your lap.' She made a wry face at the little screen before turning it off. 'But the champagne is kind of overkill. No woman I know wants to be thought tacky. Who's she trying to appeal to, women who can afford her lingerie or teenage boys?'

'I have no idea.'

'Well, you should probably get up to speed on that, seeing you're her major investor.'

Nik grunted, but she could feel him watching her as if he was gauging the right time to say something to her. Only Sybella didn't want to hear it. She was afraid to hear it. She just wanted to go home.

'I want you to forget those photos,' he said as he closed her bedroom door. 'Because I'm not a regular in the tabloid press, Sybella. I leave that to my brother.'

Sybella slipped off her shoes and lost about three inches in height. 'Well, that's one blessing, I guess.'

'Give it a week and they'll be onto something else.'

'I guess.'

She was feeling vulnerable, any woman would, but Nik didn't seem to see it that way. But why would he? He came across as the guy who either pulled the sexiest woman in the world or, in his words, turned her down. She was the girl who had to live in a small village where everyone was going to pity her.

'But how would you feel if that was me in my underwear with another man?'

He began to chuckle. 'You?'

A flash of white-hot shame went through her, immediately followed by a huge rush of anger at the unfairness of it all. Because, no, she would be humiliated to see images of herself like that, and only two men had seen her in her underwear. And he knew that. She'd trusted him in the intimacy of their relationship to let him know how special this was for her. And now he was laughing at her?

'That's an entirely improbable scenario,' he said.

'Why? Because I can't get another man?'

He frowned. 'No, because I don't date women who flash their assets for profit on the Internet.'

'Funny, the world now thinks you do.'

Nik sighed. 'If this is about issuing some kind of public statement, you know I can't do that, Sybella. I don't play that game.'

'Well, no,' she said awkwardly, because she agreed with him in principle, 'but what about me?' Her voice went small. 'I'm put in a very difficult position.'

She hated having to say it, hated more that he didn't say it first!

'It's just I have to live here, Nik, and now I'm poor Sybella who can't hold her man.'

'Do people still think that way? I suspect that's more in your head than what's actually going on.' He sounded exasperated.

'Oh.' It came out on a little puff of pain.

'I am sorry,' he said, coming over and drawing her to him, his hands resting possessively around her shoulders. As hard as his words were sometimes, when he touched her he communicated a kind of tender restraint that never failed to move her. 'But do you really care what a few locals are saying about you? If I paid attention to the number of people who cursed me out I'd be a pretty poor businessman.'

'I know, but—'

'No buts.' He began unpinning her hair. She released a shaky sigh and tried to relax and let him do this for her, because she knew her hair was her greatest claim to beauty and he did admire it, but try as she might she kept seeing Marla's dark tide of glossy designer hair swaying over her perfect, lace-framed behind moving away from the camera.

She ducked her head. 'I—I can do that. Just leave it, Nik.'

Nik let her go and she scooted over to her dressing table and sat down to put some space between them.

She didn't know how she was going to climb into that

bed with him, because she kept having flashes of those images behind her eyes and everything about her body felt lumpen and unfamiliar to her.

'Sybella, you know there's nothing in this, don't you?'

She shook her head. 'I trust you, I do, it's just you told me nothing intimate had happened between the two of you, and now the photos exist. Why didn't you just tell me then?'

'Because it was tacky. Because I didn't want you having an excuse to call time on us.'

Sybella opened her mouth to tell him she wouldn't have done that, but the truth was it was the sort of thing she might have reacted badly to. It was only now, after more than a couple of months together, falling asleep in his arms and waking up beside him in the morning, that she felt she truly knew something of him.

'Back then, Sybella, I was just the rich guy who made things happen, remember? You would have gone home and never answered my calls.'

She didn't respond because he was right.

'There won't be any more tacky stories, *dushka*. I've always been far more interested in the bottom line than dating models.'

'The bottom line being women's underwear,' she said, trying to be funny but failing. 'Is there that much money in it?'

'Not really. Frankly, I'm more interested in seeing it fail than succeed.'

'Sorry?'

She met his eyes in the mirror and discovered he was looking at her as if gauging something.

'You want it to fail?' she pressed.

He was silent.

'Nik?'

'One of the investors is Galina Voronov.'

'Oh.' The evil witch in Nik's story. The woman whose child hated her.

'When I told you she took everything, I didn't tell you I had a plan to get it back.'

Sybella suddenly felt as if she'd missed some important facet of this conversation.

'But you have your father's film archive now—you paid for it.'

'*Da*, but now she must pay.'

CHAPTER FIFTEEN

NIK HAD FOLDED his arms and, with his height and the breadth of his shoulders, for a moment Fleur's childish nonsense about a giant in their garden flared once more to life.

'Pay?' she echoed. 'How?'

Nik looked back at her. His eyes were narrowed, his mouth taut and he appeared almost wolfish in this light. 'For her sins, of which there are many.' Then he smiled, although it didn't reach his eyes, and unfolded his arms to put a reassuring hand on her shoulder. 'Don't look so worried, *dushka*, I only want the money.'

Sybella gently dislodged his hand. 'No, you don't. You've got more money than the Bank of England.'

'You know me too well.'

Only she was starting to feel she didn't.

She jerked the chair around. 'What's going on, Nik?'

'Galina has invested all her cash assets in another one of Marla's projects. It's how Marla found her way to me. I'm pulling out of Marla Mendez Lingerie and when that happens all Marla's debt is going to come crashing through like a tsunami and it will swallow up the warehouses Galina's money paid for and as Marla's silent partner she will be responsible for those specific debts too. She'll have to sell the villa on Lake Geneva and the money I gave her will be gone.'

'But what about Ms Mendez?'

'Marla will land on her feet, *dushka*, and I'm not doing anything to her that she hasn't already done to herself. I didn't build that debt.'

'She has a little boy, Nik. This is going to impact on him too.'

'As I said, I didn't build her debt.'

'No, but haven't you agreed to sponsor her—surely you entered into a contract?'

'With everything built in I need to withdraw if I feel compromised.'

Sybella's face must have shown what she was feeling because he said more gently, 'It's business, Sybella. It happens.'

'But—but what about her sister, the one you said is the creative behind the label?'

'She's a woman with real talent. I'll make sure she lands on her feet and is given a new opportunity.'

Sybella couldn't believe what she was hearing. 'Nik, you can't play God with innocent people's lives!'

He began unthreading his tie. 'Short-term pain, Sybella, for long-term satisfaction.'

'Other people's pain, your satisfaction.'

She saw the tension rise in his shoulders. 'None of this satisfies me, Sybella. The only thing that would is if Galina had never come into our lives, but I can't turn back the clock.'

'But you can turn back now. You can change this, Nik.' Sybella stumbled to her feet. 'If you do this thing it makes you as bad as her.'

'Spare me the drama, *dushka*.'

'It's not drama, it's people's lives. Marla has a son, her son has an aunty—you're going to bring all this down on them to retrieve money you don't even need.'

'And as I said, it's not about the money.'

'No, it's something worse,' said Sybella chokily. 'If you do this it changes you. Listen, Nik, that day I came to the Hall to give your grandfather back those letters I overheard the two of you talking. You were being so tender with him, and all my prejudices about you fell away. I thought you were that man, hard on the outside because you've had to be, but with a genuinely good heart and the capacity to love your family.' Her voice got stuck. 'You are that man. Don't let her take that away from you.'

'Who are you talking about?'

'Your stepmother. You're letting your hatred for her twist you into something you're not.'

'And you're being naive, Sybella.' He began yanking at his shirt buttons, and as they gave a couple popped and hit the floor but he ignored them, as if a tailored shirt was like a tissue in terms of loss, and Sybella began to feel entirely too queasy.

He must have sensed her distress because he stopped and turned around, his hands resting on his lean hips, shirt gaping, more beautiful than any Norse god and certainly as dangerous in his power and unpredictability.

She might as well have ripped the page out of a magazine and stuck it on her wall; he couldn't have looked more unreal and out of place.

He didn't belong here. He never had. She'd let the giant into the house and only now was she counting the consequences.

'I'm a businessman and I've done some ruthless things in my time to get where I am.'

Sybella could only shake her head. 'I don't feel like I even know you.'

'Yeah, well, maybe you don't,' he threw back at her, pulling off the rest of his shirt and grabbing a fresh one from his open piece of luggage he'd brought in earlier and obviously intended to live out of. Another reminder none of this was permanent.

'But I'm not wasting any more time arguing over this. You just stick to your storybook world, Sybella.' He speared an assessing look up under those thick brown lashes. 'It suits you. I like you in it. I don't want you in this world. It can be equivocal and dark and you can't handle it.'

Sybella realised he was getting dressed again and that could only mean he was leaving, and that was when she realised what had been niggling at her.

'Is that what happened with your grandfather?'

He just kept buttoning his shirt, head down, profile pure chiselled stone.

'It is, isn't it? He climbed into his own version of a storybook to find peace in his last years, to get away from your anger.'

'Don't even start this, Sybella—'

'You probably can't see it,' she said, fumbling to make sense of concepts she'd just got her first glimpse of, 'you've been living it for so long. Nik, has everything you've done been about getting back at your stepmother?'

'*Da*, I built a multibillion-pound empire to spite Galina. You found me out.'

'No, I think you built your business the same way Mr Voronov found a picture in a book and decided he wanted to live in it. To make you safe.'

Nik shook his head, as if she was being ridiculous. 'I don't fear monsters in the cupboard, Sybella.'

'No, because you've had one living in your head. Nik, can't you see? You'll never get rid of her if you don't let it go.'

'Rid of who?'

Sybella sank onto the bed. 'I blamed myself for years after my parents abandoned me. Because they were my parents, the only ones I knew. Then I met Simon and his wonderful family, and they showed me how the people who love you treat you, and that's when I was able to let my parents go.'

Nik's features softened at the mention of her parents; at least he was listening to her, although he didn't look particularly convinced.

'Your grandfather came to Edbury because he's grieving your grandmother and *you* facilitated that by buying him the Hall, and then when things started happening that you didn't authorise, that you couldn't control, you started making a loud noise and threatening people. You were scary when you came down, Nik. You made all of us uneasy.'

'I was protecting my grandfather.'

'Understood, but there was no threat. It was all you.'

'I seem to remember finding strangers outside my grandfather's home and the house open to the public.'

But Sybella refused to be sidetracked. 'Something you would have known about if you'd talked to your grandfather. Is that what I can look forward to? Are you going to put me in a house, fence me in with staff and make sure I'm snug between the covers of that storybook you think I want to live in?'

'Now you're being ridiculous.'

'Am I? What are you protecting me from? That thing your stepmother is still managing to twist you into? What you've just told me paints you as a cold, amoral man seeking vengeance.'

'*Da*, and that is what I am.'

His eyes were hard as slate. Harder than those diamonds he drilled for. Making her feel real fear for the first time. Because she couldn't be with this man. She didn't know who he was.

She tried one last time. 'You're acting as if you have absolute power over these people. If you ruin Marla Mendez's label, you'll be bringing down stress and hardship on a lot more people than Galina. All she loses is money that wasn't hers to begin with.'

Nik felt something hot shoot through the centre of his brain and in its wake he could feel all the doubts he'd had himself, and ruthlessly crushed one by one as he'd walked this path.

But it was a different thing crushing Sybella's words. He looked at her and remembered the first time he'd seen her in full light. He'd thought she was a Christmas Angel.

He didn't even celebrate Christmas last year.

Sybella lived in a different world where people observed all the family and community gatherings, embraced the tenets of 'what you do affects your neighbour' and because of that you strove to do the right thing.

He even understood, given her past, why these things mattered to her.

He couldn't convince her he was right, and a big part of him didn't want to.

He was starting to wonder why he was even here. He zipped up his holdall.

'The moment Marla's label tanks and she moves on, so do I,' he said flatly. 'I want to hear no more of this, Sybella. It's not your concern. It's business.'

She gave him a stricken look. 'Where are you going?'

'I get the impression you don't want me here tonight, and, after three weeks in a mining camp in the Urals, I've had enough of cold, hard beds.'

The next day, hollow-eyed from lack of sleep Sybella took two tour groups through the west wing of the Hall.

After lunch she went down to the gatehouse, where builders were putting in the new exit door and a ramp for the disabled to bring the tourist centre in line with fire and safety regulations. She chatted with a few of the volunteers, trying to soak up some of their excitement and then headed home in the late afternoon just as the skies opened up.

Nik's SUV was out front when she turned up her street and the initial rush of joy was subsumed by uncertainty. She found herself sitting in her little car with the early spring rain beating down on the roof, wondering if she was ever going to find the courage to go in.

It was a lousy day, in keeping with her mood.

Catherine came out onto the doorstep and waved to her. Blast.

'Darling, Nik's here,' she said as Sybella slid past her, dumping her bags and coat in the hall. 'How is it going at the Hall?'

'We're on schedule to open the visitors' centre at the end of the month.'

Sybella submitted to a hug, then Catherine stage-whispered in her ear, 'Nik's in the kitchen. Fleur's playing with building bricks upstairs with Xanthe Miller. The coast is clear.'

'For what?' Sybella blinked at her mother-in-law.

'I think he wants to ask you something.'

This was also said in an exaggerated stage whisper. Sybella often thought Catherine was wasted in the local theatre group. She needed a bigger stage.

A little part of her lit that wick of hope that nothing—not even abandonment at twelve—had managed to snuff out in Sybella: this hope was that she would find her old, familiar Nik waiting for her and last night had been nothing but a horrible dream.

Nik was sprawled on one of her chairs in the kitchen that somehow looked extra tiny with him on it. His shirt was open at the neck and although he was wearing suit trousers, which meant he had been up in London, he looked a little un-put-together, surprisingly unshaven, which was unlike him. He was thumbing his phone.

Hard at work. On what? More plans to ruin the lives of people he didn't even know.

Sybella tried to crush the condemnatory thought. She really didn't want to fight with him.

'*Dushka*, I've got something to show you.' He patted

his knee as if she were just going to sashay over there and plant her behind down.

Sybella pictured herself doing it, Nik sliding his arm around her waist and kissing her neck and both of them pretending she knew nothing bad about him and they were all going to be fine.

Instead she came closer but not close enough.

With a slightly raised brow in acknowledgement of her decision he shifted to his feet because even being a bastard he was always a gentleman.

He showed her the screen on his phone. 'What do you think?'

It was a photo display of rooms, luxurious, spacious living areas, lots of glass, and several bedrooms that Nik scrolled through at top speed, barely giving her time to see it even if she were interested.

'Why are you looking at real estate?'

'It's an apartment in Petersburg I'm looking at purchasing.'

'Oh. It's very nice.' She wanted to tell him about the visitors' centre and she waited for him to ask.

'Purchasing for us,' he clarified. 'You and me and Fleur.'

Sybella literally rocked back on her heels.

'Why?'

'I want you to move to St Petersburg with me. We'll have no more talk about business. This will be our new start.'

Sybella just stared at him.

'Nik, I can't leave Edbury village. This is Fleur's home. This is my home.'

'It's not as if you won't be coming back—both of us have family here.'

'But I have a job here now too. I mean, the visitors' centre is due to open.' She stumbled over telling him because she'd been so excited and now it had just been rendered less important by Nik's out-of-the-blue decision.

'Great,' he said.

'There's a lot to do, but you've seen the plans. I think it's going to revitalise the village.'

'I'm sure it will.'

'The Heritage Trust have put me up for a local achievement award,' she blurted out, wondering why she needed to tell him that now.

'You've put a lot of work in.'

He was saying all the right things but he was watching her as if waiting for her spiel to be over so he could get back to what mattered. To him and his plans.

'The place will be up and running soon and I'm sure there are plenty of volunteers to take over. Hell, I'll employ people.' He gave her an intense look. 'I want you and Fleur in Pitter with me.'

'Nik, we belong here. My family, my friends, Edbury Hall is here and there won't be any volunteers unless I'm around to organise them.'

Nik was shaking his head. 'It's a job, Sybella. You can be replaced.' And with those few words he broke her heart.

Because as he dismissed her ambitions and small but significant achievement with a few tossed-aside words and voiced her worst fear, she could be replaced, the enchantment fell away and Sybella saw she'd been seeing what she wanted to see, not what was there.

A ruthless, ambitious man who got what he wanted when he wanted it.

'I worked hard to make a life here after Simon's death,' she said, finding it difficult to take a proper breath. 'I want to see Edbury Hall flourish and—and I want Fleur to grow up here, and I'm not coming to St Petersburg with you.'

'Then how does this even begin to work? You've seen

how my schedule's been. It's just not practical, Sybella.'
He sounded so cold and hard and certain.

'No, probably not, and above all let's be practical.' She
couldn't keep the bitterness out of her voice.

Nik shifted on his feet. His size no longer intimidated
her, but she could see he was pressing his advantage as a
big, tough guy who always got his own way.

'Sybella,' he said with finality, 'I have thousands of people who rely on me keeping my business interests turning
over. My working life is in Europe.'

If he hadn't told her about his plans for Marla Mendez's
label, Sybella knew she wouldn't be fighting him so hard
at this point.

If she didn't have Fleur to consider she probably would
have given in. Gone with him. Hoped they could build
something together.

But she knew now what he was capable of, and she
wasn't just planning a future for herself with him, she had
her daughter to think of.

'No one is asking you to change any of that. But you
have to give something, Nik. That's what a relationship
is. Give and take.'

At last that hard shell cracked and she saw some of the
old feeling in him.

'Give? I gave Deda a house to live in when he asked for
it. I have allowed you and on your behalf that lunatic historical society to keep the west wing of the Hall open to
the public against my better judgement. I saw this damn
apartment in St Petersburg and I thought of you. Of us.
What don't I give you?'

'Well, you could start by showing some interest in
something that matters to me,' she said quietly.

He gave her a long, hard look. 'This is what matters to
you—a tourist centre at the Hall?'

'What the Hall means to the people who live here, and

future generations. It's not about me, Nik, it's about living in a community and being a part of something bigger than you.'

He laughed derisively. 'When I came down here in January, I was convinced you had an agenda, that you were advancing some little cause of your own, and here we are, a few months down the track, and it turns out I was right.'

The unfairness of it barrelled into her.

'What cause? To keep the history of my village front and centre, so Edbury has something to be proud of? At least I'm doing this for good reasons, unlike you who thinks he can play God with other people's lives!'

'I knew we'd get back to this eventually.'

'Because it really doesn't matter to you, does it?' She broke down, tears filling her eyes. 'Ruin some strangers financially, shunt Fleur and me halfway across the world from everyone we love so you're not inconvenienced.'

'This isn't about my convenience, Sybella, it's you holding on tight to that dead husband of yours,' he shocked her by saying. 'Only think about how long it's taken you to get this far. Think about how hard you had to work to get it. Take it from me, your precious Simon wasn't thinking about you when he set up practice in a town where the only outlet for your career ambitions is some old pile you don't even have much interest in.'

'How dare you? What exactly are you accusing Simon of?'

He gave her a long hard look and she found herself reliving every tender, sweet moment between them. How she'd come to believe he saw something special in her as she did in him.

'Nothing,' he said tightly, shoving his phone into his back pocket. 'Forget it, Sybella. I wish you well with your activities in the Hall. You've fought hard for it.'

With that he walked out of her life, latching the garden gate behind him.

Her environs shrank back down to normal size and everything went back to being as if he'd never been there. Only a part of Sybella understood there would be no getting over him as she had her parents, and Simon. Because she'd found her true self with Nik, the real Sybella—strong, passionate and brave—who had been there all along, only she would have to be a little braver because she was once more on her own.

CHAPTER SIXTEEN

NIK STOOD ON the perimeter of the mine that had been the foundation of his fortune.

It was so vast and for once he didn't see the wealth it represented, the mastery over nature, the supplier of thousands of jobs. He saw it as what it would be for generations, even if he closed it now. A scar on the land. A reminder of all the destruction Sybella stood in opposition to.

She wanted to restore things, to use over what already existed, to make good on the past by bringing it into the present.

All he did was butcher and destroy the things that had hurt him. Lashing out like the nine-year-old boy he had once been, who had lost everything and wanted somebody to pay.

Anybody.

His stepmother was a convenient monster to slay.

Nik kicked a clod of earth near his boot and watched it spatter a few feet in front of him.

It had been three days since he flew out of the UK.

But not a moment passed when he didn't have the oddest feeling, as if something were screwing down in his chest. He woke in the night, chilled, furious with himself.

Every email his assistant passed on about the Mendez show in Milan next week had him visualising Sybella, the look of sheer devastation in her eyes.

He shouldn't have said what he had about her husband, even if it was true.

She thought he was trying to play God, when really all he was doing was trying to mend what was broken. Although ever since he'd told her his plans that broken thing hadn't seemed all that important. What had taken primacy was trying to fix things with Sybella.

He'd come up with the apartment on the spur of the moment. The look on her face. The way she'd pulled away from him. Her refusal to consider leaving the village. It had all coalesced to push him out, and all he'd heard was, *I came here with Simon. I stay here with Simon. You're not fit to wipe his boots.*

But if he was honest she hadn't said any of that. She'd been over the moon about the visitors' centre in Sybella fashion—quietly pleased, and then a little defiant at his complete lack of response.

No wonder she'd lost it with him.

Did he want her to fit into his life instead of making the adjustments to fit into hers?

He knew what a good, healthy relationship looked like. It was the one Deda and Baba had. It was exactly what Deda had been trying to get through his thick skull when he'd arrived down here in January.

'I've found you a girl.'

When had he started thinking he didn't deserve that? What was it Sybella had said? *'You're letting the hatred twist you into something you're not.'*

But deep down he'd always believed that he was that thing. He'd been fighting with this weapon inside him that told him he wasn't a Voronov, he could do whatever it took to play the world and people like his stepmother at their own game. Only that weapon was currently at his own throat and it probably always had been.

The day he'd left Edbury his brother had rung him. He was in the chapel in the west wing at the Hall and he'd been so frustrated after his argument with Sybella he almost hadn't picked up.

'Nice shot of you and Marla Mendez. Deda is furious.'

'Deda's the least of my worries.'

Nik had looked around the high vaulted ceiling of the chapel where apparently he'd agreed tourists could pay their *kopeck* for the privilege and gawp at the stained glass and the slabs on the ground under his feet, where he'd been told sixteenth-century inhabitants of the Hall were buried.

'He emailed me a photo, you and this woman you're seeing.'

'Sybella.'

'*Da*. You were carrying this cute little kid on your shoulders.'

'Fleur. Hang on, Deda emailed you?'

'Yeah, your Sybella got him up to speed on that. Great tits, by the way.'

Hitting his brother hadn't been going to promote family unity. Besides, he'd been a continent away. 'I'll pretend you didn't say that.'

'So you love her?' Sasha had asked.

Nik hadn't even had to think about it. 'Yeah, I do. I do love her.'

There was a pause. 'Are you going to marry her?'

'She's not very happy with me at the moment.'

'Whatever you've done, man, if she loves you she'll forgive you.'

But Nik knew one thing now as he stood on the perimeter of the road that spiralled down into the dark heart of the Voroncor seam: he had to forgive someone else first.

He needed to make a call and take a flight out to Helsinki tonight.

'What's happening, love? Has business called him away again?' asked Catherine, hovering over her as Sybella dragged out her wellies and Fleur's from the cupboard under the stairs.

It had been a week since Nik had stormed out of her

house. A week of pretending, and Sybella was running out of evasions to satisfy her eagle-eyed mother-in-law.

'I don't know.'

They'd been at the May Day celebrations since dawn and Sybella had brought Fleur home for a nap because it was a long day with fireworks tonight.

Fleur appeared at the top of the stairs.

'Ready to go, darling?'

'You're going for a walk?' Catherine demanded peevishly. 'What if Nik calls? Make sure you take your phone.'

'He's not going to call, Catherine.'

'I'll stay here in case he calls.'

Sybella handed Fleur her boots and then took her mother-in-law's face between her hands. 'Go home, Catherine. I love you to bits but please stop interfering in my love life.'

'I have to,' grumbled Catherine. 'Meg won't let me near hers.'

'I want Gran to come,' said Fleur grumpily, picking up on the adults' mood.

Sybella sagged but Catherine must have seen something in her face and, instead of arguing, she helped Fleur with her boots.

'I will see you tonight, pumpkin, at the fireworks.'

Sybella started feeling awful about her behaviour before she even herded Fleur out of the house. By the time she and Fleur were trudging across the field to the high wold she felt wretched. Catherine was the closest person she had to a mother and the older woman's anxiety over Nik's sudden departure a week earlier and determination to bring them together was only motivated by a desire to see her happy.

'Look, Mummy, pretty!' Fleur had a handful of yellow flowers she'd pulled out of the ground.

'That's called oxlip,' Sybella instructed with a smile, and leant down so Fleur could tuck a piece behind her ear.

As she straightened up she noticed properly for the first time that winter had completely melted away and the countryside was fragrant with wildflowers showing themselves among the new grass.

The village below them gleamed with the local mellow gold stonework that was peculiar to the region and the May sunshine hit the church spire.

From here she could see all the windy yellow roads with their stone walls cutting through the countryside below them and the odd car wending its way.

It wasn't a bad place to be miserable. And maybe Mrs Muir was right: there were all kinds of ways to be happy, and she would have to find a way by herself.

He wasn't coming back. And one day it wouldn't hurt this much.

Then she noticed a dark head bobbing up over the next rise directly before the valley dropped down into the village.

It was Meg.

She was running—well, hobbling, really—and as she closed the space between them Sybella saw why. She was wearing stockings and high heels, which looked odd enough as she picked and wove her way around cow pats and muddy spots. She was also carting something under her arm.

'What are you doing with a laptop up here?'

Meg was panting. Apparently cross-fit classes in a gym did nothing for your ability to run an obstacle course up a Cotswold hill.

She handed the laptop over and Sybella obligingly took it as her sister-in-law bent with her hands on her knees and huffed and puffed to get her breath back.

'You. Will. Thank. Me.' She sucked in a few more breaths and then made a gesture at the laptop. 'Fire it up. I've got something to show you.'

'You know the Internet connection is bad enough in the village. I don't know if we'll get it up here.'

'I broke speed laws to get here. Just open the blinking laptop!'

Sybella settled herself down in the grass and did as she was bid.

Meg had taken off her fancy shoes and was gingerly examining the soles, now sadly scuffed and damp.

'They're on the desktop,' Meg said.

Sybella clicked and the screen filled with two faces, one of them so familiar her throat closed over.

Nik and Marla.

'Why are you showing me these?'

'That was taken at last night's opening of Mendez's fashion label in Milan.'

'It went ahead?'

'That's not the question I expected. Why wouldn't it?'

Sybella noted the space between Nik and Marla was filled by a young boy with a shock of dark hair and soulful brown eyes, perhaps around eight or nine. It must be her son.

She could feel her sister-in-law watching her face with barely constrained glee, and then she forgot all about Meg and her entire attention was welded to Nik, and although she couldn't understand the Italian voice-over, she got a lot out of just watching the camera glide over him as he sat up front with Marla, her son, and all the other VIPs while bored-looking coat hangers strutted down the runway. Only...not all those girls were coat hangers. Several distinctly rounded, curvy girls swept the stage in just enough lace and satin to keep them decent. They looked *amazing*.

Marla Mendez's perfect face filled the frame and she said in English, 'I wanted the girls to fill out my sexier designs. I remember the day I had this exciting idea. I met up with Nik Voronov's fiancée, Sybella Parminter, and I,

Marla, looked at her and saw all the shape I wanted for my line. She is gorgeous. She is an oil painting. She has the boobs and the hips and the thighs. The definition of womanhood.'

Fiancée? Sybella felt Meg nudge her.

'So I have the nymphs, the dryads and the Venuses to embrace all body shapes. We women are many things and I want my line to reflect that.'

'How about off-the-rack pricing?' commented Meg.

Then Nik was answering questions.

He was definitely out of his comfort zone with women's lingerie, but then, given his brother was apparently the main driver of the market, he thought he might as well invest.

This brought laughter and more questions.

Then with a faint smile he said, 'No, I have no interest in living in Milan. I am taking up residency in the UK to be with the woman I love. If she'll have me.'

Sybella was vaguely aware Meg's phone was ringing but she couldn't take her eyes off the screen.

'It's Mum,' said Meg. 'She wants to talk to you.'

Sybella continued to gaze at the screen.

There was a volley of high-pitched squawking from the phone. Meg jumped. 'He's rung! Nik rang your phone. Mum says you have to ring him. She says it's no time to play coy. He's shown his hand.'

'I'm not ringing him.'

'She's not ringing him, Mum. Why *aren't* you ringing him? That's from both of us, by the way.'

Sybella had put down the lid of the laptop and was looking up into the sky. There it was, the definite thwack, thwack, thwack. 'Because he's already here.'

Nik saw the forest first and then the church steeple and finally the village spread out on the cleft of the wold.

His attention wasn't on Edbury Hall itself, but the grounds where tents and bunting had been erected. One of the lawns was covered in cars. Several weeks ago it would have been unimaginable. He'd have closed the lot down.

As the chopper flew over the village he could see the maypole on the green, no longer the solitary needle without a thread he'd seen it as when he'd driven into Edbury for the first time, but festooned with ribbons and encircled by dozens of little girls in white dresses, running happily, and not so happily as one or two took tumbles, and their parents and families and neighbours and school friends cheered them on.

He saw St Mary's Church with its glinting spire and the graveyard running up behind it with the tumble of stone markers, large and small. He saw the mass of forest where he and Sybella had first walked together and he'd fallen so completely under her spell it was astonishing he'd been able to walk without stumbling over his feet.

Then he saw her, out on the hill just as Catherine had told him when he'd rung Sybella's phone. Two small figures, but even at this distance he knew which one was Sybella.

'Take it over to the west,' he told his pilot, Max, and as the chopper came in closer the woman next to her began to jump up and down, waving her arms.

Nik was unstrapped and climbing out, the blades still rotating when he saw her coming towards him.

He didn't know where her friend had gone; he didn't care.

As he strode towards her he could see all the anxiety on her face and it tore strips from his chest.

'You didn't do it,' she said.

He came as close as he dared without touching her.

She was wearing a pretty floral dress and her hair was plaited but there were flowers threaded through it, probably for May Day, and she looked like a pagan goddess of spring in her wellington boots.

'I didn't do it.' He shoved his hands into the pockets of his jacket because it was hard to be this close to her and not touch her.

'Why not?' she asked softly, those hazel eyes as anxious as the first time he'd seen her, when he'd mistaken her for an intruder and been trying to scare her.

'I worked it all out. I kept thinking about what you said, about it twisting me, about how I use money and privilege as a weapon...'

She lowered her head but she didn't argue with him.

'You were right, I've known it for a long time, and I kept justifying it because I was angry.'

'She did a terrible thing, Nik.'

'She did, but that's old anger. Frankly, Sybella, I think I stopped expending all that energy on her when I bought back the archive. I did that for my father, by the way. It was my duty by him and then it was done.'

She shook her head. 'Then who were you angry with?'

'Deda, for taking me in when he didn't have to, and Sasha for holding it against me. But it was all me—neither of them felt that way.' His grey eyes searched her face for understanding. 'And that's when I knew I'd decided to be angry with you.'

'With me?'

'I didn't think you loved me.'

The words sounded like paupers, emptying their sacks to show the rich people how little they had. Nik, who had seemed to have everything—money, power, all the confidence in the world—was opening up his heart to her.

She realised right then and there he saw her as the rich one. The one with the love to give and bestow. Just as she had once seen Simon. But she didn't want to be that person with Nik. Because it was absolutely clear to her now that he loved her, had been trying to tell her for a long time how much he loved her, and she had been deaf.

'Do you remember what you said about being angry with Simon, for the accident, something that couldn't possibly be his fault?' He spoke slowly, as if he might stumble over the difficult words.

'Yes.'

'I know you loved him, Sybella, from the bottom of your heart, because that's who you are. What I worked out since I drove away from your house was why you were angry with me.'

'Because I love you, you silly billy,' she said, as if this were obvious.

He smiled then. That slow breaking dawn of a smile, and that he used it so rarely made her think it was only for her. And she knew now that it was.

'Where have you been?'

'I went to Helsinki and met my biological father.'

Of all the things he'd say she hadn't expected that.

'He's a geologist,' Nik added.

'Of course he is.' Sybella was smiling so broadly her face hurt as she stepped right up to him.

Nik fisted his hands because the urge to touch her was almost impossibly strong but he needed to tell her the whole story first. 'He shook my hand, Sybella, and he didn't ask his billionaire son for a kopeck. That's the kind of man he is.'

'He is your dad, then,' she said softly, 'because if the positions were reversed wouldn't you do the same?' She reached up to smooth back his hair in a gesture he'd seen her use with Fleur. It stopped the breath in his body. 'He must be so proud of you, all you've accomplished.'

'I don't know about that. He was interested in you. Do you mind that I talked about you?'

'It depends what you said.'

'I asked for his advice. I told him I was in love with

this beautiful, brilliant Englishwoman and she had a sweet little girl and she was surrounded by all these people who love her, and I'd stuffed up.'

'You're in love with me?'

Nik swallowed down hard. He wanted more than anything to take her in his arms, especially when she sounded so uncertain, but he had to get through this first. He had to give her that certainty they'd once held between them back.

'He told me thirty-five years ago he'd been in love with my mother but he could see that she loved my father more, and he let her go. He told me if he'd known about me it would have been different, he would have made a different choice. And I thought about that, Sybella. I thought about all the variables in our lives. What if your Simon was still here? What if Deda hadn't found that picture in *Country Life*? And I realised the only element in all of this that I could control was me. I had choices. If I went ahead and punished Galina I would lose you. Because you can't love the man who would do something like that, because of the woman you are, and that's the woman I love. That's the man I want to be for you.'

Sybella wasn't sure how it happened, but she was in his arms and it felt like coming home. Her whole life with its good and its bad had been leading up to this moment.

More than anything she knew now this was what the fates had had in store for her.

All the bad things that could happen to a person had rained down on her and then Fleur was born and her life had taken on new meaning, until this moment when it all made perfect sense.

Embodied in this one, extraordinary man. Who was hers.

'Oh, Nik, I've been so lonely without you,' she confessed in a fractured voice as the tears came. 'I don't care where we live. As long as we're with you it doesn't matter.'

'*Net*, it does matter.' His big hands smoothed over her back possessively. 'I want you and Fleur to be with me and I'll do whatever it takes to make that happen.'

She began to cry in earnest and he held her tighter. For once she was happy to give way to his natural dominance.

'I was so proud of you for going ahead with the show, for not withdrawing the funding.'

He framed her face, wiping away her tears with his thumbs. 'On that front I thought I'd have a lot of explaining to do.'

'No, Meg did that.' She sniffed happily, gulping on all the heady emotion surging through her. 'She explained everything, bless her.' Sybella pressed her temple to his bent one. 'I'm just so happy you're here.'

He dropped down on both knees in front of her and she heard Meg give a very un-Meg-like gasp of excitement some distance away.

'Sybella Frances Parminter, will you marry me?'

Sybella's face lit up with a smile she felt from her toes to her fingertips. 'Yes, of course I will.'

Then she fell to her knees in front of him and wrapped her arms around his neck and kissed him.

'That's my yes,' she said against his mouth, 'in case it wasn't clear.'

Then she kissed him again, and Nik wrapped her up in his arms and breathed freely for the first time since he'd driven out of Edbury.

He had her; he was home.

The four of them made their way down the hill towards the carnival atmosphere of the village.

Fleur on Nik's broad shoulders, Sybella holding his hand, Meg picking her way through the field in her heels.

Sybella's heart was overflowing with all of her blessings.

Later in the afternoon when family had been told, impromptu champagne had been drunk, her father-in-law Marcus had taken a walk with Nik from which they'd returned somewhat late, having ended at the pub, only then did Nik propose they go up to the Hall.

It was nearing the four o'clock raffle of celebratory hampers and Nik borrowed a megaphone from the guy who was going to call the prize. He walked out onto the lawn and people started to naturally gravitate towards him.

Sybella took Fleur's hand and his arm came around her.

'For those of you who don't know me, I'm Nikolai Aleksandrovich Voronov. I'm caretaker of this house.'

Sybella beamed at her daughter.

'Edbury Hall is forthwith reopened to the public—not just the west wing, but the entire estate.'

His voice carried over the assembled heads of the small crowd and a small cheer went up, interspersed with plenty of 'it's about time'.

'I'll be taking up residence in Edbury but let me put your minds at rest. I will not be turning the Hall into a compound and setting dogs on trespassers.'

Some of the children laughed but Sybella noted the arrested look on Fleur's face at the mention of a dog. She'd have to head that one off when things were a little more normal and she wasn't feeling so loved up. She looked up at her Norse god and didn't think that would be any time soon.

'And just so it's clear,' Nik said, grinning down at her, 'Sybella and I are getting married.'

At the end of the summer the bells of St Mary's pealed as the happy couple emerged into the glorious sunshine.

Sybella, in an off-the-shoulder gauze and white satin gown, her bridal veil set back on her head, and Nik, in a grey morning suit, came first, and then Fleur and her friend Xanthe swinging their baskets of rose petals, the families and friends of both bride and groom spilling out of the church behind them.

The bride had invited Marla Mendez to the wedding, as long as she brought her young son.

Twelve months along almost to the day Leonid Niko-laievich Voronov came into the world in the beautiful local stone house on the wold Nik had moved them into after the wedding.

Leo was christened in the Russian Orthodox Church in London in the presence of his Russian great-grandfather and his English grandparents, but not his parents as custom dictated. He was again christened in the village of Edbury at St Mary's and was carried in the arms of his proud older sister.

There was high tea at the Hall and the whole village attended.

Old Mr Voronov toasted his great-grandson and announced the Hall was being gifted to the National Trust and he was going to live in the new house on the wold with his grandson and his wife. The house was big enough to fit them all and small enough no one would be lonely.

Afterwards Sybella, holding her new baby to her breast, sat on the terrace in the summer sun, watching Fleur tumbling on the lawn with her friends and the absolutely ridiculously large sheepdog Nik had insisted on buying her when they'd first got married. A year down the track it was growing as big as a pony.

'What are you thinking, *moya lyuba*?' Nik's dark voice ran through her senses like dark chocolate and honey, all the things she'd craved while she was pregnant. He hunkered down beside them, stroking the fine pale quiff of hair that was all Leo currently had on his small head.

'How fortunate we are. How fortunate I am.'

'It was fate,' said Nik, a true Russian.

And Sybella was disposed to believe him.

'Although one thing still haunts me,' he mused.

She angled a curious look at him.

'What if Sasha had been the brother who came down that weekend?'

'I can't say I haven't given it some thought,' she said lightly, rubbing a finger consideringly over his lower lip.

'What did you come up with?' he growled, snapping playfully at her finger.

'Sasha's so friendly, he never would have thrown me down in the snow and shaken me like a rattle and sent me on my way.'

'Did I do all those things?' Nik's eyes kindled with hers. 'Shameful. You can never tell our son.'

'I will. I will tell him, when he's old enough to find the right girl, just so he'll know what to do.'

'He's a Voronov. He doesn't need advice about finding the right girl. It's in our blood. He'll know when the time comes.'

So spoke her alpha male. Sybella smiled indulgently.

'When did you know?' she asked.

'I believe it happened when I took off your ski mask, Rapunzel, and I looked into your eyes, but I definitely knew when I kissed you.'

'Like this?' She stroked his jaw with the backs of her fingers and Nik lost his train of thought, moving his mouth over hers once more, careful not to dislodge their small son, who was fiercely guarding his nourishment.

'Exactly like that, *moya lyubov.*'

She looked into Nik's grey eyes and wondered at the idea she'd ever found them chilly. She cocked her head to one side.

'Did I ever tell you? When we first met I thought you were a bear…'

* * * * *

THE ILLEGITIMATE
BILLIONAIRE

BARBARA DUNLOP

For Shaina, Jacob, Karl and Heidi

One

In an absurdly masculine room, deep in the halls of Clarkson Castle, Deacon Holt carefully neutralized his expression. He wouldn't give Tyrell Clarkson the satisfaction of seeing anger, envy or any other emotion.

"Drink?" Tyrell asked, making a half turn toward Deacon from the inlayed walnut bar. He held up a cut-crystal decanter that Deacon could only guess held decades-old single malt.

Tyrell was well-known in Hale Harbor, Virginia, for indulging in the finer things.

"No," Deacon answered. He had no idea why he'd been summoned today, after being shunned his entire life, but he was positive this wasn't a social occasion.

Tyrell shrugged and poured two glasses anyway. He cut partway across the library and bent at the waist to set the glasses on opposite sides of a dark wood coffee table.

"In case you change your mind," he said and gestured to one of two brown leather armchairs flanking the table.

Deacon preferred to stand. He wanted to be on alert for whatever was coming.

"Sit," Tyrell said and folded himself into the opposite chair.

Though he was in his late fifties, Tyrell was obviously in good shape. He had a full head of hair, and his wrinkles were few, giving his face character. By any objective measure, he was a good-looking man.

Tyrell was rich. He was clever. He was powerful.

He was also detestable.

"What do you want?" Deacon asked.

The rest of Hale Harbor might jump to Tyrell's commands, but not Deacon.

"A conversation."

"Why?"

Tyrell lifted his glass and turned it in the light that beamed down from the ceiling fixtures. He gazed at the amber liquid. "Glen Klavitt, 1965."

"Am I supposed to be impressed?"

"You're supposed to be curious. When was the last time you tasted fifty-year-old single malt?"

"I forget." Deacon wasn't rising to the bait, even though they both knew he wasn't in a tax bracket that would allow him to casually spend whatever 1965 Glen Klavitt cost. Not that he'd be foolish enough to blow his money on it anyway.

"Sit down, boy."

"I'm not your dog."

One of Tyrell's brows went up.

Deacon expected Tyrell to react with anger. He mentally braced himself for the onslaught, realizing he'd been looking forward to a fight from the moment he walked through the oversize castle doors.

"But you are my son." Tyrell's words, though softly spoken, fell like cannonballs into the cavernous room.

Deacon held still, half expecting eight generations of Clarksons to rise from their graves and rattle the crested shields hanging on the stone walls.

He tried to gauge Tyrell's expression, but it was inscrutable.

"Do you need a kidney?" he asked, voicing the first theory that came into his mind.

Tyrell's mask cracked, and he almost smiled. "I'm in perfect health."

Deacon didn't want to be curious about anything to do with the Clarkson family. He wanted to turn on his heel and walk out the door. Whatever was going on here, he wanted no part of it.

Tyrell had two healthy, living legitimate sons, Aaron and Beau. He didn't need to reach out to Deacon for anything—at least, not for anything that was honorable.

"Will you relax?" Tyrell asked, gesturing to the empty chair with his glass.

"No."

"Stubborn—"

"Like father, like son?" Deacon asked mildly.

Tyrell laughed.

It was the last thing Deacon had expected.

"I don't know why I thought this would be easy," Tyrell said. "Aren't you even a little bit curious?"

"I stopped caring about you a long time ago."

"Yet, here you are."

Deacon knew Tyrell had him there. Despite his anger, despite his hatred, despite the twenty-nine years of resentment, Deacon had come the first time Tyrell called. Deacon told himself he was here for a confrontation with the man who had impregnated and then abandoned his mother. But the truth was he'd also been curious. He was still curious.

He sat down.

"That's better," Tyrell said.

"What do you want?"

"Do I have to want something?"

"No. But you do."

"You're not stupid. I'll grant you that."

Deacon wasn't sure if Tyrell expected a *thank you* for the backhanded compliment. If he did, he was going to be disappointed.

"Why am I here?" Deacon pressed.

"I assume you know about Frederick."

"I do."

Tyrell's youngest son—and Deacon's half brother, though they'd never been introduced—Frederick had died of pneumonia six months ago. Rumor had it that Frederick's lungs had been seriously damaged as a child, when he'd been thrown from a horse. The fall had also broken his spine and confined him to a wheelchair.

"Did you know he lived in Charleston?" Tyrell asked.

Deacon hadn't known where Frederick lived. He'd only known Frederick had left home after college and never returned. Everyone in Hale Harbor knew Frederick had a falling out with his father and walked out of the Clarkson family's life. Deacon had silently admired Fredrick for doing it.

"Frederick has two sons," Tyrell said. His gaze didn't waver.

Deacon was surprised at that news. He wasn't an expert on spinal cord injuries, but he wouldn't have expected Frederick to father children. He supposed they could have been adopted.

He didn't know what Tyrell anticipated as a response to that particular revelation. But Deacon didn't have anything to say about Frederick's sons.

"The oldest is four, the other eighteen months," Tyrell said.

"Congratulations?" Deacon ventured.

"My only grandchildren, and I've never met them."

"I don't get where this is going." Deacon had sure never met Tyrell's grandsons.

The entire Clarkson family did their best to pretend Deacon didn't exist. Aaron and Beau knew perfectly well who he was, though he'd never been sure about Tyrell's wife, Margo. It was possible Tyrell had been successful in keeping Deacon a secret from her all these years—which begged the question of what Deacon was doing in the castle today. Surely Margo would be curious.

Tyrell took a healthy swallow of the scotch.

Deacon decided to try it. What the heck? It might be the one and only thing his father ever gave him.

He lifted the expensive tumbler to his lips and took an experimental sip. The whiskey was smooth, rich and peaty, not bad, but he'd sampled better. Then again, the company might be tainting the taste.

"I want to see my grandsons," Tyrell said.

"So see them."

"I can't."

"What's stopping you?"

"Frederick's widow."

It took Deacon a beat to comprehend what Tyrell meant. Then he grinned. Poetic justice had visited Tyrell. Deacon took another sip of the whiskey, silently toasting the widow. The scotch tasted better this time, really quite good.

"You find that amusing?" Tyrell's words were terse.

"Someone keeping the powerful Tyrell Clarkson from something he wants? Yes, I find that amusing." Deacon saw no point in shading his feelings. Tyrell couldn't possibly think Deacon gave a damn about Tyrell's happiness.

Tyrell seemed to gather himself, leaning forward, his chin jutting. "Down to brass tacks, then. Let's see if you think *this* is funny. I'll trade you what I want for what you want."

The words unnerved Deacon. At the same time, they put him on alert. "You haven't the first idea of what I want."

"Don't be too sure about that."

"I'm completely sure about that." Deacon had never even had a conversation with his father, never mind confided his hopes and dreams to him.

"I'll acknowledge you as my son," Tyrell said.

It was all Deacon could do not to laugh at the offer. "I could have proved our relationship through DNA years ago."

"I mean, I'll make you an heir."

"Put me in your will?" Deacon wasn't falling for a promise like that—a promise changeable with the stroke of a pen.

"No. Not when I die. Now. I'm offering you twenty-five percent of Hale Harbor Port. You'll be equal partners with me, Aaron and Beau."

Hale Harbor Port was a billion-dollar corporation that had been owned by succeeding generations of the Clarkson family since the 1700s. Deacon tried to wrap his head around the offer. He couldn't.

His entire childhood he'd dreamed of being a part of the Clarkson family. He'd spun fantasies that Tyrell truly loved Deacon's mother, that he secretly wanted Deacon in his life, that he would one day leave Margo and welcome Deacon and his mother into the castle.

But then Deacon's mother had died when he was barely nineteen, and Tyrell didn't so much as send condolences. Deacon accepted the reality that he meant nothing to Tyrell, and he stopped dreaming.

And now this offer came completely out of the blue. What could possibly be worth twenty-five percent of a billion dollars? Nothing legal, that was for sure.

"You want me to kidnap them?" Deacon asked.

Tyrell shook his head. "That would be too easy. Also temporary, because we'd be sure to get caught."

"But you're not morally opposed to it?" Maybe it should have surprised Deacon that Tyrell would consider committing a capital crime. It didn't.

Tyrell drew in an impatient breath. "Give me credit for a little finesse."

Deacon knew he should walk away from this conversation. "I don't give you credit for anything."

"But you're still listening."

"I'm curious, not tempted."

Tyrell gave a smug smile, polishing off his drink. "Oh, you're tempted all right."

"Spit it out, or I'm leaving." Deacon rose to his feet. He wasn't going to play this game any longer.

"I want you to romance and marry Frederick's widow and bring my grandsons home." Tyrell watched intently for Deacon's reaction.

Deacon didn't have a reaction. He would have bet he hadn't heard right, but Tyrell's words were crystal clear.

"Why?" Deacon tried to fathom the complexity that had to lie behind the request.

Tyrell was reputed to be a master conspirator.

"Why would she marry me?" Deacon voiced his own thought process as he searched for more information. "And what does it gain you? Just offer her money to come home."

"I can't offer her money to come home. I can't even risk contacting her. I'm positive Frederick poisoned her against the family. If I make that play and fail, it's game over."

"You have a whole lot of money to offer."

However Frederick might have disparaged his family, surely most mortal women would be attracted to the family's immense wealth.

"Frederick may have walked away from the company," Tyrell said. "But he didn't walk away from his trust fund. She doesn't need money."

Again, Deacon smiled. "Something you can't buy. Must be frustrating."

"She doesn't know you," Tyrell said.

"Does she know Aaron and Beau?" Deacon still wasn't getting the play here. It had to be galling for Tyrell to approach Deacon for anything.

"Aaron's already married," Tyrell pointed out. "And Beau... I'm not naïve where it comes to my children, Deacon. Beau's nobody's idea of a good husband and father."

Deacon didn't disagree with that statement. Beau had always been the wild one, parties every weekend and a different girlfriend every month. His exploits had been splashed across local gossip columns dozens of times.

"You, on the other hand," Tyrell continued. He gestured Deacon up and down with his empty glass. "I recognize you have a certain sophistication. Women seem to like you. Nice women seem to like you."

Deacon couldn't help but be amazed that Tyrell had paid any attention to him at all.

"You're not publicly connected to the family," Tyrell continued. "You can move in under the radar, romance her, marry her."

"Then blindside her with the news about you?" Deacon had always questioned Tyrell's morality, but this was beyond belief.

Tyrell rolled his eyes. "Ease her into it, boy."

"No." An ownership position in Hale Harbor Port might

be Deacon's lifelong dream, but he wasn't going to use Frederick's widow as a pawn.

Tyrell came to his feet. "You have a moral objection?"

"Yes. And you should, too." Deacon peered into Tyrell's eyes, searching for some semblance of a soul. "You do know that, right?"

"Go meet her," Tyrell said.

Deacon started to refuse again, but Tyrell talked right over him. "Just meet her before you decide. If you don't want to do it, don't do it. But don't give up hundreds of millions of dollars without looking at all the angles."

"You're the angles guy, not me."

"You're my son," Tyrell repeated.

Deacon wanted to protest. He might be saddled with Tyrell's DNA, but he wasn't anything like him. He had a moral compass. He got it from his mother.

But he found himself hesitating.

In that second, it was clear he'd inherited some traits from his father. And they couldn't be good traits. Because he was weighing the harm in meeting Frederick's widow. Was there any harm in meeting her before refusing Tyrell's offer?

It was on days like these that Callie Clarkson missed her husband the most. Frederick loved springtime, the scent of roses wafting in the bakery windows, mingling with the cinnamon and strawberries from the kitchen. Today the sun was shining in a soft blue sky, and tourists were streaming into Downright Sweet for a midmorning muffin or warm berry scone.

Their bakery, Downright Sweet, occupied both floors of a red brick house in the historic district of downtown Charleston. The first floor held the kitchen that they'd refurbished when they bought the place five years ago. It also held the front service counter and several tables, both inside and out on the porch. The second floor was a dining room with screened windows all the way around, plus a covered sundeck that over-looked the tree-lined, shade-dappled street.

The lunch crowd was diminishing, and Callie's manager, Hannah Radcliff, breathed an audible sigh of relief.

"My feet are killing me," Hannah said.

She was in her early forties, with rounded curves from a self-described weakness for buttercream. Her voice was soft. Her eyes were mocha brown, and she had a perpetual smile on her very pretty face. Both of Callie's sons, James and Ethan, loved her to death.

"Go take a break," Callie said. "Nancy and I will be fine."

"Rest your feet," Nancy echoed from where she was wiping down the espresso machine. "I'll do the tables."

"I'll take you up on that," Hannah said. "Wait. Hello."

Callie followed the direction of Hannah's gaze to see Mayor Watkins striding past the front window, toward the Down-right Sweet entrance.

Nancy gave an amused laugh. She was a college student who had come back to her family in Charleston for the sum-mer. She didn't see the attraction of the Mayor.

Hank Watkins was single, slightly younger than Hannah and equally quick to smile. His dark hair was short at the sides, with a swoop across the top that didn't particularly appeal to Callie. But he was attractive enough, in a distinguished way that was beneficial for a politician.

She'd describe him as burley, with a deep, booming voice. He was the son of one of Charleston's most prominent families. They traced their ancestry all the way back to the Mayflower.

The classic little gold bell jingled as the door opened.

Callie stepped away from the cash register, busying her-self with tidying the displays of cupcakes and giving Han-nah a clear field.

"Hello, Mr. Mayor," Hannah said.

"You know to call me Hank," the Mayor answered.

"Hank," Hannah said. "What can I get you?" She gestured

to the glass case on her left. "A lemon puff pastry? Or coconut buttercream? The cupcakes are popular today."

"What do you recommend?"

"You can't go wrong with the pecan tart."

"Done."

"Whipped cream?" Hannah asked.

"Of course." The Mayor pulled his wallet from his suit jacket pocket. "Callie?" He turned his attention to her.

"Whipped cream is always a nice addition," Callie answered lightly. She kept her attention on the cupcakes, not wanting to intrude.

"I was hoping I could talk with you," Hank said, his tone going more serious.

She went immediately on edge. "Is everything okay?"

Following the unexpected death of her husband six months ago, Callie's optimism had taken a hit. She realized her years with Frederick had made her complacent. She'd forgotten life mostly dished out pain and disappointment. She intended to be braced for it from here on in.

"Nothing too worrisome," he said, handing Hannah a ten-dollar bill. He smiled again as he spoke to her. "Keep the change."

"Thank you, Hank," Hannah said.

He looked at Callie again. "Will you join me?"

"Sure." She untied her hunter green apron and slipped it over her head.

Beneath, she was wearing a white blouse and a pair of pressed khaki slacks. Her hair was up in a casual twist, and her earrings were small diamond studs that Frederick had given her for her birthday last year. She wore them every day. And as she walked around the end of the display case, she twisted her engagement ring and her wedding band round her finger.

She feared Hank was here with bad news about her deck permit.

He had offered to talk to the board personally to advocate for its quick approval. She'd turned down the offer, but now she wondered if that had been a mistake. Maybe she should have let him help.

Frederick had always advised her to keep the local politicians on their side. *You might not love them,* he'd said. *You might not even like them. But it costs nothing to be congenial, and you never know which way the wind will blow.*

If Downright Sweet didn't get the permit to renovate the deck, they couldn't replace the support beams, meaning they'd have to close the deck down while they came up with a new plan. It was May, the beginning of tourist season, and she was counting on running at full capacity by the end of June.

They took an empty table next to the window.

"Is this about the permit?" she asked.

"I'm afraid so."

Callie's heart sank. "It's been denied."

Hank organized his napkin and fork. "Not yet. But Lawrence Dennison is hesitating."

"Why?"

The bakery, along with all of the buildings in the historic district, was subject to stringent renovation conditions. There were bylaws to protect the character of the area. But Downright Sweet's plans had taken that into account. The deck would be larger, but it would be in keeping with the existing architecture.

"Lawrence is Lawrence," Hank said with a shrug. "He remembers the 1950s fondly."

"I can't believe he keeps getting re-elected."

While she spoke, Callie's mind pinged to potential solutions. She could shrink the size of the deck, maybe do only the structural renovations and keep the cosmetics exactly as they were. But it would be a shame to spend all that money and not improve the functionality. And to do a modified application, she'd have to start the process over again, losing time, and she'd definitely have to close the deck for the entire summer season.

"His pet project is the City Beautification Committee," Hank said, a meaningful look in his eyes.

Callie squinted, trying to read his expression. "And?"

"And, if somebody was to…say…join that committee and show a particular interest in city beautification, Lawrence might feel kindly toward that person." Hank took a forkful of the whipped cream and slid it into his mouth.

Callie found the suggestion unsavory. "You want me to bribe Lawrence to get my permit."

Hank gave an amused smile. "Joining a committee is not a bribe."

"It might not be money."

Hank reached out and covered her hand with his.

It was a startlingly familiar gesture. Her first instinct was to pull back. But Frederick's words echoed in her mind. *It costs you nothing to be congenial.*

"Do you have something against city beautification?" Hank asked.

"Of course I don't." Who could have anything against city beautification? "But I'm busy, the boys, the bakery, taking care of the house."

When they'd first moved to Charleston, she and Frederick had bought a roomy, restored antebellum house. It was beautiful, but the upkeep was daunting.

The bakery door opened again, and a tall figure caught Callie's attention. The man glanced around the room, seeming to methodically take in every aspect.

For some reason, he was fleetingly familiar, though she was sure she hadn't met him before. He looked to be a little over six feet, with thick dark hair, blue eyes and a strong chin. His bearing was confident as he took a step forward.

"It wouldn't be much work." Hank's words forced her attention back to their conversation. "I'm the chair of the committee, and I promise not to assign you anything onerous. We meet once a week. There are six members. Depending on the topic, there's usually some public interest, so citizens attend, as well. It's all very civilized and low-key."

Once a week didn't sound like much, but it meant skipping story time with the boys that night, getting a babysitter, doubling up on housework on another evening.

"It's not a bribe," Hank repeated, giving her hand a light squeeze. "It'll demonstrate your commitment to the city, your participation in the community and that you care about the culture and flavor of the historic district."

"I do care about the culture and flavor of the historic district. I live here, and I work here."

"I know." He gave her hand a firmer squeeze. "So join the committee. Join in a little. Make Lawrence happy, improve your city and unblock the permit for your deck."

When he put it that way, other than the babysitting challenge, there seemed little wrong with the plan. It felt opportunistic, but she wouldn't call it unethical.

Hank leaned in and lowered his tone. "With Frederick gone, I'm sure you want Downright Sweet to be as successful as possible."

"I do."

Callie had grown up severely impoverished, never knowing from week to week how her dysfunctional family would afford food, never mind clothes and electricity. Frederick had pulled her out of all that. He'd been a wonderfully sweet man, vital and full of life. The wheelchair had never held him back.

He'd had enough of a nest egg to buy both their house and Downright Sweet here in Charleston. The business had no capital debt, but it was still a struggle to keep operating costs manageable.

A shadow crossed the table, and a deep male voice interrupted. "Excuse me?"

Callie glanced up, startled to see the tall stranger. She looked into his blue eyes and felt a strange pressure build against her chest.

"Are you Callie Clarkson?" he asked. "The bakery owner?"

"Yes." She slipped her hand from beneath Hank's, wondering if the man was a lifestyle reporter or maybe a restaurant critic.

He held out his hand to shake hers.

She took it, and felt a surge of comfort and strength. He was gentle. He didn't squeeze her hand. But his palm was solid, slightly rough, not too warm, not cool, but an identical temperature to her own.

"Deacon Holt," he said.

Hank pulled back his chair and came to his feet, putting on his practiced political smile. "I'm Mayor Watkins. Are you new to Charleston?"

"A tourist," Deacon Holt said, without breaking his eye contact with Callie.

She knew she should look away, but there was something in the depths of his eyes that was oddly comforting.

"Well, welcome," Hank said in a hearty voice. "I hope you've checked out the Visitor Centre on Meeting Street."

"Not yet," Deacon said, slowly moving his attention to Hank.

"They'll have everything you need—hotels, dining, shopping and, of course, the sights."

"I've already found dining," Deacon said.

Callie felt a smile twitch her lips.

"Well, then I hope you have an enjoyable stay."

Deacon didn't seem fazed by Hank's dismissive tone. He looked back to Callie. "What do you recommend?"

"Everything's good."

He grinned at her answer, and the feeling of familiarity increased. "That was diplomatic."

Hank cleared his throat. It was obvious he wanted to get back to their conversation, to hear Callie's decision.

She'd made a decision, but it could wait two minutes for whatever Deacon Holt wanted. On the chance he could offer free publicity, she was going to make him feel more than welcome.

"The sourdough is terrific," she said. "Any sandwich made with that. If you have a sweet tooth, I'd try a cupcake. The buttercream frosting is to die for."

"Buttercream frosting it is," he said. "Thank you."

"Callie?" Hank prompted as Deacon walked away.

"My answer is yes," she said.

Hank beamed. He really did have an extraordinary smile. He took her hand in both of his. "I'm so pleased."

"When's the next meeting?"

"Thursday. Six thirty."

"I'll be there."

Deacon had been surprised to find Callie in an intimate discussion with Mayor Hank Watkins. Deacon had only been in town a couple of days, but he'd already learned all about the Watkins family. They were the Clarksons of Charleston—all the power, the prestige and the local money.

He'd also been surprised, even more surprised, that Callie was poised, polished and so stunningly beautiful in person. He hadn't expected that of Frederick's wife. Frederick hadn't exactly been suave with the opposite sex.

Deacon had gone to a different high school than Aaron, Beau and Frederick. Deacon had been at PS-752. His three half brothers had gone to Greenland Academy. But there had been enough cross-pollination through sporting events and in social circles, that he'd known the basics of each of them.

He and Beau were the same age. Aaron was a year older, and Frederick was two years younger. Aaron was blond, Beau dark like Deacon and Frederick had ended up with ginger hair and freckles. He was thinner than his brothers and shorter, and always seemed to live in Aaron's intellectual shadow, as well as Beau's athletic one.

Even in the best circumstances, Deacon couldn't see a woman like Callie falling for a man like Frederick. He supposed it could have been the money. It was often the money. Heck, it was usually the money.

For some reason, Deacon didn't want to think that of Callie. But he'd be a fool if he didn't consider the possibility.

After first meeting her yesterday, he'd waited overnight, waited through the morning, and now he was eating lunch at Downright Sweet for a second time. He was looking for more information, particularly for information on her relationship with Mayor Hank Watkins.

From what Deacon could see, Callie was way out of Hank's league. But Hank obviously thought he had a shot. She must have given him encouragement of some kind.

Fact was, Hank had money just like Frederick. There was a chance Callie's charming personality was an act, hiding a shrewd woman who knew exactly what she wanted.

She was behind the counter now, serving customers and looking as enchanting as yesterday. Her dark blond hair was in a jaunty ponytail. Thick lashes framed her blue-green eyes, and her cheeks were flushed with heat and exertion. Her apparent work ethic didn't dovetail with a gold digger. Then again, most people had contradictions in their personalities. And he hadn't even begun to get to know her.

She'd been right about the sourdough bread. It was beyond delicious. Yesterday he'd gone with black forest ham. Today he was trying sliced turkey and tomato. He hadn't decided on dessert yet. There were too many choices.

His gaze moved from the tarts to the cupcakes to the pastries and cookies. He was tempted by the peanut butter white chocolate. Then again, he could practically taste the strawberry cream tarts. Maybe he'd have two desserts. Maybe he'd have to run ten miles before he went to bed tonight.

He was just about to bite into the second half of his sandwich, when the café door opened. Two young boys rushed inside, followed by a perky teenage girl in a T-shirt, shorts and white runners.

Deacon set down his sandwich and watched the boys with amazement. There was no question that they were Callie's two sons. The four-year-old was a mini version of Aaron, while the eighteen-month-old looked exactly like Beau.

"Mommy, mommy," the younger one called out. He trotted through the maze of tables, while his brother followed at a more measured pace.

Callie smiled at her toddler. "Hello, my little darling."

"We were going to stop for ice cream on Parker Street," the teenage girl said.

She looked to be about sixteen. Her blond hair had a flashy blue streak in it that swooped across her forehead. "But the lineup was nearly an hour long, so they decided to bring all the kids back to the preschool early."

"Did you have fun at the waterpark?" Callie asked.

"Sprinkley," said the compact Beau.

"I went down the big slide." Little Aaron made a long swooping motion with his hand.

"Ethan squirted everything that moved." The teenager ruffled Little Beau's dark head. "He has good aim."

"Squirted James head," Ethan sang out with pride. He turned his thumb and index finger into a gun and pointed at his brother.

Deacon watched the interplay with amazement.

"I was already wet," James said philosophically.

"I'm glad you had fun," Callie said.

"Can we have cookies?" James asked.

"Since you skipped the ice cream, you can each have one."

"I want peanut butter," James said.

"Color candies," Ethan sang out.

"What about you, Pam?" Callie asked the teenager.

"I'm fine."

"We just took some oatmeal monster cookies out of the oven."

Pam laughed. "You talked me into it."

She ushered the boys to a table by the wall.

Deacon rose and crossed to the counter.

"Those are your sons?" he asked Callie.

The question obviously took her by surprise. "Yes, they are."

"They seem terrific."

Her expression stayed guarded. "Thank you."

"Did I hear you say you had warm monster cookies?" Deacon asked.

"Fresh from the oven," she said, putting on a professional smile.

"I'll take one."

"Coming up." She pressed some keys on her cash register.

He held up his credit card. "Your advice was good yesterday."

She looked puzzled.

"You suggested the sourdough bread. You were right."

"I'm glad to hear you enjoyed it." She pointed to the small terminal, and he swiped his credit card over the window.

"I'm back today for more."

"That's what we like to hear."

The machine beeped its acceptance of his payment, while another staff member set his cookie plate on the counter.

He knew his time was almost up.

"I was wondering," he said to Callie.

Her pretty brows went up in a question.

"Would you join me for coffee?"

The question clearly unnerved her. She touched her wedding ring, and her gaze darted to her sons.

"I don't mean right now," he clarified. "Maybe later?"

Her forehead creased.

"Or tomorrow," he hastily put in, sensing her imminent refusal.

"It's really nice of you to offer," she said.

"I hear a *but* in there."

Was she dating the Mayor? She'd certainly say no to coffee with Deacon if she were dating the Mayor.

"The *but* is that I'm really, really busy."

"I understand," he said, pocketing his card.

Being busy was probably just an excuse. It likely had more to do with Mayor Watkins. But pushing her wasn't going to get Deacon anywhere—better to regroup.

Not that he'd made a decision to romance her. He was still assessing the situation.

He wasn't about to take advantage of an innocent woman. But if she was gaming the rich Mayor now, she might have been gaming Frederick before him. And that changed the equation entirely.

"Maybe another time," he said to her.

"Are you staying long in Charleston?" she asked.

"I haven't decided." He gave her an intimate smile. "It depends on how well I like it."

Her cheeks flushed.

He lifted the plate with his cookie. "Thanks for this."

"Any time."

"I'll hold you to that."

She didn't seem to know how to respond.

He backed off. He'd ask around town. Maybe he'd get lucky and someone would know if Hank Watkins was in a relationship with Callie.

Two

In the small office in the back of the bakery, Callie's gaze rested on the framed photo of Frederick and the boys. She was struck by how much the boys had grown since Frederick passed away. She lifted the picture into better lighting.

It was the last one taken of her sons with their father. It was on their road trip last September. They'd traveled north along the coast, all the way to Virginia Beach.

Frederick had loved driving holidays. She suspected that sitting in a car made him forget about his disability and feel just like everyone else.

James was patient with the long rides, but Ethan was less than enthusiastic about spending so much time in his car seat. Frederick had done his best to entertain Ethan, who had just turned one that trip, while Callie had done the driving. It seemed like such a long time ago.

In November, Frederick had come down with a cold, just a routine cold that James had picked up in preschool. It settled in Frederick's chest, which was normal for him. He insisted it was nothing to worry about, since both James and then Ethan had run fevers with the bug, coughed a few nights and then recovered.

But in the morning, Frederick's fever had spiked alarmingly. Callie had rushed him to the hospital, where he lost consciousness and was diagnosed with pneumonia. They started antibiotics immediately. But his lungs had been severely bruised in his fall as a young teenager, and the scarring had left them weak.

He never woke up, and she'd said a final *goodbye* to him within hours.

Now she looked at the photo, Ethan grinning on Frederick's lap, James standing with his head on Frederick's shoulder. James still remembered Daddy, but Ethan only knew him from photos and video clips. Both boys had changed so much, grown so strong, learned so much. Frederick would be proud of them both.

"Callie?" Hannah poked her head through the open doorway.

"Is it getting busy out there?" Callie set the picture back down.

It was nearing the lunch hour. Pam had the boys until two today. With Frederick gone, Callie had modified her schedule. Pam was a godsend of a babysitter, and Hannah kept the bakery running like a well-oiled machine when Callie had to be at home.

"The lineup's growing," Hannah said. "The Spring Berry Cheesecake is still really moving."

Callie was happy with the news. They'd created the recipe and introduced the new item just this month. It was gratifying to hear it was a success.

"I'm on my way." Callie rose and followed Hannah through the kitchen to the café.

The lineup was halfway across the seating area. A few tables had just been vacated. Callie moved quickly to clear them and make room for more customers to sit down.

As she freshened the last of three tables, she was surprised to spot Deacon Holt sitting in one of the window booths. It had been a week since he was last in the café, and she'd assumed his vacation had ended and he'd left town.

Since she never expected to see him again, she'd allowed herself to fantasize the past few nights. Her fantasies ranged from hand-holding in the park to kissing under the stars to more, much more. She felt her face warm thinking about it. She knew he couldn't read her mind, but looking at him now felt oddly intimate.

He spotted her. "Hello, Callie."

She shook off her discomfort and went to his table. "Hello, Deacon."

His smile went broad at her use of his name.

"I thought you would have left town by now," she said.

"Still here in Charleston."

She glanced at his sandwich plate. "And back for more sourdough?"

"I couldn't stay away." His tone sounded flirtatious, and she raised her gaze. "I was hoping you'd reconsider my invitation."

She wished she didn't feel the same way. She knew she had to fight it. It would be unseemly to rush out and date this soon after her husband's death.

It wasn't that Frederick had been the love of her life. They were dear friends, companions, parents together. Frederick had rescued her from hopeless poverty, and she'd given him the family he desired.

"I wish I could," she said honestly.

"Something is stopping you?" His tone was gentle, even concerned.

"A full and busy life." She wasn't about to get into details.

"Someone else?" he asked.

She drew back in surprise. "What?"

"Are you dating someone else?"

"I don't date." She glanced over her shoulder to check the lineup, feeling suddenly guilty for standing and talking while Hannah and the others were so busy.

"Everyone dates," Deacon said.

"No, they don't. Case in point, me." Why was she still here? Why was she indulging herself in something that couldn't happen?

"Maybe not in the formal sense, but the opposite sex is always checking each other out."

"I'm not checking you out," she lied.

There was a gentle amusement in his blue eyes. "Well, I am most definitely checking you out."

"Don't."

"It's not something I can control. But to be clear, I'm only suggesting coffee and conversation."

She gestured to the lineup. "I have to get back to work."

"Okay."

"I can't go out with you. I don't have time." The excuse was perfectly true. Between the bakery and her sons, she had no time for a social life.

"Okay." He gave up easily.

She didn't regret saying no. She wouldn't allow herself to regret it.

She gave him a nod and firmly turned herself around, heading behind the counter.

"What was that?" Hannah asked in an undertone.

"Just a customer." Callie wished she didn't feel overheated. Then again, she was in a bakery, and it was May. It would be odd if she didn't feel overheated.

"He was in last week."

"He was," Callie acknowledged.

Hannah finished ringing up a cheesecake order and handed a customer some change.

Callie took a clean plate from the stack and loaded it up with a slice of Spring Berry Cheesecake, a drizzle of chocolate sauce and a generous dollop of whipped cream. She set it on top of the case, then assembled another identical one.

"What did he say?" Hannah asked.

"Nothing," Callie answered.

"That was an awfully long nothing."

"He asked me to coffee," Callie admitted.

"That's fantastic."

"I said no."

A new customer stepped up. "Two pecan tarts and a dozen peanut butter cookies. Can you make the cookies to go?"

"Cookies to go," Hannah called over her shoulder.

Callie plated the tarts. "Whipped cream?" she asked the man.

"Only on one."

She decorated the tart, while another staff member bagged the cookies.

The staff worked efficiently until the lineup disappeared.

Hannah followed Callie into the back, where cinnamon twists were cooling on racks, and the bakers were rolling out pastry.

"Why would you say no?" Hannah asked her.

Callie knew exactly what Hannah was talking about. "I'm not going to date a tourist. I'm not going to date anyone. I don't have time, and it's only been six months."

"It's been a lot more than six months."

"Nobody knows that." Callie and Frederick had never let on that their marriage was anything other than normal.

Hannah's voice went singsong. "I'm just saying, what's wrong with a little flirting, a little kissing, a little...whatever with a handsome stranger?"

"I'm not answering that."

"Because the answer you wish you could give is opposite to the answer you want to give," Hannah said with authority.

"That didn't even make any sense."

"Your hormones want one thing, but your brain is fighting it."

"I have two sons, a bakery and city beautification to think about."

"Callie, you're a healthy and vibrant young woman who's never—"

"*That* has nothing to do with anything."

Hannah knew Frederick hadn't been able to engage in intercourse. James and Ethan were conceived through in vitro fertilization.

"You're going to have to take the plunge someday."

"Sex is not the only kind of intimacy."

"I get that," Hannah said, backing off.

"It doesn't sound like you get that."

"I'm not trying to push you."

Callie let out a laugh at the absurdity of Hannah's last statement.

"I'm only saying…you know…don't write off a guy like that too quickly. Think about it."

Callie had thought about it. She was still thinking about it. That was her biggest problem. She couldn't seem to stop thinking about it.

Deacon recognized a losing strategy when he was engaged in one. Callie wasn't going to date him. It was probably because of the Mayor, but it could be something else. In any event, if he wanted to get closer to her and find out, he had to change tactics.

He spent another week in town, researching Callie and Hank Watkins. People considered them both pillars of the community. They hung with the same crowd, attended the same functions. People mostly thought the Mayor was a good catch, and a few seemed to have speculated on the two of them as a couple.

When Deacon learned Callie was on the City Beautification Committee, he jumped on the opportunity and showed up at a meeting. He sat in the back, obscured by the shape of the room. But he was close enough to watch her interactions with Hank.

Hank whispered in her ear at one point, and she smiled in return. He touched her arm, and she didn't pull away. He filled her water glass and offered her a pen. She took the pen and drank the water.

Watching her cozy up to the wealthy, powerful, but much older, Hank Watkins renewed Deacon's suspicion she'd married Frederick for his money. It also confirmed that Deacon had competition.

He realized he didn't have the Watkins name and power, and he sure couldn't tell her he was a Clarkson. But he'd achieved a reasonable level of success in life, and he could make himself sound better than he was—richer and more powerful.

But he was going to take a more subtle approach this time, let her come to him. At the end of the meeting, when coffee and cookies were served over friendly chitchat, he struck up a conversation with a few Charleston citizens. He stood where he was sure he'd be in Callie's line of sight.

"Deacon?" Her tentative voice behind him said the approach had worked.

He turned, feigning surprise. "Callie. It's great to see you again." He cheerfully excused himself from the others.

"Exactly how long is your vacation?" she asked, brow furrowed as they moved a few steps away.

He feigned a guilty expression. "I'm afraid I have a confession to make."

She waited.

He'd rehearsed his lines. "I'm more than just an ordinary tourist."

She looked apprehensive. "Who are you?"

"I'm thinking of relocating to Charleston."

The words seemed to put her off guard. "Why didn't you say so?"

"It's complicated. There were things to check out, arrangements to make. I didn't want people to know I was considering the city."

"Considering it for what?" Now she seemed annoyed and distinctly suspicious.

He realized he was messing this up. "I'm a partner in a national transportation company."

The claim was an exaggeration, but not a huge one. He was a minor partner, and they were more regional than national. But it was true enough to get by.

"We're based out of Virginia," he continued. "But we're looking to expand. We'd need a lot of land, commercial industrial land. If the real estate community knew we were in the market, well, funny things happen to prices when a large corporation expresses an interest."

He stuck as close as he could to the truth. Mobi Transport was always looking to expand. It could as easily expand into Charleston as anywhere else. And local land prices did get jacked up when the real estate community knew a big corporation was in the market.

"You're saying dishonesty was in your best interest."

He wasn't sure how to answer that. "I wouldn't call it dishonesty."

"You're keeping Charleston citizens in the dark about the value of their property."

"I'm keeping the value realistic."

"By lying about your intentions."

"I'm not—"

"That's how market forces work, Deacon. When something is in demand, it becomes more valuable."

He was surprised the conversation had taken this turn.

At the same time, he was curious about her immediate leap to skepticism. Honest people were trusting. Devious people looked for deceit in others.

"I don't want to have to pick another city," he told her. "I like Charleston. If land costs too much here, we'll choose another city where it costs less."

She gave a little shrug, as if the easiest solution in the world was at hand. "Just tell the people that's the case."

"That's one way to approach it."

"It's the honest way to approach it."

"Are you an honesty-is-the-best-policy type?" He watched her reaction.

She hesitated, her expression flinching ever so slightly. "It *is* the best policy."

She hadn't exactly answered, but he didn't press.

"Check out the Mobi Transportation website. See if you think it would be good for Charleston."

The Mobi website was slick and professional. It was designed to encourage sales by making the company look bigger than it was.

"We do long-haul trucking. We have six terminals across the northeast."

Her expression relaxed a little. "That sounds…interesting."

"In the internet age, goods transportation is primed for expansion. There's a whole lot of opportunity in the sector."

Out of the corner of his eye, he could see Hank Watkins making his was toward them.

Deacon gestured to the refreshment table on the other side of the room. "Would you like a coffee? A cookie? They're okay, but not as good as yours."

"Flattery, Deacon?"

"The truth, Callic." He didn't have to exaggerate there. "Your cookies are the best I've ever tasted. How long have you been a baker?"

She made a move toward the refreshment table. "I worked in a café from the time I was fourteen."

He fell into step beside her. "That young?"

"We didn't have much money when I was growing up. I did whatever it took. I lied about my age. I bused tables at first, but then I was promoted to waitress."

He was starting to form a picture of her. She was a survivor. He could relate to that.

"Did you grow up here in Charleston? Decaf?" He reached for the labeled pot.

"Decaf would be best."

He poured them each a cup.

"It was a small town in Tennessee, Grainwall." She flinched almost imperceptibly as she said the town's name.

He kept watch on Hank's progress. "You didn't like it there?"

"Nobody likes it there. My husband, Frederick, and I chose Charleston because it was so beautiful." A look of sadness passed over her face.

"I was sorry to hear about your husband."

Deacon was genuinely sorry about Frederick's death. Frederick had seemed like the nicest of the entire Clarkson clan. He was certainly the most honorable. Neither of his brothers seemed to ever stand up to their father, who—if employees of the company were to be believed—was an ill-tempered, self-centered control freak.

"Thank you," Callie said, her expression pinched. "We miss him. He was a wonderful man."

Deacon silently acknowledged that she played the delicate widow very well.

"I met him at the Fork 'n' Spoon," she said.

"You worked somewhere called the Fork 'n' Spoon?"

"It was aptly named, since we provided both forks and spoons." She gave an engaging smile. "It was mostly burgers and chili—not the best clientele. I don't know how Frederick found it, but he kept coming back."

Deacon wasn't surprised that Frederick kept coming back, and it sure wouldn't have been for the burgers. Callie was enough to draw any man back again and again. Like Hank, who was slowly getting closer.

"He said he liked the chili." Callie held her coffee mug in both hands, but didn't take a drink.

"Was it good?"

She laughed lightly. "I've seen it bring down a man twice Frederick's size. He may have been in a wheelchair, but he had the stomach of an ox."

Deacon decided to let the wheelchair comment slide. "So you moved to Charleston together?"

"That's when we opened the bakery. We had no idea what we were doing. But Frederick had a little bit of money."

A little bit? Deacon couldn't help but be curious about her definition of a lot of money.

"I knew something about the café business," she continued. "And I wanted to work somewhere nice, somewhere pleasant, somewhere that customers were happy. Desserts seemed like a good idea. When Hannah came on board, we managed to make it come together."

Hank was closing in, only one persistent senior citizen holding him back. Deacon glanced at his watch, wondering how he might get Callie outside.

She followed suit and glanced at her watch. "I've got a babysitter waiting."

Perfect.

She set down her cup and started for the door, and he went along.

"You're interested in city beautification?" he asked as they walked.

"I am now."

He held open the door, taking note of Hank's frustrated expression. "Well, that answer has me intrigued."

"I…" She looked flustered.

He couldn't imagine what would fluster her about city beautification. Had she joined the committee to get close to Hank?

"I thought… I should…get engaged and support my community."

Well, that was the worst lie Deacon had ever heard. She was all but begging him to call her on it.

"Will you tell me the real story?" he asked, assuming that's what she expected him to do.

Her face flushed under the community center's porch lights. "It's embarrassing."

"We all do embarrassing things. I promise, I'll understand."

Deacon was ready for her to walk to the parking lot. Instead, she turned the opposite way down the sidewalk. That worked for him.

She took an exaggerated breath, as if she was about to own up to grand larceny. "I joined the committee to butter up Lawrence Dennison."

The unexpected answer threw Deacon. "Isn't Lawrence pushing eighty?"

"Downright Sweet is in the historic district. My deck needs repairs, or I'll have to close it down. I can't do the repairs without the permit. Lawrence is holding up the permit. And the beautification committee is Lawrence's pet project. I'm buttering him up by joining the committee."

Deacon was impressed. By guiltily confessing to such a trivial lie, she looked like the most honest woman in the world.

If Deacon didn't believe she was using the story to manipulate him, it would have been enchanting.

For the next three days, Callie glanced up every time a customer walked through the bakery door. She thought Deacon might stop by Friday. He'd walked her all the way to her door Thursday evening.

He hadn't judged her for joining the committee. He'd understood. He'd even told her his own story about planning a lavish party when a particular state politician was in town, with the aim of getting an introduction to him in order to help Mobi Transportation expand. He couldn't say for sure if it had worked, but he'd definitely put out the effort.

They'd laughed and talked for ten blocks. She would have invited him in, but she had to tuck the boys into bed. She'd found herself hoping he'd kiss her. But he didn't.

Then she'd fully expected him to show up at Downright Sweet and ask her out again. He didn't do that either.

By Monday, she feared he'd left town. Maybe the right land wasn't available. Or maybe taxes were too high. There were a hundred reasons why he could have decided against Charleston.

"Callie?" Hannah came out of the kitchen with a phone in her hand. "It's for you. Lawrence Dennison."

Callie didn't know whether to be optimistic or worried. Was Lawrence calling to thank her for joining the committee, or had he seen right through her ruse?

"Does he sound annoyed?" she asked Hannah.

"Not that I could tell."

"Happy?"

"No. What's going on?"

"Nothing." Callie took the phone. She steeled herself. "Hello?"

"Hello, Callie." Lawrence sounded happy—maybe too happy.

"Hello, Councilman Dennison."

"Please, please, call me Lawrence."

She couldn't help but think the invitation was a good sign, but she didn't want to hope. "All right. Lawrence."

"I'm calling to thank you personally."

She felt a wave of relief. "For joining the committee."

"For the donation."

"The donation?"

Hannah, who was watching, cocked her head in curiosity.

"Two-thousand dollars was very generous of you."

Two-thousand dollars? Had Callie accidentally signed something, or agreed to something? She couldn't afford to donate two-thousand dollars. "I—"

Lawrence didn't seem to hear her. "The beautification committee will definitely put the money to good use."

"Lawrence, I think there's been—"

"And on your building permit, I've reviewed the architectural drawings, and I'm optimistic it can be approved this week."

"Approved?"

She knew she should protest. She hadn't made any donation. And if she had, would it have been a bribe?

Hannah's brown eyes went wide as she whispered. "The permit?"

Callie wanted to nod, but she was afraid to jinx it. Could this really be happening?

"You should hear something by Wednesday. If the office doesn't call, feel free to contact me directly."

Hannah touched her arm, pointing to the bakery door.

Callie turned to see Deacon walk in. He looked tall, handsome and crisply cool in a pair of designer jeans and a dress shirt with the sleeves rolled up and the collar open.

"I…uh…" Her gaze met Deacon's secretive, self-satisfied smirk, and she immediately knew what had happened. "Thank you, Lawrence."

"My pleasure. Goodbye, Callie."

"Goodbye." Without taking her gaze off Deacon, she handed the phone to Hannah. "I have to talk to Deacon."

"Are we getting our building permit?"

"Looks like we are." Callie wasn't sure how to feel about that: happy, guilty, annoyed, grateful?

What kind of man would do that for her?

While she wondered, he came to a stop on the other side of the display case. "Hello, Callie."

"Can we talk?" she asked.

"Sure." He glanced around at the customers. "Can you get away for a few minutes?"

"Yes." She untied her apron and lifted it over her head.

He gave an admiring glance at her white, short-sleeved blouse and fitted black skirt. The interest in his eyes sent a pleasant sizzle down her spine. He had a casual, earthy sexuality that reached out to her.

She had to remind herself she was…at least possibly…annoyed with him.

A good person would be annoyed with him.

Wouldn't they?

Winding her way through the dining tables, she followed him to the door. Her gaze moved involuntarily from his broad shoulders, down the taper of his back, to his attractive rear. He had to be in incredible shape. A good person wouldn't be watching his rear end either.

She wanted to be a good person.

"It's a hot one," he said as they exited to the sidewalk.

"It was you, wasn't it?" she blurted out.

"I don't know," he said easily. "What are we talking about?"

"The *donation*."

It was clear from his expression that he immediately understood. "Ahhh."

"I'm taking that as a yes."

"Yes. It was me. Can I hold your hand?"

"What?" Her brain stumbled on the question.

"Your hand. I'd like to hold your hand while we walk."

"Why are you saying that?"

"Because it's true."

"We're talking about *you* letting *Lawrence* think I made a big donation to the beautification committee."

"We can't do that while I'm holding you hand?"

"Deacon."

"What?" Instead of waiting for an answer, he took her hand as they walked beneath the arching oak trees.

She knew she should pull away, but she didn't seem to have it in her. "Lawrence just called me," she persisted.

"Good." They took a few more steps. "Right?"

It was definitely good holding hands. In fact, it was great holding hands. His was strong. It felt manly. It was a manly hand, and she liked that.

"Callie?"

"Huh?"

"What did Lawrence say?"

"Oh." She put her focus back on track. "He said my permit will be approved on Wednesday."

Deacon squeezed her hand, lifting it to his lips to give it a kiss. "That's fantastic!"

She let his action sink in for a moment.

He'd kissed her.

It was on the hand, sure. But he'd kissed her, and she'd liked it. Her lips tingled as she thought about the kiss. They were jealous of her hand.

She ordered herself to get a grip. She got a grip, tamping down her wayward reaction.

"You bribed him," she said, making sure she sounded disapproving.

"That wasn't a bribe. It was inspiration."

"It was *money*."

"A bribe would be if you called him up and said 'I'll give you two-thousand dollars if you approve my permit.'"

"I didn't *do that*." Her brained clicked through the implications. "Did I break the law?"

He chuckled. "You're too much." Then he lifted her hand to kiss it again.

He held it still against his lips. He stopped walking, and she stopped too.

He turned to gaze into her eyes. She felt a wash of helpless desire warm her body and flush her skin.

He wrapped his free hand around her upper arm, urging her gently backward into a narrow, cobblestone alley.

"Can I kiss you?" he whispered. "I want to kiss you."

She didn't even think to refuse. "Yes."

Three

Deacon's anticipation of the kiss went way beyond the role he was playing. He truly wanted to kiss Callie senseless. But he forced himself to take it slow.

He brushed the back of his hand over her cheek, marveling at the softness of her creamy skin. "You're beautiful."

Her red lips parted, softening, while her blue-green eyes went opaque. She looked slightly tremulous, compellingly innocent. Even as he questioned her authenticity, he reacted to the sensual image with a rush of passion and an overwhelming surge of possessiveness.

He leaned down and brought his lips to hers.

She tasted like honey. Her lips were tender and malleable. She returned his kiss, and a tidal wave of desire hijacked his senses.

He spread his fingers into her hair, releasing its lavender scent into the summer breeze. He placed his palm on the small of her back, drawing her close, reveling in the touch of her soft, toned body. She molded against him.

Her head tipped to the side, and he deepened the kiss. She welcomed his tongue, answering it with her own. He could feel his arousal build. He was dimly aware they were on the street, barely masked by the stone buildings on either side. He could feel himself stop caring.

But then her palms went to his chest, and she gave the lightest of pushes.

He immediately broke the kiss and backed off. His breathing was deep and ragged, and his head was swirling with a cocktail of hormones and emotions. What on earth had just happened?

"I'm sorry," she said, with a tremble to her tone.

He took another half step back and blew out a breath, struggling to get his bearings. "I'm the one who's sorry. That was my fault."

"It's just…" She glanced to the sidewalk behind him.

"Anybody could have seen us." He finished her thought.

"It's complicated," she said.

He couldn't help but wonder if she meant it was complicated because of her feelings for Mayor Watkins or because of Frederick's recent passing. She still wore her wedding ring.

"I understand," Deacon said. Whether it was Hank or Frederick, Deacon's job right now was the same, behave like a perfect gentleman. "I wasn't trying to rush you or push you. I'd be happy just to take you out for coffee."

A man's voice sounded behind Deacon. "Callie?"

Concern crossed her face.

Deacon turned to see Hank Watkins on the sidewalk behind them.

"Hello, Hank," she said, shifting from behind Deacon, putting some more space between the two of them. "You remember Deacon Holt?"

Hank's attention shifted to Deacon for a brief second, just long enough to be dismissive.

"I was looking for you at the bakery," Hank said to her.

"Oh?" Guilt was pretty clear in her voice.

Deacon would bet she was either dating Hank, or at least stringing him along.

He decided to test his theory by shifting closer to her. "I don't know if Callie mentioned it, but my company, Mobi Transportation, is looking to open a new terminal in North Carolina."

As Mayor, the prospect should have pleased Hank. But as Callie's boyfriend, it would annoy him.

It annoyed him.

"I see," Hank said, jaw tightening and eyes going hard. "Am I to understand you're considering Charleston?"

"He wanted to keep it quiet," Callie said in a rush, putting the space back between her and Deacon. It sounded suspiciously like she was making an excuse for keeping the information from Hank. "For business purposes," she finished.

"Callie has been very kind in helping me understand the city," Deacon said.

Hank's nostrils flared.

"Did you need to talk about something?" she asked Hank.

Hank refocused his attention on her, and his expression smoothed out. "I spoke with Lawrence this morning. I understand it's good news all around."

"You mean the permit?"

"I mean the donation. Well played, Callie."

"It wasn't—"

"She was just telling me about the positive outcome," Deacon put in.

Hank's gaze hardened on Deacon. "She was, was she?"

"I agree with you," Deacon told Hank, pretending to be oblivious to the undercurrents. "The donation was a good move. The permit should be in place this week, and she can get moving on the renovations."

"*She* doesn't need your support," Hank said.

"I'm standing right here," Callie said.

"Forgive me." His tone dripping with remorse, Hank stepped forward and took her hands.

Deacon wanted to rip her from Hank's hold. He waited for her to break it, but she didn't.

Part of Deacon wanted to repeat his invitation for coffee, nail it down here and now. But the smarter part of him wanted to keep Hank in the dark about his intentions. If Hank knew Deacon was interested in Callie, he'd block him from every angle. Better to make a strategic temporary retreat and let Hank feel overconfident.

"I have to be on a call in a few minutes," Deacon told Callie.

"Sorry to have kept you." She finally withdrew from Hank's hand-hold.

"See you later," Deacon told her in a breezy tone that masked his frustration.

He left them, taking swift, long strides along the sidewalk.

Half a block away, he pulled out his phone. He dialed Tyrell's private number.

"Yes?" came Tyrell's gruff answer.

"I'm in," Deacon said.

There was a silent pause on the line. "You'll romance Callie?"

"Draft the paperwork." Deacon ended the call.

Callie wasn't going to think of this as a date. It was true that coffee with Deacon had turned into dinner. But that was only a matter of convenience. It was easier for her to get away in the evening. Downright Sweet catered to the breakfast and lunch crowd, closing at six, after patrons picked up takeout on their way home.

She didn't know where she and Deacon were going for dinner, so she'd gone neutral with a sleeveless midnight blue cocktail dress. Its scoop neckline sparkled with a spray of subtle crystals. The waist was fitted, and it flared slightly to mid-thigh.

She'd popped her little diamond studs into her ears, pairing them with a delicate gold diamond chip pendant. Her black, high-heeled sandals were classic and comfortable. Her makeup had turned out a little heavier than usual, and when she caught a glimpse of herself in the mirror, she realized there was a shine of anticipation in her eyes.

She spotted her wedding set in the mirror.

She lifted her hand, spreading her fingers and touching the solitaire diamond.

She was too jazzed tonight for something that wasn't a date.

She closed her eyes. Then she pulled off the rings. Before she could change her mind, she opened her jewelry box and set them on the red velvet. She'd already kissed Deacon once.

If she was going to do it again, she had to admit to herself that Frederick was in her past.

She smoothed her dress, taking a last look at herself in the mirror.

Then her phone rang, and she felt a sudden rush of anxiety. Was it Deacon? Had he changed his mind?

She was afraid to look at the number, afraid to see it was him.

"Hello?"

"Callie?" It was Pam.

Callie breathed a sigh of relief. "Are you running late?"

"Yes. I mean, no." Pam's tone was high, her words rushed. "I mean, I'm not running at all."

"Whoa. Slow down. Is everything okay?"

"I fell down the front stairs."

There were voices in the background.

"Are you hurt?" Callie asked. "Who's there with you?"

"I twisted my ankle. My mom's taking me to the hospital for X-rays. It's swelling up fast."

"I'm so sorry." Callie's heart went out to Pam.

Pam was an avid cyclist and tennis player. A broken ankle would be devastating for her.

"I can't babysit tonight," Pam said.

"Don't worry about it. Take care of yourself."

"I'm so sorry."

"It's fine. Get to the doctor. Call me when you know something, okay? And if there's anything I can do."

"Ouch! Mom, I can't bend that way."

Callie cringed in sympathy.

"I better go," Pam said.

"Good luck," Callie called as Pam signed off.

"Mommy, Mommy," James shouted up from the kitchen.

"I'm coming, honey."

The front doorbell rang.

"Ethan squirted his juice box," James cried out.

"Ethan," Callie admonished her youngest son as she trotted down the stairs. "You know better than to squirt."

"Purple," Ethan said with an unrepentant grin.

"Do you want to use a sippy cup instead?"

Ethan's smile disappeared, and he shook his head.

The doorbell rang again.

"Then don't squeeze," she told him firmly.

"Can we have macaroni?" James asked, opening the refrigerator door. "With orange cheese?"

"We'll see," Callie said, swooping the juice box out of Ethan's hand to set it on the counter.

"Juice box!" Ethan cried, reaching up for it.

So much for her date. Or her non-date. Whatever it was, she was sorely disappointed to miss it.

"I have to get the door," she told James.

"Juice box!" Ethan screeched.

"You'll have to wait a minute," she said to Ethan, walking quickly down the hallway to the entry foyer.

She drew open the door to find Deacon on the porch.

"Hi," he said. Then his attention was immediately drawn to Ethan's cries from the kitchen. "Is everything okay?"

"Juice box disaster," she said, pulling the door wide and standing out of the way. "Come on in."

He wore a white dress shirt, a steel blue blazer and dark jeans.

"You look fantastic," he said, closing the door behind him.

She smiled, her heart warming at the compliment. She hated to tell him the night was over before it even got started.

"I'll be right back." She headed for the kitchen to quiet Ethan.

He'd come up with another plan of attack and was pushing a chair toward the counter.

She retrieved the juice box. "No more squirting?" she asked him in a grave voice.

"No squirt," he agreed, abandoning the chair to trot over to her.

"I'm hungry," James said.

"I know." She rubbed her hand over his tousled hair. "Pam can't come tonight."

Ethan took a pause in his drinking. "Pam, Pam."

"Pam hurt her ankle," Callie told them both. "She has to go see a doctor."

"Does she need a bandage?" James asked. "We have horsey bandages."

"Yes, we do," Callie agreed.

The boys were currently big into cartoon bandages. Since they got a lot of cuts and scrapes, it was helpful that they thought of the bandages as a treat.

"The doctor will probably give her a white bandage. It might be a big one."

"Big owie?" Ethan asked.

"I hope not," Callie said.

She was already thinking about tomorrow morning and what she could do about work. With Pam out of commission, she was going to have a problem.

Deacon's voice joined the conversation. "Somebody has a *big owie*?"

Callie turned to see him in the kitchen doorway.

Both boys fell silent and stared at Deacon.

"I didn't mean to abandon you," she told Deacon.

"No problem."

"James, Ethan, this is my friend Deacon Holt."

"Hello," James said.

Ethan stayed silent.

Deacon stepped into the kitchen and crouched on his haunches. "Hello, James. Hi, Ethan. You probably don't remember, but I saw you at Downright Sweet last week. You were having cookies."

"Color candies," Ethan said.

"That's exactly what you had."

"I had peanut butter," James said.

"I had a warm monster cookie," Deacon said.

"Purple juice," Ethan said, holding up his juice box as proof.

"I see that." Deacon's gaze took in the purple streak that ran across the white patterned linoleum.

"Oh, dang," Callie said, remembering the spill. If she didn't get it wiped up, it would stain.

She crossed to the sink and soaked a cloth with hot water.

"I'll get that." Deacon's voice directly behind her made her jump.

"Oh, no you don't." She wasn't about to let him scrub her floor.

"You look way too good to be cleaning floors." He gently but firmly took the cloth from her hand.

"Deacon, don't," she protested.

But he was down on one knee, wiping up the spill.

"Ethan squirted," James said.

"I see that," Deacon answered.

"He got in trouble."

"Trouble," Ethan called out with glee, jumping in place.

"Careful," Callie said, afraid of another stream of purple, afraid it might hit Deacon's white shirt.

"Gone, gone," Ethan said and shook the box.

Callie took it from him, while Deacon rinsed out the cloth.

"It's my babysitter that got hurt," Callie told Deacon. "She's getting an ankle X-ray. I'm sorry, but I'm afraid we'll have to postpone dinner."

Deacon shut off the taps and squeezed the excess water from the cloth. "You're going to have to eat something."

"The boys want me to make them macaroni." It wasn't Callie's favorite, especially when she'd been anticipating music, wine and adult company.

"With orange cheese," James said.

"How do they feel about pizza?" Deacon asked.

Ethan's attention immediately perked up. "Pizza?"

"It has white cheese," Deacon said to James.

"Pineapple," Ethan called out.

"With pepperoni?" James asked.

Callie couldn't believe Deacon was making the offer. Was he actually willing to stay here amongst the grape juice stains with two rambunctious boys and eat take-out pizza?

"What's your favorite topping?" he asked her.

"I don't think you know what you're doing," she said.

"I have ordered pizza a time or two."

"You're volunteering to stay?"

"You're staying."

"Of course I am."

He gave a shrug. "Then that's settled. What's the best pizza place in the neighborhood? And do you want me to run out for some wine?"

On the sofa, Ethan's sleeping head cradled in her lap, Callie sipped a glass of cabernet sauvignon.

"It's the biggest castle in all of England," James said, putting a final colored building brick on the tower he was assembling with Deacon.

"Who lives inside?" Deacon asked, making Callie smile.

"The King," James said. "And the Queen, and five little princes."

"Five? That's a lot of princes."

"They play together in the tower. It has winding stairs, and they have practice swords."

"Are there any princesses in the castle?" Deacon asked.

"Nah. Girls are no fun."

Deacon looked up to catch Callie's eye and give her a light-hearted grin. "I think girls are pretty fun."

"They play with dolls," James said, scooting backward on the living room carpet to survey their creation.

"I suppose that's true. But boys can play with dolls," Deacon said.

"I know they *can* play with dolls. But why would they?"

"They could pretend they were the daddy."

"My daddy had a wheelchair," James said matter-of-factly.

Callie's breath caught for a second. James rarely mentioned Frederick.

"I heard he did," Deacon said with a nod.

"I sat in it once. I like my bike better." James took the remaining few blocks and built a square near the front gate. "That's the statue."

"Guarding the front gate?"

"It's a statue. It can't guard."

"Some statues are built to look fierce and scare off the bad guys," Deacon said. "Like lions."

"Or dragons."

"Or dragons."

"James," Callie said softly, so as not to disturb Ethan. "It's bedtime, honey."

"It's always bedtime," James said on a whine.

"Same time every day," Callie said, although it was half an hour later than usual. She hadn't wanted to interrupt the castle building.

"It's not fair," James said, screwing his mouth into a mulish frown.

"Why don't we take a picture of the castle," Deacon suggested, producing his phone. "That way, you can always remember it. Do you want to be in the picture?"

Callie couldn't help but admire Deacon's distraction technique.

"I want to be in the picture," James said, coming up on his knees beside the castle.

"Smile," Deacon said as he snapped a few pictures. "I'll send these to your mom, and you can see them in the morning."

"Okay," James said, and then he magically came to his feet.

Grateful, Callie gathered Ethan in her arms.

"Do you need help?" Deacon asked in an undertone.

"He's not too heavy." She stood, wrapping her arms beneath Ethan's bottom, supporting his head with her shoulder. "I'll be right back."

"I'll be here."

She followed James up the stairs, where he tiredly climbed into his pajamas, alternating between jabs with an imaginary sword and wide yawns.

She tucked Ethan in, and then supervised while James brushed his teeth. James was asleep as soon as his head hit the pillow.

Barefoot now, but still wearing her dress, she padded back downstairs to the family room.

Deacon was on the floor, disassembling the castle and packing the blocks into their bins.

"You don't have to do that," she said. "I can clean it up in the morning."

He kept at it. "You're not going to Downright Sweet in the morning?"

"I will if I can find a substitute babysitter."

"Then you don't need to be picking up toys before breakfast."

"Fine. We'll do it now." She lowered herself to the floor to help.

"Am I doing this right?" he asked, indicating the various sizes of bins.

"You're doing it very right. I never thought to ask, but do you have children?" She didn't know why she'd assumed he didn't.

"No."

"Nieces or nephews?"

He hesitated over his answer. "No children in my life."

"Funny."

"Why?"

"Because you're very good at this." She was definitely impressed.

"Good at building toy castles?"

"Good at dealing with children. James was about to make a huge fuss about going to bed, but you distracted him. And you didn't ask if he wanted to demolish the castle. You asked whether or not he wanted to be in the picture. Either answer was a de facto agreement to end the game."

She finished talking and realized he'd stopped putting the building blocks away and was watching her.

"I really hadn't thought it through," he said.

"So it's instinct."

"I don't know what it is, logic and reason, maybe."

She leaned forward, stretching to put a handful of blocks in a bin. "Then I admire your logic and reason."

He didn't respond, and when she looked up at him, she realized the neckline of her dress had gaped open, giving him an expansive view of her lacy bra.

She knew she should move or cover herself. She didn't.

"Wife?" she asked him.

"Huh?" He didn't wear a ring, but that didn't make it a certainty.

"Are you married?"

He raised his gaze to meet hers. "I wouldn't be looking at you like this if I was married."

"Girlfriend?" she asked, not ready to take anything for granted.

"I *kissed* you."

"That's not a guarantee."

"It is in my case. I wouldn't have kissed you if I had a girlfriend." He eased closer. "Boyfriend?"

"No."

"Potential boyfriend?"

She drew back in confusion. Did he mean himself?

She wasn't sure how to answer.

"I don't really know. I haven't given it much thought."

As she said the words, she recognized they were a lie. She'd given plenty of thought to Deacon. Maybe not as formally as a boyfriend, but definitely in the romantic sense, absolutely in the sexual sense.

"Okay," he said. His gaze returned to her neckline. "You're killing me, Callie."

"You want to kiss me again?" She saw no reason to be coy.

"And how."

She straightened to her knees, and he scooted forward, rising to wrap his arm around her waist, meeting her lips in a deep kiss that sent instant arousal zinging through her. She wobbled for a second, but he held her tight.

On their knees, their thighs were pressed together. Her breasts were flush against his chest, their bodies pressing intimately.

His kiss deepened. She tipped her head back, giving herself up to the taste and scent and sensation of Deacon.

She wrapped her arms around his neck, and he eased them both to the carpet. The strap of her dress slipped from her shoulder. He kissed the tip. The intimacy of his hot lips on her skin made her soften with escalating desire.

Her body liquefied, melted against him. He slid his hand up her bare thigh, firm, certain and direct. He kissed her neck, then her mouth. He traced her lips with his fingertip. She touched his finger with her tongue, and he groaned, his other hand flexing on her inner thigh.

She knew what was coming.

She wanted it badly.

But she had to be honest. She had to be fair.

"Deacon," she tried, but no sound came out.

"Deacon," she tried again, managing a whisper.

"Hmm?" he asked before kissing her neck.

"You know," she said on a groan as his tongue laved her tender skin.

"I know," he said.

She ordered herself to focus. "You know Frederick."

Deacon interrupted the kiss.

She wouldn't allow herself to stop. "Frederick had a spinal injury."

Deacon drew back, looking somewhat dazed. "Are we really going to talk about your husband right now?"

"No. I mean…" She was afraid of getting this all wrong. "Yes."

"Why?"

She could feel the atmosphere cooling. She had to get on with it. "Because…well…there's something you should know. The boys were conceived through in-vitro fertilization."

Deacon didn't move. He didn't say a word.

"I'm not telling you I'm a virgin," she rushed on. "I mean, not technically. I've had two children. But…the truth is… I've never…" She felt her face heat in embarrassment.

He took his hand from her thigh.

"I'm afraid of doing this all wrong." She took in his stunned expression. "I'm doing this all wrong, aren't I?"

His mouth worked for a moment. "You've never had sex before?"

"I was young when I met Frederick."

"That's a yes? I mean, a no? I mean…"

"I've never had sex before."

He rocked into a sitting position, raking a hand through his hair. "I like you, Callie."

She hated where this was going. She was embarrassed and hurt. "But not enough to have sex with someone so inexperienced."

"*What?* No. *No.*" He emphatically shook his head. "I'm angry with myself. I keep trying to take you on a date. I want to take you on a proper date. I don't want to just—" He gestured around the family room.

She felt instantly better. "Have a quick roll in the toys?" She reached beneath her shoulder blade and extracted a stray building brick, holding it up as her sense of humor returned.

He gave a self-deprecating half smile as he took it from her. "Not my most charming moment."

"It felt pretty good to me."

He reached out to smooth her hair from her face. "Let me take you to dinner."

"I tried to let you. Events conspired against us."

He chuckled low. "They did. Let's try again." He put her strap back onto her shoulder and smoothed her hem into place.

"Is our date over?" she asked, telling herself not to be disappointed.

He was being noble. She should appreciate that.

"Tonight might be over, but our date hasn't even started."

Four

Deacon wanted to get it right this time. He couldn't remember ever having so much trouble getting a woman on a date.

He wasn't big on labels and designers, but he spent an afternoon in Columbia decking himself out with the subtle symbols of wealth and privilege. He bought a ridiculously expensive watch, a beautifully cut suit, a pair of diamond cufflinks and shoes that cost as much as a new refrigerator.

He hated to admit they were comfortable.

Callie hadn't denied having boyfriend prospects, and Deacon could only assume she'd meant Hank. It seemed she was carrying on with an upwardly mobile life. Frederick had lifted her from poverty, and now she was moving to the next rung, power and societal position.

Deacon could understand that. He might not admire her methods, but he had no quarrel with her objectives. And if wealth was what she wanted, wealth is what Deacon would project.

It was dead easy to guess at Hank's interest. Callie was absolutely a prize. She would be good for his political career—a beautiful young widow, a business owner in the community, the mother of two little boys. The four of them would look spectacular on the Mayor's Christmas card.

She'd suggested they meet at the restaurant, so he'd arrived at the Skyblue Bistro a few minutes early. When he saw her coming across the walkway, her motivations flew from his mind.

Her hair was loose, billowing around her face in the fresh breeze. She wore a burgundy cocktail dress, slim fitting, with a halter neckline. It molded over her breasts and hugged her trim waist, highlighting a shape that made men turn their heads. The skirt showed off several inches of toned thigh, while her shapely calves ended in strappy sandals that decorated her ankles and polished toes.

He walked forward to meet her. As she drew closer, her turquoise eyes sparkled under the hundreds of little lights in the trees around them.

"Hi." He held out his crooked arm, anticipating her touch. She took it. "Hi, yourself."

"You look stunning." He covered her hand with his, impatient for skin-on-skin contact.

She cocked her head and took in his outfit. "As do you."

"The most attractive thing about me is walking beside me."

She grinned, and he felt her essence rush through him.

"How was your day?" He told himself to get a grip.

"Hectic. One of the ovens broke down, and we had repairmen there for three hours."

"I'm sorry to hear that."

Before she could respond, they came to the hostess podium.

The woman gave them a professional smile. "Good evening."

"A reservation for Holt," Deacon said.

"Would you like to sit inside or on the patio?" she asked.

He looked to Callie.

"It would be nice to overlook the river," she said.

"The wind's coming up," the hostess said, as she stacked two leather-bound menus. "But I can put you behind a plexiglass divider."

"Does that work for you?" he asked Callie.

"It sounds perfect."

"We'll take it," he said.

The hostess led them to a small table at the edge of the patio. The wind was gusty, but it was calmer behind the divider, and they had a great view of the lights across the river. Clouds were gathering to block out the stars, but the roof above them would keep away any rain.

"Did they fix the oven?" Deacon asked, picking up the conversation thread, as Callie got settled into the padded chair.

"Not yet. They had to order a component from Philadelphia."

"How long will that take?"

"About three days. We bought that oven used when we remodeled the kitchen. I'm not sure it was good value."

"You bought a used oven?" Deacon was confused by that decision.

She gave an absent nod as she opened her menu. "I'm sorry we did. It's been a money pit ever since."

"Why would you buy a used oven?"

"It was reconditioned. We also bought two that were new, smaller ones. To get *that* size, in a decent brand, would have cost the earth. You probably haven't eaten here yet. The steaks are amazing, but the fish is their feature. It's always market fresh."

"Frederick bought a *used* bakery oven?"

She looked up, her brow wrinkling. "Why is that so surprising? Back then, we had to economize where we could."

"Why?"

It took her a moment to answer. "The usual reasons."

Deacon gave himself a shake, realizing he was grilling her. "I'm sorry. I don't know where I got the impression Frederick had a lot of money."

"He had some. Way more than I ever imagined having, that's for sure."

Deacon wanted to probe for more information, but he didn't dare.

"Shall I order a bottle of wine?" he asked instead.

"I'd drink a glass or two."

"Red or white?"

"What are you ordering for dinner?" she asked.

"You say they're good with fish?"

"It's hard to go wrong with the catch of the day."

He flipped to the white wine page and turned the list toward her. "What looks good to you?"

"I don't know anything about wines."

"Frederick did the wine ordering?" Deacon guessed.

"We weren't that big into them. We pretty much went with what was on sale."

That didn't sound even remotely right to Deacon. She was obviously downplaying her lifestyle. The question was why?

The waiter appeared, along with an assistant who filled their water glasses.

"My name is Henri, and I'll be serving you tonight, along with Alex and Patricia," he said, gesturing to the woman beside him. "Can I start you off with a cocktail or an appetizer?"

Deacon looked to Callie. "A cocktail?"

"Wine is fine for me."

Deacon looked down at the wine list and pointed to the most expensive white on the page.

"The Minz Valley Grand Cru," Henri confirmed. "We receive excellent feedback on that one."

He placed their napkins in their laps before withdrawing.

The wind picked up, flickering the flame in the glass hurricane lamp and billowing the tablecloth.

Callie brushed her hair from her face, but it blew right back again. "Will it totally ruin my look if I pull my hair back?"

"Nothing could ruin your look."

"Good answer."

She fumbled with her purse, producing a clip that she set on the table. Then she worked against the wind to pull her hair to the back of her head.

"Do you need some help?" he asked.

"Can you hand it to me?" She nodded to the tortoise shell clip.

He handed it over, and she snapped it into her hair.

"That's better," she said.

"We can go inside," he offered.

"No, I like the breeze. I just don't like my hair blowing into my mouth while I'm trying to eat."

"Understandable."

Henri arrived with the wine, along with Patricia, who set up an ice bucket in a stand next to the table.

Henri showed Deacon the label. It was pretty dark, and Deacon couldn't really read it. But he decided to trust the waiter wasn't substituting an inferior bottle.

At Deacon's nod, Henri opened it with a flourish, pouring a small amount into Deacon's glass. Deacon offered the taste to Callie, but she waved him off. So he did the honors. It tasted fine to him.

"Good," he said to Henri, who seemed inordinately pleased that the wine hadn't gone off.

Henri poured some for Callie, then filled Deacon's glass.

As Henri and Patricia left the table, Deacon raised his glass.

"To a beautiful woman, on a beautiful night." As he finished the toast, the wind suddenly gusted, and a splatter of rain hit the deck's roof.

Callie glanced above them at the worsening weather. "I'm not quite sure how to take the comparison."

"To a beautiful woman, on a not-so-beautiful night?" he tried.

"That works." She touched her glass to his, and they both drank.

"Oh, that's good." She kept her glass aloft, gazing at the wine inside.

His second taste was more impressive too. He had to admit, it was a very fine-tasting wine.

"Nice choice," she said.

"Thank you." He pretended there'd been some level of knowledge behind it.

Henri appeared again. "Excuse me, ma'am."

Callie tipped her head to look at him. "Yes?"

"The gentleman over there." Henri pointed. "Would like to buy your wine tonight."

Annoyance flared in Deacon. He looked past the waiter to the table Henri had indicated.

It was the Mayor. Hank Watkins was going to buy Callie a drink? Deacon didn't think so.

He set his napkin on the table, rising from his chair.

"The wine stays on my bill," he told the waiter as he passed.

Then he crossed the patio to Hank and his party of four businessmen.

"Deacon Holt, isn't it?" Hank asked heartily as he arrived.

"I know you consider yourself a bigshot around here," Deacon said to Hank, keeping his voice low, ignoring everyone else at the table. "But where I come from, you don't buy a woman a drink when she's with another man."

Hank squared his shoulders, setting his beefy hands on the tablecloth. "I'm only being neighborly, sir."

Deacon leaned slightly forward, keeping his gaze locked on Hank's. "And I'm being neighborly by telling you plain. Back off."

"Touchy?"

"You don't know the half of it."

Henri arrived, looking concerned. "Mayor? Mr. Holt?"

"It's fine, Henri," Hank said. "Mr. Holt was just leaving."

"So long as we're clear," Deacon said, hardening his gaze.

"I believe you've been perfectly clear." Hank gave a practiced smile to the rest of his party. "Mr. Holt prefers to take care of his own bill."

"Indeed, he does," Deacon said. He straightened and turned away.

Back at the table, Callie looked puzzled. "Is everything okay?"

"It is now." He sat down and repositioned his napkin.

"Why did Hank want to pay for the wine?"

"It was a power play. It had nothing to do with the wine."

She looked confused.

"He wanted to impress you by proving he's rich."

Now she looked amused. "By paying for a bottle of *wine*?" She lifted her glass. "Exactly how much did this cost?"

"Seven-hundred dollars."

Her expression fell. The glass slipped from her fingers, bouncing on the table.

She gasped, while Deacon reached for the glass, saving it before it could roll into her lap.

She stared at the widening, wet circle in horror. "I just spilled a hundred dollars' worth of wine."

"Good thing it was white."

"*Deacon*. What were you thinking?"

"About what?" He used his napkin to blot the spill.

"Spending so much money?"

"I thought it would be good. And it was good. It *is* good. Don't worry about the price."

"How can I not worry about the price?"

"I can afford it," he said. "I can easily afford it."

It was true. Just because he didn't choose to spend his money on luxury items, didn't mean he couldn't afford to buy them.

Alex and Patricia bustled over to the table.

"We can move you to a new table," Alex said.

"It's fine," Callie said.

"If you're sure," Alex said.

Patricia blotted the spill, replaced Callie's wineglass and produced a new napkin for Deacon.

In the blink of an eye, the table was almost back to normal.

Henri joined the trope. "Is there anything I can do to help?"

Callie started to giggle.

Henri raised his brow, looking concerned.

"We're really not batting a thousand on this, are we?" she said to Deacon.

He felt himself relax. He could see the humor in the situation, and he chuckled along with her. "But we do keep getting up to bat."

"You have to admire that about us."

Henri looked from one to the other. He didn't seem to know what to say.

"I think Mrs. Clarkson might like some more wine," Deacon said.

"Indeed, she would." Callie held up her glass.

"Of course," Henri quickly answered, gesturing to the bottle.

Patricia retrieved it from the ice bucket, dried it and poured.

"I can take your order whenever you're ready," Henri said, seeming to recover his poise.

"Give us a few minutes," Deacon said.

As Henri withdrew, Deacon raised his glass again. "To…?"

There was a spark of mischief in her eyes as she put her glass to his. "To a slightly crazy man, on a slightly crazy night."

"I'll drink to that."

"You have to tell me about last night." Hannah sidled up to Callie at the front counter.

It was the late-morning lull, and Callie was refilling the coffee-bean dispensers.

"I had a good time," Callie said, feeling a warm surge of emotion at the memories: laughing over dinner, then walking along the river path, Deacon's jacket draped around her shoulders against the cold.

"You gotta give me more than that." There was a thread of laughter in Hannah's voice. "I like the way your eyes are shining. So, did you…"

Callie glanced up from her work and immediately understood Hannah's meaning. "No, we didn't."

"Too bad. Why not?"

"It didn't seem… I don't know. It wasn't what I expected. He wasn't what I expected."

Deacon had called her a cab. His good-night kiss was passionate and wonderful, and it lasted a very long time. But he hadn't suggested anything more.

Hannah's enthusiasm dimmed. "Oh. Not so good, then?"

"Not *not* good. More…" Callie searched for the words. "Intriguing, maybe. It's like he's got this polished thing going on at the surface, but you break through and he's super down to earth. He's got a good sense of humor. He seems smart."

Hannah cocked her head. "I'm not hearing any good reason to hold back."

"I'm not holding back. I wasn't holding back." Callie hadn't made any overt sexual moves, but she hadn't been standoffish either.

"He's holding back? That seems odd. I mean, for a guy."

The bell on the door tinkled, and Hannah looked in that direction.

"Oh, heads up," she said.

Callie looked, her chest contracting with the expectation of seeing Deacon. It had only been twelve hours, but she was more than ready to see him again.

But it was Hank who walked in.

"I got this," Hannah said, stepping up to the counter.

Disappointed, Callie went back to scooping varieties of coffee beans into the glass cylinder dispensers.

"Hello, Hank," Hannah said behind her.

"Good morning, Hannah."

"What can I get for you today?"

"A cappuccino and one of those chocolate-dipped shortbreads."

"You got it." Hannah rang up the order.

"And, Hannah?"

"Yes?" There was an expectant lilt in her voice.

"Can you ask Callie if she has a moment to talk?"

Hannah paused for a second. "Sure."

You had to be looking for it, but Callie caught the disappointment in Hannah's response. Hannah was such a fun, compassionate and beautiful woman, and Hank had never been married. Callie didn't understand why he couldn't seem to see the potential for the two of them.

Hannah turned. "Callie?"

Callie pretended she hadn't been paying any attention to the conversation. She glanced over her shoulder. "Yes?"

"The Mayor wants to talk to you."

"Sure." She washed her hands and dried them on a towel.

Hank had moved partway down the counter while Hannah worked on the cappuccino, so Callie followed him there.

"I won't ask you to sit down," Hank said.

She was relieved. "We are pretty busy today."

She would rather keep Hank at arm's length.

She might agree with Frederick on the wisdom of having a cordial relationship with the city's politicians. But getting too close was inviting trouble. And Hank had been unusually friendly the past few weeks.

She'd already joined a committee and been a party to a donation. She didn't want to be drawn any further into any political web.

"I can see that," Hank said. "I just wanted to make sure there was no misunderstanding."

She could only assume he was talking about the building permit for the deck. As far as she knew, everything was in order.

"My gesture at dinner last night, it was meant to be friendly and welcoming, nothing more. I fear Deacon Holt misconstrued my motives. I don't want you to think badly of me."

The unexpected turn of the conversation surprised her. "I don't think badly of you."

Even if Deacon was right, and Hank had been showing off that he was rich, she wasn't going to worry about it. It seemed unlikely Hank had known the price of the wine. In fact, it would be odd if he had. In which case, Hank's version was the more plausible. He was trying to be welcoming to a potential city investor.

"I'm very glad to hear that," Hank said. "Will you be at the meeting Thursday?"

Callie wished she could skip it. But she'd promised herself she was joining the City Beautification Committee for more than just her permit. It was how she'd soothed her conscience. She wasn't about to stop attending now that she had her permit in hand.

"I'll be there," she said.

"Good. That's good. You should know there's talk of putting a rose garden and a water feature at Fifth and Bay Street."

It took Callie a moment to picture it in her mind. "Do you mean blocking off the through traffic?"

"Traffic would reroute on Balsam Crescent."

"But…" A feeling of dread slid through her. "Whose idea was that?"

Blocking off Bay Street would significantly impact traffic flow to Downright Sweet. They'd stand to lose a huge percentage of their tourist business.

"I'm looking into it," Hank said, concern clear in his expression. "Can I get back to you?"

"Yes, please do."

Hannah broke into the conversation. "Your order is ready, Hank."

Hank put his public smile back on as he turned to Hannah. "Thank you so much, Hannah. You're a treasure."

Hannah looked pleased by the compliment.

Callie was still absorbing the news. She counted on impulse purchases from the passing tourist traffic. Her local customers were a stalwart base to her business, but Downright Sweet couldn't survive without the money they made from tourists in the summer months to offset losses over the winter.

Frederick hadn't had life insurance. His health condition had made premiums far too expensive. And they'd spent all they had buying the house and the bakery.

He'd once told her he'd donated significantly to charities before they'd met. He'd said he regretted that decision. At the time, he'd never expected to have a family to support. She never imagined she'd someday be sorry he'd donated.

But what was done, was done. Now she needed the bakery

to be profitable. She had the boys' education to worry about, upkeep on the house and day-to-day living expenses.

"Something's wrong," Hannah muttered to her as Hank chose a table.

"Nothing huge." She sure didn't want to worry Hannah.

"What is it? What did Hank want?"

"It's the beautification committee. Some of their ideas are pretty out there."

"That's because they're all geriatrics with short-term memory loss. Well, except for you and Hank, of course," Hannah hastily added.

"I am definitely going to have to keep attending those meetings."

Beautification was one thing. But the city's economy was important, too. If the committee's decisions started impacting businesses, everyone was going to suffer.

"Maybe Deacon will come with you."

"Maybe."

The meetings would definitely be more fun if Deacon came along. And perhaps he'd be willing to lend a voice of sanity. His transportation business wouldn't need property in the downtown core. But if he was planning to live here, he'd probably care about the overall success of the city. Maybe he'd be willing to side with her.

"And then, after the meeting…" Hannah let her voice trail off meaningfully.

Callie rolled her eyes. "You have a one-track mind."

"You should have a one-track mind, too. You're dating a hunky guy, and your level of sexual deprivation has got to be off the charts."

"Hannah!"

"I'm just calling it like it is."

"That's not *like it is*." Callie didn't have a one-track mind. She wasn't obsessed with sex. Okay, she was a little obsessed with Deacon. And she'd like to have sex with Deacon. And she did think about that an awful lot.

But she wouldn't say she had a one-track mind.

She thought about other things.

A little bit.

Sometimes.

Deacon accepted the video conference call from Tyrell, bringing the man's face up on the tablet screen in the hotel suite. Tyrell was obviously in his office.

"I need an update," Tyrell said without preamble.

"I'm here. I've met her. I'm making progress."

"What kind of progress?"

"The getting-to-know-her kind of progress." Deacon wasn't about to share anything personal with Tyrell.

"I heard you went on a date."

"What do you mean, you heard?"

Who would Tyrell have heard from? Did Tyrell have contacts in Charleston?

"Are you spying on me?" Deacon demanded, rocking back in his desk chair.

"Of course I'm spying on you. I don't trust you. And I need to know what's going on down there."

"Then ask your spies."

"My spies weren't on the date. And they're not inside her house. What's going on with the Mayor?"

Deacon told himself not to be surprised by Tyrell's behavior.

"I don't exactly know," Deacon answered honestly. He'd been giving a lot of thought to the Mayor. "Hank is definitely interested in Callie. I can't tell for sure if she has any interest in him."

Deacon couldn't definitively say she wasn't. Hank was quite a bit older than her. But it was possible she was drawn to political power. It was an explanation that had been rolling around in Deacon's head.

"Get her interested in *you*," Tyrell said.

"I'm *trying*." Deacon found it easy to get annoyed with Tyrell. "I'm succeeding. I think."

Callie had seemed to enjoy their date.

Deacon had been the one to stop at a good-night kiss. It wasn't like she'd pushed him away. In the moment, he'd thought taking it slow was the best decision. But he was only guessing at that, as well.

"You've met my grandsons." Tyrell's words weren't a question.

"A couple of times. I don't know if you've seen pictures—"

"I've seen pictures."

"Then you know they're Aaron and Beau 2.0."

Tyrell gave a genuine smile.

Deacon wasn't sure he'd seen that before. "What can you tell me about Frederick's trust fund?"

"What do you want to know?"

"How much was in it? Ballpark?"

"Enough. Millions. Why?"

The answer hit on the heart of Deacon's confusion. "Because Callie doesn't act like a woman with money."

"Oh, she's got money all right."

Deacon tapped his index finger on the desktop. "Why doesn't she want me to know she has money?"

"Did you mess up? Does she think you're a gold digger?"

"I didn't mess anything up. I've done everything in my power to prove to her that *I* have money. I pointed her at Mobi Transportation. I've upgraded my wardrobe, my accessories. I've got the most expensive hotel suite in town, a high-end car. There's no way she thinks I need money."

"Well, you better figure it out."

"I am going to figure it out. Millions, you say?" Deacon's brain went back over the bakery oven conversation. It didn't make any sense.

"She was a waif when Frederick found her," Tyrell said.

"That's what she told me."

"It worked for her once."

"So you think she's playing the part of the damsel in distress."

"Yes. Go rescue her, Deacon. Time's a wasting."

Tyrell's theory didn't feel right to Deacon. But he didn't have a better one, and something was definitely up with Callie and money.

"And get that mayor out of the picture," Tyrell demanded.

"I'm working on it."

"Work harder. My people tell me she's with him right now."

"She's *what*?" Deacon glanced at his watch. It was only five fifteen.

On Mondays, Callie didn't leave the bakery until six thirty.

"They just left the bakery together."

"I'm on it." Deacon signed off the call, grabbed his wallet and phone and left the hotel.

It was a short walk to the bakery, and he was there in minutes, looking up and down the street for signs of Callie.

It didn't take him long to find her. She and Hank were at a table on the patio of a nearby café. They sat side by side, heads close together, intense emotion in their expressions.

Callie was upset about something.

Hank seemed to be comforting her.

He took her hand.

She shook her head.

He spoke at length, clearly trying to talk her into something.

Deacon took two steps forward before stopping himself.

What could he say? What could he do? What was she up to?

She raised her head, and Deacon quickly stepped back, shielding himself from her view with an oak tree.

Then she nodded, and Hank squeezed her hands with his. Hank smiled, and Deacon wanted to punch him in the teeth.

Deacon acknowledged the danger in his reaction. He should be frustrated that he had competition from the Mayor. But he shouldn't be jealous. It shouldn't hit him on an emotional level.

Callie was a means to an end. She was a complicated woman, who obviously had an agenda of her own. He needed to harness that. He needed to use it by pursuing their relationship. But he also needed to stay detached.

The smart play was to coolly and dispassionately focus her attention on him, instead of Hank. Whatever Hank could do, Deacon would do better. That meant eliminating the differences between them.

He pulled his phone from his pocket and dialed Tyrell.

"Yes?" Tyrell answered in a gruff tone.

"It's Deacon."

"I know."

Deacon could hear male voices in the background. "Can you talk?"

"Give me a minute."

It went silent.

"What is it?" Tyrell asked.

"I need a political future."

"Explain."

"It needs to be something convincing, maybe a shot at the state legislature. I want Callie to believe there's a powerful political career in my future. Who do you know who can help?"

"Everyone."

"Okay, who do you trust?"

Tyrell was silent for a minute. "Senator Cathers."

"Seriously?" Deacon couldn't help but be impressed. Senator Cathers was the Senior Senator from Virginia.

"He's speaking at a Chamber of Commerce event in Richmond tomorrow. I'll have him mention your name."

It took Deacon a second to respond. Just like that, Tyrell could put words in a Senator's mouth?

"Make sure you record it," Tyrell continued. "Figure out a way to put it in front of her. Yada, yada."

"Yeah, I get it. I get it."

"Good."

Deacon glanced back at Callie and Hank. Every instinct he had told him to march up to the table and drag the two of them apart. But he had to be smart about this. He had to be methodical. He had to make her come willingly to him.

Five

Callie left the City Beautification Committee meeting, anger propelling her forward. She made it through the door and half-way across the porch before she heard Hank's voice.

"Callie, wait."

She ignored him and kept walking.

"Stop." His hand clasped around her upper arm.

"Let go of me." She tried to shake him off.

"Just listen for a minute."

"*Listen?*" she demanded, rounding on him. "I *have* listened. I listened really good back there while you threw me and Downright Sweet under the bus. I didn't ask you for anything, but you promised to support me."

If she'd known what he was going to do, she could have been better prepared.

"There was nothing I could say to them that would have made a difference," he said.

"You didn't even try. Never mind try, you jumped on the bandwagon with the other side."

They hadn't formally voted on the rose garden tonight, but it was only a matter of time until they did. It would pass, and her business was going to suffer. She was going to lose money. She couldn't afford to operate at a loss, and Hank knew that.

"This is only the first round," he said.

"No, Hank. This was a knockout punch. There's nobody on my side. Everyone loves the rose garden proposal. Nice PowerPoint by the way."

"You have to look at the long game, Callie."

"There's no long game. There's no game. There's only the demise of Downright Sweet."

"You're getting hysterical."

"No. I'm getting angry."

"Please calm down." His patronizing tone was offensive.

"I'm leaving." She looked pointedly at where he held her arm.

He let go of her arm but took her hand. "I know what it is you need."

Why did he insist on touching her so much? It was really annoying. But his grip was firm enough that she couldn't easily slip out of it.

"It's hardly a secret," she said.

"What I mean is I know how to help you."

"You didn't help me." When she'd needed his help, he'd sat mute in the committee.

He seemed to gather his thoughts. "This is going to sound bold, but I think there's a way we can help each other."

She wanted to jerk her hands from his. Every instinct she had told her to ignore Frederick's advice and walk away. Being friendly to the Mayor wasn't helping her one little bit.

"You're an incredibly beautiful woman, Callie."

His words took her by surprise. "What's that got to do with—"

"Let me rephrase," he rushed on. "You're a wonderful woman. And your boys, well, I think they're terrific."

Unnerved, she searched his expression. Was he threatening her boys?

He eased a little closer, lowering his voice. "You and I, Callie. We should think seriously about teaming up."

"What do you mean?" But she was afraid that she knew exactly what he meant.

"I'm saying that I'm attracted to you."

Something shriveled inside her.

"I'm more than just attracted to you," he continued.

She'd always considered him a fairly distinguished man. But she'd never had a single romantic thought about him.

"You, me, a perfect little family…think of the possibilities."

Forget Frederick's advice. She jerked her hand free of Hank's.

"Nobody knows this yet." He talked faster. "But I'm running for Governor next election."

She couldn't think of a single response.

Should she have seen this coming?

He'd been friendly, sure. But he was friendly to everyone. She'd never given him the slightest cause to think she was romantically interested in him.

His enthusiasm was obvious. "I have dozens of well-placed supporters. Contributions are pouring in. Our future would be—"

"I can't," she blurted out.

What had she ever done to make him think she'd be swayed by his political aspirations?

He took a moment. "Is it the age difference?"

"Yes." It seemed like the simplest answer. It was the age difference and so much more.

"There are a few years between us, I know. But it happens all the time."

"Hank, please stop. I'm sorry." She didn't know why she was apologizing. She only knew she wanted out of this conversation.

"You're a practical woman, Callie. It made sense for you to marry Frederick when you needed him, and it makes sense for you to marry me now."

There was no comparison between Hank and Frederick—none at all.

"You and your sons will have everything you could ever want."

"This isn't going to happen, Hank."

His gaze narrowed. It seemed like his patience was wearing thin. "You've considered it for all of two minutes."

"It's not something I'm—"

"Is that all I get? A whole two minutes of your time?"

She didn't know what to say that wouldn't make the situation worse.

His voice took on a harder edge. "The rose garden would get out of your way." He snapped his fingers in the air. "Just like that. Gone. I can do that. I can fix things."

"You think I'd marry you to move a rose garden?" The idea was both preposterous and revolting.

"It's not just the rose garden. That's small time. I'm talking about the Governor's mansion, Callie."

She took a small step back. Like there was a house in the world that would entice her to marry him.

His voice turned gravelly, his expression darkening. "I make a much better ally than an adversary."

A chill ran through her, and she realized she might be better off with another tactic. She forced herself to lighten her tone. "Hank, I'm flattered. But you have to know this is very sudden."

The words seemed to mollify him, and he gave a thoughtful nod. "Fair enough. You need to think about it. I can understand that."

"I'll think about it." She would. But not in the way he meant.

She wanted to appease him for the moment, to put an end to the drama. She wanted out of this conversation and to go home to her boys.

Luckily, three people chose that moment to exit the main door and join them on the porch.

Callie took advantage of the distraction. "Good night, Hank."

She trotted down the stairs and walked quickly to the sidewalk, resisting the urge to break into a sprint. She wanted to leave Hank far, far behind.

She made it fifty yards.

"Whoa," came a voice from the street side.

It took her a second to realize it was Deacon. Her heart was beating fast, and she was breathing deeply.

"Where's the fire?" he asked.

She ordered herself to pull it together as she looked over at him. "You missed the meeting."

He fell into step beside her. "I was hoping to catch the tail end. How did it go?"

"Not great."

"No? What happened?"

She opened her mouth. Then she hesitated, unsure of how much to share.

Deacon had felt an immediate lift in his mood when he spotted Callie.

She had energy. She sparkled. The air seemed lighter around her, the world a more interesting place.

If something had gone wrong for her, he wanted to help.

"Tell me?" he prompted.

"Everyone *loves* that rose garden," she said, her sarcasm crystal clear.

Deacon had heard about the garden, and he knew it was going to be a big problem for Callie.

"What about Lawrence?" he asked. As far as Deacon was concerned, Lawrence owed Callie his loyalty.

"Lawrence and Hank put on a PowerPoint together. It swayed everyone who might have been on the fence."

"I'm really sorry to hear that." Deacon impulsively took her hand as they walked along the edge of the park.

It felt good. It felt ridiculously natural to be connected to her.

At the same time, it was disturbing to learn that Lawrence had abandoned her. Could Lawrence be naïve about politics? Or maybe two-thousand dollars didn't buy much goodwill these days.

"They didn't vote yet," she said. "But it would have been seven to one if they had."

Deacon looked for a way to help. "What's your next move?"

A pained expression came over her face.

"Is there more?" he asked.

It took her a second to answer. "No. Not exactly." Then she rushed on. "I don't know *what* to do next. All I want to do is run a business, a simple little bakery that gives people tasty treats. I don't want political intrigue. I don't want favors and tactics and counter-schemes." She abruptly stopped and turned to face him. "Is that so much to ask?"

"No." His answer was simple.

And she was beautiful in the moonlight.

He smoothed her windblown hair. "How can I help?"

"You're listening to me complain. That's a help."

"I'm happy to do it. But it's not very practical."

"Hank's offered to help." There was an odd inflection in her voice.

Deacon's hackles rose. He didn't want Hank anywhere near Callie's problems.

"How?" Deacon asked, his question clipped and short. Too late, he wished he'd been more careful with his tone.

But Callie didn't seem to notice. She gave a dismissive wave with her free hand and started walking again. "He wasn't any help tonight, that's for sure."

Deacon wanted to press, but he also wanted to move past the topic of Hank.

"What about you making a donation?" he asked, watching for her reaction to the suggestion. With this much at stake, would she finally admit to having money?

"Even if I could afford it, I'm not going down that road."

"There's no way for you to come up with the money?" He covertly watched her expression.

"No. I'm not taking out a loan against my business to bribe a city politician. Wow. That sounds really unsavory, doesn't it?" Her expression was inscrutable.

He knew she was lying about the money. She could be faking the moral outrage, as well. She seemed completely genuine, but he had to be smart about this.

"Can I ask you a question?" he asked.

She hesitated. "You can."

"It's about Frederick."

"I don't mind talking about Frederick."

Deacon weighed the pros and cons in his mind. "Were you in love with him?"

Callie slipped her hand from Deacon's hold, and he could have kicked himself.

They walked in silence for a several minutes, passing the end of the park and turning onto a residential street.

He was about to apologize, when she spoke.

"It was complicated," she said. "I was young. I'd been through a lot. My family was severely dysfunctional. My mother died, and I was all alone in the world with nothing. I'd already dropped out of high school. I could barely keep a roof over my head. And Frederick was kind. He wanted children. And I, well, I wanted security. We each wanted something the other could provide. Frederick was a decent man. I respected him. And I liked him."

She made it sound almost noble, marrying a handicapped man for his money to give him children.

"I don't regret it," she said.

The cynical part of Deacon wondered why she would. She had two boys she clearly loved, all of Frederick's money, and she was free to embark on a new relationship and better her circumstance even more.

He shouldn't care. He didn't care. It wasn't like she was robbing banks. And her pragmatic attitude suited his purposes. All he had to do was make sure he was the next rich husband on her list.

"I understand," he said.

She paused once again, turning toward him. "Do you?"

He took both her hands in his, happy to pretend he was buying the image she projected. "You're kind. You're generous. You're devoted, a paragon really." It wasn't hard for him to say those words. He believed them.

She smiled with self-deprecating humor. "That's ridiculous. You should see what goes on inside my head."

"I'd like to," he said, moving in. "I'd love to hear your innermost thoughts."

That wasn't the only thing he'd love. His gaze focused on her lips, dark and soft under the faraway streetlight.

"Deacon," she sighed, her eyes fluttering closed.

He cradled her cheek with one hand, leaned forward and kissed her soft mouth.

He instantly stopped caring who was pretending and who was playacting. It didn't matter. Nothing mattered except the taste of Callie.

"Come in," she whispered against his lips.

It took a moment for her words to penetrate, and he realized they were in front of her house.

"You're sure?" he asked, not wanting to seem too eager.

"I'm sure."

He held her hand as they took the walkway and entered the house.

There, Pam said a breezy good-night before she limped to her car.

"She's off the crutches," Deacon noted, moving closer to Callie in the living room.

"The sprain is healing fast."

"That's good." He couldn't stop himself from touching Callie, so he brushed her shoulder.

The fabric of her simple T-shirt was thin, and he could feel her warmth on his fingertips.

"A drink?" she asked, the slightest quaver to her voice.

"Whatever you're having." He kissed her temple.

She stood still for the length of the kiss.

Then she turned toward him and tipped her chin. "I think I'm having you."

As her words hit his brain, the world disappeared. Passion obliterated everything.

"You are incredible," he whispered as he drew her into his

arms, kissing her mouth, slanting his head to deepen the kiss. Her taste filled his senses.

He pressed her fast against him, sliding his palms down her back, reveling in the tone of her body, the indentation of her waist, then the flare of her hips and her rear.

He held her close, his arousal building.

She moaned in response, the sound vibrating against his lips.

His hands convulsed against her.

"Upstairs," she whispered.

He didn't need another invitation. He scooped her into his arms and headed for the staircase.

"Right," she said. "End of the hall."

He walked as fast as he dared, and in seconds they were through the double doors, into an ornate, cream-toned bedroom with a fireplace and a massive canopy bed. It was lit by a small Tiffany lamp on the dresser. Impatience screeched inside his head.

Instead, he set her on her feet. His hands all but trembling, he cradled her face. He kissed her tenderly, ordering himself to take it slow and gentle. She'd never done this before.

Her hands went to the buttons on his shirt. They were trembling.

"Are you okay?" he asked, worried he'd frightened her.

"Huh?" She looked up at him, her blue-green eyes glazed in the dim light.

"You're hands are shaking."

"Help me," she said.

It took him a second to realize she meant with his buttons.

"I can't get them." She looked at one of her hands. "Is this normal?"

"Are you afraid?"

"What? No. *No.* I'm… I don't know what I am. But could you please take off your clothes?"

"Yes, ma'am." He practically ripped his buttons open.

While he did that, she peeled her T-shirt over her head,

revealing a lacy white bra. It was irresistible. She was irresistible.

She pulled off her slacks and stood in front of him in equally tempting panties, wispy and lacy, minuscule and sheer.

"Deacon?" she asked.

He gave himself a shake. "Yeah?"

"You're overdressed."

"I'm in awe." He drew her toward him, wrapping his arms around her, feeling her melt into him. "You are stunningly beautiful."

"You might be, too," she said, pushing his shirt off his shoulders. "But I can't tell yet."

He chuckled, half at himself and half at her. She wasn't anywhere near what he'd expected.

He quickly stripped to his black boxers.

"That's nice," she said, gazing at him, reaching out to stroke his chest.

Her fingertips sent flares of passion across his skin. He closed his eyes, arousal hammering along every nerve. Her hand moved lower and lower, until he grabbed it to stop her.

"Pace yourself," he rasped. "Pace me," he corrected.

He wrapped one arm around her waist, and with the other hand, he covered her breast.

She gasped, and when he kissed her mouth, she met his tongue, tangling with it.

He unhooked her bra, sliding it away to touch her skin, skimming his knuckles over her nipple, drawing it between his thumb and forefinger, watching in satisfaction as her head tipped back, her eyes closed, and her mouth dropped open.

He settled her gently on the bed, lay down beside her.

"Let me," he whispered, using his hands and his lips to kiss and caress her, finding her sensitive spots, doing his utmost to bring her to a perfect arousal.

She touched him back, exploring his body, testing his concentration and his resolve.

When her hand wrapped around him, he spun her onto her back, knowing he was beyond his limit.

He looked deep into her eyes. "Now?"

She nodded.

He was quick with a condom, and then he was above her. Her legs went around him, and he slid them to a slow and perfect meld.

Her eyes were wide, her cheeks flushed, and her lips formed a perfect *oh*.

"Good?" he asked her, loving the expression on her face.

"Oh, Deacon."

"I know." He cupped her breast again, touching her nipple, bringing it to a peak.

He withdrew and surged, withdrew and surged.

Her fingertips grasped his shoulders, clinging tightly.

"What?" she gasped. "What do I…?"

"Nothing," he told her. "You're perfect. You're amazing. You're wonderful. Just let go." He kissed her deeply, canted her hips toward him, pressed deep, pulled back, feeling her body, listening to her sounds, guessing what made her feel best.

Her chopped moans guided him. He increased his pace, driving harder and harder. Insistent waves of pleasure drove deep in his abdomen. He lost his focus, lost control, lost his very mind.

Then she cried out his name, and he tumbled with her, wave after wave after wave of infinite pleasure washing through him and over him and all around him.

When he came back to earth, she was panting in his ear.

He eased his weight from her, giving her lungs some space.

"You okay?" he asked between his own gasps.

"Wow."

"Is that a good *wow*?"

She seemed to blink him into focus. "Wow. So that's what people were talking about."

He struggled not to laugh. But her expression was amazing, endearing and funny all at the same time.

He turned them together, putting her on top, wrapping himself around her and wishing he never had to let go.

He didn't know what to say. He couldn't find any words. So he stroked her hair and whispered her name, while her body went lax on top of him.

Callie woke up alone. The ceiling fan was whirring above her head. Two windows were open, and she was buried in a comforter, in the middle of the big bed.

She threw off the blanket, squelching her disappointment that Deacon had left while she was sleeping. Last night had been nothing short of magical. He was passionate, attentive and so incredibly sexy. Whatever happened between them after this, she would never regret making love with him.

It was bright in the room, brighter than normal. She glanced at her clock, shocked to see that it was nearly nine. The boys never slept this late.

She sat upright, worried something was wrong.

But then she heard their voices.

Ethan laughed, while James whooped.

Then she heard another voice. Deacon. He hadn't gone home last night.

She dropped her head back down on the pillow. Instead of going home, he'd gotten up with her boys, letting her have a rare sleep-in. Could he have made himself any more perfect?

She brushed her teeth, pulled on a pair of exercise pants and a T-shirt and wandered downstairs.

The voices were coming from the kitchen, and she walked to the doorway to find Deacon and the boys clustered around the stove. James was on the step stool, Ethan on a chair, while Deacon wielded a spatula in one hand. The kitchen counter was a mess of bowls and utensils and baking ingredients.

James spotted her first. "Deacon's making pancakes. They're shaped like race cars."

"Zoom cars, Mommy," Ethan called out.

Deacon turned with a smile. "Morning."

"Morning," she said, walking barefoot into the room. "Looks like you've been busy."

He glanced around the room, and his smile dimmed a little. "Won't take long to clean it up."

"Smells good," she said, realizing she should be appreciating his efforts, not criticizing them.

"They're banana," James said.

"And tasty syrup," Ethan sang out.

"I'm guessing that's a quote," she asked Deacon.

"Tasty syrup is the very best kind of syrup." He carefully flipped a pancake. "We're going to need plates."

James started to hop down.

"I'll get them," Callie said. "Can you get forks and knives?" she asked James.

"Wheels," Ethan announced, pointing to the pan.

Callie noticed Deacon was using a back burner, and the position of Ethan's chair made it impossible for him to reach the hot surface. More points for Deacon.

She set four plates out on the table, while James carefully arranged the cutlery. She added butter, syrup and juice to the mix. Then she started the coffee maker.

"I hope we're not keeping you from something," she said to Deacon.

He reached along the counter and wrapped his hand around her forearm, urging her closer, while leaning in, speaking in an undertone. "There's nowhere else I want to be."

After a quick glance to make sure the boys weren't watching, he gave her a tender kiss.

She smiled, her heart feeling light.

"Pancakes one and two are ready for eating," he announced to the boys.

James put his arms out like wings and made an engine noise as he trotted to the table. Deacon wrapped an arm around Ethan's waist, making a matching noise as he swooped Ethan to the table, settling him in his booster seat.

He took their plates to the stove and placed an impressively shaped car pancake on each of them.

"Where did you learn to do that?" Callie asked.

"My mom was creative."

"I can see that." She spread some butter on Ethan's pancake and added a drizzle of syrup.

"Any requests?" Deacon asked her.

She didn't understand the question.

"What shape do you want your pancake?"

She smiled as she cut Ethan's car into careful squares. "Round is fine for me."

"I'm going to need more information," Deacon said.

"You need me to explain round?"

"Do you want an orange, a beach ball, the moon? You're going to have to be specific."

"Get the moon, Mommy. Get the moon," James called.

She couldn't help laughing. "I'll take the moon."

"One moon, coming up."

"What are you having?" she asked, moving to stand beside him at the stove.

"I'm going with a base drum."

"You must be hungry."

"I am." He paused. "I worked up an appetite last night."

Her cheeks grew warm. "Yeah." She didn't know what else to say.

"Don't tell me you're feeling shy."

"A little," she admitted. She'd never had breakfast with a lover before. She had to wonder if children were often part of the equation.

"You should feel great. I feel great." Deacon put a hand on her shoulder. "You're amazing."

"You're pretty amazing yourself."

She could see him smile out of the corner of her eye.

"Any chance you can take the day off?" he asked.

She hesitated. She wasn't sure she wanted to hop immediately back into bed. Well, part of her did. But part of her wanted to take a breath.

Deacon must have guessed the direction of her thoughts, because he nudged her playfully with his hip. "I thought we could take the boys to the beach."

"Oh, uh, let me check with Hannah."

"I didn't mean *that*." His tone was teasing.

"I know."

"Don't get me wrong. I'd do it again in a heartbeat. But that wasn't where I was going."

Her self-consciousness rose again. Then she told herself to quit being foolish. She wasn't some blushing teenager.

"Juice, Mommy, juice," Ethan called from the table, his little heels banging against the chair legs.

She stretched up to whisper in Deacon's ear. "I would too."

Then she sashayed across the room to pour the orange juice. Deacon was right behind her with the pancakes.

He set them down and pulled out her chair. Then he leaned in behind her as she sat. "Teasing me?"

She gave him an unrepentant grin. "Just being honest."

His blue eyes twinkled in response.

"Anybody want to go to the beach today?" she asked the boys. She was confident Hannah wouldn't mind holding down the fort at the bakery.

"Beach," Ethan shouted.

"Can we build a sand castle?" James asked.

"We sure can," she said, cutting into her pancake.

"Castle," Ethan sang out.

"He doesn't seem as noisy when you're outside," Callie told Deacon.

"I don't mind. I get it. I was a boy once myself."

She took a bite of her pancake. It was delicious. "Secret recipe?"

"It's all yours if you want it."

"I do."

"Mommy, can I take my orange wagon?" James asked.

"I don't think the wheels will roll on the beach."

"They might."

"They might get stuck in the sand."

"Why do you want your wagon?" Deacon asked.

"It's big. It'll fit a whole mountain of sand." James made an expansive gesture with both hands.

"Watch your fork, honey." Callie could live without syrup drops flying through the kitchen.

"Do you have buckets?" Deacon asked James. "Your mom's right. The wagon wheels will probably get stuck. But I'm pretty strong, I can carry big buckets."

"Can we take the bubble tub?" James asked, his eyes wide with excitement.

"The bubble tub?" Deacon asked.

"It's a laundry tub. We play bubbles in it in the backyard."

Deacon lifted his brow to her in a question.

"I have to warn you, it's pretty big," she said on a laugh. She didn't imagine the beach would do it any harm.

"Done," Deacon said. "Let's see how much I can lift."

Six

Callie's sons were slightly sun-kissed, thoroughly exhausted and now sound asleep. Deacon gave one last look at Ethan in his crib and James in a sports car bed, still marveling at how much they looked like their uncles, Aaron and Beau. Then he followed Callie out of their bedroom.

"You wore them into the ground," she whispered to Deacon.

"They were the ones who did that to me." He'd been impressed at their energy levels all day long.

They'd slowed down around one o'clock, but half an hour of shade, a couple of hotdogs and some hydration, and they were ready to go all over again. They'd built a sandcastle, rented bikes, tossed a beach ball around and played endlessly in the waves, finding tiny shells and sea creatures.

"Should we eat something?" she asked.

"I don't know. Are we hungry?" He smoothed back her hair and kissed her neck, like he'd been dying to do for hours.

Her creamy, copper limbs and bare midriff had been teasing him all day long.

"You want to stay?" she asked, stopping at the top of the stairs and turning to face him.

"Do you mean overnight?" He didn't want to misunderstand.

"Yes, I mean overnight."

"Absolutely." He couldn't think of anything he'd rather do.

"Then, we can probably take time out to eat."

"I suppose I can wait."

"Yes, you can wait." Her tone was mock-stern. "It's barely eight o'clock."

"I can wait." In fact, he wanted to wait. He wanted to hang

out with her in this big, comfy house, enjoy her company, have a little dinner, all the while anticipating that he would be holding her in his arms, making love with her, sleeping curled around her lithe body.

"I can order something in," he offered as they started down the stairs.

"There are leftover pancakes."

"You've been living in mom-world way too long."

She grinned over her shoulder.

"I was thinking of braised duckling and wild mushrooms," he said.

"You can get that delivered?"

"You can get anything delivered. They'll throw in salad, wine and dessert."

"I leave it in your capable hands."

He gave her a mock salute. "On it, ma'am."

"I'll pick up the toys."

He gazed around the jumble of the living room. He didn't mind the lived-in look, but he knew Callie was more comfortable when things were tidy.

"I'll help in a minute," he told her, borrowing her tablet and bringing up a food delivery app.

It was quick and painless to place the order. And then, though he preferred to stay with her in the fantasy and forget about the outside world, he did his duty and set the tablet to a Virginia political news page.

"We've got thirty minutes," he told her, placing the tablet on the coffee table.

"No," she said, seeming to randomly throw the word into the conversation, as she finished lining up stuffed bears across an armchair.

"No what?"

"No, we're not tearing our clothes off for thirty minutes, while we wait for dinner."

"Did I say that?" Not that he'd turn her down. He definitely wouldn't turn her down.

"It's in your eyes."

He moved toward her. "You haven't even looked in my eyes."

"Then it's in your tone."

He looped an arm around her waist. "The only thing in my tone is a desire to get you to sit down and stop working. You have to be just as tired as I am."

She let herself be led to the sofa. "I didn't carry anywhere near as much sand. And you had Ethan on your bike."

"He's not heavy." Truth was Deacon had been entertained by the little guy's chatter throughout the ride.

She sat at one end of the sofa, while he moved to the other to keep himself away from temptation. Because, despite his protests, he was having a very hard time keeping his hands off her. And it was time for him to focus on impressing her.

He pretended to bump the tablet as he sat down, lighting the page he'd queued up. He'd enlarged his name in the title of the article, hoping she'd notice.

She didn't, and the page soon went dark.

"Are you thirsty?" he asked, looking for another excuse to touch the tablet. "I ordered wine, but I can get you something while we wait."

"I'm fine."

"Well, I'd like some water." He rose, touched the tablet screen again, surreptitiously turning it her way. Then he headed into the kitchen.

"You sure I can't grab you one?" he called back.

"No, that's…okay, maybe, sure. Bring me one."

He took two bottles of water from the fridge door, breaking their seals as he returned.

Bingo. She was reading the article.

She looked up. "What's this?"

"Hmm?" He set a water bottle down close to her and took a drink from his own.

"It's about you."

"Me? Really?" He feigned surprise. "I must have typed my name in the wrong box. Is it the Mobi Transportation family picnic? I killed in the ring toss."

"No. It's Senator Cathers. He was talking about you."

Still pretending to be confused, Deacon reached for the tablet. "When?"

"At some event last week."

He scanned the article. "Oh, man. This is embarrassing. I told him not to do that."

"Is it true? Are you going into politics?" She didn't look particularly happy at the prospect.

"No. Well, maybe someday. There are a few people out there who think it's a good idea."

"For the power and influence?" she asked.

"To help my fellow Virginians." It was such a pat answer, it was almost laughable. But it was still the best answer. "There's a lot of work to be done in streamlining regulations, cutting red tape and creating jobs."

"Are you sure it's not for the power and influence?"

He lounged back, trying his best to look nonchalant. "That's not my focus at all. Why so skeptical?"

"I don't know."

He didn't buy it, and he wanted to get to the bottom of her thought processes. "Why?"

It took her a minute to answer. "I don't… It sure seems to be working for Hank Watkins."

Deacon tried to read her expression, but it was carefully neutral. For some reason, she was hiding her feelings about Hank's political power. Deacon couldn't tell which way to play this. So he waited.

She leaned forward and lifted her bottle of water, twisting off the cap and setting it down. "Hank says he can make the rose garden go away."

Deacon hid his reflexive annoyance. "He offered to fix your rose garden problem?"

"He did."

"Did you take him up on it?" Deacon hated the thought of Hank having leverage over her.

She frowned, her eyes hardening. "No."

"Good. I'll donate to the committee again." And this time, he'd make the donation big enough to make sure Lawrence stayed loyal.

"No," Callie said.

"What do you mean no? That's how we do an end run around Hank."

"It feels too much like bribery."

"It's not bribery. It's maybe, at most, gaining a little influence."

"You just said you didn't care about power and influence."

"I don't." What he cared about was helping Callie and disempowering Hank.

"Then why are you using it?"

"I'm not a politician, Callie." Deacon could see that he'd gone down the wrong path on that one, but it didn't mean he'd leave the field open for Hank to fix her problem.

"Not yet," she said.

"Maybe never. I'm a long, long way from a decision like that."

The doorbell rang.

She rose.

He stood with her. "I'll get that."

She nodded, looking sad and dejected. Their mood was completely ruined.

He moved to face her and took her hand. "I'm sorry."

"I am, too." Her eyes were wide and glassy.

"I won't make another donation."

"Thank you."

"Do you want me to leave?"

She hesitated. Then she slowly shook her head. "Stay."

He felt a huge weight come off his chest.

* * *

Callie had postponed long enough. It had been nearly a week since Hank had showed his true colors, and she owed it to Hannah to tell her the truth. The last staff member had just gone home for the evening, so it was only Callie and Hannah finishing the paperwork and calculating the day's bank deposit.

"You should get home to the boys," Hannah suggested as she sorted through the cash, putting it in neat stacks into the deposit bag.

Callie pulled a second chair up to the small round table in the compact office. There wasn't much room next to the bookshelf, so she leaned forward. "There's something I've been wanting to tell you," she opened.

Hannah smiled without looking up. "About a certain hunky tourist who's been hanging around every day, gazing at you like a lovesick calf?"

Callie didn't think that was a particularly accurate description of Deacon. But she was determined to stay on topic. "It's about Hank."

Hannah did look up. "Is something wrong? He hasn't been in for a few days. Did he catch that flu that's been going around?"

"It's not the flu."

"What is it? What's happened?"

"I saw him last Thursday, at the beautification committee meeting."

"Uh-huh."

"I didn't say anything to you then, but he went against me on the rose garden."

Hannah straightened a stack of twenties and put a band around them. "I'm sorry he did that. But maybe he had his reasons."

Callie slid a round mesh pencil holder over in front of her, absently separating the pens by color as she talked. "You really like him, don't you?"

"Everybody likes him. He's a great guy."

"Thing is." Callie put the four reds pens in a row. "He might not be such a great guy."

"Just because he's in favor of the rose garden?"

"I was mad about that. I admit it. But then…" Callie drew out a black sharpie that didn't match anything else and tapped it on the table. "He said something, Hannah. I'm so sorry, but he… I guess…propositioned me."

Hannah's chin dropped.

Now that she'd broken the ice, Callie wanted to get it all out in the open. "He told me he was attracted to me. He said we could be a perfect little family, and if I agreed to be with him, the rose garden and all my other problems would go away."

Hannah swallowed. She seemed to be having trouble finding her voice. "What did you say?"

"I said *no*."

"Okay."

"I'm not interested in Hank." The only man Callie was interested in was Deacon.

She didn't want to insult Hannah by sharing her true feelings about Hank. She only wanted to stop Hannah from fantasizing about him. Hank was no good for Hannah. But Callie hated to hurt her friend's feelings.

Hannah began flipping through a stack of fives. "I sure called that one wrong, didn't I? Oh, well, what could I expect? The good ones always go for younger women."

Callie covered Hannah's hand with hers. "That's not always true. And Hank isn't one of the good ones."

"Just because he's attracted to you instead of me? That's perfectly normal. Look at you. You're extraordinary."

"I'm not extraordinary. I'm completely ordinary. And Hank was more interested in how the four of us would look as a family for his political career than he was in me personally. He doesn't even know me."

"Well, I know you," Hannah said with conviction. "And you are amazing."

"So are you. And you're beautiful. And any man would be beyond lucky to date you. But it's not Hank. You're way too good for Hank."

"That doesn't seem to be the way Hank sees it."

"Hank's a fool."

A sheen came up in Hannah's eyes. "I'm the fool for thinking I had a shot."

Callie squeezed her hand, not sure what else to say.

"You should go home," Hannah told her. "James and Ethan will be waiting."

"I wish this hadn't happened," Callie said.

"Well, I'm glad it did. No point in an old woman like me pining for someone who's never even noticed her."

Callie smiled, hoping to lighten the mood. "You're not old. And you're not pining. You just had a misguided crush."

"Crushes are for high school."

"Crushes are for everybody. And you'll have another one. And it'll be soon. It's almost June, and the town's filling up with tourists, and new customers walk through that door every day. Heck, if Mobi Transport opens up a new terminal, the town may be crawling with single men."

Hannah cracked a smile. "You are an optimist."

"Not really." Callie was mostly a pessimist.

Before Frederick, her life had been a series of disasters and disappointments. She'd simply learned how to move forward in life, no matter what happened. A person could take a lot of hits and still get up.

Hannah went back to counting the cash. "I'll be fine. I'm glad I know. Thank you for telling me."

"Do you want to stop for a drink somewhere? We could grab something to eat." Callie had planned to meet Deacon after work for the sixth night in a row. But she was sure he'd understand if she cancelled.

"No thanks," Hannah said. "Do you mind if I take home a couple of the red velvet cupcakes?"

"Take as many as you need."

Hannah gave a brave smile. "Nothing a little buttercream won't fix. I'll see you tomorrow."

"If you're sure."

"I'm sure."

Callie's phone pinged with a text message.

"That'll be your hot guy," Hannah said.

Callie checked. Sure enough, it was Deacon. The message said he was out front waiting.

"Go do something wild," Hannah said. "I'm going to live vicariously through you for a few weeks."

"Something wild, huh?"

"Tell me all about it in the morning."

"If it's what you want, I will gladly share." Callie texted back to Deacon that she was on her way.

Then she logged out of her computer and headed through the dimmed dining room.

It felt good to see Deacon's face.

"What's wrong?" he asked, as she locked the door behind herself.

"Long day." She forced a smile. "I'm glad you're here."

He swung an arm over her shoulders. "I'm glad to be here."

They took a few steps along the sidewalk, but Deacon slowed, stopping.

"Tell me," he said.

"Tell you what?"

"Your shoulders are tense. Tell me what's wrong." He turned to face her head on.

She didn't want to tell him, but she didn't want to hold back either. "I had to talk to Hannah about Hank."

Deacon's eyes narrowed. "Hank?"

"At the meeting Thursday. I didn't want to make a big deal about it. But she's had a thing for him for a while now, and after what he said to me on Thursday…"

"About the rose garden?"

"Partly. He also…" Callie hesitated. She wasn't sure telling Deacon was the right thing to do. "He kind of, sort of, propositioned me."

Deacon drew back, his expression turning to thunder. "He *what*?"

"It wasn't exactly that blatant. He suggested a relationship between the two of us. He seemed to think I would be a political asset, and he could use his power as Mayor to solve problems for me."

Deacon was still. "What did you tell him?"

The question surprised her. "That I wouldn't even consider it."

"In those exact words?"

"Yes." Then she rethought the vehemence of her answer. "I mean at first, yes. That's what I said. But I may have hinted later, a little bit, that I'd think about it. But—"

"*Are* you thinking about it?"

"It was a ruse. I wanted to get out of the conversation."

Deacon leaned in a bit. "Does he believe you're still thinking about it?"

"It doesn't matter. I'm not."

"Don't."

"I won't."

"Good."

"Deacon?"

"Yeah?"

"Are you angry?"

He looked angry. "No."

"That wasn't very convincing."

He wrapped her hand in his and started walking again. "Hank ticks me off."

"I used to think he was a decent guy."

"He's not."

"I know that now."

"You shouldn't—" Deacon raked his free hand through his

hair and gave his head a quick shake. "You know what? We're not going to talk about him anymore. Home to the boys?"

She liked the way that sounded. It was a relief. "Yes. Home to the boys."

Deacon knew he had to speed up his plan. Hank wasn't going to go away quietly. He was going to use every bit of leverage to win Callie over. She might not particularly like Hank, but Deacon couldn't be sure what factors she'd take into account. He couldn't afford to wait for Hank's next move.

Though it was too early in their relationship, making it more of a risk than Deacon would like, three days later he headed into a jewelry store.

It was quiet and cool inside. Thick grey carpet cushioned his feet, and he was surrounded by bright turquoise tones and curved glass display cases that sparkled under suspended lights.

"Can I help you, sir?" A crisply dressed and very professional-looking thirtysomething woman approached him.

"I need something fantastic," he said. He didn't have a particular style in mind. He only knew he wanted to knock Callie's socks off when she opened the box.

"In a ring?" the woman asked.

"An engagement ring," he clarified.

She gave him a warm smile. "You've definitely come to the right place. Were you leaning toward traditional or modern?"

"I was leaning toward fantastic."

Her grin widened. "Did you have a price range in mind?"

"No. If it's the right ring, price doesn't matter."

"Okay." She gestured to a round display case in the middle of the store and moved gracefully to it. "Let me show you what we have here in the 'fantastic' case."

Her joke got him to smile, and he felt himself relax. It was a strange situation to be sure. But there was no reason he couldn't be friendly with the clerk.

"Please do," he said.

She slipped through an opening into the middle of the round display. Then she unlocked a glass door and selected one…and then two…and then three diamond rings.

"These are the most common solitaire shapes," she said. "Round, emerald and marquis. If you're interested in overall brilliance, the round cut is most popular."

"What about quality?" he asked.

She pulled out a fourth ring. "This is a D flawless, excellent cut."

She handed him a magnifier.

He dutifully took it, and he had to admit the diamond looked great. But he didn't think Callie would look that closely.

He handed back the magnifier and set down the ring. "How about this? If I was asking you to marry me, which ring would you want me to buy?"

The sales clerk looked surprised by the question.

"You must have a favorite," he said.

"I have a few favorites. What are you trying to say? Beyond the proposal itself, what are you trying to say to her with the ring?"

"That I'm the best choice, and I'll take care of her and her children forever." The answer popped out before Deacon could think it through.

"Ahh." The woman's eyes danced with delight. "I know just the ring."

She crossed to the opposite side of the display, slid open another case, before returning with a snow-white leather box. It held a ring with a large, round center stone, set within a whimsically swirled and twisted band of platinum and yellow gold, further decorated with tiny diamonds.

"It's our finest stone," she said, her voice almost reverent, as she leaned forward to look with Deacon. "In a timeless but modern setting." She drew back. "I'd marry you if you gave me that."

Deacon chuckled. "Sold."

"Really? Do you want to know the price?"

He drew out his wallet to extract his credit card. "Not particularly."

She laughed as she took the card. "I'd so marry you." As she backed away, she waggled the card in his direction. "If she turns you down, keep me in mind."

Deacon grinned in acknowledgement of her joke, but inside, he was anxious all over again. Callie could turn him down. She could easily turn him down.

The sales clerk rang through the purchase and packaged the ring. She seemed to see something of the uncertainty in his expression.

"It is returnable within sixty days," she told him gently.

"I'll know the answer a whole lot before then."

"Good luck."

"Thanks." He returned his credit card to his wallet and his wallet to his pocket.

On the way out of the store, his phone rang.

A glance at the screen told him it was Tyrell. He didn't want to talk to the man right now.

He had good news. Tyrell would be thrilled to know Deacon was about to propose. But Deacon didn't want to share that information.

He wanted Callie to be the first person to hear.

The ring box tucked in his shirt pocket, he pulled his rental car from the parking space and entered the downtown traffic. Downright Sweet was only ten minutes away, and he'd arranged to meet her for a late lunch.

A fancy candlelight dinner might be a better choice. But he didn't want the audience they'd have in a restaurant. He could ask her at home, after the boys went to sleep. But as much as he found the toy-cluttered living room relaxing and comfortable, it didn't exactly shout romance.

He'd take her to the patio of the View Stop Café. They could take the winding river path from the parking lot. They could step off into the flower garden. Amongst the bright azaleas and the swaying willow trees, he'd pop the question.

He drove to Downright Sweet and saw Callie standing on the sidewalk. She was gorgeous in the sunshine, her hair freshly brushed and taken down from her usual ponytail, a soft white lace-trimmed blouse topping a pair of fitted dark slacks.

She'd changed her shoes. He knew she wore flats in the bakery, but she was wearing a pair of strappy black heeled sandals. They accentuated the length of her toned legs and showed off her pretty feet.

He came to a halt.

Before he could hop out and open the door, she was inside, buckling up.

"Having a good day?" he asked.

"Hank came by."

"What? Why? What did he do?" The last thing Deacon wanted to think about today was Hank.

"I didn't come out of the back. Hannah gave him the cold shoulder. He didn't stick around long."

"He'll be back." Of that, Deacon was sure.

Deacon touched his hand to the bulge in his shirt pocket. He wanted Hank out of the picture for good.

"View Stop Café?" he asked.

"Perfect."

Deacon drove the mile to get them there. Traffic was light that summer afternoon, and the lights seemed to be in his favor. He was breezing through the second green in a row, counting his good fortune, when a white pickup barreled through the intersection, against the red, heading straight for Callie's door.

Deacon spun the wheel to turn her out of the way a split second before the pickup smashed into the back quarter panel, sending them into an uncontrolled spin. His car slammed into a light pole on the passenger side, all but folding in half.

Deacon shook his head to clear his vision as he turned to Callie. "Are you all right?"

She moaned.

"Callie?" He was afraid to touch her.

He released his seatbelt and leaned around to look at her. People were rushing to the windows, shouting at him from outside. He barely heard them.

Callie's eyes were closed, she was slumped sideways and her forehead was bleeding.

Callie had only been stunned for a couple of minutes. She tried to tell the ambulance attendant that she was fine, but he only responded with soothing words, telling her to lie back on the stretcher and relax. Eventually she gave up, closing her eyes while the vehicle swayed beneath her.

She didn't hear sirens. She had to think that was a good sign.

Her head did hurt, but it wasn't unbearable. She reached up to touch the spot, but the attendant gently grasped her hand, stopping her.

"You'll need stitches," he said.

She opened her eyes again. "Really?"

"Only a few. Your hair will hide the scar. Does anything else hurt? Can you wiggle your fingers and toes?"

Callie tested. Everything seemed to work fine. "I think I hit my shoulder."

"You did," he said. "You have a bruise. But it doesn't seem to be broken. They'll x-ray you at the hospital."

"I don't need a hospital." Now that the shock was wearing off, embarrassment was setting in. She was about to arrive at the hospital on a stretcher. It really was overkill.

"Deacon is okay?" She looked for confirmation. "The driver?"

She remembered him talking to her in the car, and then she'd seen him speaking to the police while she was wheeled away. He'd looked okay, but she didn't know for sure.

"I can tell you there was only one ambulance called to the scene."

She assumed that was good.

"Here we are," the paramedic said.

The ambulance slowed and came to a stop.

The back doors opened, and sunlight flooded in.

Callie closed her eyes against the glare. The movement of the stretcher made her dizzy, so she kept them closed.

She could feel the temperature change when they entered the hospital. She heard voices, a nurse directing them and then the swoosh of a privacy curtain closing. The movement stopped, and she opened her eyes.

There was a woman standing over her.

"Hello, Mrs. Clarkson," she said. "I'm Dr. Westhall. You've been in a car accident."

"I remember," Callie said.

"Can you tell me what day this is?"

"Wednesday. It's May 30th."

"That's good," the doctor said, flashing a little light in Callie's eyes.

"I didn't lose my memory."

"I'd be surprised if you had. But you've had a good bump, and you'll need three or four stitches."

Deacon suddenly appeared beside the doctor, his face pale, his expression grave. "Callie. Are you all right?" He took her hand.

"Are you Mr. Clarkson?" the doctor asked.

A pained expression crossed Deacon's face. "No. I'm her boyfriend."

The words surprised Callie. Her boyfriend? Deacon considered himself her boyfriend?

Her chest warmed, and she couldn't hold back a smile.

He sat down on the opposite side of the bed to the doctor and held Callie's hand in both of his.

"I'm fine," she said.

"I'm so sorry."

"It wasn't your fault. The guy ran that light."

The doctor wrapped a blood pressure cuff around Callie's arm, and it whined as it tightened.

"I should have seen him coming."

"You turned," she said. She had a sudden memory flash of the truck's heavy duty grill coming straight at her. "If you hadn't turned..." She would have been crushed.

He pressed her hand against his lips.

"I'm going to put in some freezing," the doctor told her as she inspected Callie's forehead.

"Sure."

"I'm thinking I'll go with five stitches. The smaller the scar, the better."

"I'm not worried about a little scar," Callie said.

Deacon's attention went to the cut. "Your hair will probably cover it."

"I'm really not worried." She wasn't sure why everybody seemed so concerned about a little scar on her forehead.

Life happened. People got banged up. Nobody stayed pristine.

"When I'm done, we'll take an X-ray of that shoulder."

The concern came instantly back to Deacon's face. "You hurt your shoulder, too? Anything else?"

"It's just a bruise," Callie told him. She could feel the freezing start to work, and the stinging went away from her forehead.

"I'll feel better when we get an actual medical diagnosis. What else did you hit?"

"Everything else feels normal. Did you call Hannah? Can Pam stay with the boys?" Callie glanced at her watch. She didn't know how long an X-ray would take, but Pam was due to drop the boys off at the bakery at four.

"I've talked to Hannah. And I've talked to Pam. She has plans, but I'll pick up the boys. I can take them home. Unless you want me to bring them here?"

"No." She started to shake her head.

"Hold still," the doctor said.

"Sorry. Don't bring them here. I don't want to scare them." Callie couldn't help but think that the last time her sons were at a hospital, their father had died.

Not that Ethan remembered. But James might.

"I'll arrange for a car to take you home," Deacon said.

"I can call a cab."

"I'll set something up."

His offer warmed her. She felt cared for. It was an odd experience.

From her earliest memory, she'd struggled to take care of her sickly mother. Her older brothers had been lazy louts. At eight years old she'd already been cooking and cleaning for them.

Frederick had been wonderful. But his physical limitations meant she was the caregiver. She was the one who managed the physical necessities of life for herself, the boys and Frederick.

But now Deacon was her boyfriend. That's what boyfriends did. They took care of their girlfriends, and their girlfriend's sons. She couldn't help but smile again.

Deacon was her boyfriend.

Seven

Deacon finished reading a story to James and Ethan. He'd told them their mommy had a headache and was going to bed early. Luckily, they didn't ask any questions. They both seemed content to let Deacon give them a bath—an exciting experience for Deacon—and get them into their pajamas and tucked into bed.

Ethan had fallen asleep during the last pages of *Wilbur the Little Lost Pony*, and James was giving slow blinks, looking cozy under his rocket ship comforter. Deacon quietly closed the book and left their bedroom.

He made his way to the opposite end of the hall, through the open double doors to Callie's room. She was sitting up in bed, with a tablet on her lap and a small white bandage on her forehead. She was wearing a pretty pastel nightie with lace around the shoulders and across the neckline. Her hair was lustrous in the yellow lamplight.

"You're awake," he said softly.

"It's only eight o'clock."

He came forward to sit on the edge of the bed. "Sleep would be good for you."

"I have a boo-boo," she said. "I'm not sick."

"You almost got a concussion." He couldn't help himself, he smoothed her hair back on the uninjured side of her forehead.

"I came nowhere near to getting a concussion." She paused, and her eyes shadowed. "Thanks to you."

"I'm just glad you were okay." He moved closer and drew her gently to him.

She set aside the tablet and hugged him back. She felt perfect in his arms.

"Did the boys fall asleep?" she asked against his shoulder.

"Ethan did. James is almost there. I read them the pony story."

There was a smile in her voice. "They love that one."

"They're amazing kids."

"I'm so lucky to have them." She wiggled against him, then suddenly drew back. "What *is* that?" She pointed to his shirt pocket.

It was the ring box bulging out against her.

The circumstances were hardly ideal. He knew he should wait a couple of days. He knew he should give her a chance to feel better. He knew he should do it somewhere more romantic.

He wanted a yes.

Above everything else, he wanted a yes.

But he suddenly didn't want to wait another second.

He let his emotions rule his judgement and reached into his pocket. He extracted the box and handed it to her.

Looking half perplexed, half intrigued, she flipped it open.

Her expression froze as she stared at the diamond ring.

He knew immediately that he'd made a mistake, and he had to fix it somehow. "I know this might seem sudden. But, Callie, if one thing has become clear to me these past weeks, it's my feelings for you. I'm crazy about you. I'm crazy about your sons. We're good together. We belong together. We can have such an amazing and wonderful life together."

She lifted her gaze to his. "Are you…"

"Marry me, Callie. Make me the happiest man in the world."

"I…" She seemed to stumble over her words. "When… Why… How…"

"Why? Because you're amazing. When? I think the second I saw you. And how, well, a very nice woman at the jewelry store helped me buy this."

"Deacon, this is…" She hadn't said yes, but she hadn't said no either. She was hesitating.

He couldn't tell if she was simply acting the part of a tentative, newly widowed woman, or if she thought another man, someone like Hank, would be better for her.

"I can give you a fantastic life," Deacon said. "Both you and the boys. You'll have everything and anything you need."

Her voice was soft, cautious, nervous. "Do you love me, Deacon?"

He couldn't bring himself to utter the ultimate lie. "I am head over heels," he said instead.

"I love you, too." Clearly, she was a woman who could go all in.

He admired that, even as it put him slightly off balance.

"Is that a yes?" he asked.

"Yes. It's a yes." She wrapped her arms around his neck, and he gathered her close against him.

"Don't let me hurt you," he said, restraining himself, trying to be gentle.

"You're not hurting me."

There was a sheen in her eyes as she drew back, holding out her hand. It trembled ever so slightly.

As he took the ring and slipped it on, a cramp formed in the pit of his stomach.

It was happening. She was going to marry him, and his impossible childhood fantasy was going to come true.

He should have been thrilled.

He should have been over the moon.

But something didn't feel right. No, something felt too right.

Callie was too good at playing her part. She was taking his emotions along on the ride, and there seemed to be nothing he could do to stop it.

"Make love to me, Deacon."

He hesitated, his conflicting emotions trampling all over each other. "I don't want to hurt you," was his excuse.

But she stripped her nightie over her head. "You're not going to hurt me."

She was beautiful. She was beyond beautiful. She was perfect.

There was nothing he wanted more than Callie in his arms.

He wanted this to be real. Once again, he asked himself, *where was the harm?* She was getting what she wanted. And he was definitely getting what he wanted.

Why not delve completely into the fantasy?

He kissed her mouth, wider, longer, deeper. He closed a hand over her breast, feeling her nipple bead into his palm. He firmed his forearm across her lower back, easing her down on the mattress, resting her head on the white pillow.

The words *I love you* formed inside his brain. But he didn't dare let himself go that far.

His phone rang in his pocket. He knew deep down it would be Tyrell.

He shut if off without looking, then he stripped off his clothes, pulled back the covers and lay down beside Callie.

She cradled his face with her hands. "The boys adore you."

"I'll do right by them." He promised himself as much as he promised her.

He'd bonded with her sons in a way he hadn't expected. They'd be his responsibility from here on in. As his half nephews, they were his blood relatives on top of everything else. No matter what happened, he'd make sure they were cared for and protected forever.

She kissed him. "I can't believe this is happening."

"Neither can I." That part was the absolute truth.

Callie's life galloped forward at breakneck speed.

The Mobi Transportation project was still just an idea on paper, so Deacon wanted Callie and the boys to move to Hale Harbor. Deacon said it made sense to keep her house in Charleston, because they'd be back and forth quite often.

At first she didn't see how she could up and move out of Charleston. But Hannah eagerly offered to take over management of the bakery. Deacon confessed to having made another donation to the City Beautification Committee to get them to move the rose garden.

At first Callie was stunned and annoyed that he'd gone

against her wishes. But then she saw Hannah's reaction, and she knew he'd solved a big problem for them. He'd also circumvented Hank. And, on Hannah's behalf, Callie appreciated that. So she decided to forgive him.

Before long, Callie realized that living in Hale Harbor was a realistic option.

She'd expected they'd have a small wedding, but Deacon was in a hurry for that, too. He wanted to rush down to the courthouse and sign the paperwork. She found the idea sorely lacking in romance.

But Deacon argued that couples were wrong to fixate on the wedding. Personally, he was focused on the marriage, and he wanted to get to the heart of their relationship as quickly as possible.

She had to admit, he actually made the courthouse idea sound romantic. She also had to admit she admired his practicality. She also admired his efficiency. And she found herself anxious to get started on their new life.

So newly married, they'd landed at the small airport in Hale Harbor. Deacon had chartered a plane, explaining that the number of connections they'd need to get in and out of small airports would be hard on the boys.

She hadn't stopped to think about Deacon's wealth before now. She knew he had money, but somehow, she hadn't expected it to be at this level—maybe first-class tickets and maybe five star hotels, but chartering an entire jet? She experienced a new wave of uncertainty at the pace of everything.

But when they arrived at his house, she was relieved. It was nice. It was beautiful. It was even generous in size. But it wasn't a mansion. She'd been worried that he might have a household staff and a dozen luxury cars lined up in air-conditioned garages.

Then when he showed her into the boys' bedroom, her heart nearly burst.

It was larger than their old bedroom, and the windows were

in different places, and there was a connected bathroom, but otherwise, it was identical to their room in Charleston.

"I wanted them to feel at home," he told her as the boys hopped onto James's bed.

"How did you do this?" She took a step inside, even James's rocket ship comforter and the train pictures hanging on the wall were the same.

"I took some pictures and sent them to my housekeeper. She's a miracle worker."

"You have a housekeeper?" Callie asked, getting nervous again.

"She comes in a couple of times a week."

James scooted across the blue carpet to his dresser. "Our clothes go here."

"Don't tell me you changed the carpets," Callie said, realizing it was a near match to her house.

Deacon shrugged. "They were getting worn anyway. I wanted to go all in." He raised his voice a little. "If your mom wants to give you a bath, I'll bring up your suitcases and unpack."

"You're too much," she said.

She wanted to ask him exactly how much money he had to throw around on frivolous things, but the question was going to have to wait. It had been a very long day, and the boys were going to get cranky soon. She wanted to have them tucked into bed before exhaustion set in.

By the time she had them bathed and toweled off, Deacon had their clothes unpacked and their pajamas laid out on the bed. Callie couldn't help but appreciate the extra help. It took only minutes for the boys to be happily tucked into bed.

Outside the boys' room was a loft overlooking a curved staircase, with a spare room next door, facing out the front of the house. Past the staircase, a short hallway led to the master bedroom. It was magnificent, a very large room with a high ceiling, an adjacent sitting room, a huge master bathroom and a giant walk-in closet that was only about a third filled with Deacon's suits and clothing.

"This is gorgeous," Callie said, turning to look from all angles.

"It was one of the things that sold me on this house plan. I like space around me. I don't like feeling cramped."

"When did you buy it?" she asked.

"Three years ago. The company had a good year, and the dividend payment was unusually high. Besides, I'd never intended for my apartment to be permanent."

"Was it new when you bought it?" Callie hadn't seen anything in the house that looked remotely worn.

"I'd bought the building lot a while ago, so it was just a matter of finding the right plan. Do you want to unpack, or look around a bit first?"

"Can I look around?"

"You can do whatever you want."

She made her way back to the staircase, passing another loft that overlooked the two-story living room. At the bottom of the stairs, the foyer opened to a library on one side and a formal dining room on the other. Moving to the back of the house, she came to the two-story living room with an arched bank of windows facing the yard and connected to an open-concept kitchen, breakfast nook and family room.

"There's a covered porch off the family room." Deacon flicked a switch and lit up a generously sized deck with padded all-weather furniture and a hot tub.

"Is the hot tub secure?" The thought of Ethan accidentally falling in made her nervous.

"I put a lock on the cover."

She turned to glance behind her, taking in the sparkling kitchen, the pristine family room furniture, the art work and fixtures.

"I don't know how to ask this," she said, walking back, trailing her fingertips along the burgundy leather sofa.

He followed. "Ask away."

She abruptly faced him. "I didn't think… I mean, we never discussed… How, um, rich are you?"

"On a scale of one to ten?"

"You know what I mean."

His expression became a little guarded. "I have enough to support us."

It was a nonanswer.

From what she'd seen, he had far more than enough to support them.

She tried to put her concerns into words. "It's a little… This wasn't exactly what I was expecting."

He crossed his arms over his chest, his lips pursing as if she'd annoyed him. "You don't waste any time, do you?"

She didn't understand. She struggled with how to phrase it. "I can't help wondering how much my life is going to change."

"I didn't really want to do this tonight," he said.

"This?"

He kept talking. "I hoped we could have a little dignity about it."

"Dignity?"

Was he secretive about his money? If he wanted to keep it private, she supposed she could live with that. But it was an odd way to start a marriage.

"Why don't you go first?" he said.

The question baffled her. "Go first at what?"

"Why did you hide Frederick's money?"

"Hide it where?"

Did he mean by buying the bakery? That wasn't hidden. And hidden from whom?

"I think we're past playing coy, Callie."

"Deacon, if you don't want to talk about your money…"

"I don't want it to be one sided."

She peered at his expression, trying to figure out what was going on. "Okay…"

"Good," he said. "What's your net worth?"

The question confused her even more. He'd seen her house, her business. He knew her lifestyle.

"You mean the house and the bakery?"

Deacon looked impatient. "I mean Frederick's money."

She cast around for an answer. The few thousand dollars in her savings account didn't seem worth talking about.

"Frederick didn't have a life insurance policy," she said. "Not with the injuries to his lungs."

"I meant his family money."

"What family money?"

He threw up his hands. "This is getting us nowhere."

She was feeling as frustrated as he sounded. "Then tell me what you want? What are you talking about?"

"I'm talking about the Clarkson family fortune?"

He was joking. He had to be joking.

She waited for him to laugh, but he didn't.

She braced her hand on the back of the sofa. Something was terribly wrong with this conversation.

Deacon couldn't figure out what Callie had to gain by continuing to pretend. They were married now. The deal was done.

They'd played each other. But they'd both done it. They were both bringing something to the table, and they were both getting what they wanted.

"I know all about Frederick's family," he said. "So let's just figure out how this is going to work."

She still didn't drop the act. "What about Frederick's family?"

"I grew up in Hale Harbor."

She didn't respond. If anything, she looked even more confused.

"Everyone in Hale Harbor knows the Clarksons. The castle, the Port, their history, their *money.*"

"Frederick's family lives in Miami."

The statement stopped Deacon cold.

Either she was the greatest actress on the planet, or she believed what she'd just said.

Plus, there was no reason for her to have made that up. There was no benefit to that particular lie. Was there?

"They don't have a fortune," she continued. "They sure don't have a castle."

A feeling of unease crept into Deacon. If Frederick had lied to her, where had his money gone?

Deacon frantically reframed a world where Callie hadn't known about Frederick's money.

Her hold on the sofa tightened. Her expression hardened, and she gestured around the room. "Is this all a sham, Deacon? Are you a con artist? Are you under the impression that, by marrying me, you'll get your hands on a fortune? Are you in debt, is that it?"

"No!"

"You didn't want a prenup. I thought that was odd. I should have listened to myself." She turned to leave the room.

His brain was struggling to make sense of everything. "Callie, something's wrong."

"You bet it is," she called over her shoulder.

"Frederick lied to you."

She gave a slightly hysterical laugh. "It's *you* who lied, Deacon." She kept walking.

He rushed across the living room and caught up to her in the foyer.

"You can divorce me," she said. "And go find yourself some other rich woman to marry."

"I don't want your money."

The front doorbell rang.

"I'll be out of here in the morning," she told him.

"Deacon?" a man's voice called through the door.

Deacon recognized Tyrell's voice and swore under his breath.

Callie started up the stairs.

"I can explain," he called after her.

She didn't answer.

"Deacon," Tyrell called out again.

Deacon was torn between going after her and getting rid of Tyrell. The last thing he needed was Frederick's father in the mix of all this.

He dragged open the door. "*What* are you doing here?"

Before the words were even out, he saw that Margo was with him.

"Where are my grandsons?" she asked, a desperate hunger in her eyes.

"They're asleep," Deacon said.

"But they're here."

"You were supposed to call," Tyrell said.

"And I *will*," Deacon countered.

Margo started forward.

"You have to *leave*," Deacon said, blocking her from entering and glancing behind him.

He was fairly sure Callie wouldn't come back downstairs, but he didn't dare chance it.

"I want to see them," Margo said.

"I told you, they're asleep."

"I won't wake them."

Deacon looked at Tyrell. "Take her home or you'll blow everything."

He could see the hesitation on Tyrell's face.

"Now," Deacon said.

"I've waited so long," Margo wailed.

"Darling." Tyrell put a hand on his wife's arm. "We have to—"

"You can't make me wait," she cried, shaking Tyrell off. "And *him*." She pointed to Deacon. "He's the last person who should stop me from seeing my grandsons." She surged forward.

Deacon planted himself directly in front of her. "You may not like me. You may even hate me. But this is my house, and Callie is my wife, and you are not getting past me to see those boys."

"How *dare* you."

He heard a noise behind him.

"Deacon?" Callie asked.

His stomach turned to lead.

"What's going on?" she asked.

"Is that her?" Margo asked.

"Go," Deacon hissed.

"Grandsons?" Callie asked.

He turned to face her, blocking the opening of the door. "I told you I could explain."

"Who are those people?"

Deacon fought it for several seconds, but then gave in to the inevitable. "They are Frederick's parents."

The color drained from Callie's face.

"They've been estranged from Frederick for years," Deacon quickly explained. "He didn't tell you about them, because he didn't speak to them."

She looked like she might keel over, and he rushed forward to support her. He grasped her shoulder and put an arm around her waist.

"Are you Callie?" Margo asked.

Deacon saw that the door was wide open, and Margo had stepped inside.

"I'm sorry," he whispered in Callie's ear. "I'm so sorry."

"I'm Frederick's mother," Margo said.

Tyrell entered, as well. "I'm Tyrell Clarkson. This is my wife, Margo."

Callie tipped her head to look at Deacon.

"Can we do this tomorrow?" he asked Tyrell.

"I've waited so long," Margo said. "Can I please see my grandsons?"

"They're asleep." Callie's whisper was paper dry.

"I promise I'll be quiet," Margo said. Her longing was so painfully obvious, that even Deacon felt sorry for her.

"You don't have to do this," Deacon said to Callie. "She has no right to ask."

Margo glared at Deacon.

"You're their grandmother?" Callie asked Margo. The bewilderment was clear in her tone.

Margo nodded.

"You knew this?" Callie said to Deacon.

"I was trying to figure out how to tell you. I thought—" Deacon stopped himself. There was no way he was having this conversation in front of Tyrell and Margo. "I'll explain. But not right now."

"I don't have Frederick's money," Callie told Deacon.

"I don't want Frederick's money."

"What happened to Frederick's money?" Tyrell asked.

"Back off," Deacon ordered.

"He gave it to charity," Callie said. "Spinal cord research."

"His entire trust fund?" There was skepticism in Tyrell's tone. "Millions of dollars?"

"He never told me how much. He once said he regretted it. He didn't know he'd have the boys."

"I have no interest in Frederick's money," Deacon said to Callie. To Tyrell, he said, "Can you not see that you should leave."

"But—" There was a tremor in Margo's voice.

"Not tonight," Deacon said.

"You can come up and see them," Callie said.

Deacon looked at her, dumbfounded.

Hope rose in Margo's expression.

"For a quick minute," Callie said. "If we're really quiet."

Margo gave a rapid nod.

Callie disentangled herself from Deacon. "This way."

She started up the stairs, and Margo was quick to follow.

"You better start talking," Callie said to Deacon as she marched into the family room.

She'd sat in the boys' room for an hour after Margo left. Instinct had told her to curl up next to James for the night and try to block out everything she'd just learned. But she knew she'd never sleep. There was no point in putting off the confrontation with Deacon.

"Will you sit?" he asked.

He was in a leather armchair, next to the stone fireplace, a tumbler of amber liquor on the table beside him.

There was nothing to be gained by standing. So she took the opposite chair. The thick cushions cradled her weight.

"Something to drink?" he asked.

"No."

"Okay." He sat forward. "From the beginning. When I first came to Charleston, I already knew who you were."

"What did you want from me?"

"I wanted to meet you. Tyrell was curious about his grandsons. He was also afraid of approaching you. He thought Frederick had turned you against them, so he didn't want to introduce himself."

"Why you?"

Deacon hesitated.

She peered at him. "Are you making up a lie?"

"I'm thinking about how to phrase the truth."

She scoffed at the semantics, wishing now that she'd said yes to a drink.

"It was because I'm only tangentially connected to the family," Deacon said. "Tyrell thought you'd know the rest of them, but not me."

"What does *tangentially* mean?" She hated the way he was talking in riddles.

Deacon was hiding something. He was probably hiding a lot. When she let herself think about what she'd lost here tonight, her stomach curled into a ball, and tears burned behind her eyes.

"I'm Tyrell's illegitimate son."

Callie sat up straight, nearly coming out of her chair. "You're Frederick's *brother*?"

"Half brother. And we never knew each other. I'm not sure he knew I existed."

"But his father did."

"Oh, yes. Tyrell has known about me all along."

Callie sat back, trying frantically to digest the information.
Deacon rose and crossed the room.

When he came back, he handed her a glass.

"Brandy," he said.

She thought about refusing, but it seemed like a better idea to drink it down.

She accepted the glass and took a healthy swallow.

"You don't love me," she noted as he sat down. Of everything that had been revealed, that was the fact that burned most sharply in her mind.

Deacon sat back down and again took his time responding. "I was amazed at how much I liked you."

"Am I supposed to be grateful for that?" She could add mortification to her list of unwelcome emotions. She'd honestly thought she loved him, that she was *in love* with him, that he was the love of her life.

He, on the other hand, had been faking it the whole time.

"I thought you were after my money," he said.

"I wasn't."

"I don't mean that in a bad way."

"There's a good way to accuse me of being a gold digger?" She took another drink.

"You as much as admitted to marrying Frederick for his money. I thought I was the next step on the ladder."

"But you stayed after that. It doesn't make sense that you stayed."

She knew she was tired. She was emotionally drained. This was probably the very worst day of her life, and her brain was foggy. But it was nonsensical that he'd stuck around if he thought she was using him.

"There are a lot of different relationships in the world. I guess I didn't mind that you were pragmatic about bettering your circumstances."

"You thought I was pretending to fall for you?"

What kind of a man was he? She thought back to the time they'd spent together, the fun they'd had, the nights in her house, the beach with the boys. All that time, he'd thought she was playing him?

"I liked you a lot," he said, toying with his glass, turning it in a circle on the wooden coaster. "I didn't know where it was going, and I wanted to find out."

"So you *proposed*? You *married* me to find out where it was going?" She took another healthy swallow of the brandy.

"I knew Watkins was pursuing you, and, well… I couldn't afford to wait."

"I had no interest in Hank." She was revolted by the thought of even kissing Hank. There was no way she would have embarked on a relationship with him.

"I know that now," Deacon said.

She polished off her drink. "I don't know what you thought was going to happen here. But I'm leaving in the morning. I'm filing for divorce. You've messed up my life—"

"I wish you wouldn't do that."

"Too bad."

"I think we can make this work."

She laughed. It sounded a bit hysterical. It probably was.

"Make it work?" she repeated. "In what universe is there anything here to make work?"

"I was wrong. I thought I was giving you what you wanted, another wealthy husband."

"It had nothing to do with wealth." She didn't know why she made the point. She didn't care anything about Deacon's opinion of her. "Frederick begged me to marry him. He knew I wasn't in love with him. But he was kind, and he said I made him happy, and I wanted to be a mother. I didn't want to stay in Gainwall and—"

"You don't have to explain it to me."

"I hate what you thought of me."

"I was wrong. I knew the Clarksons wanted their grandsons. I thought you wanted money. We got along fine. We got along better than fine."

Memories of their lovemaking—the ones she'd been desperately trying to keep at bay—suddenly surfaced. She felt her body heat up from her toes to her cheeks.

"Is that how you see it?" she asked. "You had everybody's best interests at heart?"

"I'm saying I knew what they wanted. I thought I knew what you wanted. And it was easy to talk myself into doing it."

"You got it completely wrong."

"I just admitted that."

It was true. He had. She didn't know what else to say.

"Don't leave right away," he said. "It's always an option. It'll stay an option. But there are a lot of people..."

She waited, wondering how he'd intended to end the sentence.

"More brandy?" he asked instead.

She looked down at the empty glass in her hand. She wasn't leaving in the next five minutes. She still had to make it through tonight. "Why not?"

He rose to pour. "You saw how Margo feels."

Callie couldn't help but think back to Margo's expression when she saw her sleeping grandsons. There had been tears in her eyes. She'd slowly crouched down beside James's bed and just stared at him.

"There's no love lost between me and Tyrell, but he is their grandfather. And they have two uncles, Aaron and Beau." Deacon finished pouring her brandy and turned back. "James and Ethan are the spitting images of their uncles."

"I don't care," she said.

This wasn't about uncles. It was about her and her sons. Her chest tightened again thinking about what this would do to her boys. They adored Deacon.

They were barely recovering from the loss of their father. She'd just ripped them away from their lives in Charleston, and now she was going to ruin their foundation all over again. How had this gone so wrong?

"Family matters," Deacon said as he handed back her glass.

A question rose up in Callie's mind. "What happened with Frederick and his family?"

"Something between Frederick and Tyrell. Beyond that, I don't know."

"I don't believe you."

"All I know is that Frederick went off to college and didn't come back afterward. There were rumors that he'd had a falling out with his father."

"You never asked?"

"Asked Tyrell?"

She nodded.

"Tyrell and I don't talk much."

Callie was struggling to put the pieces together. "But he sent you to Charleston."

"That was an anomaly. I was probably his last choice."

She gazed into her glass, the rich amber glowing in the lamplight. "I am leaving." She had no other choice.

"I know," he said softly. "I'm only asking for a few days."

Her heart actually hurt. "I'm not sure if I—"

"You can have your own room. I'll stay out of your way. Let the boys meet their grandparents. Just take it slow, methodical, make the best choices for the three of you. It'll be the right thing in the long run."

She studied his expression, wondering if he was playing her all over again. "What do you get out of this?"

"I like you, Callie. I adore the boys. We're…compatible." The sensual glow in his eyes told her what compatible meant. "We could make it work."

He wasn't wrong. They were compatible in every way possible.

But staying with him, knowing all this, accepting what he'd done and how he felt about her? She couldn't do it. It was more than her heart could take.

"That's not going to happen," she said, her voice breaking over the words.

Eight

It was 4 a.m. Deacon was in bed, but he wasn't anywhere near to sleeping.

How had he judged her so wrong? Callie wasn't acting. She's wasn't playing him or Hank or anyone else to work her way up the societal ladder.

Down the hall, Ethan cried out in his sleep.

Deacon was on his feet and halfway across the room before he realized he couldn't go to the boy. Callie would go to him. Deacon no longer had the right.

He sat on the edge of the bed, his gaze going to the glowing red numbers on his bedside clock. It was four eleven.

Her heard Callie's voice, indistinct as she tried to soothe Ethan.

Deacon rose again, moving to his open door, listening while Ethan continued to cry.

He heard James's voice, and realized Ethan had woken him up.

He started down the hall. He didn't care how Callie might be feeling about him. It was clear she needed help.

He walked into the room and went straight to James, who was sitting up in bed. Deacon sat down, and James climbed into his lap. He hugged the boy close and looked to Callie.

"He's burning up," she said in a hoarse voice.

"Does he need a doctor?"

"There was a bottle of acetaminophen drops in one of the suitcases."

"I put them in the medicine cabinet." Deacon rose, carrying James with him into the bathroom.

In the glow of the nightlight, he located the medicine. Behind him, Ethan coughed weakly and cried harder.

"Owie," Ethan whimpered.

"I know, sweetheart," Callie said. "We're getting you some medicine."

Ethan sobbed, coughed and sobbed some more. He sounded wretched, and Deacon's heart went out to the poor little guy. Deacon measured out a dose and brought it to Callie.

"We can call a doctor," he said.

"Let's see if this helps first."

Deacon would rather call a doctor right away, but he knew he had to leave the decision to Callie.

She put the medicine dispenser to Ethan's lips. "You need to swallow this, honey," she crooned.

"Yucky," Ethan cried.

"You can have some juice after."

"No."

"It'll make you feel better."

"No, Mommy, no," Ethan wailed, turning his head.

"Ethan." Callie's voice was firm.

"Daddy," Ethan cried, launching himself to Deacon, catching Callie completely off guard.

Deacon quickly grabbed for him, holding James fast in his other arm, gathering the sobbing Ethan against his chest before he could fall to the floor.

Deacon locked onto the staggered expression in Callie's eyes.

"Let me try," he told her softly. "James, can I put you down on the bed?"

Ethan's sobs turned into an uncontrollable cough.

"Mommy?" James asked, his voice trembling. "Is Ethan going to die?"

Callie's eyes filled with tears. She reached for James, taking him from Deacon to hold him in her arms. "No. No. Sweetheart, Ethan is going to be fine. I promise. We just have to give him some medicine."

Deacon took the medication from Callie and sat down on

James's bed, holding Ethan close, the little boy's damp face against Deacon's bare chest.

"Does your throat hurt bad?" Deacon asked in a calm voice.

Ethan gave a miserable nod.

Deacon kissed the top of Ethan's head. "I'm sorry, buddy. Do you want it to go away?"

Ethan nodded again.

Deacon was vaguely aware of Callie and James watching him.

"I think I can help." Deacon smoothed Ethan's soft hair. "Do you like honey?"

"On toast," Ethan rasped.

"Not on toast right now. On a spoon. It'll help. Do you think you could swallow some honey on a spoon?"

Ethan nodded.

Deacon rose, carrying Ethan. "Let's go to the kitchen and find some."

"Owie," Ethan whimpered again, as Deacon walked out of the bedroom.

"You know what will work even better than honey on your owie?" Deacon took the stairs. "The yucky medicine."

"Nooo."

"The trick is, you swallow just a little bit of medicine, and before you can even taste it, you pop the honey in your mouth."

James spoke from Callie's arms behind them. "Can I have honey?"

"Sure," Callie said, sounding dazed.

Deacon turned on a small light in the kitchen. He located a bottle of honey and a spoon.

"What do you say, buddy?" He looked down at Ethan. "A quick squirt of yucky medicine and then a big spoon of honey?"

Ethan looked skeptical, and Deacon was afraid his ploy wouldn't work. If it didn't, he was calling a doctor whether Callie liked it or not. Ethan was burning up. They had to get his fever down.

"'Kay," Ethan said in the quietest of voices.

"That's my boy." Relief rushed through Deacon. He held up the medicine dispenser. "I know you can do it, buddy."

Ethan gave a brave nod.

Deacon squirted the medicine into Ethan's mouth.

Ethan screwed up his face in a scowl, but he managed to swallow it.

Deacon quickly put the honey to his lips, and Ethan sucked the spoon into his mouth. His expression slowly cleared.

"That was fantastic," Deacon praised him, wrapping his arms fully around Ethan's sweaty little body.

Callie slumped against the counter, James still in her arms, a single tear escaping to run down her cheek. He held her gaze, and she gave him a shaky nod of thanks.

"Do you want to go back to Mommy?" Deacon asked Ethan.

"'Kay," Ethan squeaked out.

Callie set James down, and Deacon handed her the limp Ethan.

Then Deacon crouched to talk to James. "Honey for you too?"

"Is Ethan okay?" James asked.

"He's going to feel better really soon," Deacon said. "After your honey, you'll need to brush your teeth again."

"Okay," James agreed.

Deacon got a fresh spoon and gave James a small dollop of honey.

He grinned as he licked it.

Callie was sitting at the breakfast table, rocking Ethan in her arms.

Deacon took James's hand. "Back to bed for you."

"Okay," James said, with a last look at his brother.

Deacon helped James with his teeth, got him tucked back in and then returned to the kitchen. Callie was still at the table, rocking Ethan.

Ethan had stopped crying. But his eyes were open, and he cringed in pain as he swallowed.

Deacon crouched beside them.

"Thank you," Callie said, her voice breaking.

"No problem." Deacon was incredibly glad to have been here to support her. "We can still call a doctor."

Callie glanced at her watch. "Let's give the acetaminophen time to work."

"Do you want to move to the family room?" He rose and held out a hand to help her up. "It'll be more comfortable."

She hesitated, but then accepted his offer.

Deacon resisted the urge to put his arm around her. Intellectually, he knew their relationship had irrevocably changed. But emotionally, he still felt protective of her. He still felt close to her. He still felt like her husband.

She sat down in the same armchair as earlier, leaning back with Ethan stretched across her chest.

"Do you want a blanket?" Deacon asked her.

"He called you daddy."

"Yeah." Deacon's chest tightened with the memory. It had taken him completely off guard.

Callie looked wretchedly unhappy, her voice half whisper, half wail. "What am I going to do?"

After Ethan recovered, circumstances seemed to conspire against Callie.

The boys were very obviously bonding with Deacon, and Hannah called full of excitement and ideas as she ran the bakery solo. Margo had had a playroom specially built, and couldn't wait to show it off to her grandsons.

So on Saturday, with Ethan back at full strength, Deacon pulled the car up to the front of the castle.

Callie couldn't do anything but stare in awe at the imposing stone structure. "It looks like a hotel."

"This is where Frederick grew up."

"Daddy used to live here?" James asked in wonder from the back seat.

"He did," Deacon confirmed.

"Was Daddy a prince?"

"He was just a very lucky little boy." There was something in Deacon's voice, but Callie couldn't pinpoint the emotion.

"I wish I was a prince," James said.

Callie had to fight a smile. It was the first time she'd seen humor in the world since she'd discovered the truth.

"When I was a boy, I wanted to be a prince, too," Deacon said.

"There's a tower," James said, excitement growing in his voice. "A real tower. Can I have a sword?"

A part of Callie couldn't help being interested in Frederick's childhood home. But mostly she was plotting their exit from Hale Harbor. The sooner she moved the boys back to their old life, the better it would be for them.

While she helped Ethan out of his car seat, Deacon opened the opposite door for James.

The castle's grounds were vast. Summer flowers were blooming in dozens of garden beds. The lawn was a smooth emerald carpet. Oak trees lined the wide, exposed aggregate driveway. And two lion statues flanked a wide staircase that led to arched oversize wood-plank doors.

The castle was three stories high, with a tower on each of the front corners. She could see at least three gardeners on the grounds. While off to the left side, there was a six-car garage.

"This is ridiculous," she muttered under her breath.

"Down," Ethan said, kicking his legs.

Callie set him down.

He immediately ran for the lawn.

"Don't touch the flowers," she called after him.

James trotted after his brother, while Ethan dropped and rolled in the lush grass.

The door to the castle yawned open. Callie half expected a butler to emerge. But it was Margo and Tyrell who appeared.

With them was a young woman who looked to be in her early twenties.

"Who's that?" Callie asked Deacon, dividing her attention between the porch and the boys.

Ethan had spotted a row of rhododendron bushes, and she could almost see his little mind working.

"I don't know. It's not Aaron's wife."

"Another long-lost relative?"

"Not that I know about."

The trio started toward them.

Although it was a warm Saturday, Tyrell was dressed in a business suit. Margo wore tan slacks and a sleeveless patterned silk top. Her grey hair was wispy around her face, while a pair of designer sunglasses were perched on her nose. The other woman was dressed in jeans, a white capped-sleeve T-shirt and flat sandals. She had long blond hair in a sporty ponytail.

"James," Callie called out. "Can you bring Ethan back?"

James trotted over to his brother and took his hand. Ethan pointed at the pink rhododendrons, but James tugged him along.

"I just can't get over it," Margo said as she watched the boys come toward them.

"The genes are strong," Tyrell said.

Callie had learned from Deacon that James and Ethan bore an uncanny resemblance to their uncles, Aaron and Beau.

"I'll have to show you some pictures," Margo said to Callie.

Although she greeted Callie with a squeeze on the arm, Margo didn't acknowledge Deacon.

It was growing clear to Callie that Margo didn't like Deacon. It didn't take a genius to figure out why. It wasn't Deacon's fault that Tyrell had an affair with his mother. But it seemed as though Margo was determined to hold Deacon responsible.

"Callie, this is Dee Anderson," Margo said. "Dee has a degree in early childhood education, and she's joined our household staff."

Callie let the phrase "joined our household staff" roll around in her brain for a moment.

"Hello, Mrs. Holt." Dee offered her hand.

The name jolted Callie, and she stumbled in her response. "Please, call me Callie." She studiously avoided looking Deacon's way.

Deacon had spent a lot of time at work the past few days. In the evenings, he'd been a big help with the boys. But they'd tiptoed around each other when they were alone. She hadn't talked to him about her immediate plans to stay or go, and he hadn't brought it up.

"Grandma has something special to show you," Margo said to James and Ethan.

James hung back, but she captured Ethan's attention.

"Candy?" asked Ethan.

"It's not candy," Margo said with an indulgent smile.

Ethan frowned.

Callie moved to take each of her sons' hands, putting a cheerful note into her voice. "Why don't we see what Grandma wants to show us?"

James hung on, while Ethan tried to pull out of her hold.

"Do you want some help?" Deacon asked Callie.

"We'll be fine." Margo waved him away and started walking.

"My name is Dee." Dee introduced herself to the boys as she fell into step. "You must be James, and you must be Ethan."

"Ethan," Ethan said.

"It's nice to meet you, Ethan."

"Have candy?"

"Ethan," Callie warned. "You've only just finished breakfast."

"Dessert," Ethan said with authority.

"You know we don't have dessert with breakfast."

"Do you like slides?" Dee asked.

James spoke up. "I like towers." He craned his neck as they walked toward the castle.

Instead of heading for the front door, they took a walkway along the south side of the castle, coming to a chain-link gate that led to a fenced area with a giant, colorful playset of swings, slides, bridges and ladders with safety rails.

James's eyes went wide.

"Slides!" Ethan squealed.

Dee opened the gate, and both boys dashed inside.

"It's…" Callie didn't even know what to say.

"It's consumer tested and very highly rated," Margo said.

"The best safety rating," Dee said.

"I was going to say enormous." Callie stared at straight slides, covered slides, curving slides.

Ethan started up a ladder.

Callie checked his path, looking for the danger zones, deciding where best to stand to spot him. But she didn't see any flaws in the design. There were no spaces where it looked like he could fall. And Dee was right behind him, laughing and asking him what he wanted to try first.

"They seem to like it," Margo said.

"I don't know any kids who wouldn't." Callie looked a little further around. The area was completely fenced. The boys couldn't wander away.

"Would you like to sit down?" Margo gestured to an umbrella-covered table. "I'll have some iced tea brought out for us."

Callie got the feeling she'd been separated from Deacon for a reason. But the boys were happy. Margo was being very hospitable, and Callie preferred to keep her distance from Deacon anyway.

It didn't matter where he was, or what he was doing. She wasn't even going to think about him.

As Deacon signed the paperwork at the boardroom table in the castle's business wing, Beau burst through the door.

"You can't *do* this," Beau shouted at his father.

Tyrell glared at his son for a beat before answering. "Hello, Beau."

"Aaron just told me what's going on."

Tyrell's tone was clipped and even. "Had you not missed the last three board meetings, you might have known sooner."

Beau stalked across the room, making a beeline for the paperwork in front of Deacon.

When Beau reached out to grab it, Deacon jumped from his chair, grabbing Beau's lapel and pushing him back into the wall.

Beau doubled up his fist, and Deacon braced himself for a hit.

"Stop!" Tyrell bellowed.

Beau glared into Deacon's eyes.

"You need a two-thirds majority," Beau spat.

Deacon narrowed his eyes, trying to gauge if Beau was bluffing.

"No," Tyrell said, staying in his seat at the head of the long table. "You need a two-thirds majority to overturn the decision."

Beau broke eye contact with Deacon to look at his father.

Deacon took a chance and relaxed his hold.

Beau pushed to break free. "Are we going to let the lawyers duke it out?"

Aaron appeared in the doorway, and Deacon felt distinctly outnumbered.

"Do you have the authority to make this deal?" Deacon asked Tyrell.

"Yes," Tyrell said, his voice definitive.

"I will fight you," Beau said. "You are not having this…" He rounded on Deacon. "This *person* replace Frederick."

"He's not replacing Frederick," Tyrell said.

"No?" Aaron walked in and took the chair to the right of his father. Aaron's tone was far more reasonable. "You're giving him Frederick's company shares. He married Frederick's wife. He's here. What more is there to replacing Frederick?"

"We should throw him out," Beau said.

"Beau," Tyrell snapped.

"You're not helping," Aaron said to his brother.

"You're welcome to try," Deacon said easily.

"I'll tie you up in court so long, you'll be bankrupt or retired before we're done."

Deacon sat back down and signed the final paper with a flourish. "Do that, and you'll never see my sons again."

Deacon knew full well Callie could walk away at any moment, and he'd be the one who'd never see James and Ethan again. But for the moment, they were his best leverage point with the Clarksons.

"The price is too high," Beau said to his father. "Even *you* have to know it's way too high."

"They're my grandsons," Tyrell said. "They're the future of this family."

Beau walked around the table and dropped into a chair. "I'll get married," he said. "You win. I'll get married and give you legitimate grandchildren."

"You had your chance," Tyrell said.

Deacon couldn't help but glance at Aaron. Aaron was married. Was there some reason he wasn't having children? From the tight expression on Aaron's face, Deacon guessed that must be the case.

The reason for Tyrell's offer to Deacon was becoming clearer. James and Ethan weren't just his first grandsons. They might well be his only grandsons.

"What's your beef with me?" Deacon asked Beau.

Beau shot a sneer across the table. "Are you kidding me? The mere sight of you is a knife in my mother's heart."

"Not my fault," Deacon said.

"Shouldn't we be talking about his credentials," Aaron asked. "What does he know about running the port? We don't need a useless drain on the system with twenty-five percent voting power."

Deacon was getting tired of this argument. He looked to Tyrell. "Do we have a deal, or don't we? Because I'm the legal guardian of those two boys, and their mother is madly in love with me." The last part was a gross exaggeration at this point, but Deacon liked the way it added to his threat.

Tyrell stood. "There's something you need to see."

At first, Deacon thought Tyrell was talking to him. But it was clear he meant Aaron and Beau.

"What?" Beau asked.

"You can't run this place by decree," Aaron said.

"Will you follow me?" Tyrell's exasperation was clear.

Both men reluctantly followed their father out of the room.

Curious, Deacon went along. Whatever it was Tyrell had up his sleeve, Deacon could only hope it settled the deal.

They made their way along a hallway, through a formal dining room, to a set of glass doors. The doors led to a patio. And when they walked outside, Deacon could hear James's and Ethan's shouts. He also heard a woman's laughter. He guessed it was Dee.

The play area was off the edge of the patio, and both Aaron and Beau moved closer to look. They stopped at the concrete rail, and Deacon watched their expressions as they stared: Aaron at James and Beau at Ethan. It was clear they saw what everyone else did. It was as if they'd been cloned.

Aaron spoke first. "How could that…"

Beau brought the heels of his palms down on the rail, a note of awe in his voice. "Do you think Frederick could see it?"

Tyrell's bet seemed to have paid off. It looked like Aaron and Beau would close ranks around their nephews.

Deacon caught a glimpse of Callie. She was laughing, looking relaxed while she chatted with Margo. She looked unexpectedly happy, and he was jealous. He saw her every day, but he missed her desperately.

His fingertips itched from wanting to touch her. He was

longing to hold her. Every time she smiled at her sons, he wanted to kiss her. And at night, he lay awake in a near-constant state of frustration.

She was only steps down the hall in the guest room. He pictured her silk nightgown, her creamy shoulders. In his mind he saw her sleeping, eyes closed, cheeks flushed, lips slightly parted. He'd kissed her awake more than once. And then…

He gritted his teeth and gave himself a shake, focusing his attention on reality.

As he did, and as he surveyed the scene, a cold realization came over him. It was the boys they wanted. It was Callie they needed. If Callie walked away from him, the Clarksons would welcome her with open arms.

Deacon was entirely expendable.

Callie had let ten days go by.

First Ethan had been sick. Then Margo wanted some time with her grandchildren. She'd asked to take them shopping and to the funfair at the pier. Dee always came along and lent a hand, making Callie feel quite spoiled.

Deacon had stayed busy, working all day, coming home late, making it easy for her to push their problems to the background. He never asked if she was staying, never asked if she was going.

She wanted to leave. But leaving meant telling the world she'd made a mistake, telling Hannah and everyone back in Charleston she'd been a fool. Telling Margo she was taking the boys away. It meant giving a final decision to Deacon and maybe fighting with him about it.

She didn't want to fight with Deacon. She wanted to laugh with him again, talk to him about anything and nothing. She wanted to hold him, kiss him, make love with him and sleep in his arms again. Her soul ached with missing him.

She walked back out onto the deck, in the cool dark of the evening. She'd played with the boys in the hot tub before bundling them off to bed. Now, she picked up the discarded towels and reached in for the floating toys.

Her hand skimmed the warm water. She'd pulled on her cover-up, but her bathing suit was still damp underneath. She was chilled now, and the hot water felt wonderful.

She knew that just inside the door was the wet bar, with wine and brandy, and anything else that might strike her fancy. The moon was full, the lights in the garden glowing, with a view overlooking the town and the dark ocean beyond.

She hadn't spent much time, really no time at all appreciating her surroundings. Deacon had a wonderful house, in a beautiful spot, with every amenity a person could wish for.

Making up her mind, she padded inside, the carpet soft against her bare feet. She found a small snifter, chose a pretty brandy label and poured herself a drink.

She dimmed the lights, discarded her cover-up and lowered herself into the hot water, turning the jets to high and facing the view. She sipped the brandy as the water pulsated against her lower back and surged between her shoulder blades.

"You look comfortable," Deacon said from behind her, his voice deep and melodious.

For a moment, she let the sound wash over her, leaving her skin tingling.

"I didn't know you were here," she said, craning her neck to look at him.

He moved into her view. "I just got home."

"Working late?" A part of her wanted to laugh at the banal conversation, as if they were a normal couple, on a normal night, in a normal circumstance.

He crouched on his haunches and trailed his hand through the water.

She watched with rapt attention, imagining it on her skin.

"Growing pains," he said.

"Hmm?" She forced herself to look up.

"The port is growing, and there are some tough decisions to make."

She was surprised he was sharing. He didn't seem to ever talk about work. She knew he'd lied about Mobi Transportation looking at relocating to Charleston. It was a minor lie in the scheme of things.

It was true that he was a shareholder at Mobi, but his real job was in the family firm of Hale Harbor Port. That was where he worked, with his half brothers, Beau, who seemed hostile, and Aaron, who seemed cold to everyone, not to mention his father, who had, despite Margo's resentment of Deacon, apparently brought him into the family business anyway.

"Mind if I join you?" Deacon asked.

Her heart skipped a beat.

He took in her expression. "I won't if it makes you uncomfortable."

"No. It's fine. It's your hot tub."

He looked like he wanted to say something, but he clamped his lips together.

"Please," she said, gesturing to the water. "It's nice."

He rose. "I'll grab a suit."

She watched him walk away, wishing she could tell him to forget the bathing suit. She'd seen him naked dozens of times. And he'd seen her. And it was silly for them to feign modesty now.

She lowered herself deeper into the water and sipped the brandy, while her mind went on a flight of fancy about making love with Deacon.

He was back before she expected, startling her.

She sat back up, while he climbed into the hot tub with his own glass of brandy. He also set the bottle at the edge.

"Margo mentioned a ball today," Callie said, latching onto a neutral topic.

"The Summer Solstice?" he asked.

"That sounds right."

"It's famous around here, the social event of the year. Everyone wants to be invited to the castle to dance in the grand ballroom."

"The Clarksons apparently have a tailor. She wants to make matching suits for the boys."

Deacon blinked at her. He didn't have to ask the question. They both knew what it was.

The ball was a week away. Would James and Ethan be here to wear their custom-made suits?

"I don't know," Callie told him honestly. "I don't know what to do."

Deacon might be the source of her problem, but he was also the only person who knew the truth. Everyone else thought their marriage was real.

"You know what I want." His tone was deep, sincere, like the words had been pulled from his very core.

She couldn't take her gaze from him. She couldn't speak. She couldn't move.

When he shifted to the seat next to her, her pulse jumped. The water temperature seemed to inch up several degrees.

"Stay," he said. "For as long as you want. I'll give you space." Even as he made the promise, he seemed to grow closer. His gaze moved to her lips. "I'll give you—"

And then he was kissing her. And it was magic. It took her breath away. And she kissed him back, the water sloshing between them. His arms went around her. Her body slid against his. Her breasts plastered again his chest.

A crash shattered the night around them.

They jumped apart, and she realized she'd dropped her brandy snifter on the concrete deck.

"I'm sorry." She couldn't believe she'd been so careless. She rose to her knees to look over the edge.

"Don't move," he told her, setting his own glass down.

"I'm so stupid," she said.

"I'll clean it up."

"You have bare feet."

"I'll get some shoes."

He turned back to her, wrapping his hands around her

shoulders, gazing into her eyes. "I will give you space," he promised.

"That was my fault, too." She had to make the admission.

"What do you want?" he asked. "Just tell me what it is, and I'll do it."

What she wanted was impossible. She wanted the fantasy that had never been true. She wanted their marriage to be what he'd pretended.

"I don't think you can," she whispered.

"Okay," he gave a nod of acceptance. "Okay. But that doesn't mean I won't stop trying."

She watched him rise from the water, the droplets sliding off his broad shoulders, the arms that held her so tightly, his abs, his thighs, everything she'd kissed and touched as they'd made love so many times.

How could he try? What could he possibly do?

There was no way to go back and turn his lies into the truth.

Nine

Deacon dug in and worked hard to learn about Hale Harbor Port. Callie didn't know that his interest in the company was tied to her. She assumed he'd been working there for years, and he hadn't corrected her. So he was on eggshells, thinking she might ask a question he couldn't answer.

Aaron and Beau sure hadn't made the learning curve easy. They wouldn't answer a single question, and Deacon was convinced they were actively turning staff members against him.

But he'd persisted. He'd poured over their billing, accounts payable and receivable, their terminal schedules, traffic volume, even cargo manifests. After hours and hours of work, he'd come to a simple but startling conclusion. Hale Harbor Port was losing money.

He presented his findings to Tyrell, Aaron and Beau at the boardroom table in the castle's business wing.

Tyrell showed little reaction. "We're aware of it," he said.

"It can't continue." Deacon didn't have to fully understand the port business to know that much.

"It's won't continue," Beau said. "It's a temporary slump."

"You have to revise your pricing structure." Deacon didn't buy that it was a temporary slump. He knew from his work at Mobi that the transportation sector had fundamentally changed over the past decade. Everyone had to look at new approaches.

"And price ourselves out of the market?" Beau asked. "It's competitive out there."

"That's obviously not what I meant," Deacon countered.

"What do you mean?" Aaron asked.

Beau turned on his brother. "You're going to take him seriously? He's been here all of five minutes, and you're ready to take his advice."

"Nobody's taking his advice," Tyrell said.

Deacon rocked back in his chair. "Sure. Ignore me. Stick your head in the sand and—" As he spoke, he caught a glimpse of movement through the boardroom window.

He could see all the way across the courtyard, through a window into another part of the castle. It looked like… It was. Callie was in the next wing. He leaned forward for a better view.

"We should at least monitor it," Aaron said.

"We are monitoring it," Tyrell said.

Then Deacon spotted James. He looked disproportionately tall, and Deacon realized he was standing on something. He raised his arms, holding them out to his sides.

"We do have accountants," Beau drawled.

A man approached James, reaching across his outstretched arms. Deacon all but cheered. The man was the tailor. The boys were being measured for suits. They were staying for the ball. Callie was staying for the ball.

A wave of relief passed through Deacon.

"Is that funny?" Tyrell asked.

Deacon refocused his attention. "What?"

"Is it funny that we have accountants?"

"Of course not." Deacon stole one more glance across the courtyard.

James and Ethan were going to look terrific in little tuxedos. Deacon was buying one for himself. He didn't think a tuxedo would come anywhere near to changing Callie's mind about him. But it couldn't hurt either.

"We're not making a major decision today," Tyrell said.

"I'm only suggesting we gather more data," Deacon said, refocusing. "We should look at options."

"What kind of options?" Aaron asked.

"Will you stop humoring him," Beau demanded.

"Vertical integration," Deacon said.

Beau threw up his hands in frustration, but Aaron looked interested.

"Again," Beau said. "He's been here five minutes."

"I've been alive longer than that," Deacon said evenly. "I've been in the transportation industry for years. There's money there. Global supply chains are growing, trade agreements are popping up all over the world. At the retail level, bricks and motor are out, delivery is in. Hale Harbor could be at the nexus of a game-changer."

"Vertical integration." Aaron's head tilted thoughtfully.

"We've operated steady as she goes for hundreds of years," Tyrell said.

"Exclusive agreements," Deacon said to Aaron. "With a firm like Mobi Transport."

"There it is," said Beau. "He wants to use Hale Harbor Port to beef up Mobi."

"It was only an example," Deacon said. "And I meant the other way around, use a company like Mobi Transportation to beef up Hale Harbor Port."

"How?" Aaron asked.

"I've had enough of this." Beau came to his feet.

"We have other business on the agenda," Tyrell said. "But let's break for lunch." He also came to his feet.

Deacon allowed himself another glance across the courtyard, seeing Callie in profile. She was talking to Margo, and the two were watching the tailor try to wrangle Ethan.

Beau and Tyrell left the room, but Aaron stayed seated. He tapped a pen on his leather folder. "How?" he repeated to Deacon.

"Does it matter?" Deacon asked. He knew Aaron was as hostile toward him as Beau. Aaron simply hid it better.

"Do you have a good idea or not?"

Deacon figured he had nothing to lose. "Buy or take an equity position in Mobi, or in another company along the chain, like a maritime shipping company. Mobi is nice because it's local, it's small. So a good place to start and test the methodology. Give them preferential pricing, so they use Hale Harbor exclusively."

"*Lower* prices? Lose more money?"

"Increase volume, streamline processes, make the port it-self revenue neutral, then get profitable through the subsid-iary businesses."

"Do you have *any* idea what you're talking about?"

"I'm only saying it's worth exploring."

"The magnitude of that change is ridiculous."

"You got a better idea?"

Aaron came to his feet. "Not yet. But there has to be a dozen better ideas than that. Beau's right. You've been here five minutes."

Squelching his disappointment, Deacon let his gaze rest on Callie. He might have lost this round with Tyrell and the boys, but Callie was staying, at least for another week. It was a win for him on that front.

"The slump could be temporary," Aaron said.

"Maybe." Deacon didn't think so.

Aaron started for the door. "It always has been in the past."

"This isn't the past," Deacon tossed over his shoulder.

Given the choice between lunch and seeing Callie, he was taking Callie.

He left the boardroom and made his way along the sec-ond-floor hallway. The castle was big and rambling, with circuitous hallways, dead ends, multistory grand halls and winding stairways. He had to go up to the third floor and make his way along an open loft hallway, then come down to traverse a kitchen, drawing curious looks from a couple of staff members.

But he finally made it to the other side of the courtyard. He found the second floor and heard the boys' voices.

They were in a dressing room of some kind, though it was the size of a dance hall. He wondered if Margo had all her clothes custom made and if Tyrell and their sons did, as well.

"Daddy," Ethan cried, jumping down from the stool to the obvious chagrin of the tailor.

"What's going on here?" Deacon asked cheerfully as Ethan trotted toward him.

"We're getting new clothes," James answered, heading for Deacon.

"Special, special clothes," Ethan spun around.

Deacon caught Callie's gaze. "You're going to the ball."

Ethan made a throwing motion with his hand.

"There will be dessert," James said.

"You know I like dessert," Deacon said, ruffling Ethan's hair.

Margo kept her attention on the tailor, doing her best to pretend Deacon wasn't there. He wondered how long she planned to keep giving him the cold shoulder. He wasn't going away.

He crossed the room to Callie. "You made a decision?" he asked her on an undertone.

"Time for lunch," Margo said brightly to the boys. "Who wants grilled cheese?"

"Me, me," Ethan said.

"Yes, please," James said.

"Let's go find Dee." Margo hustled the boys out, while the tailor retreated to a table at the far end of the room.

"I should go," Callie said, watching the doorway where her sons had left.

"I'm glad you're staying," Deacon said.

"Don't make any assumptions."

"I'm not."

"It's not for you."

"I know." He wished it was, but he acknowledged full well it wasn't.

"Margo is… She's really grown attached to the boys."

Deacon hadn't seen himself ever being grateful to Margo. But he was now. In this moment, he silently thanked her for her doting ways. It bought him some time.

He didn't know what he was going to do with that time. He had absolutely no plan. But it was better than the alternative.

* * *

As she tucked the boys into bed, Callie hoped she was doing the right thing by staying for the ball. It was a form of torture being around Deacon, wanting him, missing him, trying desperately to stay angry with him.

"Mommy," James said as she smoothed the covers around him.

"Yes, sweetheart?"

"Is Grandma very smart?"

"I think so. She seems pretty smart."

"Okay."

"Why do you ask?"

"She says a red tie will make me shine."

"I bet you'll look terrific in a red tie."

"Ethan's snoring again."

Callie listened for a moment. "Just a little bit. It's a quiet snore."

"It sounds like an angry dog."

She gave James a hug. "Your brother's not an angry dog."

"Okay. You're smarter than Grandma."

"I'm glad you think I'm smart." Callie came to her feet. She couldn't help but be warmed by the compliment. She also couldn't help but be curious about the scale James was using to make his assessment.

"Grandma gets mixed up," James said.

"About what?"

"She calls Ethan Beau."

Callie stilled, unnerved, but not completely sure why. "Ethan looks like Uncle Beau did when he was little."

"Uncle Beau looks like an angry dog. He frowns all the time."

"Does Uncle Beau frighten you?"

"No." James sounded completely unconcerned. "I bet he snores."

Callie breathed a sigh of relief. "Good night, James."

"Good night, Mommy."

She left the door partway open as she walked into the hall.

She'd heard Deacon come in while she was reading the boys a story. He was home earlier than usual. She toyed with the idea of going straight to bed. It would be better if she didn't see him tonight. It was emotionally safer to keep her distance.

But she'd left some dishes in the sink, her book was on the table in the family room and she'd been looking forward to a cup of tea. She might struggle with her feelings around him, but she didn't want to hide in her room either.

She started down the stairs.

Deacon was talking, she assumed on the phone. But then she heard another voice. It was oddly familiar, but she couldn't place it.

She followed the sounds into the living room to find the two men standing, facing each other.

Deacon saw her.

The man turned. He was shorter than Deacon, stockier, his hair was long, straggly, and he wore a pair of wrinkled jeans, scuffed black boots and a navy blue T-shirt. The skin of his face looked soft. He had a stubble beard and familiar blue eyes.

"Hello, Callie." His voice sent a shiver down her spine, and she flinched as she recognized him.

"Trevor?" It was her oldest brother, but he sounded frighteningly like her father.

"Long time, no see, baby sister."

"*What* are you doing here?" She hadn't seen or heard from him since the day he stormed out of their tacky little house in Grainwall.

He'd been eighteen. She'd been only nine.

"Is that any way to greet your brother?" He moved toward her.

She was too stunned to move, and he gave her a hug.

She was suddenly transported back to her childhood, to the screaming matches between her brothers and father, to the barked orders for her to bring them beer, make them sandwiches and *to clean that kitchen the hell up*. Everything inside her cringed.

After what seemed like an eternity, he stepped back. "I hear you got married."

She struggled to find her voice. "How did you find me?"

Why had he looked?

After her father had died, one by one, her three brothers had left home, until she was alone with her mother. None of them had ever come back. None of them had helped, not when her mother got sick, not when her mother had died. None of them ever cared that Callie had been orphaned at sixteen.

"Social media. It's a wonderful thing."

"Can I offer you a drink?" Deacon asked. "Please, sit down."

Callie wanted to shout *no*. If Trevor started drinking, he'd never stop.

"Don't mind if I do." Trevor popped himself down on a sofa and patted the seat next to him.

She took an armchair.

"What would you like?" Deacon asked.

"A brew if you've got one." Trevor glanced around the room.

"Merlot, Callie?" Deacon asked, knowing it was one of her favorites.

"I was going to make tea."

"Sure." Deacon left for the kitchen.

"Done real well for yourself, Callie," Trevor drawled.

Now that Deacon was out of the room, Trevor's eyes hardened in appraisal.

Callie's stomach started to hurt. The sights and sounds and smells of her childhood swelled up inside her head. She hadn't thought about her father in years, or her brothers, or even her mother for that matter. But now she pictured her father yelling, her mother sobbing in the corner and Trevor laughing drunkenly.

She couldn't remember who hit whom. There were frequent

fistfights amongst the boys, and her dad was quick to slap her mother. Callie herself hadn't been a target. They yelled at her and shoved her, but she didn't remember getting hit.

She did remember being terrified.

"Cat got your tongue?" Trevor asked.

She swallowed. She wanted to tell him to leave, to go away, to never come back. But she couldn't bring herself to do it. The frightened little girl inside her didn't have the courage to stand up.

"Never mind." Trevor looked her up and down. "You don't have to say anything for me to get how it is. You've landed on your feet. I've got my trouble, but you landed on your feet."

Deacon came back, and Callie was incredibly grateful to see him. He carried a mug of tea in one hand and two bottles of beer in the other. He set her tea down beside her, then handed Trevor a beer.

"Are you visiting Hale Harbor?" Deacon asked Trevor. Deacon chose the armchair opposite Callie and twisted the cap off his beer.

"Came to look in on Callie," Trevor said. "Been kicking around Alabama for a while now." He guzzled half his beer.

"Oh. What is it you do?"

"Little of this, little of that."

Deacon glanced at Callie.

She was frozen. She couldn't speak, and she couldn't move. A part of her knew it was ridiculous to be afraid of Trevor. He couldn't do anything, especially not with Deacon here. But she couldn't shake the visceral fear.

Deacon guzzled a good measure of his beer, and Trevor grinned at him in a way that said he'd met a kindred spirit.

"You married my sister," Trevor said.

"I did."

"Didn't get a wedding invitation."

"It was a small wedding."

"Really." Trevor seemed surprised. "I thought you well-to-do people put on posh parties."

"Sometimes," Deacon said politely.

Callie ordered herself to speak up, to say something. It wasn't fair to force Deacon to carry on this conversation with her brother.

Trevor took another long guzzle of his beer.

Callie asked, "Are you married?"

Trevor swung his gaze to her. "Never met the right gal."

Callie was silently grateful on behalf of womenkind. If Trevor had turned out anything like her father—which it seemed he had—then no woman deserved to end up with him.

"No kids either," Trevor said.

Callie did *not* want to talk about her sons. "Have you heard from Joe or Manny?"

She lifted her mug of tea, willing her hand not to shake.

"Can't say that I have. But maybe we should look them up. Maybe we should have ourselves a family reunion."

Callie immediately regretted asking the question.

Deacon polished off his beer and pointedly set down the bottle. "It was nice of you to drop by," he said to Trevor and came to his feet. He glanced at his watch. "Why don't you leave your number, and we'll be in touch."

Trevor looked flummoxed and then annoyed. "Well…" He looked to Callie, but she focused on her tea. "I was…" He didn't seem to know how to counter Deacon's dismissal.

Callie was immensely grateful.

"Sure," Trevor said, polishing off his beer.

He set the bottle on the end table with a thud and rose to his feet.

Deacon walked to a side table and produced a pen and paper. "Just write it down," he said to Trevor.

Trevor scrutinized Callie as he passed, but thankfully he didn't say anything to her.

She was vaguely aware of Deacon seeing Trevor out, and then Deacon was back.

He dropped to one knee in front of her, concern in his expression. "What on earth?"

"They're *awful*." The words burst out of her, and she started to shake.

Deacon quickly took the mug from her hands and set it aside.

"All of them," she said. "They're mean and violent."

"Did he hurt you?"

"Not me. Not physically. Not much."

Deacon pulled her into his arms, holding her close.

She couldn't help herself. She tucked her head against his shoulder and closed her eyes, absorbing his strength as fear and dismay shuddered through her.

"I thought I was over it," she said.

"Tell me what happened."

Everything inside Deacon told him to go after Trevor. Whatever it was that Trevor had done to Callie in the past had hurt her badly. He should be held responsible. Deacon wanted justice for the way Callie was shaking in his arms.

But Callie needed him.

He eased her to one side of the big chair and sat down himself, drawing her into his lap, cradling her close and rubbing her arms.

"Tell me," he gently urged.

Whatever it was, he was going to make it better. Somehow, some way, he was going to make it better.

"How could they do that?" she asked, her voice a rasp. "How could they be so cruel? I was just a little girl."

He listened while she told him about the family's abject poverty. There was never enough money for food and clothes. She'd gone to school in castoffs from the church rummage sale. Their electricity was often turned off. They barely had heat, never mind air conditioning in the summer. And she'd slept for years on a damp mattress on the floor.

Meanwhile, she and her mother had waited on her father and brothers hand and foot, enduring shouts, curses and shoves. She told Deacon about the terror she felt when her parents fought, how her father slapped her mother, and how she'd been relieved when her father had died of a heart attack.

But her brothers hadn't let up. It wasn't until they finally left home, one by one, that she had any peace. Money was still tight, and then her mother got sick. At fourteen, she'd found a part-time job and tried desperately to hold it together financially. But then her mom died, and the hospital bills came due, and Callie had quit school.

While she spoke, her shaking slowly subsided. "Frederick was the first person to care for me. He was so kind. He was so gentle. I was never afraid of him."

She was a limp bundle of heat in Deacon's arms. Twin tear tracks glistened on her cheeks. Her hair was tousled, her legs were curled up.

"Have you ever told anyone about this?" he asked gently.

"There was no one to tell. Frederick had more problems than I could imagine."

"He had different problems."

"I couldn't tell him. I didn't want to tell him. It was in the past by then." She gave a shaky laugh. "I wanted to pretend it had happened to someone else. I wasn't her anymore, that defenseless little girl, exploited like a servant." She fell silent.

"I'm glad you told me." Deacon kissed her temple.

She sighed and rested her head against his shoulder.

He kissed away the tear track on her cheek. Her lips were dark and soft and sweet, and he gave in to temptation, kissing her tenderly, trying to will away her pain and heartache.

She kissed him back.

But then she gasped and turned her head away. "Deacon."

"I know," he said, wrapping his arms fully around her, holding her desperately close. "I won't let it get away from us. I promise."

"We can't."

"We won't." He rocked her. "Just let me hold you."

Minutes ticked past before he felt her relax.

He wanted to kiss her again, but he knew he'd be lost. And

he couldn't let himself do that. She needed his comfort, not his lust.

He sat for an hour.

He didn't know exactly when she fell asleep, but she did.

He didn't want to put her down. He didn't want to let her go. But he had something to do, and he wasn't going to let it wait.

He carried her upstairs, laid her gently on her bed and pulled a comforter overtop of her.

Then he set his jaw, trotted down the stairs and took the paper with Trevor's phone number. He dialed as he walked to his car and opened the driver's door.

"Yo," Trevor answered, music twanging in the background.

"It's Deacon Holt." Deacon climbed in and shut the door, pressing the ignition button.

There was a brief pause on the line. "Well, Mr. Holt. That didn't take long."

"I want to meet," Deacon said, an adrenalin buzz energizing his system. He pictured Trevor in a seedy bar.

"Sure. Can do. When would you like this meeting?"

"Now. Where are you?"

There was another pause and a muttered voice. "It's called The Waterstreet Grill."

Deacon knew the place. It wasn't a dive. Too bad.

"I'll be there in ten minutes."

"You got it," Trevor said.

Deacon hung up the phone and pulled out of the driveway. It was after ten o'clock, so the roads were mostly clear. He lowered the windows and let the breeze flow in, trying to cool his temper. He kept picturing Trevor, who was six feet tall, shouting at a miniature Callie, her lugging cans of beer, and him chugging them down.

He smacked his hands on the steering wheel, swore out loud and pressed his foot on the accelerator. He made it to The Waterstreet Grill and swung into the curb out front. It was a no parking zone, but he really didn't care if they towed him.

He left the car, crossed the sidewalk and shoved open the heavy door.

It was dim inside the grill. The restaurant section was almost empty, but the bar was full. Country-pop came out of ceiling speakers, and cigarette smoke wafted in through an open door to the side alley.

He spotted Trevor talking with two other men at the bar. He made his way over.

"Yo, Deacon," Trevor said with a wide smile. He held up his hand to shake.

Deacon ignored it. He cocked his head toward the open door.

"You can talk in front of my friends," Trevor said. He clapped one of the men on the back. "This here's—"

"I don't want to talk in front of your friends," Deacon said.

Trevor's expression fell. "Chill, bro."

Deacon grimaced. "Shall we step outside?"

"Is this a fight?" Trevor asked with an uncomfortable laugh.

"No. But it can be." Deacon turned for the side door, confident that Trevor would follow.

Deacon passed two groups of smokers in the alley and went a few feet further.

"You're the one who called me," Trevor said as he caught up.

Deacon pivoted. "Callie is not your gravy train."

Trevor's eyes narrowed and crackled, his passive demeanor vanishing. "She's my sister. We're family."

"What you were to her isn't family."

"Got a birth certificate that says different."

"She owes you nothing."

"Let her tell me that."

Deacon stepped forward into Trevor's space. "You're never speaking to her again."

"Are you threatening me?"

Deacon reached into his jacket pocket and withdrew a check. He knew exactly why Trevor had come back into Callie's life, and he was taking the most direct route to sending him away.

"Consider this the carrot," he said, planting the check against Trevor's chest. "If it doesn't work, I've got a stick."

Trevor stepped back, grabbing at the check. He looked down, his widening eyes giving away his surprise at the amount.

"You're gone," Deacon said. "And you're never coming back."

"Is this good?" Trevor asked.

"Gone," Deacon repeated and turned to walk away.

He hoped he'd made his point.

Ten

James and Ethan looked adorable in their matching tuxes. James wore a red bowtie, while Ethan's was royal blue. Callie was a ridiculously proud mom.

Deacon looked magnificent, while Callie couldn't help but feel beautiful in her designer gown, with its glittering bodice, peekaboo back and flowing chiffon skirt. Deacon had insisted she buy it. And she'd been inclined to make him happy, since he'd been so supportive about Trevor.

Deacon said he had spoken to Trevor and promised her that her brother wouldn't be back. She hadn't asked Deacon what he'd said. She didn't care. It was enough that she didn't have the weight of her family hanging over her head.

"Mommy, Grandma gave us pudding," James said with excitement as he arrived holding Dee's hand.

"Mousse," Dee told Callie.

"Chocolate?" Callie asked.

"We were careful of their white shirts."

"It's nearly eight o'clock," Callie said. She didn't give the boys sugar, never mind chocolate, after five.

"Oh, don't worry so much," Margo said, arriving with a fluttery wave of her hand.

"We should probably take them home soon." Callie looked around for Deacon. She didn't mind driving the boys home on her own if he wanted to stay.

"What's the rush?" Margo asked.

"They'll be getting tired," Callie said.

"I'm not tired," James said.

"They're doing fine. Their grandpa and I still want to show them off."

Callie hesitated. The boys did seem to still have energy. It was probably the chocolate, but she understood Margo's perspective. She had gone to a lot of trouble for tonight.

"A little while," Callie agreed.

"I'll stay with them," Dee said.

"I can come along." Callie knew she should keep an eye on their moods.

"Don't be silly," Margo said. "Go find Deacon and have a dance."

In the face of the onslaught, Callie gave in. A selfish part of her did want to dance in her new gown. A foolish part of her wanted to dance with Deacon.

To do that, she'd have to throw caution to the wind.

She paused to give her saner side an opportunity to talk her out of it. Instead, she admitted this was a caution-to-the-wind kind of night. Her toddler had just eaten chocolate pudding at eight o'clock.

She caught sight of Deacon across the room.

He met her gaze and smiled.

She felt the attraction arc between them. She returned his smile and started toward him.

He must have seen something in her eyes, because he looked puzzled. Then he looked pleased, then he looked flat-out sexy.

"Dance?" she asked without giving herself a second to hesitate.

"Absolutely." He took her hand and led her toward the dance floor.

There was a small orchestra in the corner of the grand ballroom. The polished floor was smooth under her feet. Deacon's lead was sure, his steps perfect, his arm wonderful around her waist.

"This is some party," she said as they twirled across the floor.

"It's been a tradition for two hundred years."

She drew back. "Seriously?"

"The Clarksons are big on tradition. Take a look at the

walls. Those are real swords and shields from the ancestors back home. The Clarksons came over on the Mayflower and fought in the civil war."

"Which side?"

"This is Virginia, ma'am. Both sides."

Callie grinned. "That's hedging your bets."

The music changed to a slower rhythm, and Deacon went quiet. His hand moved against the small of her back, gently stroking, his thumb touching the skin revealed by the open back of her dress.

She knew she shouldn't sink into the sensation, but she couldn't help herself. She shifted closer and closer, until she was flush against him. He put his cheek to her hair, and she burrowed into the crook of his neck.

Desire pulsed deep into her body. The music flowed louder. Voices around them disappeared. The other dancers faded to a swirl of color.

Then she heard it, faint but unmistakable. It was Ethan's cry.

She jumped back from Deacon.

He seemed stunned. "What?"

"Ethan," she called. "Something's wrong." She rushed toward the sound.

"No," Ethan was shouting.

Callie rushed as fast as she could on her high heels.

She could see Margo talking to Ethan.

Ethan screwed up his face and shook his head.

Tyrell said something, and Ethan looked up. At first he looked scared, but then he dropped to the floor and squealed.

Tyrell reached down and pulled him back to his feet as Callie came within earshot.

"—and behave yourself!" Tyrell's tone was sharp.

Callie quickly crouched to put her arms around her son. "Sweetheart? What is it?"

Ethan started to cry.

She stood, wrapping him in her arms.

"I don't think coddling him will help," Tyrell said.

Callie glared at him. She didn't care that this was his house, and that he was the party's host. Ethan was her son, and her parenting choices were none of Tyrell's business.

This was all her fault, not Ethan's. It was nearly nine o'clock.

James was watching the whole thing with wide eyes.

She took his hand. "It's time for us to go home, honey."

"Oh, there's no need for that." Margo's tone was soothing.

Deacon arrived. "Is everything all right?"

Margo spoke directly to Deacon. It was the first time Callie had seen her do that.

"I was just telling Callie there's no need for her to leave early. We've set up the nursery for the boys."

Callie didn't want the nursery. She didn't want to stay here any longer. She wanted to take her boys home to their own beds.

"Ethan?" Dee came up close to him. "Would you like me to read you a story? You can have a bubble bath, too."

Callie didn't like the idea. "I think it's better if we—"

Ethan's voice was watery. "Which story?"

"The Pig and the Duck."

"The whole thing?" Ethan asked.

"I like *The Pig and the Duck*," James said. "And I like bubbles."

Ethan stopped crying and raised his head, looking at Callie.

"Do you want Dee to read you a story?" she asked.

Ethan nodded.

Deacon touched her shoulder and whispered in her ear. "It's completely up to you."

"There's a room made up for you, too," Margo said. "It's right across the hall from the nursery. You wouldn't have to disturb them at the end of the party."

Against her better judgement, Callie took the path of least resistance. They were only moments from the nursery. It would take at least half an hour to get the boys loaded into the car and back home. By the time they got there, Ethan would be truly miserable.

"Okay," she said. "Dee can put you to bed." She handed Ethan to Dee, who took James's hand to walk away.

"You shouldn't encourage that kind of behavior," Tyrell said to Callie.

"Don't," Deacon warned him. "Callie is a fantastic mother."

"It was the chocolate." Callie felt the need to defend Ethan. It might not have been his finest hour, but he wasn't the one to blame.

"Shall we dance again?" Deacon asked her.

She took him up on the offer. It might not be the smart thing, but she missed Deacon's arms, and she wanted to get away from Margo and Tyrell.

She knew Tyrell had a big personality, that he preferred things his own way, but this was the first time it had touched her personally. And on the heels of her brother's unsettling visit, it was more than she could take.

Deacon heard Callie open then close the bedroom door. She'd been across the hall, checking on James and Ethan, and now she set the baby monitor on a small table.

It was after midnight, and the party was quickly winding to a close. Although there were still dozens of guests, not to mention the staff, in the halls below, the castle walls were thick, and here on the second floor, it was completely quiet.

The room was large, with warm wooden walls, recessed windows showing the original stone structure, heavy ceiling beams and a thick woven carpet. There was a massive carved wood canopy bed in the center, flanked by two armchairs around a fireplace and a small table and chair set. The walk-in closet and the connected bathroom were at opposite ends of the room.

Callie looked tired but beautiful in her flowing gown. Her upswept hair was wispy around her face, and when she reached down to strip off her high heels, Deacon felt a surge of desire. It was pathetic, really, finding her bare feet that sexy.

"Are the boys okay?" he asked as a conversation opener. He didn't want to address the sleeping arrangements head on.

"Did it seem weird to you?" she asked. "Earlier, I mean." She looked around the floor, settling on putting her shoes beneath the upholstered bench positioned at the foot of the bed.

"Did what seem weird?" All Deacon remembered was holding her in his arms on the dance floor, watching her talk and smile with the other guests, not being able to take his gaze off her all night long.

"Margo with the boys. I mean, Tyrell was a jerk. I don't want him alone with the boys, especially Ethan."

"I understand." Deacon had no intention of letting Tyrell babysit.

"But Margo." Callie perched on the bench. "Does she seem a bit possessive to you?"

"She adores her grandsons." That had been obvious to Deacon from minute one.

"That nursery." Callie pointed across the hall. "It's full of toys and clothes. They could live there forever if they wanted."

Deacon moved closer to Callie. "The Clarksons do have a lot of money."

She tipped her chin to look up. "I know. It's just a funny feeling I get around her lately. She called Ethan *Beau*. James told me that."

"They do look alike."

"Yeah. You're right. I guess it's not that strange."

"Are you okay staying here?" he asked.

"It doesn't make any sense to wake the boys up."

Deacon looked meaningfully to the big bed, the only place in the room for either of them to sleep. "I mean..."

It seemed to occur to her for the first time. "Oh." She drew a sigh. "I'm so exhausted, I don't even care. Will it bother you?"

"Not in the least." He was surprised by her pragmatic acceptance.

She sized up the bed again. "I doubt we could find each other if we tried."

He'd find her in about half a second. But he wouldn't.

He'd already hung up his jacket, and now he stripped off his tie. As he removed his white shirt, her gaze seemed to stall on his chest. He wanted it to mean something, but he doubted it did.

He held out the shirt. "Here."

"What?"

"You can sleep in this."

She blinked. She paused. "Oh. Okay. Thanks."

He gestured to the bathroom. "Go ahead."

She rose and took the shirt.

She shut the door behind her, and a vision of her changing bloomed in his mind. To distract himself, he removed his shoes and set them next to hers. Then he pulled the curtains on four separate windows. He flicked on a bedside lamp and turned off the overhead lights.

He turned down the bed and fluffed the pillows, folding the heavy spread and laying it across the bench at the foot of the bed.

The bathroom door opened, and Callie emerged. He told himself not to look. It was going to kill him. But he couldn't help himself.

She was backlit, his white shirt slightly translucent, falling to her mid-thigh, the sleeves rolled up along her slender arms, the top button open to make a V-neck.

The world seemed to stop.

"Is there a hanger...?" She removed the gown from a hook inside the door, the motion bringing his shirt against her breasts.

He nearly groaned out loud.

"The closet's over here," he managed.

She draped the gown over her arms.

"I can get that." He quickly took the gown from her arms.

"Thank you."

It took all his strength not to touch her, not to hold her like he had on the dance floor. Her green eyes met his in the shadowy light. She'd scrubbed off her makeup, and there was a fresh glow to her skin.

She was so incredibly, naturally beautiful. And she'd once told him she loved him.

But he'd ruined all that. Right now, he'd have done anything to rewind time, to fix his mistakes, to find a way back to where they'd been in Charleston.

Instead, he had to find a way to keeps his hands off her.

"Deacon," she said in a tentative voice.

"I can do this," he vowed on a whisper.

She looked at the dress, obviously misunderstanding his words.

He gave himself a mental shake. "Go to bed," he told her softly. "You should sleep."

She nodded.

While he hung the gown, she climbed under the covers.

Deacon shut off the bathroom light, stripped to his boxers and joined her, lastly turning the switch on the bedside lamp and plunging the room into darkness.

The blankets rustled, and he felt her move.

"I don't like it here," she said.

"Do you want me to leave?"

There was a short silence. "No. I mean I don't like this place, the castle. It feels, I don't know, dark."

"It is dark." He couldn't see his hand in front of his face.

He wondered if he'd made a mistake in drawing all the curtains. If the boys woke up, he and Callie would probably trip on the furniture getting to them.

"I mean somber. It feels like the walls want to suck the very joy out of life."

"It is cold and hard. Funny, from the outside it always looked grand."

"It's grand on the inside, too."

"It has no soul."

"That's it," she said.

He couldn't see her, but he heard her come up on her elbow. He did the same, facing her in the dark, barely able to discern her outline as his eyes adjusted.

"Do you think it could be haunted?" There was a joking note to her voice.

"By eight generations of Clarksons?" He gave a chuckle. "Now there's a daunting thought."

"Would you protect me?"

"From the ghost of Admiral Frederick Baines Clarkson?" Deacon deepened his voice, speaking with exaggerated drama. "Legend has it that Admiral Clarkson was murdered."

She matched his tone. "Here in the walls of Clarkson Castle?"

"I believe we may be in mortal danger." He gave a pause, glancing around at the tiny rays of light below the curtains. "Shh. Do you hear that?"

The wind was blowing through the battlements.

"Are you trying to scare me?"

"It's his ship's whistle. He's calling his men, still angry they didn't save him."

"You have a vivid imagination." She batted her hand against his shoulder.

The second she touched him, his world stopped.

She stopped.

Then she moved.

Her hand smoothed over his skin, to his neck, to his cheek.

"Callie," he breathed in desperation. "I can't... I won't..."

"I know," she said. "It's..." She shifted closer. Her breath brushed his face. Her lips touched his.

His reaction was immediate. His arm went around her waist, he pressed her into the soft mattress, his mouth opened wide, his kiss went deep. Every sense he had zeroed in on Callie.

Her hand burrowed into his hair, anchoring. Her arm

wound around his neck. Their bodies came tight together, and he absorbed her heat, her softness, her essence.

He kissed her mouth over and over again.

Then he moved to her neck, her shoulders, her breasts.

She gasped his name.

He stripped off her shirt, kicked off his boxers, and they clung naked to each other, limbs entwined. He breathed in her essence, tasted her skin, felt the softness of her lavender-scented hair between his fingertips.

"I've missed you so much," he rasped.

"Oh, Deacon." There was a catch in her voice.

He reached beneath her, tilting her body toward him. Her thighs softly parted. Her legs went around him.

He stopped, poised, holding himself back, wanting the magic to go on forever.

"Deacon, please," she moaned, and he plunged them together.

Her breaths pulsed against him. He kissed her deeply. He cradled her breasts, smoothed the backs of her thighs, captured her body, her core, over and over again.

Her arms convulsed around him, and her hips surged to meet him. Their passion heated the air of the cold castle. The thick walls absorbed their cries. The darkness cocooned them, and every shadow of his heritage disappeared.

The past didn't matter, only the future. And the future was Callie. It had to be Callie.

Her body contracted, pulling him over the edge, and he spiraled irrevocably into paradise.

Coming back home the next day, Callie realized how much she loved Deacon's house. It was welcoming, comfortable and functional. It was roomy, but really just the right size. The kitchen was brilliantly laid out, with every convenience. She could clean up from lunch while watching the boys play with building bricks in the family room.

It had been Deacon's idea to add a toy box to the family

room décor. So the boys could play and easily help clean up afterward. She was even getting used to a housekeeper twice a week. She was over the guilt of having someone else dust, vacuum and scrub her shower.

Now Deacon appeared by her side. She knew he'd been in his study making calls. He'd mentioned he was at odds with Beau over something, and he was trying to put together his own side of the argument. She'd learned he worked seven days a week. He might dial it back a bit on the weekends, but the port never closed, so there was always some problem to be solved.

He gave her a gentle touch on the shoulder. Still on a high from last night, she simply enjoyed the feeling. She'd have to come back down to earth soon. She couldn't simply pretend their marriage had turned normal. But not today—she wasn't going to let reality intrude just yet.

"I thought I'd take them outside for a while," Deacon said. "Maybe run around with the soccer ball and burn off some energy."

"I'm all for that," she said.

"Do you want to take a nap?"

She couldn't help but think the offer was a veiled reference to how little sleep she'd had last night. She'd slept in Deacon's arms, but mostly they'd made love and talked and made love some more. He'd said he missed her. She missed him more than she could have imagined.

"I'm fine," she said now. She really was. There was a spring in her step and energy in her veins.

"I think I'll call Hannah."

"Whatever you want." Deacon gave her a quick kiss on the temple and helped himself to the leftover cheese. "Who wants to play soccer?" he called to the boys.

Ethan jumped to his feet. "Soccer, soccer!"

"I need my red runners," James said.

"Let's gear up." Deacon swung Ethan up on his shoulders, giving Callie a parting wink as they headed for the foyer.

She returned the cold cuts to the refrigerator and wiped down the counter.

After stacking the dishes in the dishwasher, she took the kitchen phone and wandered onto the sundeck, where she could see Deacon and the boys playing on the far side of the yard. The sunshine was warm, and she stretched out on a padded lounger in her shorts and T-shirt. She put on a pair of sunglasses against the glare and dialed the bakery.

"Good afternoon, Downright Sweet Bakery." It was Hannah's voice.

"Are you busy?" Callie asked.

"Callie! Hi! How are you?"

Callie could hear the familiar sounds of the lunch crowd in the background. "I don't want to interrupt."

"It's steady but not bad."

The sounds faded as Hannah obviously moved into the back, probably into the office.

"I just wanted to check in," Callie said.

"It's turning into a good summer. Tourist business has been steady. The city rose garden is under construction. There wasn't another word about putting it at Fifth and Bay Street. I don't know what you said to the Mayor."

"It was Deacon."

"Well, he's magic."

Callie knew the magic was really Deacon's check book. She didn't like it, but she'd gotten over it. The important thing was that business was going well for Hannah.

"Speaking of the Mayor," Hannah said. "He has a serious challenger for re-election."

"I thought he was going for governor."

"Ha! That didn't pan out. Rumor has it his opponent has the support of two Congress Members and some financial backers."

Callie was afraid to hear the details. One thing she'd learned was that she wanted no part of the backroom power and deception, or the deals and betrayals, which often came along with politics.

"So long as he's staying away from you," she said to Hannah.

"Far away. We started a new product line this week."

"Do tell."

"I found a steady source of haskap berries in Colorado. They're supposed to be a superfood, all the rage and a wonderful color and flavor. We've done a muffin, a rainbow lemon loaf and syrup for the vanilla cheesecake."

"I can't wait to try them."

"How are the boys?"

"They're good." Callie focused on the soccer game. "They're kicking a ball around in the backyard with Deacon."

"He's super. You got yourself a great guy there, Callie."

"Yes," she managed. There were so many things about Deacon that were great.

If he hadn't lied about who he was, what he wanted, and his feelings for her, things would be downright perfect. Her heart hollowed out as she watched him laughing with James, passing the ball to Ethan. It was heartbreaking that it all had to end.

"Not yet," she whispered.

"What was that?" Hannah asked.

"Nothing. He's great." Callie could ignore his flaws, at least for a little while.

In the early morning, before Tyrell and Beau arrived in the business wing of the castle, Deacon sought Aaron out in his office. Tyrell occupied the large CEO's office in the corner, beside the boardroom. Tyrell's assistant and three other staff members worked in a common area outside. Aaron, Beau and now Deacon had offices along the north wall, overlooking the harbor and the port in the distance.

"I've fleshed out some more details," Deacon told Aaron, setting a file folder on his deck.

"The vertical integration?" Aaron asked.

"Yes."

"I thought you gave up on that."

"Why would I give up on it? It's a solid solution."

"Because without either Beau or my father's support, it's a nonstarter." But Aaron did open the folder.

"Tyrell might come around," Deacon said.

"You don't know him very well."

Deacon couldn't argue with that. Aaron knew both Beau and Tyrell far better than Deacon did. Aaron was probably right. But Deacon had to try.

Things were going so much better with Callie, that Deacon was beginning to see a future with her: a future with her, a future with the Clarksons and a future managing Hale Harbor Port—both for him and for James and Ethan.

That meant he had to take a long view, to push for what was best. Even if the odds were stacked against him, he had to try.

Aaron was his best bet. Aaron was smart. He was methodical. He wasn't anything like his hotheaded brother, Beau.

Aaron thumbed through the top sheets. "How optimistic are these numbers?"

"They're realistic. We've done a low, medium and high case scenario."

"It might be a range, but it's still only speculative."

Deacon was prepared for the question. "The base data was derived from—"

"Is this a private meeting?" Tyrell's tone from the open doorway was clearly a rebuke.

Deacon had learned Tyrell was an exacting man, a cantankerous man and also a paranoid man.

Aaron closed the file. "Volumetric data and route statistics."

It wasn't a lie, but it wasn't the full truth either. Deacon appreciated Aaron's discretion. It also told him Aaron wasn't completely opposed to pursing the idea of vertical integration. That was encouraging.

"I need to talk to you," Tyrell said to Deacon.

"Sure." Deacon left the file with Aaron in the hopes that he'd read further.

He followed Tyrell to his office, where Tyrell shut the door after them. Tyrell took his position behind the massive dark walnut desk. Beyond him were big recessed windows, the glass so old, it warped the city and mountains behind.

Sounds echoed in the big room, because unlike most of the rest of the castle, Tyrell had not covered the stone walls with paneling. Instead, he'd covered them with vintage oil paintings and coats of arms. The stone floor was worn, and the guest chairs were red velvet and ornate wood, anything but comfortable.

Tyrell sat down, and so did Deacon.

"You've had time to settle in," Tyrell said.

"I have."

"And Callie? And the boys?"

"Them, too." Deacon couldn't help but be curious about where this was going.

It wasn't like Tyrell to ask after anyone's welfare.

"It's been nearly a month," he said.

"Not quite," Deacon said. He was acutely aware of time passing, as he worried about Callie's ultimate decision to stay or go.

"Nevertheless," Tyrell said.

Deacon waited.

"It's time to make some changes."

Deacon's senses went on alert. "Changes to what?"

"To your circumstance. Margo and I have discussed it, and we want you to move into the castle."

The request gave Deacon a jolt. "That was never part of the deal."

And it wasn't something Deacon would ever consider. For one thing, Callie would hate it. For another, Deacon valued his independence far too much. And most importantly, it wouldn't be good for James and Ethan. Deacon planned to keep their exposure to Tyrell at an absolute minimum.

"It's not negotiable," Tyrell said.

"I wasn't planning to negotiate with you. The answer is no. We're not moving into the castle. I don't even know why you'd want us here. Margo can barely stand to look at me."

"That's not her fault."

"No, it's your fault."

"Nevertheless," Tyrell said.

"*Nevertheless* is not a rational argument for anything."

"You *will* move in."

"What part of *no* is getting past you?"

"What part of *will* is getting past *you*?"

"You can't force the issue," Deacon said. "You can't undo the contract. The shares are mine."

Deacon's lawyer had assured him that Tyrell could not renege on the contract.

"That may be true." Tyrell sat forward, bracing his hands on the desk. "But I have the power to change the class of your shares."

Deacon narrowed his eyes, focusing on Tyrell's unyielding expression, trying to imagine where this threat was going.

"With a two-thirds majority vote, I can change your shares from Class A to Class D. That means no voting rights, no position in the company, no dividends. Your interest in the company would be effectively worthless."

Deacon held his composure, refusing to let Tyrell see the news rattled him. Tyrell wouldn't be bluffing. Somehow, in the hundreds of pages of the contract agreement, Tyrell's lawyers had planted a loophole.

"I could sell," Deacon said.

There was nothing Tyrell could do to make the shares completely worthless. And Deacon could throw a wrench in the works by threatening to sell to someone hostile.

"You're forgetting the buyback clause. Hale Harbor Port would be happy to reacquire the shares at the price you paid for them."

"I would sue."

Tyrell laughed at that. "My dear boy, you can try. But you will lose. It will take years and the legal fees would break you."

Deacon clenched his jaw. He racked his brain, but he didn't immediately see another option. And deep down, he knew Tyrell's army of lawyers would have thought through every strategy.

Tyrell truly had no soul.

"I gave you everything you wanted," Deacon said. Though his effort was most certainly doomed, he had to try to reason with Tyrell.

"I wanted my grandsons."

"And they're here."

"No. They're not *here*. They're with you."

"They're with their mother."

"And she can live here."

"She won't agree to it." Deacon was completely sure of that. She'd probably walk out the minute he asked her.

"That's *your* problem," Tyrell said.

He took a pen from the ornate holder in front of him, slipped on his reading glasses and pointedly picked up a report.

"And if I can't convince her to do it?" Deacon asked.

Tyrell peered over the top of his glasses. "Then I convert your shares."

Deacon came to his feet. "You're the real bastard in this family."

"Is that a yes?"

"It looks as though I have no choice."

A smirk twitched Tyrell's mouth. "I'm glad you see things my way."

Eleven

Callie's heart sank as she stared at her brother Trevor in the doorway. Deacon had promised her Trevor wouldn't be back. And she'd believed him.

The boys were playing on the staircase behind her, building jumps for their little race cars.

"You shouldn't be here," Callie said to Trevor.

She felt instantly alone and vulnerable. Deacon wouldn't be home for hours.

"You're gonna want to hear what I have to say," Trevor drawled.

"No, I don't." She started to close the door.

He blocked it with a stiff arm, and her heart thudded hard against her chest.

"What do you want?" she asked, hating the fear in her voice.

"I want to know your game."

"What game? There is no game. Just go, Trevor."

"He paid me off. He paid me good."

Callie hadn't known Deacon had bribed Trevor. But it shouldn't have surprised her. At the moment, she was even grateful.

"So go away. You got what you came for."

Trevor gave a cold laugh. He unexpectedly shoved the door open and walked inside.

James and Ethan both looked up.

"Are these the little tykes?"

"James, take Ethan to the family room. You can watch cartoons."

Trevor moved toward them. "No need for them to skedaddle."

Callie's fear for her own safety evaporated, and she bolted between her brother and her sons. "James, honey, take Ethan. You can each have a cookie while you watch."

"Candy cookies," Ethan sang.

"Okay, Mommy."

"Thank you, sweetheart." She glared at Trevor and listened as the boys left the foyer behind her. "What do you want?" she demanded.

"More of the same."

"Deacon's not going to give you more money."

Trevor took a few steps across the foyer, his black boots glaring against the polished white tile. "I met a guy at the bar, a new drinking buddy of mine."

Callie kept herself between Trevor and the hallway that led to the family room.

"He's a gardener down there at that castle. Word is out on your scam, baby sister."

"I don't know what you're talking about." She wanted him out. She wasn't exactly afraid anymore, but she wanted Trevor out of the house.

"Oh, you know exactly what I'm talkin' about. The two of you are taking that family for millions."

She'd had enough. She marched back to the door and pulled it wide. "Get out."

"Not a chance."

"There is no scam," she said.

Trevor moved closer. "Then why's Deacon never been to the castle before? Why'd nobody even speak his name until he showed up with you? Now he's got the run of the place. Because of your kids." Trevor cast his gaze toward the family room.

"They're Tyrell's grandchildren," she said. "It's not a scam."

"Then it's a bribe," Trevor said with conviction. "And I want in on the action."

"It's not a—"

The word *bribe* echoed ominously inside Callie's head.

Bribes were Deacon's go-to tool. He did it all the time.

"You bribed the old man," Trevor said.

Callie hadn't bribed anyone. But had Deacon? Could Deacon have used the boys to worm his way into the Clarkson family?

If he had, everything suddenly made sense.

Deacon's voice boomed through the room. "What are you doing here?" He grasped Trevor by the collar and hustled him onto the porch.

Trevor only barely kept his footing. "Hey, man, I'm—"

"You're trespassing on private property." Deacon slammed the door in Trevor's face. He whirled to Callie. "Are you all right? Where are the kids?"

"Am I a bribe?" she asked, her voice quavering.

The enormity of what Trevor had just accused Deacon of, and the reality that he could be right, had shaken her to the core.

"What?" Deacon looked dumfounded.

"Trevor said—"

"You're listening to *Trevor*?"

"He said you bribed your way into the Clarkson family, using me and the boys."

The expression on Deacon's face told her it was true.

She gasped and took two steps backward.

He reached for her.

"No! That explains it all. It explains everything. You finding me, pretending to like me, lying to me, manipulating me."

"You have to listen, Callie."

"I don't. I really don't."

James came running through the foyer with his arms outstretched, as he made airplane noises.

Ethan followed in the same posture. "Hi, Daddy."

The two of them did a loop and left again.

"What have you done?" Callie whispered through a throat closing with emotion.

"Tyrell came to me with the offer. He promised me my

birthright, and I was tempted. I admit, I was tempted. It was everything I ever wanted in my life. Everything."

"You took it," she said. "You *took* it."

"No. I didn't. I only agreed to meet you."

"You lied to me and married me, and brought us home like some prize."

"By then I thought you wanted to marry me. I thought you had your own agenda."

"Your money," she said woodenly. "Yeah, I remember that lie, too."

"It all went horribly wrong," he said.

"Not for you. For you, it all went horribly right."

He turned from her and raked a hand through his hair. "Not anymore."

She didn't need to listen to this. She needed to get her boys, pack her things, get out of Hale Harbor and never come back.

Deacon was a liar, and she was never going to see him again. Ever.

Her heart shouldn't hurt this much.

"He wants us to live at the castle," Deacon said.

Callie mutely shook her head. No way, no how. That was *not* going to happen.

"He gave me an ultimatum today. I move you to the castle, or I lose it all."

"They want the boys," she found herself whispering. "They're trying to steal my sons."

"I told him yes."

"What?"

"Only to buy us some time. I came home to tell you everything. And to tell you, you need to leave."

James and Ethan buzzed through, playing airplane again.

"I *am* leaving," she said as her sons trotted out of earshot.

"Today. Right now," Deacon said. "I was going to tell you everything that happened, and then tell you to take the boys, take them to Charleston and never come back. I made a deal with the devil, and I was wrong."

"*Yes*, you were wrong!"

"Thing is…" he said, his tone turning reflective.

She refused to listen. "There's no *thing*. There is nothing."

"I kept trying to stay logical, to stay detached."

"Bully for you." She hadn't had the opportunity to stay logical and detached, because she'd been conned from minute one.

"But I couldn't."

"Stop talking."

"It took me way too long to recognize it, but I fell in love with you."

What was left of her heart shattered into pieces.

"You can't do that," she cried. "You can't say that. You can't wait until after everything else has failed and then throw that out on the table."

"I know."

"You can't."

"I can't. And I won't. Callie, I'm so sorry I let you down."

If the banging on the front door hadn't been so insistent, Deacon wouldn't have bothered answering. The house was eerily quiet with Callie and the boys gone. It had been less than twenty-four hours, and Deacon hadn't yet decided how to move forward.

This morning, he'd found one of Ethan's socks under a sofa cushion. He'd stared at it for a long time, trying to decide whether to wash it and mail it to Charleston or toss it out. Right now, it was sitting on a table in the family room, while he made up his mind.

Through the prismed window of his front door, he recognized Aaron. Deacon didn't particularly want to talk to him, but he didn't care enough to make an issue of it either. He'd rather face Aaron now and send him away than risk him coming back later and disturbing Deacon all over again.

Deacon opened the door.

He was shocked to see Beau standing next to his brother.

"What are you doing here?" he asked them bluntly.

."We want to talk," Aaron said.

Deacon coughed out a laugh of disbelief. "We've got nothing to talk about."

"I think we do," Beau said.

Deacon took in their determined stares. He didn't care enough to fight this either. He stepped back. "Come on in."

They glanced at each other, then stepped into the foyer.

The library was closest, but it was a small room, too intimate for Deacon's liking. He led them back to the living room, with its generous size, cavernous ceilings and huge bank of windows. Whatever they had to say could get lost in the space.

He gestured to a burgundy leather sofa and took the armchair across from it, putting a wide glass-topped table between them.

"We brought you something," Aaron said, placing a document on the table.

"You don't expect me to sign off on converting the shares." Deacon couldn't believe they had the nerve to show up and ask that. He was beginning to work up the energy to fight.

"It's not the shares," Aaron said. "After the last time you and I discussed vertical integration, I did some research."

"Why are you telling me this? I'm out. You both know I'm out."

"Will you listen?" Beau barked.

"Shut up," Aaron told his brother.

"He makes everything difficult," Beau said.

"You can leave anytime," Deacon told Beau.

"I remembered something Frederick worked on six years ago." Aaron pointed to the document. "It's dated, but it has a lot of the same ideas you had. It even mentions Mobi Transportation. Back then, Frederick suggested bringing you into the family fold."

Deacon tried to make sense of that statement.

"Now he's listening," Beau said.

"Frederick didn't even know me," Deacon said.

"He knew of you. He went off to college and came back with a sense of social justice and some big ideas for the port. He shared them with Father, who crushed him like a bug. Father called Frederick *pathetic.*"

Beau sat forward. "But Frederick stood up to him. He said we had to modernize, and he said it was the family's responsibility to include you, because you were Father's son. Father went ballistic."

Deacon was speechless.

"I should have stood up for him back then," Aaron said.

"*We* should have stood up for him back then," Beau said.

"He was right about modernizing," Aaron said. "And he was right about you."

"That's why he walked out?" Deacon asked, trying to wrap his mind around it.

"He had more guts than either of us," Beau said.

"We didn't stand up for Frederick," Aaron said. "We're not going to make the same mistake again. Not with our long-lost brother."

Deacon couldn't believe he'd heard right.

But Beau came to his feet and stuck his hand out to shake. "We're with you in this, brother. We want to stand together."

Deacon rose, and so did Aaron.

"I'm out," Deacon said. "Didn't Tyrell tell you? I won't move to the castle, so he's converting my shares."

"Callie can't move to the castle," Aaron said.

"No kidding," Deacon said.

"Miranda's wanted to leave for a while now," Aaron said. "She's tired of dealing with Mother and Father all the time. I didn't have it in me before, but I do now. We're moving out."

"Well, I'm not staying there by myself," Beau said.

"What will the old man do?" Deacon asked Aaron.

"He can't do anything if we stick together."

"Are we going to shake on this?" Beau asked, sticking his hand out more firmly.

Deacon shook. "I'm flattered. I'm really overwhelmed." His emotions couldn't seem to sort themselves out. "But, like I said, it's too late."

Aaron smiled. He shook Deacon's hand then added his other hand overtop. "You haven't been paying attention." Aaron paused for what looked like effect. "Tyrell needs a two-thirds majority to convert your shares. We won't give it to him."

Beau pointed around the circle at the three of them. "And between us, we've got more than two-thirds."

Deacon could not believe what he was hearing.

"We're in favor of vertical integration," Aaron said. "Want to come with us and tell Dad?"

"We?" Deacon started speaking slowly. "The three of us? We're going up against Tyrell?"

"He's traveling, but will be back in two days," Aaron said. "I think we should do this in person. You in?"

"He's going to flip." Beau grinned as he said it.

"Where's Callie?" Aaron asked, glancing around.

"She moved back to Charleston."

Beau frowned. "Why?"

"She left." Deacon saw no point in hiding the truth. "She didn't like being used as a pawn. She particularly didn't like me exploiting her children for personal gain."

Aaron looked confused. "But I thought the two of you were…"

"Not so much," Deacon said, fighting to hide his despair.

"Man, I'm going to miss those little guys," Beau said.

Deacon missed them so much, he could barely breathe.

And Callie, Callie…

He might have his birthright and two new brothers, and he was grateful for both of those things. But none of it made up for losing Callie.

He'd made mistake after mistake. He'd hurt her badly, and he deserved his misery.

* * *

Being back at the bakery was surreal for Callie. In some ways, the past two months seemed like a dream—a breathtaking, bewildering, heartbreaking dream.

Her chest was hollow where her heart used to be, but everything else was normal. She looked the same. She talked the same. She acted the same. And the world around her hadn't changed at all.

Hannah nudged her elbow, and Callie realized she was standing at the counter, staring off into space, while a customer waited for service.

"Nancy?" Hannah prompted, gesturing to the customer.

Nancy stepped up to help.

In the meantime, Hannah reached into the display case and extracted two oversize vanilla cupcakes with mountains of buttercream and caramel sprinkles.

"We need to talk," she said to Callie.

"About what?" Callie asked.

"This way." Cupcakes on plates, Hannah headed around the end of the counter, into the dining area.

When Callie joined her at a corner table, Hannah handed her a fork and pushed one of the cupcakes in front of her.

"If ever there was a woman in need of buttercream…" Hannah said.

Callie had to admit, the cupcake looked unusually appealing. "I haven't had one of these in a very long time." She took a forkful of the rich, fluffy frosting and lifted it to her mouth.

"You haven't been this despondent in a very long time," Hannah said, digging into her own cupcake.

"I'm not despondent." Callie thought she was putting on a very brave front, especially considering how she felt inside.

Deacon was out of her life. It had only been three days, but it felt like a year. She'd lost count of the times James and Ethan had asked about Deacon.

Hannah's expression was full of sympathy. "What really happened?"

"It didn't work out." Callie had decided to keep her explanation simple.

"You were head over heels for that guy."

Callie felt her eyes mist up, and she covered her emotions with a bite of cupcake.

Hannah waited.

"It was a mistake," Callie said.

"It's never a mistake to fall in love."

"It is with the wrong guy."

Hannah tilted her head, her puzzlement clear. "Deacon was the right guy. He wasn't Hank, he wasn't—"

"He was worse than Hank." The words were out before Callie could think better of them.

"You're going to have to explain that." Hannah's tone was gentle but implacable.

Callie stopped eating. Her stomach couldn't take it.

"It was a con, Hannah. It was all a ruse." Once she started, she couldn't seem to stop herself. "Deacon's biological father, the rich and infamous Tyrell Clarkson—Frederick's father, too, by the way."

Hannah slowly set down her fork.

"Frederick was legitimate, but Deacon wasn't. Frederick hated his father, so he never told me anything about his family. I'm glad he didn't. It was the right decision to keep us apart. It would have been better if I'd never met any of them. But then Tyrell promised Deacon a share of the family fortune if he brought me back to Hale Harbor."

"How big of a share?"

"*That's* your question?"

Hannah gave a shrug. "Don't you wonder how much it took?"

"It was a lot."

"Millions?"

"Hundreds of millions."

Hannah's brow shot up.

"I suppose it's good to know I'm worth that much." Callie

gave a slightly hysterical laugh, quickly covering her mouth. "It wasn't so much me. It was the boys. Tyrell's grandsons. His only grandchildren."

Hannah's palm went to her chest. "Oh, Callie. Deacon only pretended to love you?"

Callie gave a miserable nod.

"I'm so sorry."

"He told me he didn't love me."

"That's brutal."

"It was…" Callie's brain flashed a kaleidoscope of Deacon. "And then…in the end…when it was all falling apart, he even used that as a tactic."

"I don't understand."

Callie felt her misery turn to bitterness. "When Deacon couldn't deliver, when he couldn't get me to move the boys to the castle, Tyrell pulled out the rug. He took back Deacon's share of the company. And at that point, Deacon said he loved me." She snapped her fingers in the air. "Suddenly, he'd fallen in love with me."

"The castle?"

Callie gave a small shudder at the memory. "The Clarksons have an actual castle. You should have seen it. It's positively medieval. I could never in a thousand years live there."

As she spoke, her mind was drawn back to the night she'd spent in Deacon's arms, making such sweet sexy love with him in that castle. Their whispered conversations, the laughter, his warmth, his scent, his taste—for those few short hours, she thought it was going to work out. She thought they could make a life together.

"Callie?" Hannah interrupted Callie's memories. "You zoned out on me there."

Callie dragged herself back to reality. "It was nothing but a ruse."

"He admitted he didn't love you."

"Yes." Callie picked up her fork and determinedly dug into

the cupcake again. She wasn't going to let Deacon, or anyone else, ruin buttercream.

"But then he said he did," Hannah confirmed.

"Only to get me to the castle."

"Walk me through it."

"What do you mean?" Callie asked.

"I'm trying to figure out why he'd change his story."

"It's simple. When Tyrell said 'move her to the castle or lose all the money,' Deacon suddenly decided he'd loved me all along."

"So he tried to convince you to move to the castle?"

"No." Callie cast her mind back to the conversation. "He told me to take the boys to Charleston and never come back."

She went over it a second time in case her memory was flawed. But that was how it had happened.

"Before or after he told you he loved you?" Hannah asked.

"Before. It was before."

"So, he'd already given up the money." Sounding like she'd made an important point, Hannah scooped a bite of her cupcake.

"No. He still had the option of getting me to change my mind."

"Which he didn't do. You said he didn't even try."

In the strictest sense, Callie knew that was true. But it was more complicated than that. "He didn't bother, because he knew it was hopeless."

"That's not what I'm hearing."

"What are you hearing?"

"I'm hearing he gave up hundreds of millions. He told you to go back to Charleston. *Then* he told you he loved you."

"Which, *believe me*, if I'd let it, would have led to a pitch to move me to the castle."

"Maybe," Hannah said, sounding unconvinced.

"I was there."

"You were upset."

That was true enough. Callie didn't think she'd ever felt

more upset in her life. Trevor's revelation had rocked her to her core. She hadn't told Hannah about Trevor. She tried to calculate how that would change the situation.

"You don't know what might have happened," Hannah said, polishing off her cupcake. "Eat."

"I know what *did* happen."

"Eat," Hannah said.

Callie took a bite.

"When you finish that cupcake," Hannah said. "I want you to consider that a man who gives up hundreds of millions of dollars for your well-being, then tells you he loves you, might…in fact…"

Callie couldn't let her mind go there. She couldn't survive another fantasy, another disappointment, another heartbreak.

"Love you," Hannah finished.

Callie took another bite of the cupcake, and another, and another, until it was gone.

"Well?" Hannah said.

"I can't go back. I can't let myself hope…" Callie wanted so desperately to hope, but she knew the stakes were far too high. She'd never survive another heartbreak.

"Then don't go back," Hannah said.

Callie was surprised. She was also a little disappointed. She realized she wanted Hannah to talk her into going to Deacon. That was beyond frightening.

"Call him. Text him."

"And say what?" It was the most preposterous idea Callie had ever heard.

"Anything. Text: *What's up? Where are you? What are you doing?* All you need is an icebreaker."

"I'm not doing that."

"Then text: *Can we talk?* If I'm right, he'll be on the next plane. If I'm wrong, he'll send some lame brush off answer, and you'll know for sure."

"He wouldn't have to wait for the next plane." Callie couldn't believe she was considering it. "He'd charter his own."

* * *

Tyrell swaggered into the boardroom, his expression dark. "What's this?" he demanded of Deacon, Aaron and Beau.

Deacon's phone pinged.

"We have some information to share with you," Aaron said.

Deacon watched Tyrell's suspicions rise. Deacon didn't feel the slightest sense of satisfaction or vindication. But he did feel a sense of justice.

His phone pinged again, and he glanced down.

His heart stopped when he saw Callie's name. Everything in the room disappeared.

He focused on her message.

Can we talk? her text said.

Yes, they could talk. Of course they could talk. They absolutely could talk. He came to his feet, pushing the chair out behind him.

"Deacon?" Aaron's voice penetrated.

Deacon looked up to three expressions of astonishment.

"I have to go," he said.

"What?" Beau demanded.

"I'm…" Deacon started for the door. "I'll…talk later. I have to go."

He all but sprinted down the hall. He didn't know what would happen in the boardroom behind him, but he didn't particularly care.

He texted while he walked: I'm on my way. Where are you?

He hopped into his car, tossing his phone on the passenger seat, watching it to see her answer. It was taking too long. It was taking way too long for her to respond.

He stopped at a light and picked up the phone, thinking something had gone wrong. He'd have to resend.

But then it pinged: At the bakery. But on my way home.

He glanced at the red light and typed in a message: *Be there in an hour.*

A horn honked behind him. He hit send and switched to hands free, contacting an air charter company.

They had a jet with immediate availability. He didn't ask the price, all but threw them his credit card in the boarding lounge and leapt on board.

He barely noticed the opulent white leather surroundings. He did say yes to a single malt, hoping it would calm his nerves. The pilot was able to radio ahead for a car, and Deacon came close to his time estimate.

One hour and twenty minutes later, he was at Callie's front door.

She opened it, and he had to fight an urge to wrap her immediately in his arms.

"Hi," he said, instead, feeling breathless.

"Hi," she returned.

He could hear the boys in the kitchen.

"Is everything okay?" he asked.

He searched her expression for a sign of her mood or her state of mind. At first, he'd taken her request as a good sign. But as the minutes dragged by in the jet, he was assailed with doubts. The truth was, he had no idea what she wanted.

"You came," she said.

"Of course I came." Nothing could have kept him away. "Is it the boys?"

"They're fine. We're all fine. Well, maybe not so fine."

Deacon was leaping from hopeful to worried to confused.

"Come in," she said, stepping out of the way.

He walked over the familiar threshold, feeling more at peace and at home than he had in weeks.

"I can't live in the castle," she said.

Hope flooded him. "I would never ask you to live in the castle."

The castle was a terrible place. He had no intention of living there either.

"I know it's a lot of money," she said.

"The money doesn't matter." The money couldn't matter less. "You matter. The boys matter."

"You said you loved me."

"I do."

"What do you love about me?"

"Everything." Without conscious thought, he moved closer to her.

"You haven't talked yourself into it, have you? You know, because of the potential perks of loving me."

He couldn't help but smile at that. "I haven't talked myself into a thing. After you left, if I could have talked myself out of loving you, I would have done it in a heartbeat to save my sanity."

She tilted her head to the side as if she were considering him. "I didn't exactly understand that, but I'm going to assume it was a good thing."

"It was a good thing. It is a good thing." He gave into his desire to reach for her, cradling her face with his palm and stepping closer still. "I love you, Callie, more than anything else in the world."

"You'll give up the money, hundreds of millions of dollars."

"See, the thing is—"

She put her fingertips across his lips. "There can be no equivocation. You have to make your choice."

"There is no equivocation. It's you, Callie, and James and Ethan, over and above anything else in the world."

"Good. Then we'll get by. We have the bakery. We'll work as hard as we have to."

He opened his mouth to explain again, but then thought better of it. "I know we will."

"Good," she repeated.

"So…" He searched her expression. "We're doing this? We're making it real? We're making it work?"

"I love you," she said.

His heart sang, and his grin broke free. "Thank goodness." He swooped in for a heartfelt kiss.

"Daddy!" came Ethan's excited voice.

"Daddy!" James chimed in.

Ethan's compact body hit the side of Deacon's leg, his little arms going around it. James came up on the other side to give his hip a hug.

Deacon gave Callie another quick kiss. "Hold that thought." Then he crouched down to hug the boys.

"We *are* a package deal," she said with a thread of laughter.

"Best package in the world," Deacon said to the boys.

"Daddy, come and see the new castle," Ethan said, tugging on Deacon's hand.

"It has a moat," James added. "Mommy made us build it in the kitchen."

Deacon looked up at Callie. "Mommy's very smart."

Deacon followed the boys, his boys, to the kitchen, duly admiring their creation.

After a few minutes, he stood, leaning on the counter next to Callie. He took her hand. He touched her cheek. He gave her another kiss.

"There's something you need to know," he said.

She drew back to look at him. "Will I be unhappy?"

"I don't know. It's about the money and the Clarksons."

"That never makes me happy."

The boys squealed and zoomed rubber alligators through the makeshift moat.

"It's Aaron and Beau. They want us to be real brothers."

She searched his expression. "Is that what you want?"

"It is." It was what Deacon wanted. He was surprised by how much he wanted it.

Callie wrapped her arms around his waist. "Then that's wonderful."

Deacon didn't want to leave anything out. "That's not the crux of it. They want to join forces with me in running Hale Harbor Port. They blocked Tyrell's plan to write me out of the company."

She pulled back again. "The money?"

"It's still mine. It's ours. We own Frederick's share of Hale Harbor Port. And someday it will belong to James and Ethan." He held his breath, waiting to see if she'd be angry.

She didn't look thrilled, but she didn't look angry either.

"You don't mind?" he dared ask. "That we're rich and we're connected to the Clarksons? I promise you don't have to worry about Tyrell or Margo or anyone else. Any relationship with them will be on your terms."

"We were always going to be connected to the Clarksons," Callie said with resignation. "I just didn't know it for a while."

"Between me and my brothers—that's so odd to say. With the three of us together, Tyrell won't be able to bully anyone ever again."

James shouted out, "The alligator ate the princess!"

"Owie alligator," Ethan called.

"I'm not afraid of Tyrell," Callie said, molding against him. "I'm through being afraid of bullying men."

"Good."

She gave a little laugh. "I'll send them to you."

"Absolutely."

"You can bribe them."

"Ouch," he said.

"I'm teasing. I have complete faith in you to protect us."

"I always will," Deacon said, feeling a deep and enormous sense of satisfaction. He tightened his hold. "I have a family," he whispered in wonder. "A true and wonderful family. And I love you all so very much."

"We love you back, Deacon. All three of us love you right back."

* * * * *

A BILLIONAIRE
AFFAIR

NIOBIA BRYANT

As always, for my mama, my guardian angel, Letha 'Bird' Bryant.

Chapter 1

"Have a good evening, sir."

Alek Ansah nodded sharply at the pilot and crew of his private plane just before disembarking. Quickly he jogged down the metal stairs, not even paying attention to the crisp London night air whipping against the hand-tailored tuxedo on his well-built frame. He checked his de Grisogono watch as he strode across the airfield to his waiting black Bentley Mulsanne. By the time he reached it, his longtime driver had exited the vehicle and held the rear door open.

"Julius," Alek greeted him, his accent a blend of his Ghanaian ancestry and his upbringing in England. He unbuttoned his jacket and slid onto the smooth leather seat.

"Sir." His driver gave him a polite nod of his head. As soon as the door closed, Alek relaxed and settled his chin in his hand as he released a heavy breath and looked out the darkly tinted window as the vehicle eased forward. The sights of London were reflected in the depths of his coal-black eyes. The capital of both England and the United Kingdom had served as his home base for the last five years.

That would change tomorrow.

Alek was surprised at the slight tinge of nervousness he felt. Was it leftover anxiety about the fear of flying that he hid so well, or the day of reckoning fast approaching? He sighed, his mood now pensive.

The ride from the airport to his penthouse apartment in the heart of historical and prestigious Westminster took less than fifteen minutes. As the car rolled to a smooth stop outside the building constructed of stone, granite and bronze, Alek looked up at the illuminated floor-to-ceiling windows of his apartment. It was the lone flat on the tenth floor.

He climbed from the vehicle before Julius could even leave his seat. "Good night, Julius," Alek called over his shoulder, already loosening his bow tie and the top button of his monogrammed shirt as he strolled up the length of the walkway and entered the building.

After a full day of work topped with his evening flight to and from Paris just to attend a charity event at the Pavillon d'Armenonville, his muscles felt weak with fatigue—a rarity for him. He was strong and fit and thrived on challenge. Still, he was human and required even minimal rest.

Striding across the stylishly appointed lobby, the soles of his handmade Italian shoes beat against the marble floors as he made his way to the elevators. He entered his private code for the elevator to go to the penthouse and rode in silence. As he stood there with his legs apart and his hands behind his back, he flexed his shoulders and rolled his head to relieve the slight strain of tension he felt. He paused when he caught sight of his reflection against the bronze of the double doors.

He did a double take and then chuckled a bit. Earlier that night one of the waitresses shared with him that he should audition to be the first black James Bond. He was nearly 100 percent sure she thought he was Idris Elba. He didn't know whether to be flattered by that or insulted that he was the honoree at the very event where she worked and she had no clue who he was. That was a first in the circles in which he moved.

The doors of the elevators opened directly into his apartment; he removed his white dinner jacket and folded it over the back of one of the four modern charcoal sofas in his expansive living room.

"Your drink, sir."

Alek turned away from the view of the London cityscape to find his loyal manservant, Huntsman, still very much awake, dressed in customary black on black attire and ready to serve. With a smile, he accepted the snifter of brandy from the small wooden tray held by the bald middle-aged man. The warmed crystal felt good in his hand as he swirled the alcohol and took a small sniff of the aromas released by the heating of the glass before taking a satisfying sip.

Over the rim of the glass, he looked out at the sight of Westminster Abbey and the Houses of Parliament in the distance. At night, he often found himself standing there in front of his windows enjoying the sight.

To think there was a time when none of it mattered to him. Simplicity had been key.

With a smirk, he looked around at his lavish surroundings. Everything had changed, and sometimes he wasn't sure it was for the better. With a slight clench of his square jaw, Alek focused on his six-foot reflection, letting the cityscape laid out before him blur as he did.

Sometimes he felt he hardly knew the man in the reflection.

"Big day tomorrow, sir."

With another sip, Alek glanced over his shoulder to find that Huntsman had never moved from his spot, the serving tray still in his hand. "Very," he agreed, curving his lips into a smile.

Huntsman chuckled.

The two had been officially employer and employee over the last fifteen of Alek's thirty years of life, but they had a friendship and a mutual respect that extended beyond a work relationship and their twenty-year age difference. Huntsman knew almost everything about Alek's life and pretended to turn a blind eye to his jet-setting ways filled with a string of beautiful women that gave the international paparazzi plenty on which to report. It was well documented that Alek Ansah worked hard, but he played just as hard.

Still, Huntsman was very aware of Alek's inner struggles, and he knew Alek's imminent return to New York was a mixed blessing.

"Your luggage and travel arrangements are prepared. Are you?" Huntsman asked, stepping up to stand beside him.

"I don't really have a choice, do I?" Alek asked, and took another deep sip.

"No, sir, you do not."

In the morning, Alek would return to the corporate headquarters of the Ansah Dalmount Group in New York to officially claim his position as the cochairman of the billion-dollar conglomerate. He was fulfilling the wishes of his father, Kwame Ansah, and not his own. "You won, Dad," he mouthed as he lifted his snifter in a toast and looked up to the heavens with a small sardonic shake of his head, as a wave of grief caused his gut to clench.

Five years ago, the lives of both his father and his father's business partner, Frances Dalmount, were tragically ended in a crash of ADG's company jet. He had been deep into his grief and grappling with the lost opportunity to mend his strained relationship with his father when the reading of the will completely turned Alek's life upside down.

Alek's grandfather, Ebo Ansah, began a financial services firm in Ghana in the 1950s that grew significantly in the mid-1960s, providing a very respectable living for his wife, Kessie, and their four children. His eldest son, Kwame, grew under the tutelage of his father and was anxious for his opportunity to enter the family business. They expanded the fiscal services offered to their loyal clients and grew their business. Life was good, and with the Ansah men working together doggedly, it became even better. Upon Ebo's passing in the early 1980s Kwame took over the running of the business, aggressively taking over smaller banks and insurance and investment firms to catapult himself to wealth and prominence. When the opportunity arose in 1987 to join forces with Frances Dalmount, a business competitor from England, he accepted with the intent to use their combined resources to take on other business ventures. The Ansah Dalmount Group was formed, eventually becoming one of the most successful conglomerates in the world with its business umbrella encompassing financial services, oil, hotels/resorts/casinos and telecommunications.

Kwame Ansah relished every moment of their success because he knew his father would be proud. And he wanted nothing more than for his eldest son to join him to advance the company even further. It was their biggest point of contention.

Alek clenched his jaw in regret.

After graduating with a Master of Business Administration degree from Columbia University, Alek did not enter the family business as planned and instead fostered his love of the outdoors and sailing by working as a deckhand on a luxury mega yacht, with plans to rise up the ranks to captain his own vessel. What his father saw as defiance was just him fighting for his independence to be his own man. It was the first time he ever defied him.

Back then he felt so much pride in striking out on his own.

Back then he was pleased that his job kept him away from home so that he could avoid the look of disappointment and anger in his father's eyes.

Back then he thought he had more time to make everything right.

And now?

Five years had passed and the guilt was still palpable.

"I knew your father well, Alek," Huntsman said,

reaching up with his free hand to firmly pat his shoulder. "You have already made him proud."

Alek's smile was slight but genuine. "He threw me in the deep end and I had no choice but to sink or swim," he said with a chuckle.

Kwame Ansah had been determined to have his way, even in death.

Alek had to make the difficult choice of accepting the position as cochief executive officer of ADG or having all his father's shares in the conglomerate sold, with the proceeds donated to various charities. That would leave not only Alek but the rest of his family without an inheritance. His father had to have known he would never lose the family's legacy and financial security. *Stubborn old man.*

Kwame Ansah was relentless, and in the end, he had been right. Per his father's request he had spent the last five years training inside the company in preparation to run it. He spent considerable time within every branch of the ADG learning about it from the ground floor up. He took to it all like a fish to water. He soared, driven by a desire to make his father proud, but also pure determination to thrive and win—traits he inherited from his sire.

For so long, his stubbornness to pave his own path in life had blinded him to the innate skill and tenacity his father had seen in him all the while.

Now he was prepared to take the Ansah Dalmount Group even further.

Well, along with Alessandra, he conceded, sliding one hand into the pocket of his tailored slacks and taking another sip as he shook his head.

The news that his father's business partner had left

his shares of their billion-dollar conglomerate to his daughter had yet to sit well with him. Their power in the company was equal. Each inherited 49 percent of the shares, with the board of directors left with 2 percent of the shares to decide on a stalemate between them.

Alek felt that was inevitable.

They were completely driven.

With their fathers as both business associates and close friends, Alek had known Alessandra since childhood. Ever since they were small, Alek had found Alessandra's quiet nature off-putting. She was never friendly and seemed afraid of her own shadow. As teenagers, they were never in the same circle of friends or schools but saw each other at social functions. She was decidedly awkward and found with her head in a book more times than not. He had little patience for the mousy little introvert and was glad their time in each other's presence became nonexistent with age.

He frowned at the memory of her during their first meeting with the board of directors of ADG. Slender and petite with a head full of massive curls that dwarfed her face. Her petite figure swamped in the shirt and pants she wore. Oversize, ill-adjusted spectacles that she continuously pushed up on her nose. Nervously biting at her bottom lip. Looking confused, lost and unaware that she was completely out of her element.

He expressed his discontent with her appointment as co-CEO, so much so that the board readily agreed to his request to do his training in their London offices while Alessandra remained in New York. That was the last time he saw Miss Alessandra Dalmount.

And all of that would change tomorrow.

Everything would change tomorrow.

Alek released a heavy breath.

"It is not your last walk to the electric chair, sir," Huntsman said, taking the now-empty snifter from him to cross the polished floor to refill it.

Alek reached up to run his long fingers across his close-shaven head. It wasn't the move that Huntsman spoke of and they both knew it. It was not a "what" but a "whom."

Alessandra Dalmount.

He accepted the snifter Huntsman pressed into his hand. "What in the world was Frances thinking?" he muttered darkly, his brow furrowing as he gripped the nightcap so hard that a lesser material would have crushed in his grasp.

"Ah, the eternal question," Huntsman said softly, his tone amused.

"I will not sit back and let her destroy everything our fathers worked so hard to build," Alek said sharply, turning in his spot to face the older man.

Huntsman smoothed his hands over his vest before clasping his hands together behind his back and rapping his heels together. "And yet the firm still stands strong after five years of her working there," he said smoothly, his face almost unreadable.

"But she gains forty-nine percent control tomorrow—"

"As do you, sir," Huntsman reminded him.

"Yes, but *I* know what the hell I'm doing!" Alek snapped.

Ding-dong.

"Plans, sir?" Huntsman asked drily.

"Damn," Alek swore, dropping his head so low that his chin almost touched his chest.

He'd forgotten the beautiful woman he'd met after a business lunch out on the cigar terrace of the Boisdale of Belgravia earlier that day. It had been hard not to notice one of the few women enjoying the decidedly masculine Scottish decor, particularly her handling of the long and thick cigar in her mouth as she boldly met his stare from across the terrace. She'd made an invite back to his apartment for a nightcap completely undeniable.

He'd since forgotten all about her.

Huntsman waited patiently as Alek looked down into his drink and then toward the door before looking back at his drink again. Whatever desire he had to bed the woman had waned. He couldn't remember her name and could only vaguely recall her beauty. "Have my driver take her home and offer her my apologies," Alek said before tipping his head back to finish his drink.

Huntsman immediately turned to do as he was bid.

Alek wasn't proud of treating the woman like a disposable convenience. It wasn't usually his character, but he would not be good company for her or anyone else that night. His thoughts were centered on one thing and one thing alone: how to convince Alessandra Dalmount to willingly step down from her position at ADG.

For him, that was *all* that mattered.

Alessandra Dalmount leaned back in her leather executive chair and crossed her legs in the pin-striped pencil skirt she wore as she coolly eyed the junior executives sitting in the leather club chairs across from her at the conference room table. The two young men glanced at each other and shifted nervously in their seats as her silence filled the air.

As she continued to study them, Alessandra took the moment to ponder how hard she had to fight to prove her worth in the last five years. She was proud to finally be so respected within the company that her silence after the presentation of a business proposal elicited subtle anxiety. In the early days of stepping into the role her father had bequeathed her, Alessandra had been nervous, fidgety and apologetic. She had felt so unsure in her role. So unworthy. So judged.

Well, no more.

"As you all know, the expansion of ADG into the shipping industry has been of the utmost importance to me for the last year," she began. "I expect some resistance."

From Alek Ansah.

She forced a stiff smile and nearly snapped the pen she held in half from her tightened grasp as she shifted in her seat. She forced herself to do a mental five count as her employees watched her.

Get it together, Alessandra.

"I expect my team to gather the information and analytics I need on the list of firms I am suggesting the company acquire. I will make some notations and corrections to the report and get them back to you this evening," she said, forcing her shoulders to relax as she stood up on her sling-back Fendi heels and gave each man a hard stare. "I expect the amended reports back to me before the end of the week, sans the little loopholes I've already discovered after a two-minute cursory perusal."

"But, Ms. Dalmount…" one of them said.

"That is all," Alessandra said firmly, dismissing them as she turned to look out the window at the Empire State Building among the sprawling landscape of Midtown Manhattan.

As her staff members quietly took their leave, her focus on the neighboring high-rise buildings blurred. She pursed her lips and released a breath meant to calm her nerves. It didn't work.

Today she would assume her share of the responsibility in running one of the largest conglomerates in the country. She had the last five years to prepare, but in this moment, she felt as if that time had flown by so quickly.

And in truth she felt completely overwhelmed.

Alessandra unclasped the locket she wore on a long chain around her neck and stroked her thumb against the wedding photo of her parents nestled there. They both were lost to her. Her mother, Olivia, died when Alessandra was young, and her father had loved his wife so deeply that he never remarried. She could only find solace that her parents had reunited in heaven.

I miss you, Daddy.

As always, the thought of her father dying in such a tragic way weakened her knees. She closed her eyes as a wave of sadness and grief hit her, causing her to wince. *Will the pain ever dull?*

Not enough time had passed to properly grieve the death of a parent. In the space of a week, she lost her father, attended the funeral and then learned during his will reading that it was his wish for her to take over his position as a chief executive officer of the Ansah Dalmount Group. She'd wanted nothing more than to return to their family estate and bury her head under the dozen pillows on her bed so that she could sleep and pretend the week had never happened.

But that wasn't to be.

Alessandra had been completely moved and surprised by her father's faith in her, but her fear of it all had come with a quickness. Although she had previously graduated with a bachelor's in English, Alessandra's life had been all about her volunteer work for various charities. With one stroke of his pen, Frances Dalmount had solidified his daughter as one of the most wealthy and powerful women in the world. And now the day had arrived for her to take the reins.

Father, what have you gotten me into?

Alessandra closed the locket but kept it pressed in her hand.

Back then the last thing she wanted was the responsibility of taking over the family empire. She had hardly ever bothered herself with her father's business affairs. She was his only child, and although he loved and spoiled her immensely, she had always known he would have preferred a son to raise in the ways of business. She had never held ill will about that.

And she never assumed he would expect so much of her.

Alessandra squeezed the bridge of her nose as she turned and walked along the length of the table to leave the modern and stylish conference room. Closing the glass door behind herself, she began walked down the hall to the right to her corner office, but stopped midway with a soft curving of her crimson-painted lips. Instead she turned and walked down the opposite end of the hall to the elevator. As the wood-paneled doors opened, she stepped on and pressed the button to go to the top floor of the twenty-five-story building.

She couldn't lie; there *was* excitement blended with her fear.

The last five years she worked hard to form herself into a successful businesswoman. Between the fifty- to sixty-hour weeks she put in working in various departments to garner a firsthand knowledge of the business, to returning to college to earn her Master of Business Administration from Columbia University, to reshaping her image and bolstering her confidence, Alessandra went above and beyond to prove herself to the naysayers. It was clear that many people questioned her father's decision to have her inherit his shares of ADG—she even questioned it herself.

Pain over her father's death, anger about being openly scorned because she was a woman and a desire to win motivated Alessandra.

And she had thrived. She surprised the board members and her peers. She took pride in that. Alessandra had given up so much to live up to what her father expected of her. *So very much.*

The elevator slowed to a stop and the doors slid open, revealing the wide reception area. To her left was a sandalwood station beneath the backlit brass letters *ADG* on the wall, and to the right sat a modern sofa with sleek lines. Her eyes quickly landed directly across from her on the ornate double doors of the palatial boardroom. She smoothed her hands down her hips and stiffened her spine as she walked off the elevator.

ADG owned the entire commercial building, leasing out all but the top four floors with the penthouse reserved just for the expansive offices of the two CEOs.

That morning when she arrived, she learned one of those offices was now hers.

The receptionist, a tall redhead with glasses, rose to her feet. "Good morning, Ms. Dalmount," she said with a warm smile.

Alessandra fought her natural inclination to return the smile and instead gave her a polite nod as she passed her to enter the wide hall. She paused and turned to look back at the hall to the right of the elevator, which led to the other office now belonging to Alek Ansah.

Her heart pounded and she nervously bit the gloss from her lips. *Is he in there?*

It had been five years since she'd seen him in person, and the last time would be hard to ever forget. Her father's attorney had announced, "Alessandra Dalmount and Alek Ansah, as the newly appointed majority owners of ADG, you will both be primed within the company to take over the running of the conglomerate—together."

Behind her spectacles she had looked to Alek. He had barely spared her a glance when he first entered the office and took the seat across from her, but his dark eyes were locked and loaded on her. His square and handsome chiseled features had been unreadable, but his eyes told the story: he was not happy with having her as his equal.

Their fathers had been competitors before becoming business partners and eventually best friends. Alessandra had known Alek since they were children, although they encountered each other more as teenagers. As they moved into adulthood, she watched the surly teen grow into an arrogant and cocky man. His demeanor toward her had always been decidedly brooding, but bordered on hostile when he discovered they would run ADG together.

It's been five years; does he feel the same?

She fought the urge to ask Emily if he was in fact in his office. The board meeting was tomorrow morning and she would undoubtedly see him then. Alessandra flipped her straight hair over her shoulder as she arched a brow and released a heavy breath. If he was still unwilling to accept her role in the company, then, like their offices, they would remain at opposite ends. *The choice is his to make.*

Sighing, she continued down the hall, her heels echoing against the marble floor. The glass door leading into the outer office automatically opened upon her approach. Unger Rawlings, her executive assistant, instantly rose to his feet and grabbed his iPad, but she held up her hand and softly shook her head to prevent him from following her through the open double doors into her office. "I'm fine for now, Unger," she assured him.

"Yes, ma'am."

He had been her right-hand man and dedicated employee since her first day at ADG. The tall and slender young man, who was just a little younger than her thirty years, knew all too well of her priorities. She could think of no one else to serve as her assistant, even if there had been a push for someone with more experience and qualifications. His professionalism and loyalty were significant to her.

"Actually, you can go to lunch, Unger," she said.

"Would you like anything?" he asked.

She shook her head.

It was solace that she sought.

Alessandra paused in the doorway and took in the nearly 360-degree view of Manhattan through the three glass curtain walls of her office. The open floor plan was breathtakingly beautiful and sleek with over three thousand square feet, twenty-foot ceilings with skylights, private spa bath, small kitchen, exercise room, lounge area with a grand fireplace, library and an outdoor terrace. All was stylishly designed in luxury, but it wasn't the grandeur of the space that caused her to pause.

Although the office had been updated and remodeled in the last five years, to her it was still her father's space and he was gone.

"Deep thoughts?"

Alessandra froze. She didn't need to see the face that matched the seductive, masculine voice. It had been years, but she knew it well. Hating the feeling of nervous anxiety that plagued her as his return became imminent, she stiffened her spine and prayed her makeup and hair were still flawless. *Keep it cool*.

"Welcome back, Alek," she said coolly, slowly walking the length of the polished hardwood floors to reach her large desk. She turned to face him, leaning back against the edge of her desk and crossing her ankles.

There he stood in the open doorway in a designer suit and handmade shoes, looking every bit the man of power. Polished. Stylish. Tall, truly dark and unapologetically handsome. Black hair cut low, dark eyes, bronzed brown complexion. His groomed beard emphasized his high cheekbones and square jawline. He stood right at six feet tall with a strong, athletic build that his tailored suit couldn't hide.

Alessandra's eyes missed nothing, not even the small scar on his cheek that added a dangerous edge to his style. She had always considered him a fine-looking man, but the years made him more rugged… more handsome.

Sexy. Too damn sexy.

Alessandra had heard of and seen Alek's personal life in the press, but the photos of him and his rotation of beautiful dates had not prepared her for all of him in person. Her facade was cool as she hid her pounding heart and racing pulse. Alek Ansah was pure, raw sex appeal.

Well, I'll be damned.

"Alessandra," he said, his voice deep and rich with that British accent.

Boom-boom-boom-boom-boom.

Alessandra's heart betrayed her. She ignored the almost deafening pounding as she eyed him strolling into her office. He came over to stand at her window, his coal-black eyes locked on some spot in the distance. He had the kind of stride that hinted at his sexual prowess.

She looked back over her shoulder. Her eyes caressed his profile. *Sexy arrogant bully.*

Alek suddenly turned his head to eye her, as well.

Alessandra kept her face nonchalant. "Can I help you with something, Alek?" she asked, rising to come around her desk and pull back her chair to claim her seat behind it. Her hand was as unsteady as her pulse as she picked up her favorite Aurora fountain pen.

"There are whispers in the air that you are proposing working on a deal to shift the firm into shipping," he said, moving over to stand in front of her desk.

Alessandra glanced up at him, purposely dismissing him with her eyes as she pretended to focus on the files and forms before her. "Whispers, Alek?" she said mockingly. "I would think a man like you was above listening to…whispers."

"A man like me, Alessandra?"

She allowed herself a moment to close her eyes at how his tongue seemed to caress her name. Dropping her pen, she leaned back in her chair and looked up at him. "Your first day back and we're picking—no, no, no—*you're* picking up right where you left off," she said with a disapproving twist of her lips.

"My feelings haven't changed since my last day here," he assured her, his eyes locked on her.

"Your feelings about me, I assume?" Alessandra rose to her feet, hating the feeling of him looking down on her.

"Exactly."

She felt affronted. "And your issue with me is?" she asked, deciding to be just as bold as him.

"Your refusal to step down from a position not suited

for you," he instantly shot back with ease as if the words had been sitting perched on the tip of his tongue.

"It's too bad you feel that way, Alek," she said, her voice firm. "Because you're mistaken."

His eyes took her in. Her hair. Her face. The fit of the embroidered satin shirt she wore with a formfitting pencil skirt. A warm appreciation filled the dark depths.

In the years since she blossomed into a swan, she had learned to pick up on the unspoken cues of a man. She felt desired at his perusal, but his demeanor toward her was weakening her desire of him.

Alek reached across the desk dividing them to stroke her hair. "I like your new look. Playing dress-up?" he asked, slightly mocking.

She held his stare as she coolly raised her hand to brush away his touch. "Change is good, Alek. Particularly change of times. Why don't you and your outdated chauvinistic thinking join the rest of us in the current year."

"This should be fun," Alek said, nodding his head and smiling.

"Games are not a part of my day, Alek," she snapped. "I will not be undermined in this business by you and your return. I have earned my MBA from your alma mater. I have worked my way up inside this business. I have implemented deals that have generated ADG a steady influx of money. I have proved my worth. And, most importantly, *Alek*, I own the same number of shares as you. We are equals. And I'm not going anywhere."

He wiped his mouth as he eyed her with a hint of

amusement in his eyes. "We'll see," he said simply before turning to walk out of her office.

Even as his arrogance burned her gut, her eyes took in his smooth stride until he disappeared from her line of vision. Forcing herself to relax, she dropped down into her seat and swiveled to look out the window at the Manhattan views as she attempted to release her anger and her desire.

Chapter 2

What a difference five years makes.

Alek picked up his crystal glass of water and closely watched Alessandra over the rim as she spoke to the board members from her seat at the opposite end of the conference table. Where once she had been an ineffectual woman who seemed afraid of her own shadow, her slender face buried beneath a ton of curls and so thin that the wind could shift her like a leaf, she had transformed herself both physically and in temperament. The dull caterpillar had become a jewel-toned butterfly.

Her dark tresses were bone straight and expertly styled to complement her heart-shaped face and caramel-brown complexion. Makeup highlighted her almond-shaped eyes of brandy, blush contoured her high cheekbones, and gloss made her full lips poutier and succulent. Her height was average but the curves of her toned shape were not. She wore a dark gray chiffon blouse with sheer sleeves and a plunging neckline that was just deep enough to allude to more without revealing it. She paired it with wide-leg pants that fit close against her hips before falling straight to the floor and flaring. Her outfit was professional with a sexy edge.

His eyes dipped down to her mouth as she spoke. He liked the way the tip of her tongue caressed the small dip in the center of her bottom lip. Her oxblood lipstick gave her a dramatic flair that was hard to ignore.

Alek took a deep sip of water as he forced himself to look away from her. To not be drawn into her, into everything she had become: a mix of cool confidence and simmering sex appeal. He definitely enjoyed the look of her more than what she was saying.

"Alek… Alek…your thoughts?"

He blinked away a vision of undoing every button of Alessandra's shirt to bury his head against her breasts as he pressed her body down onto the conference table. His eyes shifted to Aldrich Brent, the president of the corporation and executive board member. "I'm not impressed," he said dismissively, rising to his feet. He smoothed his double-knotted silk tie before buttoning the jacket of his custom Tom Ford pin-striped suit. "It's clear that Alessandra is naive and amateurish in business. I am disappointed she felt competent in presenting this venture to the board."

Alessandra mumbled under her breath.

He offered her a brief glance as he reached for his briefcase and pulled a stack of twelve black folders from it. "I would like to offer an alternative that is *viable*," he stressed, walking around the table to place a report before each of the ten board members flanking the table and then Alessandra sitting at the end opposite him.

She took it from him with a hard stare.

He came to stand next to his seat at the end of the table. "Anyone with an iota of business acumen could ascertain—"

"Enough of the insults, Alek," Alessandra requested calmly.

He feigned confusion. "Insults?" he asked.

"Yes, less of them and more of your proposal is all that I'm asking," she said.

Only the fire in her eyes revealed her rising ire at him.

"Do you need a moment?" he asked, his tone mocking as he egged her on.

Her mouth tightened into a thin line and her jaw was clenched so tightly that he was sure she could bite a nail in half with ease.

Alek cleared his throat. "The interest of ADG would be better served with a move into commercial aviation," he said.

"Commercial aviation," Alessandra snapped, tossing the folder on the table where it spun like a top until it hit against a board member's glass of water.

"Yes," he answered, his gaze leveling on her. Her annoyance with him caused her eyes to shine brightly. He forced himself to look away from her as he felt his usual cool composure wane. *When did she become so beautiful?*

"And we're supposed to believe this is not just a last-minute stunt to gun for my venture idea?" she asked coldly.

"Yes."

Alessandra swore, and then winced in regret. Such language wasn't appropriate, no matter the impetus.

The chaotic energy around them seemed to whip loudly in the air with the force of lightning.

"Really?" Alek asked, his tone scolding.

"My apologies, but as you all can see nothing has changed between Mr. Ansah and me since our last meeting in this boardroom five years ago," she explained, her tone calm and composed.

The board members and the secretary taking the notes stirred in their seats as Alessandra and Alek cast each other cold glares.

"Very unprofessional, Alessandra," Alek said with a smugness at her losing her equanimity. He wasn't finished. "The boardroom is no place for histrionics."

She jumped to her feet and stalked down the length of the table with the board members' heads all turning to follow her. "Histrionics?" she spat, as she pointed her finger into his chest.

"This board does not have time for your trivial pursuits, Alessandra," he countered, looking down to take in her brown eyes lit with the fire of her anger.

"Nor your inept attempts at trying to capture the queen in a chess game you're not fully equipped to play," she said coldly.

Alek reached up and lightly captured the finger she pressed into his chest into his hand. "When it comes to business, you're no queen, my dear," he said, his voice low in the small space between them as he instinctively stroked her soft palm with his thumb.

His eyes squinted in surprise when he thought he felt her shiver.

She snatched away from his grip and stepped back from him. "Then why are you so intimidated by me?"

Alek threw his head back and laughed wholeheartedly. "Me? You? Intimidated?" he said in between chuckles.

"Enough!" Aldrich said, jumping to his feet.

Alek and Alessandra looked to the older man, his thin lips still quivering in frustration and his face now reddish with annoyance.

"Do you think your fathers would be proud of your behavior?" he asked, his English accent clipped.

"Yes," Alessandra answered unequivocally. "Yes, I do."

Alek looked disbelieving.

"My father wanted me in *this* position. He believed I could handle *this* position. And I have proven—even at the detriment of my own personal happiness—that I can thrive in *this* position," she said, stalking back to her seat. "And so, if it means standing up for myself to this archaic-minded jackass and his chauvinistic mindset then, yes, I believe my father is in heaven not only standing up and applauding, but wishing he could interject and give some more of the same."

Alek's eyes darted to the up-and-down motion of her breasts as she deeply breathed through her anger at him. His desire stirred. This woman who defied him with such fire and authority was not the mousy little Alessandra of the past. This was a different woman. And he wanted her with an intensity that surprised him. He bit back a smile as he calmly unbuttoned his blazer and reclaimed his seat.

Aldrich gave them both stern looks as he took his seat. He had been with the conglomerate since the early days and both thought of him as a family friend. It was respect for him, his position with the company and his friendship with their fathers that stopped the sparks flying between them.

"Do you both have companies in mind set up for an acquisition to become a subsidiary of ADG?" another of the board members asked.

"Yes. My team and I have been narrowing the field for the past couple of months in preparation for this being my first major act as co-CEO. As shown in the reports I gave you all, we have a strong contender," Alessandra said.

"Alek?"

"Yes."

"Liar," she mouthed at him.

That tongue on the dip of her bottom lip thing is really hot.

"I believe it would only be viable to explore *one* of these suggestions at this time," Aldrich said, looking from Alessandra to Alek. "The majority vote of the members of this board would constitute the breaking of a…tie."

Alek's and Alessandra's eyes locked across the distance.

He blinked and looked away from her. A craving to kiss her wouldn't release him.

Aldrich cleared his throat. "I suggest you both present your full proposals at next month's meeting and we will hold a vote to settle the matter once and for all."

His fellow board members gave approving nods.

"Fine," Alessandra said, picking up her pen to rotate it between her slender fingers.

Alek remained silent. He was stunned the board was even open to her proposal. And in truth, during her presentation they had been attentive. Respectful, even. *It's time to get more acquainted with Miss Dalmount.*

Over the rim of round, bright red spectacles, the board's secretary, Iris Dennis, eyed the board members from her seat next to Aldrich. "Shall we move on? The meeting does coincide with the thirtieth Jubilee celebration next month to be held at the Lake House. The meeting will be that Thursday and we have confirmed use of a conference room on-site. I would like to quickly review the final preparations for the events that weekend."

Alek tilted his head in acquiescence to Iris as he continued to watch Alessandra closely and find that he liked the look of her. She was stunning. Sophisticated and polished. Poised. She had this subtle sexy that was understated and made a man want to see more. *He* wanted more.

"I would like to make a formal offer to buy you out, Alessandra."

Long after the board meeting had ended and the members had left the conference room, Alek and Alessandra remained in their seats at opposing ends of the table. Moments ticked by and silence reigned.

Alessandra took him in. His low-cut hair, his handsome face, and the broadness of his shoulders in his tailored suit that he wore with such ease that she was sure he owned a hundred or more of them. Physically, everything about him intrigued her. *Traitor.*

"It's time you realize that there is a woman—a qualified woman—sitting at the table in the boys' club, Alek," she finally said, tapping the tip of her nail against the top of the polished wood conference table. "No more running to London to hide from the truth."

Tap-tap-tap.

"And do you like being in the company of men, Alessandra, pretending to be one of the boys?" he asked.

Alessandra arched a brow. "Are you questioning my femininity, Alek?" she asked, her voice soft but with an underlying steely edge.

He shook his head and turned his lips downward. "No, of course not," he said, rapping his strong knuckles against the table. "Femininity has nothing to do with sexuality."

Alessandra sighed and leaned back in her chair as she tilted her head to the side to look at him. "Perhaps having women with more looks than intellect fawning over you has distorted your idea of women and what we want, Alek. But please let's be clear that, although I completely understand why a woman would want to be rid of men in every way, including sexually, I am not a lesbian."

"You're not?" he asked in feigned surprise.

She rolled her eyes. "Surprise, surprise, Mr. I Can't Keep My Personal Life Out of the Tabloids. Not every straight woman flings herself at your feet. Some of us have more discretion—and taste."

Alek leaned back in his chair and rubbed his chin. "Perhaps if you stopped playing businesswoman and focused on finding a life of your own, you wouldn't have time to watch mine."

Alessandra fought hard to keep her composure.

Gone was her nervousness, replaced by the fire and indignation his attitude evoked. She enjoyed their banter. She even felt rallied by his challenge. "And perhaps your life entails such a long string of women because you're incapable of satisfying one well enough to stay around," she said, and then offered him a tip of her head. *So there.*

Alessandra rose and gathered her files and folders before turning to walk to the door without another look at him.

"Perhaps if you were my type I would show you how well equipped I am at satisfying a woman."

She froze just as her hand closed around the cool brass of the doorknob. She released a short breath as if a pressure valve had been briefly turned. Allowing herself a five count, she turned and walked the length of the spacious conference room to stand before him. She reached down to grip the back of his chair, bringing their faces just inches apart. His face within a lick of her oxblood-tinted lips, she said, "Physically I am your type, Alek. I am very much your type…and you know it. Humph, it's only my brain and my backbone that you think are a turnoff."

His face was a mask of boredom, but his eyes dipped down to her mouth, and Alessandra saw it. Her breath caught and she rose, backing away from him at the truth of her words in his eyes. She knew desire when she saw it. She turned and quick-walked to the door, trying to hide how much he flustered her.

"Qui s'enfuit maintenant?" he asked smoothly in French.

He must have known she spoke it fluently. "Who's running away now?" he'd asked.

Me. I'm running. Running fast and hard and not stopping one damn bit.

Alessandra didn't stop her hurried steps until she had left the room and pulled the door closed behind her. With her heart beating rapidly, she licked the dryness from her mouth and allowed herself a moment to press her back to the door as she fought hard to reclaim the coolness she had become known for in the last five years.

Making a pained face, she raised her free hand to lightly knock her wrist against her forehead. "Stupid, stupid, stupid," she admonished herself in a whisper.

The man was a chauvinist who made it clear he wanted her out of the company in which they equally owned the majority of shares. He had no respect for her. No desire to work with her or even be around her.

The doorknob turned against her buttocks a moment before it was opened from behind her. Alessandra's face filled with alarm as she felt her body free-fall backward.

She felt Alek's large hands wrap around her upper arms. The thin material of her shirt did nothing to protect her from the warmth of his touch as he kept her from hitting the floor. Her head landed on one of his shoulders and her back pressed lightly against his chest.

Alessandra felt nothing but strength.

Quickly she turned, accidentally pressing her body back against the open door. "Th-thank—thank you," she stuttered, her nerves completely undone by him.

He stepped up close to her.

Alessandra tried to back away more but there

was nothing but the unrelenting pressure of the door against her back.

"You're welcome, Alessandra," he said softly, before reaching up to lightly stroke her cheek and then her chin before he walked away from her.

She closed her eyes and released a long shaky breath, left with nothing but the warm scent of his cologne and the lingering aftereffects of his touch.

I wanted to kiss her.

Alek looked back over his shoulder as he walked down the length of the hall leading to his office. He stopped and turned as Alessandra closed the door to the conference room, pressed her files to her chest and then walked across the reception area. His eyes shifted down to the gentle sway of her hips and buttocks in her pants.

Alek considered himself a connoisseur of woman, and Alessandra Dalmount was top-shelf.

Very nice, he thought, not turning away to continue down the hall until she was out of his line of vision.

He walked through the open glass double doors into his outer office.

"Hello, Ms. Kingsley," he said to the woman whose very appearance was the essence of propriety and nononsense.

He wanted it that way. He'd experienced the debacle of a young, sexy secretary with her eye on the wealthy executive. He didn't need the temptation.

Ms. Kingsley gave him a smile that didn't reach her cobalt blue eyes. "I entered all your messages on the online log," she said.

Alek patted the inner pocket over his heart where

his iPhone sat. "I got the notifications. Thank you," he said, moving past her desk to open one of the double doors leading into his office.

"Please get Naim Ansah on the line."

"Of course, sir."

With an approving nod, he closed the door and tossed his briefcase on the leather sofa of his reception area before he unbuttoned his silk-lined blazer to remove it and place it on the hanger of the wooden valet standing just outside his private bathroom. Taking his seat behind his massive desk, he signed on to his iPad to check the log of his incoming messages. A few business calls, and at least one message each from his mother, LuLu, his sister, Samira, and his brother, Naim.

He smiled. His return to New York meant more time spent with the family he had left behind five years ago. They visited him often in London, but he was pleased to be back among them regularly. He was sure his mother was already preparing his favorite Ghanaian dish of yam *fufu* and *nkatenkwan*. He couldn't wait to pull off a piece of the *fufu* ball and dip into the stew of chicken cooked in a rich peanut butter sauce and tomatoes with spices.

His stomach grumbled, but he focused on work instead. It was time to get serious about his plan to shift ADG into commercial aviation, and his younger brother was just the help he needed. Naim was younger than him by five years, but he was ambitiously climbing through the ranks of the company through sheer hard work. Nepotism had gotten him in the door but Naim was out to prove that he deserved his seat at the table. In the three years since he had begun at ADG, he had moved up the ranks from a management trainee to a lead position in the marketing division.

Bzzz.

"Yes?" he said, continuing to scan the message log.

"Mr. Ansah is in a meeting. Would you like me to continue holding?" Ms. Kingsley asked via the intercom.

Alek held his finger above the tablet at the sight of his ex-wife's name. *Kenzay called?* His brows dipped as he frowned deeply.

"Sir?" Ms. Kingsley gently nudged.

"No. I'll see him later," he said before turning off the intercom.

He leaned back in his chair and swiveled to look out the twenty-foot windows. The warmth of the sunlight framed him as he looked off in the distance at the varying shapes, colors and designs of the neighboring high-rise buildings. *Is Kenzay in New York?*

Usually they reached out to each other only during those rare occasions they were in the same city.

He'd met the beautiful socialite on the elevator of the Burj Al Arab in Dubai. He'd been staying at the hotel while in the country checking on one of ADG's numerous oil refineries; she was on a massive shopping spree sponsored by her father, a real estate developer of luxury hotels and mansions. Within hours they were making love against the floor-to-ceiling windows of his presidential suite with the sapphire ocean as their backdrop. Six months later they were married in a five-million-dollar destination wedding in the Maldives. The honeymoon period came and went quickly. Although their nights were filled with hot sex, their days were nothing but bitter arguments and long stretches of cold silence. They agreed neither wanted to be married and they never truly loved each other. By their second wedding anniversary their divorce was finalized.

Over the last three years, they'd occasionally given in to the attraction that still simmered between them. Neither wanted to reunite permanently and both frequently dated other people. Kenzay's dating life was just as adventurous and well chronicled by the press as his own as she traveled the world on her father's dime and the generous divorce settlement he paid to her based on their prenuptial agreement.

If she was calling she was somewhere nearby. *Maybe an afternoon romp would relax me...*

He picked up the phone to dial her cell phone number but changed his mind with a shake of his head and a downturn of his lips. He didn't have time for the distraction of his ex-wife. He had to stay focused on another woman in his life.

Alek swiveled away from the window. His dark eyes landed on his briefcase on the leather sofa. The file containing Alessandra's proposal was in it. She surprised him with more than just her change in looks and demeanor. She was further ahead on her proposal than he thought.

He swore, leaning back in his leather executive chair and tenting his fingers beneath his strong chin.

Their stalemate in that boardroom was one of the prime reasons he didn't want to share ownership with Alessandra. He wasn't quite sure how their fathers had accomplished it for thirty years. *Because they had been equals. They'd respected each other.*

It was going to take more than an MBA and a makeover for it to sit well that he was forced to share the company and the decision-making with Alessandra Dalmount. For years, she'd shown not one modicum of business savvy and suddenly she was a savant? He refused to swallow that.

Alek jumped up from his chair, causing to it to roll back and softly hit against the glass as he made his way across the expansive office. He snatched up his briefcase and pulled out his copy of her proposal. *Why can't she just go away quietly?*

His hand crumpled the corner inside his fist before he flung it down onto the couch.

And why can't I stop wondering how her mouth would taste?

"Damn," he swore.

"Physically I am your type, Alek. I am very much your type...and you know it. Humph, it's only my brain and my backbone that you think are a turnoff."

She was almost right on that point.

He did want her...but he wanted her out of his business affairs more.

They were a month from celebrating the thirtieth anniversary of the conglomerate his father and Alessandra's father had formed. Thirty years rich with a history that had to be protected and preserved. He respected the brilliance of Frances Dalmount, but his choice to make his daughter his heir had been made with his heart and not the cunning intellect he was well respected for.

Alek was intent on correcting the error.

He would rather have Alessandra Dalmount in his bedroom than his boardroom.

Perhaps I can kill two birds with one stone.

For one moment, one *very* brief moment, he allowed himself to imagine wooing Alessandra so much that she gave up any foolish notions of being a businesswoman. His conscience won out. He was a businessman and not a man-whore using his wares to convince women to do as he pleased.

Alessandra didn't deserve to be his partner, but she definitely didn't deserve to have her heart and body toyed with, either.

Alek sat down on the sofa and pulled the conference phone closer to press the intercom button. "Ms. Kingsley."

"Sir?"

"I need to speak with each of the board members, starting with Aldrich Brent," he said. "Call each one. Give me thirty minutes and get the next on the line."

"Yes, sir."

He rubbed his hands together in the moments before his phone buzzed. It was time to gauge just what side the board was going to choose. He couldn't do anything about her ownership, but he could call for a vote for her to be officially removed as chief executive officer.

Chapter 3

Three weeks later

Alessandra closed her copies of the *Wall Street Journal* and *New York Times* and picked up her cup of lavender tea to take several deep sips before she sat it down and reached for her iPad. Enjoying the feel of the July sun blazing through the windows of her two-story penthouse apartment, she connected with the online editions of *International Business Times*, London's *Financial Times* and Italy's *Corriere della Sera*. All five newspapers were a part of her normal routine, but she preferred the feel of the print paper against her fingers as she turned the pages.

Just like her beloved books. She was still a voracious reader of those set during the Elizabethan era and had curated a small collection of rare first editions of authors of that era. There was something to be said for tradition. Respect for the past.

"You have an old soul, my Alessandra," her father would say, and then playfully pinch her nose.

She smiled at the memory as she looked around at the French country design of her luxurious apartment with its soft muted tones, high-end furnishings, fine art and sweeping views of the Manhattan skyline. She grew up surrounded by such excess, but she had never felt at ease. Her style was simplistic. It was a part of her inheritance from her father, and she could never imagine changing the decor or getting rid of the apartment. It was just as her father had left it and he'd had it designed in the taste her mother would have loved. And so, for all its grandeur, living in the penthouse made her feel closer to them both.

Alessandra looked down the length of the table large enough to seat twelve people. Every empty chair was a reminder of her loneliness. Her longing caused an ache to radiate across her chest.

She didn't long for more people in her life. She wasn't even interested in dating with her focus on her career. No, Alessandra just wanted less space to echo around her.

The penthouse was a place to stay during the week while she was in Manhattan. Home was the family estate in Passion Grove, New Jersey. She smiled. Passion Grove. She absolutely loved the small town and couldn't wait to get there on Friday evenings.

Although the vast majority of the residents were wealthy, the town was ideal for those with luxurious homes still wanting to enjoy the small-town feel. Everyone knew one another and there were many events and holidays the townspeople enjoyed together. For her, Passion Grove, with its heart-shaped lake and streets named after flowers, was ideal.

Alessandra looked up as her maid silently entered the room to begin clearing her dishes. "Tell Cook everything was delicious as always, Gia," she said before rising from the table, setting her linen napkin atop her nearly empty plate.

Gia nodded. "I will," she said warmly. "Have a good day, Ms. Dalmount."

"Same to you, Gia," she said, offering her a soft smile. "Thanks."

Alessandra was well aware her demeanor with her staff at her various homes was different than with her staff at work. She had nothing to prove at home. No one was judging her. She could be herself, and that was thoughtful and kind. At ADG, that would be taken for weakness.

She chuckled as she used a crimson-red stiletto-shaped nail to ease her hair back behind her ear. "Elsa," she said with another chuckle. The modern take on calling her the ice queen. Alessandra mockingly pretended to pout at the memory. When she discovered that's what she was called behind her back, the last thing she did was "let it go." Instead she took the chill factor up a notch. "I gave them frozen, all right."

Her footsteps echoed against the travertine stone floors. The reminder of the emptiness of the five-bedroom apartment was deafening. She passed the door leading into her father's palatial master suite and her own childhood bedroom still decorated in shades of baby pink and ivory with an abundance of ruffles. She had long ago selected the largest of the three guest suites, preferring the more adult decor.

She removed the white floor-length robe she wore, already missing the cool feel of the woven cotton as she lay it across the foot of the king-size upholstered bed. In the walk-in closet separating the bedroom from the en suite spa bathroom hung a row of clear garment bags. Thirty in all. Each was labeled with a date with a clear shoe container on the shelf above it.

This was the playland of her stylist, Shiva Delacroix. Alessandra just visited it daily to wear whatever ensemble Shiva had prepared for that day. Everything from undergarments to accessories were readied, making her mornings easy and sending her into corporate America ready for war as if her clothing were her armor.

Another facade.

Alessandra turned the first bag and unzipped it to remove a burnt-orange button-up blouse teamed with flared trousers with racing stripes. She tore the Polaroid photo from the bag and set it atop the island in the center of the room, before removing the clothing from the suede hangers and getting dressed. She hummed Beyoncé's "Grown Woman" as she checked the correct fit of the clothing by the model in the photo.

She undid the buttons exposing the top of her cleavage, pushed up the sleeves to her elbows, and made sure the multi-strand gold chain she wore just barely peeked from beneath the shirt. She rushed through slipping on the leopard-print calf-hair pumps and her favorite Patek Philippe watch and grabbing the clutch Shiva selected before leaving her suite.

In the foyer, she picked up her briefcase and keys

from the table as she checked her watch and left the apartment through her private entrance and elevator. It opened into the first level of her exclusive parking area.

Ding.

The doors slid open and as expected her driver, Roje, was already waiting outside her father's black 1954 Jaguar MK VII sedan. As a little girl, she could remember standing on the porch of their mansion in Passion Grove as her dad climbed into the back and was driven to work each day. Ever since her first day of work at ADG she had used the car, as well. It felt like a full circle moment.

With a soft smile to the tall and burly man of sixty with skin as dark and smooth as midnight and a bright white goatee, she slid inside, setting her purse on the leather seat beside her. Roje was her bodyguard and her driver. She held no fear in his presence. His name was of his Jamaican heritage and meant "a person who is a guard." It suited him perfectly.

"Shiva's showroom, Roje," she requested, as she let her head fall back on the seat. Her eyes drifted closed.

She wasn't physically tired, just weary at the thought of yet another fitting.

Thursday would see the start of the extended weekend-long celebration to mark the company's thirtieth Jubilee anniversary. It was to be held at one of ADG's properties, the Lake House, a castle resort in upstate New York. Luncheons, picnics, art exhibits, tours, bike rides, boating, rock climbing and a charity tennis game were on the schedule. All the high-ranking executives and their families were invited, along with business colleagues and the press. The weekend would culminate in a lavish ball to officially welcome Alessandra and Alek to their positions.

She was headed into Midtown Manhattan for the final fitting of her couture Zuhair Murad gown. Alessandra turned her head on the rest to look out the tinted window at the abundance of skyscrapers and hotels as Roje maneuvered the traffic on FDR Drive. The distance between Shiva's showroom and the ADG offices was less than ten miles, but the drive would undoubtedly take every bit of twenty-five minutes.

She'd barely carved out the time for Shiva, because her focus had been on her report for the board. Their meeting was tomorrow morning at the Lake House before the celebratory festivities were scheduled to begin. Their vote of approval was the last step to ADG's purchasing the controlling shares in ZiCorp, the shipping company she had personally selected and vetted for acquisition. It would serve as the perfect opportunity for ADG to branch into Greece, with personnel and an established customer base in place. She and her team had addressed every possible issue that might arise and any concern the board could have. Months of arduous work would hopefully pay off. The company was in solid shape and would be nothing but an asset to ADG, with a return on the purchase price of controlling shares of ZiCorp projected to be recouped within a year.

During her training time at ADG Alessandra had chosen to focus on mergers and acquisitions, particularly in the areas of favorable purchase price, market movement and successful integration techniques. This was the first deal she had managed, but it was solid.

She wanted to beat Alek. To humble him. To prove him wrong.

To earn his respect.

No. She purposefully pushed any thought of him aside, closing her eyes and shaking her head a bit to free her mind of any thought of the handsome—yet infuriating—rogue. He took up enough time in her life antagonizing her during the day and invading her dreams with wild thoughts at night.

"Ms. Dalmount."

Alessandra opened her eyes. They were double-parked on Seventh Avenue outside the eighteen-story building where Shiva had set up a showroom for her impressive roster of clients. Usually, Shiva would come to her for measurements or fittings, but on occasion Alessandra preferred the normalcy of going to the showroom.

Roje now stood with the rear door open and his hand already outstretched to her. Picking up her purse, she accepted his assistance as she stepped onto the street. "Thank you," she said, easing through the pedestrians, tourists and locals alike, who moved up and down the street with speed. "I shouldn't be more than an hour, Roje."

"Yes, ma'am," he said, stepping ahead of her to open the glass door leading into the beautifully tiled lobby.

Alessandra rode one of the four elevators of the beautiful office building to the third floor. Through the glass wall and the double doors of the entrance to Shiva's showroom, she took in the two thousand square feet of loft-style space lined with clothing racks and adorned mannequins with bright light streaming in from the windows.

She smiled and waved at Shiva, who was looking on as one of her three assistants adjusted the hem of an emerald satin strapless gown on a woman standing before a wall of mirrors.

"I'll be right with you, Alessandra," Shiva said, kneeling to lift the hem and then release it.

The woman before the mirror turned to look over her shoulder. She was a tall, caramel-skinned beauty with shoulder-length auburn hair and hazel eyes. She smiled at her as if they knew each other.

They did not.

Alessandra sat her clutch on the low-slung white leather couch running along the glass wall as she eyed her. The woman was stunning, and that would be a fact in or out of her beautiful formfitting dress.

"I see Shiva will be styling us both for the ball," she said with a friendly grin and an accent that was English.

Alessandra stiffened and offered her a cool smile. "And you are?" she asked politely.

"Millicent... Alek's date for the weekend," she answered smoothly.

Alessandra fought not to frown. *A date? He would.*

"See you tomorrow then," she said, deliberately softening her tone because it wasn't the woman's fault Alek was a philanderer who couldn't stand to attend an event without arm candy.

"Okay, Milli, you're all set," Shiva said, raking her fingers through her waist-length jet-black hair. "If you go get changed, we'll package the dress for you to take with you."

Millicent smiled and showed perfect teeth before she lifted the dress and carefully walked to the rear of the showroom to the curtained-off dressing room area. The woman looked like Jessica Rabbit.

"You're welcome," Shiva said, as she strolled up to Alessandra in a floor-length white tunic and army boots.

"For my dress, yes, thank you as always, Shiva," Alessandra said, her tone distracted as she drew her iPhone from her clutch and pulled up her contact list.

Shiva pressed her hand down against the screen.

She looked up in surprise at the thirtysomething Cuban woman with striking features that made her an odd beauty.

"I scheduled your fittings like this on purpose," Shiva said, waving at her male assistant, who pushed a body form covered with white silk.

Alessandra swiped Shiva's hand from her phone and scrolled through the list with the steady stroke of her thumb against the screen. *There is no way I am attending the ball alone now. No. Way. In. Hell.*

"Bring it to me but do not uncover it just yet," Shiva called across the busy showroom.

"Hill," Alessandra said, thinking of the corporate attorney she'd had lunch with weeks ago. He was boyishly handsome, well-dressed and successful. They had no chemistry, but he would suffice for the night. *Wait...would that mean I'm using him?*

Shiva gently removed her phone.

Alessandra frowned. Over the years they had become good friends and not just stylist and client.

"I wanted you to see Alek's date in her dress," she

explained with a wink. "And give you a chance to wear the dress I *first* suggested."

The two women shared a look before Alessandra adamantly shook her head, causing her hair to move back and forth against her nape.

Millicent walked up to them with her garment bag hung carefully over her arm. She looked just as striking in a simple white T and distressed boyfriend jeans with heels. "Bye, Shiva. And nice meeting you, Alessandra," she said before leaving the showroom with long, model-like strides.

"You know the good thing about having that custom body form made to your specifications is that I really didn't need you to fit the new dress to your body, *mi amiga inocente*," she said.

Alessandra spoke Spanish, as well. "Yes, I'm your friend but I am *not* innocent," she said defensively, looking toward the silk-covered form being rolled toward them.

"Humph," Shiva teased, accepting the black garb a petite pink-haired assistant handed her.

She held it in front of Alessandra's body as she steered her toward the wall of mirrors. The lace dress with long sheer sleeves and flowing A-line skirt was covered with delicate floral designed beadwork.

"This is exquisite. Beautiful and classic," Shiva emphasized. "But *that* one will make sure you are the queen of the ball…"

Alessandra looked over as the white silk drape was snatched with dramatic flair from the body form. She gasped a bit as the light from the window seemed to shine like a spotlight on the gown. The moment was very cliché, but also very fitting. The dress was amazing. "It's not...*too* much?" she asked in a whisper, like a child in a library trying not to get caught talking.

"It's *just* enough," Shiva said, her voice a whisper, as well.

Alessandra stepped from behind the black frock Shiva held to stand before the dress form.

"Millicent who?" Shiva asked.

Alessandra looked over her shoulder to give her a look, like, "Really, Shiva?"

The woman shrugged.

"I'll try it on," Alessandra said, heading back to one of the dressing rooms.

"Yes! Take that, Alek Ansah!" Shiva exclaimed in victory, well aware of Alessandra's rocky relationship with the man.

Maybe it's time for the ice queen to serve up a little heat.

Alessandra was anxious to get to the office. Shiva was having the dress delivered to the Lake House in the morning. It was time to get refocused on work. The final printed proposals were to be on her desk before she walked through the door. She had no doubt that they were.

"The side entrance, Roje," she requested, her eyes looking out the window at the busy New York traffic.

"Yes, ma'am," he said, his voice rough and his Jamaican accent clear.

He drove the vintage Jaguar down the one-way street and parked outside the art deco building that spoke to its creation in the 1930s. She tucked her clutch under her arm and slid on her shades as he left the car and came around to open the rear door for her. Sliding her hand inside the one he offered, she stepped onto the street. She wasn't in the mood to speak to anyone, and the private entrance was ideal. On the opposite side of the building, Alek had his own, as well.

She paused to look up at the bright sunlight breaking through the tall buildings. For a moment, she just enjoyed the feel of the sun and thought back to a simpler time when she would lie by the pool and read literary classics when she wasn't doing volunteer work for one of her many humanitarian efforts.

Her smile was melancholy as she turned and entered the pass code to the nondescript-looking door. The shadow of Roje's large body behind her was comforting as he reached around her to open the door to a narrow and short hall leading directly to a private elevator that only stopped on the penthouse floor. She hardly used this entrance, preferring the massive and elaborate entrance into the front lobby.

The well-worn black-and-white checkerboard tile and the ornate wrought iron door to the elevator spoke to its originality to the building. Although the security features had been updated, nothing else had been touched.

The outer door closed behind them and locked as she pressed her thumb to the fingerprint reader. The lock echoed in the small space.

Clank.

"Have a good day, Ms. Dalmount," Roje said, opening the wrought iron gate.

Alessandra stepped inside and removed her shades, tucking them inside her purse. "Same to you, Roje."

With a nod, he turned and exited. Just as the elevator began to ascend, she watched on the security monitor in the corner as he climbed into the vehicle and pulled away, leaving the street empty.

She allowed a break in her usual cool demeanor as she fidgeted anxiously and fought the urge to press the button again for the top level of the building as if that would speed its journey there. "Relax, Alex," she said, reverting to her childhood nickname.

The elevator came to a stop and opened into the hall just outside her terrace entrance. She barely spared the elegant and spacious outdoor setting a glance as she made her way across the large expanse. Her footsteps echoed her quick pace to reach her desk.

She dropped her briefcase and purse on her desk as she eyed the stack of leather folders. She immediately picked one up and sat down in her chair to pore over every word, photo and graph on every page. She hardly noticed when she heard Unger arrive to work and begin his day. Soon, he quietly entered and sat a cup of lemon tea on her desk. At home, the lavender relaxed her before a full day of work, and at the office the lemon invigorated her.

He knew her routine well.

Taking a sip of her tea, she gave the pitch a careful final perusal for error. She refused to let a typo or an error by the printer ruin her presentation to the board. Alessandra nodded her head in approval as she closed the folder and then settled back in her chair. She was ready for her presentation to the board in the morning. *Is he?*

Alessandra rose from her seat and walked over to the glass-front wine cooler to remove a bottle of 1995 Krug Clos d'Ambonnay champagne and grabbed two flutes from her bar. She tucked one of the proposal packets under her arm.

She walked behind her desk to the shelves of books lining the wall. With a gentle push against the shelf to the far right, it swung open, revealing a long, windowless concrete hallway that ran along the back wall of the boardroom and connected to Alek's office on the other end. Another of the secrets the building held.

Her father had shown it to her ages ago when she was six or seven.

It was her first time using it. Would Alek be shocked by it? Alessandra shrugged. "Well, let's see," she said.

Her heels clicked against the dull concrete, echoing against the unadorned walls, as she reached the other end.

She was surprised when the door opened suddenly and his presence filled the doorway. She felt slightly flustered at the sight of him sans jacket with his sleeves rolled up and his tie loosened.

He motioned with his hand for her to enter before turning to walk back into his office.

"I've been summoned," she whispered as she followed him, disappointed that she couldn't surprise him.

In the three weeks since they moved offices she'd never ventured into his space before. The similarities were clear, although his had more of a masculine and modern edge. As he continued on his call she looked down at the framed photos on the edge of his massive desk. She recognized his mother and siblings. *Um, Naim and Samira.*

The entire family was beautiful, brown and bold.

"Let me call you back. I have a…visitor," Alek said before swiftly hitting a button on his phone and then removing his earbud.

Alessandra set the champagne and flutes on a clear spot on his desk. "Video surveillance, Alek? Really?" she asked, spotting the digital images on his iPad. "Thank goodness I didn't sneak a nose pick."

"It's your nose, Alessandra," he said, shifting his weight in the chair before leaning back and smoothing his hand over his beard as he watched her with those dark eyes.

Her heartbeat went awry under his watchful gaze. "I thought we should celebrate," she said, lightly tapping the cork on the bottle.

Alek gave her a once-over before leaning forward to take it from her.

She instantly felt warmed by the slight touch of his fingers against her hand. "This weekend we celebrate thirty years of ADG and our official claim to the thrones of the empire our fathers created together," she said, discreetly wiping her hand against her thigh as if she could erase the slight tingle that remained from his touch.

Alek opened the rare bottle with ease and filled each of the flutes slowly.

"Even *if* you've made it clear you don't think I deserve it just as much as you just because I use the facilities sitting down instead of standing up," she said smoothly before accepting the flute he handed her.

He chuckled. "To the Ansah Dalmount Group," he said, holding his drink out to her.

Alessandra arched a brow and lightly touched her

flute to his before taking a deep sip. "And to the completion of a comprehensive report that will seal the Zi-Corp deal tomorrow. *Salute*."

Alek fell just short of taking a sip as he paused the flute and eyed her over the rim. "I'm going to hate to see such a beautiful woman filled with disappointment," he said before finally allowing himself a large gulp of the smooth champagne that was well worth the four-figure price tag.

"My beauty is of no relevance to this conversation," she said, moving to sit on the edge of his desk.

"Of no relevance but very hard to deny," Alek said in a low voice, rising from his seat to come around and lean against the desk beside her. His shoulder brushed against hers.

Alessandra's heart fluttered as if filled with the wings of a million butterflies.

"I'm not equipped to handle all this…flattery, Alek," she began, giving him a side-eye as she subtly shifted her body to place a few inches between them. "I left my boots at home."

He eased his body over to close the gap she created. The warmth of his body and his cologne were overwhelming. *Why did I come in here to play with fire?*

Her awareness of Alek Ansah wasn't diminishing. Being in his presence made her senses go on alert. And the fact that he seemed as unable to hide his desire for her as he was his antagonism was its own kind of torture.

She stood up and tilted her head back to finish off the champagne before she turned and walked to the hidden door. His mocking and all too telling chuckle followed by her. Aware that his eyes were on her, she measured her steps because she didn't want it to appear that she was running again…even though she was.

"Non abbiate paura di ottenere una regina calda e bella del ghiaccio."

She paused at his words spoken fluently in Italian. She thought of the gown she would wear to the ball and if that would prove that the ice queen was not afraid to get hot. "Just how many languages do you speak, Alek?" she asked over her shoulder.

"Five," he answered. "But I will only speak to you in one of the four you speak, Alessandra."

She turned, her hand lightly grasping the edge of the portal. "And how many does Millicent speak?" she asked.

His handsome face filled with the surprise she sought earlier.

Alessandra held up her hand when he began to speak. "Don't answer that. I'm sure when you two are together she doesn't speak because her mouth is full," she said slyly.

Alek laughed. Loud and boisterous, with his head flung back and his beautiful mouth opened wide. He clapped. "Good one, Alessandra. Very good one. You're very quick on your feet."

"Goodbye, Alek," she said.

"And you're jealous," he added.

Yes. I am.

She walked back over to where he still leaned against the edge of his desk to stand before him. With a lick of her glossed lips, she reached for his tie and gently wrapped the ends around her fist to tug him forward until their faces were inches apart.

Their eyes locked.

Their breaths mingled in that small air between their mouths.

That primal awareness between them pulsed with life.

His eyes dipped to take in her pouty mouth before rising back to her eyes. She saw the heat of desire in the ebony depths.

"I am jealous of the one thing I can't seem to get from you," she whispered, her words pressing against his hungry mouth. "And that's your *respect*."

His face filled with shock. "Huh?"

It was Alessandra's turn to chuckle as she released his silk tie and smoothed it against his chest.

Oh my God. I can feel his muscles.

She suppressed her urge to roughly tear his custom shirt open and press her hands greedily to his abdomen. "Goodbye and good luck tomorrow, Alek," she said, quickly moving away from him.

He reached out and grabbed her wrist. His touch was electrifying.

She shivered, trying in vain to tug free of his strong hold.

And then suddenly he released her and stood to move past her, tipping his head back to finish the rest of his champagne. "Leave, Alessandra," he said, his voice tight with anger. "Get out."

Alessandra hurried out of his office through the secret passageway, surprised by his anger. She had barely taken two steps into the hall when the door closed and the turn of the lock echoed around her. She looked back and then up until she spotted the small camera in the corner.

Her face was stoic as she turned and walked the length of the hall with measured steps until she, too, was behind her closed and locked hidden door.

Chapter 4

Alek was still haunted by that moment in his office with Alessandra earlier that day. Not even his attendance at a luxurious dinner party hosted by his best friend, Chance Castillo, at his estate in Alpine, New Jersey, could free him of the hot memory. Her taunt had angered him because he fell for it. In that moment with nothing but space and opportunity between them, he had wanted to feel the softness of her mouth on his own. He didn't want to hunger for Alessandra, but he did. At odd moments of the day he imagined just how he would stoke the same fire from her in passion as he did in anger. During meetings, she would distract him with the smell of her perfume or the cut of her clothing on her curvaceous body. At night, when he tried to rest she was there in his dreams, causing him to awaken with an aching erection like a virginal schoolboy.

He wanted Alessandra Dalmount. Badly. In a rushed, hot, *rip your clothes off and fill her with every hard inch you got while up against the wall* kind of way.

He swore into his snifter of Grand Marnier Cuvée 1880.

"Something wrong, stranger?"

Alek looked up from where he sat on the bench of a nine-foot Brazilian rosewood Steinway grand piano to find his ex-wife, Kenzay. She wore a white lace romper that exposed the silk bralette and panty beneath it. The color looked fabulous against her deep brown complexion and highlighted her long, shapely legs. During their marriage, they would have argued about such a revealing outfit, but now he just enjoyed the show.

Rising to his feet, he grabbed her waist to pull her close for a hug. "Hello, stranger," he whispered in her ear before planting a warm kiss to her lobe.

She squeezed his elbows. "I called you the last time I was in town," she said. "I needed a fix."

He leaned back from her to look in her eyes. He couldn't help but smile. He knew they shared the memory of hot sex in an elevator when they last saw each other months ago.

"You know what seeing you in a tux does to me," she whispered in his ear.

Yes. Yes, he did.

Ding-ding-ding.

The varied conversations of the dinner guests died down as everyone in the music room turned to Chance's butler standing near the entrance of the dining room. "Dinner is served," he said, turning to push open the double doors, exposing a table set for twenty with tall elaborate glass-blown floral arrangements and candle lighting. Chance's taste ran toward vibrant and colorful contemporary style. It was an environment that spoke to his fun-loving personality.

The crowd began to move forward.

Kenzay slid her arm around his.

"Shouldn't you care if I have a date?" Alek asked as they followed the throng.

"Not at all," she assured him.

They made their way into the dining room.

"Alek," Chance said to him from the head of the table, patting the seat to his right.

With Kenzay still attached to him, Alek made his way to his seat. He held the chair next to him for her to slide her tall frame into before he claimed his own.

"Kenzay, I didn't know you were in town," Chance said, spreading his bright red napkin across his lap.

"I just got in today," Kenzay said, reaching under the ebony wood table to massage Alek's inner thigh. "I had to come and get something I wanted."

Alek just shook his head, denying her as he removed her hand, gently setting it back in her own lap. He saw the surprise and anger in her eyes before she masked them.

Kenzay did not like to be denied.

He looked across the table at Chance's girlfriend of the last six months, Helena Guzman. She was a petite, almost waiflike, fair-skinned beauty with waist-length blond hair as bone-straight as her frame. "Have you met Kenzay?" he asked as one of the servers set his plate atop the red square charger before him on the table.

Helena smiled and looked across the table at Kenzay. "Actually, I invited her," she admitted, her Cuban accent very subtle. "We met years ago at boarding school in Switzerland."

Alek and Chance shared a brief look before they both smiled in disbelief.

"Surprise, surprise," Kenzay said, having leaned close to whisper in his ear.

Ding-ding-ding.

Alek stopped feasting on the delicious Cuban dinner as his friend and host rose from his seat with his fork and his glass in his hand. The swinging doors leading from the kitchen opened, and the uniformed servers entered the dining room carrying trays of flutes filled with champagne.

"What now, Chance?" Alek asked playfully as he accepted his flute.

Everyone seated around the table laughed or chuckled.

Chance nodded his head in acquiescence. "Well, first I would like to officially welcome my friend— my brother—back to New York. We have all missed your constant presence—and your smart mouth—over the last five years."

Alek smiled and lifted his flute slightly in thanks.

"I am surrounded by friends and family, and I could not think of a better time to share some good news," he said, holding out his free hand to Helena.

She rose to stand beside Chance and captured his hand in the middle of both of hers.

Everyone at the table stirred and murmurs rose.

Chance dropped his head and smiled. "Let me get to it, since I can tell guesses have been made," he said.

"Last week Helena graciously accepted my proposal to become my bride."

Alek's face filled with disbelief even as he rose to hug first his friend and then his fiancée. "Congratulations," he said to them both.

"I can finally wear my ring," Helena said as she drew a chain from the V-neck of her stylish jumpsuit. She pulled it over her head and unclasped the lock to drop the ring into her palm.

Chance picked it up and reached for her left hand. *"Por siempre, mi amor,"* he said, using the language of their shared Cuban heritage as he slid the ring onto her slender finger.

Helena rose up on her toes, pressing her hands to his broad shoulders before kissing his lips.

Forever, my love.

Alek frowned at the idea of his friend's words to his fiancée as he gave Chance one last strong pat on the back before moving away from them to allow the waiting guests to congratulate the couple, as well.

Picking up his glass of champagne from his spot at the table, he pressed a kiss to Kenzay's temple and moved to walk through one of the four sets of French doors lining the dining room to step out onto the terrace. As he took a deep sip of champagne he instantly recognized as Dom Pérignon, he inhaled the scent of Sicilian honey lilies heavy in the night air.

In the days before sports and girls had drawn his full-time attention, Alek had spent lots of time with his mother as she tended to her gardens. He knew many a flower by scent alone from those hours. In the days right after his father's tragic death, he had returned to spending time with his mother in her beloved terrace gardens of her apartment on the Upper East Side until she had finally sent him on his way to live life and to let her live hers without a watchdog—albeit a loving one.

Alek smiled. His mother was nothing if not direct.

"Your date looks lonely."

He glanced over his shoulder at Chance stepping out onto the paved terrace, as well.

"Kenzay is not my date, your girl…eh, *fiancée*, invited her," Alek reminded him. "I just needed a moment to let it digest that my friend is getting married."

Chance nodded as he looked out at the stars in the night sky, which was deepening from a cobalt blue to jet-black. "Just like I had to when you married Kenzay," he said with a chuckle.

"Not a good example."

They fell silent.

They were good friends and in many ways closer than Alek was to his own brother. He knew he could fill the silence with warnings of marrying too soon and urgings to make sure she was the one, but he didn't. He couldn't. *Not yet.*

"Are you that surprised? We've been seeing each other for the last six months—and locked it down to just me and her for last three of those months," Chance said, turning to lean back against the metal railing securing the solid glass that gave him unobstructed views of his landscaped garden below.

"And I've been out of the country so I wasn't aware it was that serious," Alek offered. "But I am happy for you."

"Maybe you're next," Chance said, bending to pick

up a stone that he threw across the wildflowers surrounding his villa-style home.

Alek laughed wholeheartedly at that. "Maybe not," he assured him. "I'm still recovering from Kenzay, remember?"

It was Chance's turn to laugh. "There is nothing wrong with having the life your parents had. The love. The kids. The happily-ever-after."

"Yes, but my mother was home full-time," Alek reminded him.

"And my mother worked to provide for me alone," Chance reminded him.

"Wouldn't you prefer she didn't have to work?" Alek asked.

"Of course, *but* it brought her pride that she relied on no one but herself," Chance said. "I never expected Helena to trade being an attorney for being a full-time homemaker, but that's her plan."

Alek gulped his champagne as if it were cheap swill. "Seriously?" he asked, his doubt clear.

Chance nodded with a proud smile. "She surprised me. Helena has always been career-driven, but the ring changed all of that, I suppose."

Alek turned and leaned against the low metal railing surrounding the terrace. "What if she changes her mind again?"

"I still want her to be the woman I spend the rest of my life loving."

"Then I am happy for you, my friend," Alek said with honesty.

Alek wasn't looking for a lasting love nor a long-term relationship, but he had often thought of having children of his own. For a man in his position of wealth and prominence, he knew to have one without the other was a risk he wasn't willing to take. Billion-dollar baby mama drama? A straight catastrophe. So the kids would wait until he found the right woman to marry the next time. The only thing he knew for sure was that his wife would be a traditional, stay-at-home mother.

Nothing at all like Alessandra Dalmount.

Alek frowned and shook his head. Thinking of her—even in judgment—

In that moment was an oddity.

Chance looked off into the distance. "Any preliminary votes from the board?"

Alek nodded. "I have three on board. I plan to meet with the others sometime this weekend."

Chance nodded. "So it's working?"

"I just need three more for the majority."

"And?"

"My sources tell me Alessandra hasn't even made an attempt to reach out to the board in the interim," he said, remembering a moment in a recent meeting when she absentmindedly stroked her throat as she listened intently to the president of their casino division. That one innocent move led to a vision of him pressing his mouth to the exact same spot as she stroked his bare back and cried out in pleasure.

"Don't underestimate her, though," Chance reminded him with the hint of a smile at his lips.

The hot image faded as he focused on his friend.

Unlike Alek, Chance came from humble beginnings, raised by a hardworking Afro-Dominican single mother who worked double shifts as a certified nursing assistant to give her lone son the best life she could. When he turned ten she moved them from the Bronx to the Lower East Side, taking on higher rent, to be closer to the fringes of the Upper East Side and fought hard to pay his annual tuition and fees to attend the Dalton School. It was at the elite Manhattan private school that Chance and Alek met and became the best of friends.

His mother, Esmeralda, was more than proud of her son, who went on to finish at Dalton and graduated from Harvard with a degree in accounting and finance. He was a wealthy man in his own right after selling a project management app for well over $600 million. That plus the dividends from smart investing were rocketing him toward billionaire status.

Chance was the epitome of someone using others' underestimation of him for motivation to succeed.

Alek nodded. "Never. She's no idiot."

"And not hard on the eyes," Chance offered.

This time he recalled when Alessandra flipped her hair back over her shoulder and exposed the smooth caramel expanse of her delicate neck. It played like a movie in his mind. He had been filled with a desire to press his lips to her pulse and inhale deeply of the subtle scent of her perfume. He wasn't surprised when he woke up that night from a dream of doing just that and much more to her.

Burying his face against her warm spots. Her cleavage. Her belly. Between her thighs.

Massaging her shoulders.

Teasing her nipples and then sucking them.

Licking a trail from the curve above her buttocks and up her spine.

"The awkward duckling became one hell of a swan," Alek admitted.

"Perhaps you should give her something more to love than just business," Chance joked.

"And who is this?"

Both men turned to find Helena and Kenzay joining them on the terrace.

Helena moved to Chance to massage his back. "We caught the end of your conversation and I need answers, Senor Castillo."

Kenzay took Alek's drink from him and finished it as she eyed him over the gold-trimmed rim.

"I was just telling Alek how you volunteered to put your career on hold once were married," Chance began, wrapping his arm around her waist to pull her body in front of his. She immediately leaned back against him.

"And he joked that was a good way for me to get rid of Alessandra Dalmount," Alek finished.

Helena made a face as she swatted Chance's hand in reprimand. "That's terrible," she said before smiling and kissing his chin.

"Well, speaking as someone who has *experienced* Alek, that is not a good way to get rid of any woman," Kenzay joked with a wink.

Alek took a mock bow.

They all groaned and laughed as they made their way back inside to the party.

For a moment, Alek thought of how much fun wooing and bedding Alessandra could be, but marrying her? Never. She was too firmly entrenched in her role as businesswoman to *ever* satisfy him as wife.

* * *

"Let me take this off while you watch me..."

Alek lay on the middle of the king-size bed. The moonlight cascaded in through the open ten-foot-tall terrace doors. The sultry sound of Beyoncé's song "Rocket" filled the air. A breeze filled with the scent of night-blooming jasmine wafted in, caressing the sheer curtains a bit.

He was waiting. And naked.

And anxious.

He closed his eyes and tilted his head back on the pillow as his Adam's apple rose and fell with his deep swallow. He tugged at the ties on his wrists and ankles that secured him to the four-poster bed.

"You ready, Mr. Ansah?"

His eyes opened to find Alessandra standing at the foot, her svelte body barely covered by a sheer black lace bodysuit. Her smile was soft and beguiling as she wrapped her hands around his ankles and climbed up onto the bed, her hands inching up to his thighs to massage the defined contours.

Her touch was ideal. Soft, barely there, but electrifying.

His breath was bated. His pulse soared. And his heart felt right on the edge of a soft explosion.

He felt drugged. He was addicted. He wanted—no, needed—more.

Desire hardened him until it was thicker and longer. Aching. Needing. Wanting...more.

Alessandra dragged her teeth against her bottom lip as she sat back on her knees between his open legs and took him in her hands.

He hissed between clenched teeth at the feel of her

warm hands on him, stroking him as she brought her thumb up to graze against the smooth tip.

"Alessandra," Alek cried out, his hips arching up off the bed.

With her eyes locked on him she lowered her head, bowing to him in a way, before she wet her lips with her tongue and then took his hardness into her mouth. Slowly. Inch by inch.

Sweat coated his body. His thighs trembled. His gut clenched. His bit his own lip to keep from crying out at the feel of her mouth on him until he felt the tip touch the back of her throat.

She swallowed, contracting her throat and causing the base of her tongue to rise up and put sweet pressure on him.

Alek whimpered as he felt a small of bit of release jolt in the back of her throat.

She moaned in pleasure and swallowed again.

"No!" he cried out, straining against the ties with such strength that his entire body bounced up off the bed a bit.

She hummed as she slid her mouth up to the tip. She circled it with the tip of her tongue and then sucked it deeply, again and again, as she pressed her tongue against his hard heat.

"Please," he begged her, his shame lost amid his abandon.

He dwelled somewhere between pleasure and insanity.

Alessandra gave one last one kiss to the tip before she freed him.

His body relaxed but his heart pounded with a ferocity that frightened him. He closed his eyes and re-

leased a long shaky breath. *"Damn,"* he swore in a whisper.

His respite was brief. Every muscle making up the hard contours of his body tensed in anticipation as she moved her body to straddle his hips. He looked to her as she bit down on her tongue at the corner of her mouth and began milking him with both her hands. Up and down with a soft twist that was slow and deliberate.

Up to the hot, swollen tip and down to the thick, rock-hard base. Again and again.

"Alessandra," he moaned, wishing his hands were free to touch her.

"Alek," she said in return.

Up. Down. Again and again.

"Don't make me come," he begged, biting on the side of his tongue.

Up. Down. Again and again.

"Yet?" she asked, pausing her actions.

He agreed. *"Yet."*

She rose to her feet, her hair swinging forward as she looked down at him. *"Am I everything you thought I would be?"* she asked, twisting her body this way and that seductively.

Alek was transfixed by the sight of her. The moonlight framed her body, and the sight of her nipples and the plump mound pressed against the sheer material was mesmerizing. He grunted as he tried to tear free of his restraints.

"Am I everything you want?" she asked, turning and bringing her hands up her thighs to caress her exposed derriere as she looked back over her shoulder. *"Everything you need?"*

Her teasing made him hungry for her.

"Everything you desire?" she asked, turning again to cup her breasts and tease her hard nipples through the barely-there material.

"Come and get it," she taunted, using the arch of her bare foot to stroke his stiff inches.

He roared, his muscles tense as he brought his arms and legs up off the bed, futilely straining against the cotton ties holding him captive to the bed...

"Alessandra!"

Alek awakened, raising his head from the pillow to look down the length of his body at his hardness tenting the sheets. Still somewhere between fully awake and asleep, his face was bewildered as he looked left and right to find his arms open wide across his pillow, but free of any ties like his all-too-real vision.

Relaxing his body, he closed his eyes and released a heavy breath. His dream had been vivid. And in those moments as he waited for his erection to ease and his pulse to diminish, he wished like hell that he hadn't awakened.

Chapter 5

Simply amazing.

"Pull over for a second, Roje," Alessandra said, sitting up in her seat of the back of the Jaguar.

"Yes, ma'am." He pulled the car to a stop on the curving road seemingly carved out of the mountain looming beside it.

As soon the vehicle stopped she climbed out and moved to stand at the metal railing lining the winding road. The smell of trees and earth was heavy as she looked in the distance at the view of the Lake House, seemingly nestled inside the towering trees and mountains of the Catskills with its reflection mirrored on the surrounding lake. Over the years since ADG acquired the once-small resort, the property had increased in size with more than three hundred guest rooms and suites. The additions maintained the original aesthetic of the stone castle with its pointed forest green rooftops referencing its surroundings.

It was picture-perfect.

Looking at it, for a moment, all her nerves about her presentation to the board that morning eased a bit.

"Are we having a moment, Alessandra? Please don't jump, sweetheart. There are way less messy ways to go."

Poof. The moment was gone with the same finality of a popped balloon.

She released a little moan of annoyance before looking over her shoulder at her aunt Leonora's head peeking out the rear window of one of the two Rolls-Royce Phantoms following behind her car. She wasn't surprised by the platinum flask clutched in her hand. Aunt Leonora enjoyed a good cocktail, and the alcohol made her tongue straight reckless.

Her father had been all about family, and his financial support of them had passed on to Alessandra upon his death. She loved them all, but they were quite a handful. She walked back to the car, careful not to trip on an errant rock or crack in the country road as she bent to look in the rear of the Phantom.

There was her aunt Brunela, her father's sister whom Alessandra recently put on a spending budget. She had made it clear that if she had been a man that the family business would have been hers to inherit and not her younger brother. And she seemed intent on spending as much as she could. The purchase of a five-million-dollar antique car had been a bit much, particularly when Brunela had never acquired a driver's license. *As if spending the family fortune would replace never being put in control of it.*

And Aunt Leonora, her father's younger sister who never married or had children. She had become Alessandra's mother figure in the years after her passing. Leonora's opinion and personality were much bigger than her petite stature, but she gave good advice and was a soft place for Alessandra to land when the world felt tough and unrelenting. *Even if her honesty sometimes stings.*

Alessandra eyed her cousin Marisa, lightly snoring in the corner with earphones plugged in, undoubtedly sleeping off another late night of partying and man-hunting. She and Brunela's daughter were the same age but so completely different. Marisa had never been given the same responsibility and it was clear that her mother's overindulgence had not prepared her for adulthood. *She has the freedom to mess up. Lucky girl.*

Her father's first cousin, Victor, and his sixth wife, Elisabetta, and their toddler twins were in the last car. Although he was quite experienced at getting married, he was the worst possible candidate for a husband. Elisabetta was thirty years his junior and loved being his wife, so much so that she couldn't seem to be bothered to discipline their twin toddlers who were as bad as the day was long. They were quite a little family and Alessandra wished them well. Although Victor was employed by ADG and received a hefty salary, he had yet to make an appearance in his office in the last twenty years. *God help him the day Elisabetta realizes he spends his days test-driving wife number seven.*

"I was taking a little time to enjoy the view," she finally said.

"Well, who the hell are you, Barbara Walters?" Leonora asked, easing her flask back inside her Louis Vuitton tote.

Alessandra just laughed as she turned back to head to her car. "Roje, let's get these people to their rooms," she said, her tone amused.

He chuckled. "Right away."

She picked up her iPad from the seat beside her, settling back as she continued to prep for her presentation at the board meeting.

"You're ready, you know."

Alessandra looked up to find Roje's dark eyes on her in the rearview mirror. "I wish I was sure about that."

"Your father was sure," Roje said. "Trust and believe in that."

Her emotions swelled inside her like a crescendo and she shifted her eyes away. "Yes, he did, didn't he?" she asked with the hint of a smile.

Roje said nothing else. He didn't need to. His words were few but meaningful. He had been her father's driver for many years and he knew both Frances Dalmount and his daughter very well. There was a lot to learn from the front seat of a chauffeured car by a man willing to listen.

Alessandra closed the cover of her iPad and slid it into the side pocket of her alligator Saint Laurent Sac de Jour bag. It was her first visit to the luxury castle resort, and during the two hour drive the gradual transformation from urban landscapes to acres of forest had been surreal. It was a decided change from the tall skyscrapers and frenetic pace of Manhattan.

She was looking forward to the weekend of activities and relaxation. The last five years had moved with a speed that left her bone-tired and weary at night, with her shoes kicked off and her feet up on the antique French provincial table. Some celebrating and taking some time to slow down and enjoy life wouldn't be a bad thing at all.

But first, let's get this business out of the way...

As Roje turned the Jaguar up the stone driveway, it was hard not to be impressed by the grandeur, scope and size of the resort. It was a gem in the ADG portfolio, and Alessandra could admit she was pleased with Alek's choice to hold their festivities there.

She slid on her shades and climbed from the car with Roje's assistance. She glanced at her watch and looked up. Her eyes widened a bit at the sight of Alek and his equally handsome brother helping his mother and sister from the rear of a black Maybach 62. She'd never seen him in casual clothing, and the dark blue button-up shirt he wore with distressed denims and brown burnished leather drivers looked really good against his chocolate complexion. His aviator shades shielded his expression from her when he looked up and saw her, but he stared for a long enough moment to make her gasp softly.

She looked away first.

Alessandra was surprised to discover that Roje still stood behind her. It wasn't like him to linger. She followed his line of vision to find his eyes resting on LuLu Ansah, Alek's mother, who looked stunning in a deep purple wrap shirt paired with white linen pants. A woman it would be hard to tell was in her midfifties, she always had a regal air about her that Alessandra found fascinating, and her head wrap in colors of purple and gold seemed like a crown on her head.

"Everything okay, Roje?" Alessandra asked, biting the inside of her cheek to keep from smiling.

He cleared his throat and stroked his mouth and white goatee with a hand before turning his attention to the Jaguar and finally getting in and closing the door.

"Alessandra, it's really nice to see you again."

She faced Alek and his family walking up to her. Out of respect for his mother, she stepped forward to meet them halfway. "Thank you, Ms. Ansah. It's good to see to you," she said warmly, pressing a kiss to both of the woman's cheeks and ignoring Alek standing beside his mother and staring at her.

Alessandra remembered his frustration with her just the day before and hoped it didn't linger. A weekend of Alek scowling at her at every turn would just ruin the entire celebration. *As would the board voting to implement his acquisition.*

She smiled and nodded at both Samira and Naim, both standing there looking like models in a Gucci magazine ad. "Alek," she said, acknowledging him.

He leaned forward to press his lips to her cheeks. "How are you, Alessandra?" he asked.

She covered her surprise as his well-groomed beard tickled her face a bit. "I'm good, and you?" she asked, her tone polite.

LuLu chuckled. "You two are a mess, but your politeness is very civilized," she said, her accent heavy.

Alek leaned back from her. "I'll make sure the rooms are ready," he said, looking back at his brother. "Come on, Naim."

Samira stepped forward, looking pretty in a peach

strapless sundress. "I am very impressed by you, Ms. Dalmount," she said.

"Call me Alessandra," she offered. "We're not that far apart in age."

She shrugged one mahogany-brown shoulder. "But you are in profession, so it doesn't seem that way," Samira said, easing her thick straight hair over the other shoulder.

Alessandra was confused by that statement and it reflected on her face.

Samira smiled, showing a deep dimple in her left cheek. "My brother won't allow me to work for the company as a relative," she said, her annoyance displayed in her tone if not in her eyes.

"That sounds about right," Alessandra said lightly, not wanting to fuel a family disagreement even as her own annoyance at Alek's chauvinistic beliefs surfaced.

"Perhaps you can give me the chance he won't," she said, her eyes serious as she reached out to hand Alessandra a thick cream envelope.

She took it from her, looking down at the woman's name embossed in gold.

"My résumé," Samira said.

Alessandra looked back up at her. She was no more than twenty-one or twenty-two, but she was everything Alessandra pretended to be, particularly fearless. At Samira's continued silence, Alessandra looked to her mother to gauge her take on her daughter's open defiance of Alek.

Ms. Ansah stood there with them, but her attention was elsewhere.

Alessandra glanced over her shoulder.

Roje stood there, a respectful distance back from them, and LuLu's eyes were on him.

She turned back to Samira, leaving them to whatever business they were creating. "I'm not sure what I can do, but I will look this over, maybe make some recommendation to colleagues in the industry," she said.

Samira shook her head. "I want to work for the firm my grandfather created from nothing and my father helped shape into a billion-dollar corporation," she said. "I want in at ADG."

The glass ceiling was still in full effect in corporate America, particularly for women of color. Even with the past advancements of CEOs like Rosalind Brewer at Starbucks, Ursula Burns at Xerox, Indra Nooyi at PepsiCo, Debra Lee at BET, and now herself at ADG, Alessandra realized she had joined an unspoken club of unicorns who were able to excel in spite of adversity.

Her own time at ADG had not been easy, but she was well aware in the current corporate climate that she still had not put in the work of her peers. Nepotism could not be denied as having some role in her success, nor could her business acumen.

Not in Alek's or Naim's careers, either, though.

Didn't Samira deserve the same?

Alessandra stiffened her back and squared her shoulders as she extended her hand to the younger woman. "Let me see what I can do," she said.

"That's all I ask," Samira said.

"Okay, ladies, I have to prepare for a board meeting," she said, giving Samira's hand a squeeze.

LuLu was now refocused on them, but her eyes were distant, as if she wished to be somewhere else.

Alessandra glanced back to find Roje supervising the removal of her luggage from the Jaguar. Her family's drivers had already done so and were gone, with her family now entering the resort. Alessandra turned to do the same, tucking Samira's envelope inside her tote.

"Yes, let's go inside," Samira said, following Alessandra.

LuLu followed behind them. "I didn't eat breakfast and I could eat something," she said, sounding distracted.

"The food is supposed to be delicious," she said, turning to glance back just as Ms. Ansah and Roje lightly touched hands as she passed by him.

"I love my brother, Alessandra," Samira said, as they crossed the lobby. "But good luck."

"Thank you," Alessandra returned earnestly, turning away from the small but telling moment.

Alek was in his element as he ran across the red clay tennis courts to swing his racket with force and accuracy to lob the ball. The onlookers applauded as the ball shot over his opponent and landed inside the line for the win. He raised his racket high above his head and balled his free hand into a fist to pump the air vigorously as he raced up the court.

Garrison Wyndham let out a shout of frustration as he spun his racket, coming up to the net. "Good win, Alek," he said, sweat plastering his blond hair to his head. "That wasn't retaliation for the board meeting, was it?"

Alek smiled as they shook hands. "Maybe a little," he joked, accepting the monogrammed towel from a middle-school-aged ball boy. "A win is a win, and I needed one after that loss a couple of days ago."

Garrison wiped his face and neck, leveling blue eyes on Alek. "It wasn't a loss, Alek. You both had strong presentations and the votes were evenly split, leaving it at a standoff."

Alek just shrugged as he wrapped the towel around his neck and tucked the ends inside the V-neck of his T-shirt. "It may be time to push the board to vote on her removal."

"*Or* you both can do what we suggested, in the tradition of the compromise for which your fathers were known, and decide together whose plan goes forward," Garrison offered.

"I'm going to shower and then get some lunch," Alek said, now done with the conversation. "See you at the ball?"

Garrison nodded, acknowledging the abrupt change in conversation. "My wife and I are taking the kids kayaking. They're disappointed the ball is adult only."

"Enjoy," he said, forcing warmth into his voice.

He wasn't angry about the board's decision and didn't want to appear that way.

"We will," Garrison said before walking away.

Alek turned and followed suit. He smiled when Millicent came through the plexiglass gate of the glass fence surrounding one of the eight tennis courts on the property. Onlookers sat at wrought iron tables enjoying the game or just having lunch in the floral settings.

He shoved his racket inside the bag and zipped it as he smiled at her in welcome. He'd known her since her modeling days in Paris and they'd dated often. When he learned she had moved to New York he decided to reconnect with the beauty and invite her as his date for just the ball. He was pleased she agreed because he didn't want the constraint of having a date there for the entire four-day weekend.

"Congratulations, Alek," she called over to him, looking like pure sunshine in the yellow sundress she wore with her reddish-brown hair blowing in the wind behind her.

His smile faded. Over Millicent's shoulder he spotted Alessandra walking onto the court followed by her date. His jaw clenched and the heat of jealousy burned his gut when she looked up at the man and laughed with such abandon that she seemed to radiate. The very presence of the man had irked his spirit since he first learned of his arrival the night before.

He had been distracted with the thought of them sharing her double-level suite until he checked with the front desk to ensure he had his own room. Ownership had its privileges.

He took in the sight of her in a white halter tennis tank that showed just a sliver of skin at her waist and a matching skirt with a hem that cut right across the top of her shapely thighs. That tiny sliver and the length of her legs was enough for him to overlook Millicent crossing the court to reach him until she was standing directly in front of him.

He jumped in surprise as she pressed a kiss to his cheek above his beard. "When did you get in?" he asked.

"This morning," she said.

"You like your room?" he asked.

"And *all* of the amenities," she said with a coy smile. "I had a stone massage and a facial that was absolutely beyond anything I've ever had. Kudos to the owner."

"You mean co-owner."

Alek's and Alessandra's eyes locked over Millicent's shoulder before she turned around. "I didn't mean anything—"

Alessandra grabbed her hand and smiled comfortingly. "I was just trying to pick at Alek," she reassured her.

"That sounds about right," Alek said, extending his hand past Alessandra to her date. "Alek Ansah."

"Hill Graham," he answered.

Alek gave his hand an extra firm grip and then felt petty when the man visibly winced.

Alessandra's eyes went from the men's hands and up to Alek's eyes with a slight arch to one of her eyebrows.

"We'll see you later," he said, lightly pressing his hand to Millicent's lower back to guide her past them.

"You really looked good out there, Alek," Millicent told him.

He barely heard her. His thoughts were somewhere else. Or rather on someone else.

As he held the gate open for her to step through, he glanced back. His breath caught to find Alessandra looking past Hill with her eyes resting on him.

They held that stare. Time seemed to tick by slowly.

"Am I everything you want?"

"Everything you need?"

"Everything you desire?"

"Let's go kayaking," Millicent said from somewhere outside the bubble.

"Alek. Alek? Alek!"

Millicent shook his arm roughly, jarring him. He looked down at her in question. "Huh?"

"Is everything okay?" she asked, lightly touching his chest.

"Yes," he lied, gently steering her from the tennis court as he forced himself not to look back again.

As she stood in a dress most women would crave wearing, Alessandra had never felt so unsure in her life. She pressed a trembling hand to her stomach as she eased the black curtain open just enough to peek out at the transformed east dining room of the Lake House. She smiled at the ADG employees and their spouses, dates and adult family members enjoying the live band and the elegant decor of the candlelight, warm white lighting and colorful floral arrangements on each table contrasting with the dark wood of the ceiling and the stone pillars.

The venue's event planners had done a wonderful job and she was pleased.

And nervous.

A frown marred her brow when she spotted her cousin Marisa in the middle of the dance floor with her hands high above her head as she danced to "Wild Thoughts" by DJ Khaled and Rihanna, drawing attention as the skirt of her short sequined dress rose high on her legs. She winced as the wife of the telecommunications director jerked his arm when he started to dance up to Marisa as she bent over and wiggled her bottom.

I know she didn't. No to the hell no.

She turned to look over her shoulder and spotted the resort's lead event planner in the wings of the stage reviewing something on her clipboard. "Cindy," Alessandra called out in a loud whisper.

The woman looked up and immediately walked over to where Alessandra stood behind the closed curtains. "We're just waiting on Mr. Ansah and we'll be ready to make the announcement and free you from back here," she said, her tone congenial.

"No, I'm fine, I just need you, or one of your staff, to go to the woman putting on the show in the middle of the floor and tell her *I* said for her plant her ass in a seat or she can go *home*," Alessandra stressed, pulling back the curtain to point out Marisa. "And let her know I am *so* serious about this."

Cindy's expression became pained after she peeked past the silk curtain. That spoke volumes that Alessandra was not overreacting. "Right away," she said, swiftly walking back into the wings and down the stairs leading to the dining room.

Alessandra watched on as Cindy reached her cousin and discreetly guided her from the dance floor as she spoke into her ear. Marisa did not look pleased, but she immediately reclaimed her seat next to her mother at their round table. Alessandra had no doubt that she would do as she bid. Being the one to dole out the family allowances had its privileges.

Waiters filed in carrying crystal flutes of Armand de Brignac champagne, ensuring every person was handed a glass. Alessandra wasn't surprised when Marisa insisted on two. Her life was always about excess. Everything was too much: too much drinking, too much partying and too many men.

"If you're looking for me, I'm right here, Alessandra."

Her body froze as her pulse raced, and she closed her eyes as she quickly sought control. Turning, she was surprised to find Alek standing so close behind her. He wore all black with a tuxedo obviously tailored for just his frame. His eyes seemed more intense. The cut of his jaw with his trimmed beard more masculine. His supple lips more enticing. Just handsome. Devastatingly so.

She took a step back. The curtain swayed.

He reached out to press his hands to her bare upper arms to steady her. "Damn, Alessandra," he said as his eyes moved up and down the length of her body in pure appreciation.

The sound of the Latin-flavored music was haunting. The lyrics spoke to temptation.

She was breathless. All her fears and nerves about her dress faded into the heat of his clear approval of her choice. The custom sheer figure-hugging backless gown with a plunging neckline was showered with crystal embellishments that sparkled beneath the overhead lights. Her glam squad had her hair piled atop her head, exposing her neck, and her makeup was a dark and dramatic smoky eye with a nude lip.

But it wasn't until that moment, as Alek looked down at her with hunger in his eyes, that she felt beautiful. Her nipples hardened against the dress as she fought so hard to continue fighting the tension that swelled between them, sometimes under the pretense of anger. But it was pure attraction. Heat. Desire. Want.

It pulsed with a life all its own whenever they were near each other.

In that moment, Alessandra couldn't think of one reason to fight it any longer.

"Alek," she breathed, reaching up to grip the lapels of his tuxedo in her greedy little hands as she stepped closer to him.

His grasp on her arms tightened as he lowered his head to hers.

Yes. Let me see if your mouth feels as soft as it looks, Alek.

Rapid footsteps echoed and they jumped apart just before Cindy came across the stage to reach them.

The moment was gone.

Their regret was palpable.

"Okay, if you both can move center stage," Cindy said as a waiter approached with a tray with two flutes of champagne. "As soon as this last song stops playing, Mr. Brent will come up onstage, introduce you both, and the curtains will open."

Alek barely heard the woman as he accepted the flute and moved to the spot she indicated. He glanced back at Alessandra as she did the same and was as mesmerized by the sight of her in that dress as he was when he first turned around to face him. He took a sip of the champagne to steady himself.

"Okay, good luck," Cindy said, before disappearing and leaving them alone again.

Alessandra came to stand beside him, glancing up at him.

Their eyes locked.

There it was again. That shift in the space-time continuum. Everything seemed to go still around them as they were in tune with each other.

Alek turned to face her. His heart pounded with such force. Little Alessandra the shy girl had grown into a woman who had the power to weaken his knees with a touch. His eyes searched hers, and the desire he felt for her was mirrored. "Alessandra," he said, low in his throat, as he dropped his head to hers again.

She brought her free hand up to stroke his beard as she raised up on her toes to meet his mouth with her own.

Alek's entire body felt alive with awareness as they kissed. Her mouth was just as sweet and soft as he imagined. His face tingled where she stroked his cheek. With a moan in the back of his throat, he slowly deepened the kiss and brought his free hand up to her back to press her body forward against his.

He felt her tremble from his touch. It made him heady. He sucked the tip of her tongue, and her moan of pleasure pushed him over the edge. He lowered his hand to grip one fleshy cheek of her buttocks.

He had never felt so alive.

"Good evening, ADG family!" Aldrich Brent roared into the microphone.

Alek placed soft kisses around her gaping mouth, leaning down to kiss and tease her neck, caring nothing about the acrid taste of her sultry perfume.

"Oh, Alek," she sighed, tilting her head back in abandon. "Yes. Yes. *Yes*."

"I know Frances and Kwame are here in spirit celebrating this momentous occasion. It was clearly their wish for their children to run this business together just as they did starting thirty years ago this week," Aldrich continued, his voice echoing around them.

Alek offered her his tongue.

She looked up at him as she sucked it.

Never had he wanted to be inside a woman so badly.

"Without further delay it is time to introduce the leaders of the Ansah Dalmount Group as they lead our corporation into an even brighter and more successful future with the same vision, drive and ambition passed on to them by their respective fathers," Aldrich said. "Rise and let us welcome the owners and chief executive officers of the Ansah Dalmount Group... Alessandra Dalmount and Alek Ansah!"

Someone cleared their throat. And then cleared it again. And again.

Alessandra and Alek were lost in each other.

"The curtain!"

They broke apart at the shriek, finding Cindy standing in the wings waving at them frantically as the curtain quickly opened from the left of the stage.

Alek and Alessandra shared a look as the energy they created dissipated like a mist.

"Wipe your mouth," she told him as she straightened her dress.

He did so with his thumb, feeling the sticky gloss on his lips.

The curtain swept past them and they both stepped forward with a smile, their champagne-filled flutes raised high in the air as the thunderous applause surrounded them.

From her spot at the front of the applauding crowd, LuLu Ansah squinted her eyes as she spotted the hint of sheer pink gloss on the corner of her son's mouth and cheek as he finished giving a speech promising a bright future for ADG. She shifted her attention to Alessandra standing a respectful distance from him and looking on with poise and respect.

But her hair was slightly disheveled and her mouth was free of any lipstick or gloss.

Well, well...

That amused her, and she couldn't help but smile as she rushed forward to wrap her arms around them both and pulled their heads in close as she hugged them. "Alessandra, your gloss is missing, sweet one, and somehow, it's on my son's mouth," she teased for their ears alone with a chuckle.

Alessandra stiffened. LuLu warmly rubbed her shoulder like only a mother could.

Alek immediately turned and removed his black linen handkerchief to wipe his mouth. LuLu chuckled again.

She stepped back from them and allowed their dates, family, colleagues and employees swell forward to congratulate them. Alek and Alessandra? She wasn't surprised. She'd seen it coming a mile away. Their level of animosity for each other was unnatural, and the root cause for that level of annoyance was always passion denied.

She knew quite a bit about that.

LuLu stopped a waiter for a new flute of champagne from his tray. "Thank you so much," she said with a bow of her head, before she continued out of the dining room and onto the wood terrace surrounding the entire building. She inhaled deeply of the fresh air before taking a deep sip of her drink, leaving her bright red lipstick on the rim as she did.

"You have never looked more beautiful, LuLu."

Roje.

Surprise and pleasure filled her.

She turned. "Same to you," she said, taking in the

navy suit he wore with a matching open button-up beneath it.

"LuLu—"

She smiled sadly and shook her head. "Roje, I can't," she said softly. "That one night helped me heal. Even a year after Kwame's death I was so lost. What we shared helped me forget for a little while, but I can't. And you know that. So, please, Roje. *Please*."

His eyes were filled with his regret, but he nodded.

She walked past him, but he stepped in her path. "That night I left a piece of my heart with you that I will never get back, LuLu," he said. "I just want you to know that."

For a moment, they went back in time to that long passionate night they shared in his bed.

LuLu pressed a kiss to the side of his mouth. "So did I, Roje," she admitted in a whisper, before moving past him and walking away with regrets.

Chapter 6

Alessandra could not sleep.

Memories of the passion she shared with Alek haunted her. Passion that had been stoked for weeks. Passion that may very well be hard to douse. It felt like dropping a lit match to a trail of gasoline and then trying to avoid the explosion that was to follow.

What happens now?

For the rest of the night they watched each other from across the room, unable to deny the intense attraction.

What now?

She flung back the sheets and rose from the king-size bed to cross the spacious suite and step out the wood-trimmed doors lining the room to her balcony. A warm summer breeze blew against the black lace nightgown she wore. She looked out at the moon reflected against the mountain lake. Not even the picturesque view could calm her raging emotions. At first there was pleasure that Alek couldn't seem to resist her any more than she was able to deny her attraction to him. And then there was remorse for so desperately wanting a man who didn't respect her presence in the business world simply because she was a woman.

As she remembered their fiery kiss, she touched her lips with a trembling hand. "What's wrong with me?" she said out loud, truly puzzled.

"The same thing that's wrong with me."

Alessandra was startled. She looked over to find Alek on the balcony directly to her left. She hadn't known his suite was next to hers, but it made sense they would be given the best accommodations at the resort. Her eyes took in the sight of him in nothing but navy silk pajama bottoms that hung low on his narrow hips and clung to the lengthy curve of him as he came to the end of his balcony nearly connecting with hers.

His eyes, those dark, intense eyes, were locked on her as he began to climb over the very short divide between their balconies.

"Alek," she said, her heart pounding and pulse racing as she backed away as if the distance would ease her desire for him.

He shook his head as if to say "Hell, no," as he strode over to pull her into his arms and without a bit of hesitation captured her mouth with his own.

She pressed her hands against the smooth brown skin of his chest and shoulder, but her resistance was weak and soon she kissed him back as she eased her hands up to press to the back of his head. His body, the strength and the heat, felt so good against her softness. His chest to her breasts. The length of his hardness against her belly.

He used his strength to pick her up into his arms.

Alessandra stroked his arms, loving the feel of his muscles flexing. Her core warmed more and she moaned as the pulsing bud snuggled inside her lips ached for release.

He walked them into the coolness of her suite and pressed their bodies to one of the large club chairs before the balcony doors, with no patience to reach the bed as they gave in to their craving for each other. Alek shifted her body to one side to caress and stroke her thighs as he pressed his face to her neck, feeling her racing pulse against his lips.

Alessandra was no innocent—she had experienced passion before—but nothing prepared her for the chemistry she created with Alek. Nothing. She arched her back up off the chair, gasping for breath and seeking relief from her body feeling so electrified. "Alek," she sighed, spreading her legs wide and lifting one over his hip when he hitched the hem of her delicate nightgown up to her thighs.

He looked down into her face framed by the moonlight as he palmed her core, his fingertips resting in the soft divide of her buttocks, as he massaged her deeply, pressing the fleshy part of his palm against her moist clit. "Feels good?" he asked her, his voice thick with his yearning.

"Yes," she admitted in a heated rush, pressing one foot against the arm of the chair to rotate her hips against his hand.

She lifted her head from the back of the chair to lick hotly at his mouth before she bit his bottom lip.

He grunted in pleasure.

Alessandra smiled a little as she ran her tongue inside the softness of his mouth before he tangled his own with hers. She reached for his hardness, caressing him from midway to the smooth tip as he lowered his head to suck deeply at her hard nipple through the Venetian lace. Down she stroked and then up, using the side of her thumb to softly stroke the tip.

He swore, freeing himself from her grasp just long enough to snatch off his pajama bottoms and then stand before her.

Alessandra grabbed him with both hands as she looked up at him. "It's so big," she whispered up to him in awe, before she leaned in to lick the tip.

His legs stiffened and he cried out as he flung his head back.

Knock-knock.

She froze, looking back over her shoulder at the door to her suite.

"It's Hill. Are you awake, Alessandra?" her date called through the closed door before knocking again.

"Damn," Alek swore in frustration, his long and curving length bobbing a bit as she released it. "*This* fool."

Alessandra shook her head as if to clear it as she rose to press past Alek's nude frame. "Just go, Alek," she pleaded in a whisper, her eyes dropping to take in the sight of his rock-hard body with his erection hanging from his body with a curve that looked dangerous.

Did I really lick it?

She thought of Alek's cry of pleasure.

Yes, I did, and I liked it.

"Am I interrupting something?" he asked, his voice hard and accusing.

"No," she emphasized. "I don't even know what he wants."

"I'm not going anywhere," he insisted, massaging the length of his erection with one hand as he reached for her with the other. "Ignore him."

"No," she insisted, moving quickly even as her body reacted to him. "You just have to realize how inappropriate this all looks. Remember, Millicent?"

His face said that he hadn't. "She's in her own room and I have no intention of seeing her until morning."

"Alek! A tryst with me tonight and breakfast with your date in the morning? What the hell kind of woman do you think I am?" Alessandra snapped angrily, bending down to scoop up his discarded pajama bottoms before pushing against his chest until he backed out onto the balcony. She flung them into his face. "Just go away, Alek. Good night."

She slammed the balcony door and locked it.

Relief flooded her when he casually draped the pajamas over one broad shoulder and strolled away to climb back over to his own balcony.

Alek rushed across his spacious suite, stubbing his toe against an antique coffee table. He hollered as he reached the door, pausing just long enough to pull on his pajamas before he eased the door open and looked down the long hall.

Hill, dressed in his pants and shirt, was still at Alessandra's door knocking with a bottle of brown liquor and two snifters in his free hand. *A nightcap? Yeah, right.*

Alek's frown changed into a big and broad smile; he leaned against the door frame and crossed his arms over his chest. "Everything okay?" he called.

Hill turned and smiled. "Yes, everything is fine," he said, turning back to the door.

Alek remained.

Hill glanced back at him. "Everything okay with you, Alek?" he asked, his annoyance with him clear.

He shrugged. "Your knocking kinda woke me," he said with a little wince. "I'm pretty sure if I hear it way down here she has to hear from right there. Right, kid?"

Hill forced a smile, giving Alessandra's door one last glance before he walked away.

Alek was gleeful. When the other man reached him he quickly reached out to grab one of the snifters. "Nightcap? I surely could use one," he hinted, holding the glass out.

Hill released a heavy breath as he opened the small round decanter to fill Alek's snifter.

"Thanks. Good night, Hill," Alek said with way too much glee.

Hill gave him a stiff nod before continuing down the hall to the elevator, eventually climbing on it and disappearing behind the closed doors.

Alek drank all the brandy in one gulp and entered his suite with a chuckle.

"Everything okay, Alessandra?"

She looked at Roje's concerned expression in the rearview mirror of the Jaguar MK VII sedan. She smiled at him reassuringly. "It is now that I'm home," she said, turning to look out the window at the large bronze sign welcoming them to Passion Grove, New Jersey.

The population of the town, home of many wealthy young millennials, was under two thousand with fewer than three hundred homes, each on an average of five or more acres. Its name was derived from the township being centered on a heart-shaped lake that the residents lounged around in the summer and skated on in the winter.

There were no apartment buildings or office buildings. Not even public transportation through the town. The township had tight restrictions on commercial activity to maintain the small-town feel. Each of the tree-lined, brick-paved streets was named after a flower. Care was given to its beautification, with large pots on each street corner filled with plants or colorful perennial florae.

Alessandra had grown up there and couldn't imagine moving. Now that the majority of her life was sucked into the fast pace of Manhattan, Passion Grove had truly become her respite.

As Roje drove her through the downtown area, she smiled at its comparison to Manhattan and other metropolitan cities. Most of the businesses were in small converted homes that were relics from its incorporation in the early 1900s. The police station, a gourmet grocery store that delivered, a few high-end boutiques, a dog groomer, and a concierge service that supplied luxuries not available in town.

The streets lacked the constant movement of people, and traffic was minimal at best. No highways or traffic lights. The stop sign sufficed.

A few neighbors enjoying coffee and pastries on

the sidewalk outside the bakery waved at her as they passed. In the city people waved, too, but usually their hand displayed only one finger at the time.

Passion Grove was home, and when she awakened that morning with memories of her lack of inhibitions with Alek, she had wanted nothing more than to be back in a place where she felt the most like herself. The most comfortable. The most familiar.

When she asked Alek to leave it had nothing to do with Hill's ridiculous appearance at her door. She used that intrusion to gain some clarity and give herself the distance needed from Alek…and his touch, his kisses and his hardness.

Hill's late-night intentions at her door were clear but she spared him a tongue-lashing and just ignored his knocks because she was thankful for his intrusion. He had unknowingly saved her from losing every last bit of her sense and control by having sex with her nemesis. She poured herself a stiff shot of some brown liquor from her bar in the suite and went back to bed, trying hard not to wish Alek was there with her. And in her. Deeply.

Alessandra sighed.

She had run from Alek yet again.

Early in the morning before the sun fully rose in the sky and everything was still, she had called Roje in his room downstairs and rushed into clothes. No time was wasted to summon the resort's maid to assist her, and she shoved the rest of her costly designer frocks inside her suitcase. She flew, knowing she was missing the early-afternoon brunch signaling the end of the weekend-long celebration. In her haste, she left Hill and her family behind.

Everyone's grown with vehicles. No one is stranded.

From behind her rimless shades Alessandra looked out the left passenger-side tinted window at the sun glistening on the lake. Even with the distance from the street, she could see a small fishing boat and knew it was Lance Millner, a local reclusive author, who fished every morning.

Roje made the left turn down Dalmount Lane, the private mile-long paved street leading to their sprawling twenty-five-acre estate. Her father commissioned a one-of-a-kind hybrid rose in honor of her mother that he named the Dalmount, which made it eligible to be the name of the private street. Soon she spotted the twelve-foot-tall wrought iron gate with the letter *D* in bronzed scroll in the center. Roje pulled up to the security panel and lowered his window to enter his pass code.

Moments later the gates rolled open and he eased forward with a brief wave to the security guard on duty who monitored the gate by video surveillance from the mansion. It was another half mile down a tree-lined paved road before the three-story, 24,000-square-foot stone French Tudor came into view. To the left he passed the six-car attached garage with the security office above it before following the curved driveway in front of the mansion. Roje made the left to steer the Jaguar under the carport where deliveries were made, passing the side entrance leading directly into the gourmet kitchen and continuing down the long path to the 1,500-square-foot guest cottage.

Alessandra smiled.

The estate had many amenities, including an

Olympic-size infinity swimming pool centered to the rear of the mansion with a four-thousand-square-foot pool house behind it. There were also outdoor tennis courts, a basketball court, an indoor and outdoor home theater, an outdoor kitchen and a horse stable. The rear of her family's estate overlooked the public lake, and there was a landing with two bowrider boats for fishing or water sports.

Even with all of that it was the little guest cottage with three bedrooms and two and a half baths that was her happy place. She rushed from the back of the car before Roje could leave the driver's seat and assist her. She heard him chuckle as she zoomed past him to open the door and raced inside, barely noting the way the bright light of the summer sun bounced off the neutral decor with pops of bright color and wood accents.

She entered her bedroom suite, kicking off her leopard-print heels as she reached behind her to unzip her strapless crimson Valentino jumpsuit—it was the first of Shiva's garment bags she grabbed in the darkness that morning to put on. Next went the bra.

"Your luggage, Ms. Dalmount," Roje called from the front doorway.

She began unclipping the tracks from her hair. "Enjoy the rest of your day off, Roje," she called back, before digging her fingers into her own hair and massaging her scalp.

Alessandra heard the front door close securely.

"Yesssss," she sighed, naked and feeling free as she entered her en suite to remove her thong. Although she wore no makeup, she scrubbed her face with her favorite skin-care regimen.

When she finally emerged from her guesthouse via

the side entrance, she had on cutoff shorts and a tank top, her shoulder-length hair was in an unruly pony-tail, and she wore her favorite tortoiseshell round spectacles that always slipped down to the tip of her nose. Barefoot, she made her way to her small fenced-in garden. Her smile was full and bright as she felt the warm earth between her toes before she knelt to begin tending to her vegetables.

Soon perspiration coated her body and she used the back of her forearm to wipe the sweat from her brow as she tilted her head back to accept the rays of the sun.

Peace reigned.

Her equilibrium was restored.

This was her happy place to decompress from the stressors of her family life and her career, and to enjoy some semblance of the life she wished she'd been able to claim as her own. Here she relished her privacy and was able to put away the facade she used to flourish in business. Here she was just Alex. Painting, reading and gardening were her joys.

"I needed this," Alessandra said, sitting back on her haunches to look across the small plot where she planted cucumbers.

They hung from the vine, long and thick, some curving a bit with the bundles of leaves surrounding them just like the soft hairs of a man's groin.

Just like Alek, she thought.

She shook her head to clear it of the all-too-vivid memory of the sight of his nudity.

She failed.

It's so big.

Alessandra felt her face flush at the memory of her

words just before she leaned in to lick the tip of him. Her core warmed at how he had cried out as he flung his head back.

"Damn it," she swore, rising to her feet in frustration that she couldn't free herself of wanting Alek Ansah.

She snatched off her gloves, making her way back up the path to her house as she pulled her iPhone from her back pocket to check the time. Hours had passed. It was late afternoon. She looked up the drive to the main house. *Are they back?*

Alessandra dropped her gloves onto the cedar bench running along the side of the house. Her family was loud and boisterous. It was normally the last thing she was looking for on her weekends off, but maybe sitting back and watching the top-rated Bravo reality show that they could be would keep thoughts of Alek off her mind.

She walked over to the all-black golf cart parked in front of her two-car garage and drove it up the path to the main house. She jerked her foot down on the brake at the sight of her cousin Victor's twin boys standing on the balcony of their parent's suite urinating. Elisabetta was flipping through a glossy magazine and smoking an e-cigarette as she relaxed on a padded lounge chair and basically ignored her toddlers.

"Hello, Alessandra," the boys yelled when they spotted her, both tossing water balloons as they stuck out their tongues.

Elisabetta looked up and waved her hand before returning her attention to her magazine.

She opened her mouth to reprimand the children

and their mother, but then shut it. "You know what," she mumbled. "Not today. Not one bit of it. Hell no."

She continued up the drive but stopped again at the sight of Marisa, naked as she pleased, jumping into the pool. Her left eye started twitching and her hands gripped the steering wheel, wishing it were her cousin's neck.

This time she threw the golf cart in Reverse and headed back to the guesthouse. "I can't. I shan't. I won't."

I can tomorrow, though, because it's time for a family meeting.

She wouldn't tolerate her kindness being taken for weakness. There were no provisions in the will ordering her to financially take care of her extended family, and definitely nothing saying to let them have the mansion so that she could find peace and enjoy her solitude. She did it because her father had done so, but she had to make it clear that it was her goodwill that kept them all wealthy. Nothing else.

Back in her house, she turned her phones on silent, fixed a turkey sandwich with cranberry relish on a toasted brioche bun, and poured herself a large glass of Côte de Beaune Montrachet chardonnay before settling down on her sofa with a book from her crowded shelves flanking the stone fireplace. She was determined not to think of Alek—not even her disappointment over the board requesting they confer as the joint heads of the company and decide on who should concede. Neither Alek nor Alessandra would budge, so the vote was delayed, with an urging for them to compromise with each other.

That battle would wait until tomorrow, too.

She took a bite of her sandwich and a deep gulp of her wine.

Knock-knock-knock-knock.

Alessandra cut her eyes at the door and frowned. She closed her book and sat it on her sofa before she rose to cross the room. She opened the door. "Alek?" she said in confusion, before adamantly shaking her head and stepping back to close the door.

Alek quickly moved past his shock at the fresh-faced sight of Alessandra to step forward and block her from closing the door. "Alessandra, we need to talk," he insisted, surprised at the weight she placed against the door to keep him from opening any wider.

"How did you get past security?" she asked, not re-lenting in the pressure she put against the door.

"Your aunt Leonora gave them permission to let me past the gate," he said.

"Six figures a year for security just wasted," she mumbled in disgust.

"I'm not a threat, Alessandra," he insisted.

"Alek, just go. The way my life is set up right now I cannot deal with you today. Seriously, Alek," she stressed.

He closed his eyes, wondering if he should use his strength to overpower her and push the door open. He decided against it. "Alessandra, I'd rather we talk today than do it tomorrow at the office or even pretend last night never happened," he said, tempering his voice.

After a few moments of silence, the door opened and he stepped inside. He eyed her from ponytail to bare feet, pausing at the sight of the back-and-forth mo-tion of her buttocks in her cutoff shorts as she crossed the room to pick up her glass of wine. This pared-down version was more like the little Alex he remembered, but still his appreciation of her was not diminished. Not one bit. He liked that she was capable of going from Instagram-model-level beauty to a regular girl just chilling at home with a fresh face.

She took a sip, looking at him over the rim.

His heart tugged. She was adorable. He looked around her living room, searching for a distraction from the butterflies in his stomach.

"One comment on my appearance, today or any other day, and I will spare no cost to find out something just as embarrassing about you," Alessandra told him with a hard stare over the top of her glasses as she sat down, tucking one foot beneath her bottom.

"You have no reason to be, Alessandra," he said, coming around the living room to stand beside the sofa and look down at her.

You're beautiful.

His heart skipped a beat.

What's wrong with me?

"I think we both know last night was a mistake that we should blame on the alcohol and just move forward—"

"Our first drink was the champagne toast." He cut her off smoothly, denying her excuse.

Alessandra took another sip of wine and then placed her glass on the table. She looked nervous.

"And alcohol doesn't explain away the last few weeks, Alessandra," Alek reminded her, sliding his hands into the pockets of the denims he wore with a crisp white button-up shirt.

"What do you want, Alek?" she asked, rising to her

feet. "Because I can tell you that what I want from you has nothing to do with what happened last night. I can't earn my respect from you on my back. So I will not sleep with you, Alek. I will not. I won't. No."

He stepped close to her and instantly felt drawn into her. "Are you convincing yourself or me?"

Her gaze fell to his mouth but she jerked it back up to his eyes and took a step a back from him. "Both," she admitted softly. "I am your equal, your partner, and should be your ally but you have never wanted that even though I deserve it for so many reasons, Alek Ansah."

He bit his bottom lip and nodded his head, pushing away the desire to smooth away the tightness of her jaw. He moved over to the bottle of wine on the counter, seeking distance from her for his own clarity. "I was wrong, Alessandra," he confessed, his back to her as he noted her wine selection. "You have proven to be more adept at business than I thought."

"Say what now?" she asked in rush, the words blending together.

He looked over his shoulder and smiled at her shocked expression. He saw her stance soften, and she pressed her fingertips to the bridge of her nose.

"This has not been easy for me, Alek," she said, her eyes becoming bright with unshed tears. "I just need you to respect that. I won't lie. I was *so* afraid and… and I knew I had to work twice as hard as you, and I *did*. I couldn't fail. I *didn't* fail, Alek, even when everyone sat back and waited for me to fall flat on my face."

She closed her eyes and raised her face to the vaulted ceiling as she released a long and shaky breath and her shoulders drooped under the weight of her feelings.

A pain radiated across his chest as he forced himself not to go to her and pull her into his embrace. He wanted to comfort her. To alleviate her pain. He balled his hands into fists in his pockets, futilely trying to erase the desire to touch her.

She looked at him. "Don't you understand that you have treated me as nothing but an enemy when I had no *choice* in this," she stressed, splaying her hands, as she eyed him with eyes filled with the fire of her emotions. "I gave up so much of myself to do this for my father, and I *will not* fail him."

Alek nodded in understanding, turning from her as her confession struck a nerve about his own feelings of sacrifice and obligation. He moved to stand in front of her window seat. "I wanted to sail, to captain my own boat. To pave my own way in this world," he admitted with a little grunt. "My father and I were not getting along at the time of his death because of it. I, uh, could either accept the position or my father's shares would be sold and all proceeds donated to charity."

He'd never told that to anyone before. No one knew but his father's attorney and with so much ease, he handed Alessandra his biggest secret. It felt like a misstep.

"Oh, Alek," she sighed in compassion, coming over to stand beside him, and grabbed his arm as she looked up at him.

He looked down into her eyes and felt comforted by her understanding.

"You were forced into it, and Samira *wants* to be a part of the company—"

His body stiffened and he frowned deeply. "What do you know about my sister?" he asked, his tone hard.

"This weekend Samira asked for my help in gaining a position at ADG," she explained. "I looked at her résumé and I plan to help her, Alek."

He threw his hands up in exasperation. "Samira will not undermine my decision through you, and if she does I will cut her off," he said, feeling disrespected and annoyed.

Alessandra eyes widened in disbelief. "You *cannot* be that archaic, Alek. That closed-minded backward-ass thinking should *not* sit well with you," she spat, her ire matching his. "What do you have against women?"

"My issue is not all women, just unqualified ones," he shot back, and then felt small and petty. *Damn.*

"Unqualified," she said, standing in front of him to poke her finger into his chest.

"You must be out of your mind, *Captain Crunch*, when you just admitted you'd rather be sailing a dog-gone boat, but I and your sister with a Harvard degree and internships at some of the top companies in the world are unqualified?"

"Alessandra," he began, feeling regret.

"Alek, what kind of mess is that?" she asked, her face incredulous.

Again, the urge to comfort her filled him. "I spoke in anger about you and my sister," he confessed, as his eyes dropped to her mouth. "I can't think straight around you, Alessandra."

"Is that why you're so averse to women in the workplace, because you can't control your urges?" she asked him, moving to cross the room and pick up her wine goblet. "Well, bully for you, because I'm a woman who can control hers, and I don't date or screw anyone in the workplace. Not you or anyone else."

Alek eyed her standing there with one hand on her hip and one knee bent as she sipped from her wine, her chest heaving with her anger.

Damn, she's sexy.

"What?" she said, looking down at herself and then up at him in confusion.

The tension around them was thick and heady; passion and anger swirled in the air creating energy that pulsated against the walls of the house and their bodies.

He continued to stare, his eyes feasting on her. A tendril of hair escaping from her ponytail and caressing her neck. Even her bottom lip pressed against the glass. The fit of her tank on her full and high breasts. The high cut of her shorts, exposing her shapely thighs.

She squinted before her face filled with understanding. "No, Alek. No," she stressed.

"Your body says different," he said, taking in her nipples hardening and straining against the thin material.

She looked dismayed and covered her breasts with her forearm. "Go home, Alek," she said, quickly moving to the front door to open it wide.

"I will," he said, coming to stand before her. "But this thing between us will happen one day. I will make love to you, Alessandra, and we will enjoy it together."

She stepped back and felt the door, taking a deep swallow as she released a shaky breath.

She wanted him just as badly as he wanted her as he stepped close to her. It was hard to miss as she looked into his hot eyes. "It's better sooner than later so we can get it out of systems and focus on work, right? You're just as curious as I am. Will it be as good as we think?"

Alessandra's eyes dropped to his mouth and lingered there.

"Is curiosity killing that cat?" he taunted softly, his breath fanning against her mouth from their closeness.

She pouted before she released a little cry of alarm as she shifted her head to keep them from kissing.

He turned to stride away.

Alessandra reached out for him. "Yes, it is," she answered.

Alek turned and took one look at the surrender on her face. He pulled her body to his and kissed her passionately as he backed them into the house, closing the door behind them with one strong push.

Chapter 7

Am I crazy? Is this crazy? Should I stop it? I can't stop. I. Can't. Stop.

"Just once," she pleaded in a whisper as Alek turned her around in his embrace and brought his hands up to slide beneath the hem of her shirt. His fingers softly trailed up her belly to stroke the underside of her breasts before palming them.

"Just once," he agreed.

She grunted in pleasure at the warmth of his touch as she let her head fall back against his chest and brought her hands up to stroke the back of his head. She shivered and cried out as he stroked her taut nipples with one hand before easing the other down to undo the button and zipper of her jean shorts. She arched her hips to shimmy her denims over her buttocks and down the length of her long legs.

"No panties?" he asked thickly.

She shook her head.

"Damn," Alek swore, easing his hand across the smooth and plump V of her core before he opened her moist outer lips with his middle finger to seek and find her clit.

Alessandra hissed between clenched teeth, her fingers briefly digging into his neck as she trembled.

"It's so wet," he moaned, pressing the fleshy bud between his forefinger and thumb as he eased his middle finger inside her.

Her body slackened against him as she gasped.

"Alessandra," Alek moaned in wonder.

She felt the length of him harden against her buttocks and rotated her hips, dragging her soft cheeks against him as she dropped her chin to her chest to look down at his hand buried between her thighs.

He pressed a sizzling kiss to her nape, licking her there before he sucked the same spot as his beard lightly tickled her.

"That feels good," she whimpered.

"What does?" he asked, bending his head to the side to look down at her face.

"Everything," she exhaled, opening her legs.

Alek followed her lead and slid his finger inside her more, until his knuckle rested on that small area between her core and buttocks. In and out. Circling against her walls. Then in and out again. And again. And again, even as he never stopped sliding her thick bud back and forth between his other fingers.

She ached. It was sweet torture. Her body craved release. Her senses said hold on for more.

He nodded against her hair, feeling the change in her. Her walls clutched and released his fingers. She got wetter. Hotter. She shivered nonstop.

He wanted it just as badly for her as she needed it for herself. "Come for me," he begged, his voice throaty from his own yearning. "Let me feel you come."

Alessandra closed her eyes and brought her hands up to squeeze and tease her own nipples as Alek lowered himself behind her to plant kisses to her lower back and softly bite the flesh of her buttocks. "I'm coming, Alek," she admitted with a whimper, her knees losing strength. "I'm coming for you."

He settled her buttocks on one shoulder to brace her as he continued to finger her to an explosive climax.

She thrust her hips forward against his hand as wave on top of wave of pleasure filled her. She floated. Her heart hammered. Her pulse raced. Her senses were on high alert. Her clit throbbed. She felt every bit of that white-hot explosion. It was pure bliss. "Yes. Yes. Yes," she cried out, the room fading to black.

Alek was persistent.

In and out. In and out. Again and again. And again. Fast. Hard. Pounding.

"No more," she cried out, thinking she might just lose her mind. She dropped her arms to try to push his hand away from her.

With a wolfish smile, he freed his finger, leaving a moist trail across her clean-shaven mound and then her belly as he wrapped his arm around her waist and stood to pick her shuddering body up against his.

Alek walked her over to the padded window bench

and sat her down on it. He quickly undressed with anxious, jerky movements before he spread her legs wide as he lowered himself to his knees. She leaned her head back against the wide railing and pressed a foot to each wall as she eyed him.

Amid the heat and passion, it was clear he appreciated the sight of her nudity. She completely lost her inhibitions as she lay before him. Ready for him. Still dealing with the aftereffects of coming for him. Hoping her body was everything he dreamed that she hid with her clothing.

"I'm aching for you, Alessandra," Alek said, the sight of her core open and wet for him, making his loins ache. "I can't wait any more to be inside you."

With heart pounding with so much force, Alek grabbed her ankles, locking her in place as he guided the smooth head of his steel inside her. She was tight. Wet. Hot. He barely gave her an inch before he stopped, afraid he would spill his seed too soon. He closed his eyes, seeking control.

Every nerve ending in his body seemed connected to electricity. There was a fine balance between pleasure and agony. It was maddening.

The moment his nut ebbed, Alek eased his hardness inside her, feeling her walls spread to allow him in. To fit him like a second skin. To grip him. Inch by inch until he filled her with it all.

She grimaced and bit her bottom lip with wide eyes as she waited for the discomfort to fade. "I feel it. I feel it. I feel it," she moaned with a whimper.

Alek's mouth formed into a circle as a small drizzle

of his release shot out against her walls. He freed her ankles and bent his body, loving the feel of her soft breasts against his chest as he kissed her as he began to stroke inside. Deeply. Slowly. Enjoying every moment. Every thrust.

The suspense was over. And being inside her was better than anything he could have ever dreamed.

"Alessandra," he moaned against her mouth before lightly biting the tip of her tongue.

Goose bumps raced across his skin as she stroked the sides of his face before trailing her fingertips down his neck, shoulders and arms with deliberate slowness that was addictive.

He eased back out of her, leaving just the tip resting at the throbbing opening of her femininity before he thrust his hips forward and filled her again, quickening his movements until he could outpace a piston.

She arched her back and broke their kiss to cry out in amorous abandon. "Alek," she gasped.

Alessandra stroked his bottom lip with her thumb, and he quickly turned his head to capture it in his mouth to suck deeply as he circled his hips, pressing his hard inches against her walls like he wanted to feel every possible spot inside her. He looked down at her, fueled by the hunger and pleasure on her face as he continued his onslaught. He had never felt so alive. So complete.

The moment just before a climax was the sweetest anticipation ever and Alek felt it coming on. Steady and strong. He wrapped his arms around her tightly, crushing her breasts against his chest as he captured her plush mouth with his own. She wrapped her legs around his buttocks and dug her fingers into the strength of his back as she rocked her hips in unison with him, causing her walls to pull down on his hardness and rush him toward his climax.

He felt it leave his hardness and coat her walls as he moaned with a wildness that only hinted at the dam that broke inside him. The spasmodic clutching and releasing of his tool by her silk walls, drained him.

They held each other tightly, as if afraid to release the other. As if the moment would fade or be found to be unreal.

Hours later, Alek eased the sheet off Alessandra's body, as she slept on her stomach in the middle of her king-size bed. He had awakened already hard for her, the lit lamp on her nightstand making his erection a long, curving shadow on the wall behind him. He wanted more of her.

He opened her legs and knelt between them, massaging the back of her thighs and buttocks before he bent to lick and lightly bite both soft round cheeks. Her skin was fresh and clean from their earlier shower. She awakened with a soft smile and a purr as Alek grabbed a pillow and lifted her up by the waist to shove it under her, causing her buttocks to arch higher in the air.

Alek licked his fingers and then stroked the tip of his erection to wet it before he gripped the thick base to guide it inside her from behind. He lay down flat atop her, loving the feel of her soft buttocks against him as he rocked inside her body.

Alessandra lifted her head from the pillow and clutched it with both her arms as she snaked her lower body, matching his powerful rhythm stroke for stroke.

He could only shake his head in wonder as he pressed kisses and tender bites from one brown shoulder to the other. "You ready?" he asked, his lips to her cheek.

She shook her head. "No, not yet."

Not wanting to leave her behind, Alek slid his hands beneath her soft body. With one he rolled her tight nipples between his fingers and with the other he teased her moist clit.

Alessandra bit down into the pillow with a grunt.

Using his chin, he moved her hair from her neck and buried his face there, sucking at that tender spot under her ear. "Now?" he asked, breathless as he continued to thrust inside her as she lay prone beneath him.

"Yes," she gasped.

Alek stroked her deeply, working hard with each thrust for his climax until his sweat coated both their bodies. He hollered out harshly as Alessandra clawed at the bed and muffled her own screams of release into her pillow.

Depleted, he rolled off her body. His chest heaving and his erection fading as he threw an arm over his eyes.

Soon their snores were as matched as their strokes.

As Alek slept, Alessandra sat on the opposite end of the bed and watched him. Broad shoulders. Toned arms. Hard chest. Chiseled abs. Long and thick hardness even at rest.

Just beautiful. And sexy. And all mine…at least for the night.

Soon the morning would come and their one night of passion would be over.

She rose from the bed and padded barefoot across the floor to her bathroom to make a sudsy washcloth. She carried it back into the bedroom, with a dry hand towel under her arm, uncaring that she left a wet trail on the wood floor.

Carefully she washed him.

Alek awakened with a start, looking up at her with wide eyes. "What are—"

"Sssssh," she said, holding a foam-covered finger to her mouth.

He relaxed his frame as she finished her task, smiling when he hardened in her hands.

Alessandra wiped away the suds with the dry cloth and flung it over her shoulder as she climbed on the bed, straddling his hips. Arching a brow, she squatted above him, holding his hardness straight with her hand as she eased down onto him.

She began her slow ride, sliding up and down the length of him as she looked at him with her hands pressed against his hard chest.

"Alessan—"

She pressed a hand to his mouth to quiet him, leaning down to replace her hand with her mouth. Their tongues lightly danced together as she worked nothing but her lower back and hips in a quick and steady pace that stoked that now-all-too-familiar fire. She broke their kiss to shift up enough to dangle her breasts above his mouth. Quickly he latched onto one and deeply sucked at her hard nipple, intensifying her pleasure as she felt her release rise. Cupping his head, she rode him fast and hard until she felt him stiffen inside her before his release filled her. With a cry she couldn't contain, Alessandra brought her core up and down his shaft as she came with him.

Trembling and shaken, they held each other tightly as she rode him until he went soft inside.

"Damn," they swore in unison before they both laughed.

Late into the night, Alessandra and Alek slept in her bed, their limbs entwined as if feeding a simple need to know the other was still there. Their passion for each other seemed limitless. Both had lost count of just how many times they mated. At times, it was slow and passion-filled. Other times, fierce and fast. Each time, they were completely lost in each other. Inhibitions released. Passion reigned.

Sleep was their only respite.

Alek was the first to rise the next morning. He didn't awaken Alessandra as she slept with a pillow snuggled beneath her upper body. He didn't dare believe he would be able to walk away from her if she even looked at him. As he got dressed he watched her, missing not one detail.

Her mussed hair, long since freed of her ponytail. The way she slept with her mouth slightly ajar. The love bite on her shoulder. The curve of her body under the sheet as she lay on her side. One brown nipple peeking from under the sheet to tempt him.

I better go now.

He carried his shoes and moved around the bed, pausing long enough to press a warm kiss to her lower back—a spot he discovered was one of her erogenous zones. With one last glance over his shoulder, he left her bedroom, quietly closing the door behind him. He slid on his shoes and left her house, still perplexed that she chose to live in the guesthouse and give free run of her mansion to her family.

He was fast discovering that she was a woman of complexities.

Alek stood there outside her house with his hand pressed to the door. He dropped his head and wiped his hand over his beard as he desperately fought the urge to retrace his steps and climb back in Alessandra's bed.

Alek gripped the doorknob for long, torturous moments before finally releasing it and climbing into his glossy dark blue Bugatti Chiron. As he reversed the car and then turned forward to accelerate the sports car up the drive, leaving her felt like one of the toughest things he ever had to do. Last night with her had created a hunger in him that he doubted any other woman could satisfy.

Just once?

He shook his head at their naïveté.

Alek looked ahead at the mansion framed by the blue, lavender and streaks of orange in the sky as the sun inched its way to prominence. In the distance, he spotted a male figure hurrying down the steps leading from a wrought iron balcony wearing nothing but a robe. Frowning, he slowed down. "Is that Victor?" he asked aloud.

He eased forward enough to watch as the older man scurried across the back lawn to a small stone home that he vaguely remembered as the servants' quarters from visiting the estate decades ago with his family. The front door opened and a young woman dressed only in a short nightie smiled up at him as he reached her. "That slick old bastard," he said.

He sped away, driving under the carport and eventually down the paved drive until he reached the security gate. He lowered the window to show his face to the monitor. If the system were anything like his own security, it was just as important knowing who exited the estate as it was to know who was entering.

Seconds, later the gates opened.

"Have a good day, Mr. Ansah," one of the guards' voices came crystal clear through the intercom.

Alek nodded and raised the window as he sped forward.

As he drove through the serene streets of Passion Grove, Alek had to admit there was something charming about the small town even in the wee hours of the morning before daylight. The town was a well-known secret for those with big dollars seeking a small-town setting. Still, his lifestyle moved at a faster pace and he enjoyed his penthouse apartment in Tribeca. Everything about Passion Grove spoke of family and settling down, even if it was still in the lap of luxury.

He wasn't ready yet.

He slowed down when he spotted the lit window of one of the businesses under the row of black canopies. *La Boulangerie* was etched on the door. It was French for bakery. His stomach grumbled and he lowered the window to inhale the scent of fresh baked goods and coffee that filled the air. He immediately pulled the car into a parking spot on the brick-paved road and climbed out to jog across the street.

Alek entered and felt like he was in an old-world pastry shop from Europe with its brick walls, wood beams, polished hardwood floors, metal accents, and black bistro tables and chairs. He wasn't surprised. Passion Grove was a small town with big-time character.

A tall man with a blond man-bun, who looked more like a sun-kissed California surfer than a man from the East Coast, came from the rear of the bakery. His black apron was embroidered in white with *Bill the Pâtissier.* "Sorry, we're not open for a couple hours. Just getting some baking done," he said, his accent decidedly Jersey.

Alek nodded in understanding, but his stomach protested. "Listen, I have a little ride to Tribeca ahead of me and I am starving," he said. "I will purchase whatever you have that's done and a cup of coffee."

Bill smiled and shrugged. "I feel you, bro," he said. "Nothing fresh is ready yet, but I do have some petits fours left from yesterday."

Alek gave him a small mock bow. "My forever gratitude."

"Your English accent is awesome, bro," he said as he filled a black paper cup with coffee from one of six French press coffee makers lining the counter.

Alek chuckled. "Yours, as well," he mused.

The laid-back baker pressed a lid on the cup and handed it to him over the butcher-block counter before turning to walk through a black swinging door.

Alek tasted the coffee. His face filled with surprise as he sipped again. He looked up at the sound of a chuckle.

The baker set a tray of a variety of petits fours on the counter. "Coffee's good, right?" he asked with confidence.

"*Damn* good," Alek stressed, taking another deep sip as he stepped forward to eye the tray of treats.

"The secret is all in the beans, the right farmer with the right packaging of the right arabica bean," Bill boasted, reaching for a small box under the counter.

"Do you know Alessandra Dalmount?" Alek asked, his thoughts returning to her.

The baker looked incredulous. "Of *course*, bro," he said. "As a matter of fact, she loves these citrus petits fours glacés."

Alek envisioned her tucking one of the small square treats in her mouth. "Let me get all of those, too," he said, reaching in his back pocket for his billfold, pulling out his American Express Centurion card.

"Sorry, dude, I haven't turned on my register yet," Bill said. "Listen, the coffee and petits fours are on the house. Enjoy."

"Wow. Thank you," he said, replacing his card.

"No problem," he said, handing over a large black pastry bag.

Alek pulled five hundred-dollar bills from the wallet and folded them to slide into a glass carafe on the counter. "Consider this a tip, then," he said, before turning to walk out of the bakery.

He chuckled at Bill's exclamation from behind him.

Once back behind the wheel of his sports car with the box of pastries safely on the passenger seat, Alek settled in and enjoyed the feel of driving as he made his way back to lower Manhattan. With a yawn that spoke to the lack of real sleep he had gotten last night, he enjoyed the taste of the coffee and welcomed any energy it gave him. He rarely drove because it was such an inconvenience in the city, but he welcomed the feel of handling the sports car. It was almost as smooth a ride as Alessandra.

His gut clenched as he glanced at the pastry box. He planned to leave the box of treats on her desk as a surprise, but outside of that he didn't know where they went from there. How would they interact? Would it be awkward?

And businesswise, would she expect him to change his views on her place in the business after last night? Because he hadn't. Would that anger her?

Alek released a heavy breath.

As much as he enjoyed last night, as much as he craved being with her again, Alek was fast realizing that he had just made things far too complicated.

Once she heard the front door close and the roar of the engine of Alek's car, Alessandra opened her eyes and stopped feigning sleep. She hadn't been ready to face Alek just yet. That would come later. She rolled over to the side where he had slept and pressed her face into his pillow. His scent lingered, and she inhaled deeply of it.

Last night was magnificent.

One time with Alek Ansah had done anything *but* get him out of her system.

Alessandra climbed from the bed, wincing at the tenderness between her thighs as she walked across the long expanse of the bedroom to her en suite bathroom. She took a shower, enjoying the feel of the massive rainfall showerhead pouring down on her while the heads on the walls pulsed against her body. Once done, she made sure the glass door was sealed tight and pressed the digital button to fill the oversize stall with

steam. She took a seat on the marble-tiled bench, leaning back against the wall as she awaited her own type
of therapy. Soon eucalyptus-scented steam swirled
around her until it was thick as clouds.

What she usually saw as just calming had become
erotic last night as Alek bent her over the bench and
stroked her from behind as the steam caressed their
bodies.

His imprint was now on her entire house. No place
was free of a steamy recollection of him.

Aware of the time, Alessandra wrapped a towel
around her damp body and left the shower. She quickly
dressed in leggings and a baggy T-shirt before driving
her golf cart up to the main house. Victor was lounging by the pool with a satisfied smile on his face as
he smoked a cigar.

"See you in the office today, Victor?" she called
over to him as she passed.

He laughed like she'd told a Kevin Hart–level joke.

"Of course not," she said drily, speeding ahead.

Alessandra parked by the stone water feature and
jogged up the steps to walk in through one of the towering double doors of the front entry. The lights of
the chandelier high above in the entrance hall were
dimmed. The quiet was unusual. As she picked up a
stack of mail from the table in the center of the round
foyer, she paused to smell the fresh flowers arranged
in a tall vase atop it.

She smiled up at the massive painting of her parents on the wall as she tucked the mail under her arm
and crossed the tiled floor to the elevator. The ride
up to the third floor was brief. She passed the double
doors leading into her master suite and instead went

to the room at the end of the west wing. Her hairstylist would arrive at six as she did every Monday morning to do Alessandra's hair for the week in her home salon.

She picked up the phone and dialed the kitchen, "Good morning, Olga," she said. "Breakfast for two, please, and I would love some pancakes."

Olga, the estate's house manager of the last twenty years, chuckled warmly. "With or without walnuts?" she asked.

Alessandra smiled. "With," she insisted, using a finger to push the styling chair. It circled.

"I missed you at dinner last night," she said. "Chef made roast pork. Your favorite."

"I wasn't up for the peanut gallery last night," she said with a shake of her head as she turned to play with her hair in the mirror.

"Are you ever?"

"No," she stressed.

"I'll bring the plates up so I can see you before you're gone for the week."

"Thank you."

She hung up the phone and leaned against the rear of the chair as she continued to study her reflection. *Do I look different because I feel different?*

"Here you are."

Alessandra turned to smile at her aunt Leonora. The silver-haired woman with freckled skin the color of shortbread was in a floor-length satin robe with an unlit cigarette in one hand and in the other, a champagne flute of orange juice that undoubtedly was a mimosa with more Veuve Clicquot than anything else. "I saw you drive up and wondered where you'd gotten to in this goliath we call home."

"Getting my hair done for the week ahead," she explained, taking a seat in the chair.

Leonora nodded, taking a sip and eyeing her niece's hair over the rim of the crystal. "I know hair messed up during sex when I see it. *That's* a sweat out," she said, running the tip of her tongue over her teeth. "Good for you."

Alessandra grimaced as she reached up to smooth the wildness from her mane.

"Alek has a strong African back and good abs— it should have been a-maz-ing," she drawled with a wink. "Right?"

"Wrong," she insisted, rotating the chair to avoid her aunt's all-too-knowing eyes.

"Oh no," Leonora sighed, wiggling her pinkie finger at Alessandra with a question in her eyes.

Definitely not.

"Aunt Leonora, didn't you attend finishing school?" she asked.

"Yes, I finished off everything they taught me with my love of a good dirty martini," she said, taking a deep sip of her drink with a satisfying—and completely unruly—smack of her lips.

Alessandra hid a smile behind her hand. Leonora had moved to Passion Grove from her villa in Paris— and a lover twenty years her junior—when Alessandra's mother passed away. She took on raising her niece, and for that Alessandra was loyal to her and endlessly forgiving of her lack of tact.

"You deserve love, my beautiful niece," Leonora said in a rare moment of seriousness as she came over to lightly stroke Alessandra's chin. Her eyes became bright. "The kind of love your parents had for each other. I never had that."

Alessandra's heart tugged at her aunt's hint of a sad smile and the tears brimming in her wide-set eyes.

"I want that for you. A lifetime without love—real love—is not easy. Please believe me," she pleaded, her voice barely above a whisper.

Alessandra rose to pull her thin frame into a tight embrace. "Aunt Leonora, I'm okay," she lied.

She was far from okay. At times her loneliness was draining, but with her busy life of tackling the business world, keeping up with her demanding family and carving out a few hours for herself, Alessandra didn't have the time or inclination to date. Last night with Alek had been her first passionate rendezvous in nearly two years. She was so driven to prove her detractors wrong that she felt dating or a relationship would diminish her focus.

And love?

That was weakness and a gateway to heartbreak.

Leonora's body began to quiver, and Alessandra rolled her eyes heavenward as she shook her head. "What, Auntie?" she asked, knowing the moment of deep reflection had passed.

"I *know* you're okay this morning after the night you had," she said, barely getting it out between her bawdy giggles.

Alessandra hugged her tighter and pressed a kiss to her smooth cheek as she reached down to lightly swat her buttocks in playful reprimand.

"Gave you some of the good ole African loving that had you thinking drums was playing in the background," she joked.

Alessandra leaned back and smiled down at her. "I love you, Aunt Lenora," she said. "See, I do have love in my life."

"As long as I'm alive and even after I'm gone, Allie," she promised, going back to her childhood nickname for her. "Just make sure that's enough."

"Okay," Alessandra agreed, wondering if it was.

Chapter 8

Two weeks later

Alessandra dropped her Aurora pen atop the feasibility studies for each of the subsidiaries under the ADG umbrella. She sat her chin in her palm as she looked over at the secret doorway behind the bookcase that led to the passageway between her office and Alek's. She bit her bottom lip, glancing down at the report and then back at the door as she stroked the back of her tight topknot.

The first time she used it had also been the last.

Is it still locked?

She leaned back in her chair and clasped her hands in her lap as she crossed her legs in the acid-green printed crepe de chine Valentino dress she wore, causing the kick pleats at the hem to open and expose black silk. For the last two weeks, it had been business as usual between them. Business meetings. Corporate luncheons. Cordiality. Distance. Pretense.

Like *it* never happened.

Alessandra lightly stroked her throat with the tips of her black-coated fingernails, turning from the hidden portal. She was an actress. Being around Alek and keeping herself from staring at him, touching him, or pretending her heart was not racing with the speed of one of his sports cars was a Viola Davis–level brilliant performance.

Was he giving a tour de force performance as well, or had that one night been enough?

If so, what were the petits fours about?

She had found them on her desk that morning, immediately recognizing the box from the bakery back home in Passion Grove. Through the day she had devoured the six citrus petits fours. Licking her lips, she opened the top drawer of her desk and withdrew the card that had been attached to the box. "Your fave, huh? Now I know another one of your secrets, Alessandra," she read. "Enjoy them slowly like I did my sweet treat last night. A."

She tilted her head back at the hot memory of him tongue-kissing her down below that night two weeks ago. Her climax had been achingly slow and completely mind-wrecking.

"Whooooooo," Alessandra breathed, as her tiny bud pulsed with new life.

She'd thought she wasn't going to ever stop climaxing.

"Alessandra," she admonished herself, picking up her pen and forcing her attention away from memories of Alek stroking deep inside her to the reports on her desk.

And then there was the elephant that stayed posted up in any room both she and Alek were in. The next board meeting was in two weeks and they were expected to make the decision on who would concede on their acquisition plan. They had yet to discuss it since the board meeting during the Jubilee weekend. She pushed aside the report and reached down to pick up the bright red hardcover folder holding Alek's report, sitting it in her lap and rotating in her chair to face the bright light of the window. She squinted in concentration, lightly biting the tip of her nail, as she read through the entire report for what had to be the third time in the past two weeks. This time when she was done she went back to the beginning and read it again.

She closed the folder and lightly drummed her fingernails against the top of it as she looked out window, lost in thought. His choice of airline to acquire was solid. All his reports substantiated his selection. The stocks were priced aggressively, making it an ideal time to acquire those necessary to gain majority ownership and have less risk of a low return. His market research showed an upsurge in the viability of the airline industry. He even researched the current executives in place to ensure that keeping them in their current position would ease the transition period.

She was willing to admit his venture was a better acquisition for ADG.

"But *something* is nagging at me," she whispered aloud.

Think. Think. Think. Think.

"Come on, Alessandra. What is it?"

Bzzzzzz.

"Damn," she swore, her chain of thought broken.

Alessandra whirled around in the chair with the velocity of the cartoon Tasmanian Devil. She hit the intercom button on her conference phone. "Yes, Unger," she said forcing civility into her tone when she felt like being belligerent.

"I don't have any lunch plans on your schedule and I wondered if you wanted to order in?" he asked.

She glanced down at her watch. Three hours had passed. "Um, yes, I'll be staying in," she said, searching for clarity. "Um, I'll have my usual from that sandwich place."

"Pisillio," he offered. "I'll go get it. I have a coupon."

Alessandra arched a brow. "A coupon?" she balked. "Unger, just use the card I gave you for expenses."

"I am, but a deal is a deal," he said. "Why pay more for something if you don't have to?"

"Right. Thanks, Unger." She removed her finger from the button and sat the folder atop all the paperwork on her desk.

Okay, where was I? Think. Think. Think. Think.

She rose from her seat and began pacing the length of her office, her heels echoing against the hardwood floors.

Tap-tap-tap-tap-tap...tap...tap...tap.

Alessandra came to a stop with her hands outstretched and her eyed closed. "I got it," she said, rushing back over to her desk and quickly flipping through the pages of the proposal until she reached the financial sections. "Thank you, Unger."

When her lunch arrived, Alessandra used one hand

to flip through and search sites on her touch screen computer and with the other she held her delicious panini of Parmacotto ham and fresh mozzarella with tomatoes, arugula and lemon dressing on fresh-baked bread. She was a dog on the hunt and her entire body tingled, letting her know she was close to her prey.

It was late afternoon when she finally dropped her pen and rubbed her eyes. She laughed a little as she looked down at the proposal with red slashings and notes in the margin. She felt exhilarated. It was such moments that she felt business was in her blood, and maybe—just maybe—her father had seen it in her.

And now maybe Alek will, as well.

Alek closed his eyes as he lay on the low-slung bright red sofa in the lounge area of his office. Jay-Z's song "4:44" played from the wireless speakers and he was lost in the music and the words. He needed a break from the world, and for him, music offered that.

As the jazz-influenced beat swelled in the air, he had an image of Alessandra flinging her head back and laughing before she smiled with a carefree and pleased look in her beautiful brown eyes.

In the last two weeks, he'd seen her nearly every day and still he missed her. There had been a shift after that night. A subtle change that maybe no one else noticed, but he had. Even as they avoided each other's eyes and made sure to never be alone with each other, his desire to just be in her atmosphere had intensified. The need to berate, embarrass or lessen had faded. Most moments of the day he wanted nothing more than to see her smile, and all moments of the night he wanted a replay of *that* night.

The scent of her hair and her neck and her femininity haunted him.

The discovery that she was far more than even his dreams captivated him.

The struggle not to stride in her office and press her body to the floor tortured him.

He sat up and swiped his finger across the tablet to end the music abruptly.

Still the opening refrain played in his head, nagging at him and speaking to his life.

He rose to slide his hands in his pockets and walk over to stand at the windows lining his office. Was he running the way he accused her? Definitely. He had never wanted to just be with a woman the way his mind and his body craved Alessandra.

That didn't sit well with him. That feeling was a doorway to emotions he didn't want to allow.

He shrugged and shook his head as his focus became his refection and not the sky-reaching buildings before him. His office door opened behind him and he shifted his eyes to the right to see Alessandra standing in the doorway. His body stiffened and his heart double-pumped as he licked his lips and freed one of his hands to stroke his bearded chin. And just like that, with the sudden appearance of her in his space, he felt rejuvenated…and if he was honest with himself, also nervous and unsure. That was unfamiliar territory.

"Hello, Alessandra," Alek said as he turned to face her as she strolled in with the hem of her skirt swaying back and forth across the thickest part of her thighs.

She stopped before his desk and held a large red binder against her chest. Her eyes shifted to the hidden door of the secret passageway.

He looked at it and then back at her before he walked over to release the latch locking it. "How can I help you?" he asked, coming back to take a seat behind his desk.

"You win," she said, setting the wide binder on his desk and opening it to a certain page.

He recognized his proposal. "Win what?" he asked, frowning at the sight of her bright red markings on the pages.

"I agree that we go forward with your proposal and not mine," she said.

Alek was surprised and he didn't bother to hide it. "That really was one helluva night, wasn't it?" he quipped, and then instantly regretted it. Nothing but male bravado and his uncertainty about their relationship brought it on.

Alessandra's face tightened in annoyance. "Your immature ego is exactly why I don't normally mix business with pleasure," she said, her voice ice-cold.

He nodded. "My apologies. That was childish, Alessandra, and I'm sorry," he said, looking up to lock his eyes with hers, hoping she saw his sincerity in the depths.

Her body relaxed. "I came in to talk business and how I have a discovered a way to improve an already solid deal and save ADG another million dollars during the acquisition," she said, coming around the desk to lean over him a bit to press her fingertips to the page.

The scent of her perfume, with its warm citrus notes, surrounded him. He leaned back a bit to look down the length of her legs, and his palms itched to stroke the softness of the back of her knees.

"Really, Alek," she said.

He shifted his eyes up from her legs to find her looking back over her shoulder at him. "'I can resist everything except temptation,'" he quoted, as he waved a hand by way of asking her to remove the enticement.

"Oscar Wilde," she said, moving around the desk to take a seat in one of the black club chairs before it.

"I am a fan of the playwright," he admitted.

"As am I," she said, crossing her legs.

His eyes dipped to take in the move.

Alessandra sighed and uncrossed them, leaning forward to tap the proposal. "Focus, Alek," she said.

He pulled the binder closer and began to seriously consider her revisions. With every passing moment, his brows dipped into a frown. He looked up at her before double-checking her facts, figures and notes. "So, we would be able to purchase the stock directly from them at a savings of a little over a million," he said.

"Why pay more for something if you don't have to?" she said with one shoulder shrug.

"And you discovered this on your own?" he asked, shocked that she discovered something he and his team had missed.

Alessandra threw her hands up in exasperation. "Alek, seriously. Come on," she moaned.

He leaned back in his chair and eyed her. He knew in that moment that it was time for him to concede, as well. Alessandra Dalmount had just finessed an already strong deal and deserved respect for that.

"Alek, it is time to put aside your resistance and your ego to accept that we can make ADG more successful as a team—the same way our fathers joined forces and worked together to start the company," she said, sitting on the edge of the chair and not at all hiding her passion and conviction. "If we just take our focus and energy off the constant battles with each other, then we could both do our jobs better."

Alek remained silent.

Alessandra stood. "I truly would love to end the war between us, Alek," she said before she turned to take her leave.

He hurried across the office, reaching out to catch her arm before she opened the door, turning her body and pressing her against it with his own. The flutter of her lashes and the quickness of her breath from their closeness was revealing. "Love conquers war," he stated in a low voice.

"We don't love each other," she countered, her eyes dropping to his mouth.

"No, but we want each other, and that's close enough," Alek said as he lowered his head to hers.

Her resistance was weak at best. She breathed his name into his mouth in that second just before he kissed her. Her body went soft against his as she snaked her hands up around his neck to splay her hands on the back of his head.

Alek's heart felt like it was fueled with pure adrenaline as he pressed his hands between her body and the door to raise her hem and cup her soft buttocks. He swallowed her gasp of pleasure as he lifted her up against the door and pressed his hips against her so that she could feel his aching hardness. Being there with her, caught up in their heat, kissing with a passion that was a feast after a famine was intoxicating.

Bzzzzzz...

The intercom broke through their haze.

Alessandra ended the kiss, tilting her head back against the door as she shook her head.

"No, no, no," he pleaded, leaning in to lightly bite her chin.

Alessandra pressed her hands against his shoulders, still shaking her head, as she dropped down to her feet. She glanced at him briefly as she corrected the fit of her black lace panties before she smoothed her skirt down. "Business always comes first, Alek. Our fathers didn't put us in charge just to sex each other in the office," she said, her voice shaky as she walked unsteadily to the door leading to their private hall.

Bzzzzzz...

He stood there with his erection straining against his zipper, watching her leave, and already felt the loss of her. "Thank you for your help, Alessandra," he said. "You proved me wrong."

She turned and leaned against the door as she looked at him in surprise.

"Promise me we will have dinner tonight to celebrate our teamwork on this deal?" he asked, his heart pounding as he watched her closely.

Alessandra said nothing and just nodded as she licked her lips before turning to leave him.

Hours later, long after night reigned, Alessandra lightly bit the side of her finger as she watched Alek easily steering his Bugatti. He was looking ahead, focused on the road, and she allowed herself to enjoy his profile. His beautiful brown skin all the more flawless by his faded haircut and his groomed beard that couldn't shield the square cut of his jaw. Long lashes that resembled small wings whenever he blinked. Supple mouth. Beautiful.

He glanced over the small divide between them, catching her eyes resting on him, and he smiled.

Alessandra looked away, her nervousness causing her teeth to dip a little deeper into the flesh of her finger.

"We're here," Alek said, driving through the entrance to a marina.

"I thought we were just having dinner?" she asked, her eyes taking in the sights of the boats and yachts lining the docks with the lit Lower Manhattan highrises in the distance as he pulled into an assigned parking spot.

"Don't worry," he said, opening the car door. "I'm going to feed you."

She waited as he came around the front of the sports car and opened her door for her. Taking his hand, she left the car and inhaled of the scent of the river. She walked beside him, quiet but curious, as they made their way down the dock to a sixty-foot white motor yacht.

Alessandra smiled at *LuLu's Baby* inscribed in gold-trimmed turquoise lettering on the bow. "This is pretty humble for you, Mr. Bugatti," she teased. "I wouldn't have expected that."

She pointed to a sleek all-black mega yacht of close to two hundred feet docked on the other side of the marina.

He chuckled. "That's *Black Joy* and it is mine as well, Alessandra."

Her nod was smug. "Of course."

"We're having dinner on *LuLu's Baby* because it requires less crew," he explained.

"How many?" she asked as she looked up at a tall, stout man with skin as brown as chocolate coming out of the covered main level of the vessel.

Alek gave her a wide smile. "Me," he said. "And that's the chef."

Alessandra glanced at the boat and then back at him. "So you never really let go of your dreams of sailing?" she asked.

A warm breeze blew in from the river as he looked up at the yacht with his anticipation clear. "It's not in the way that I wanted, but it knocks the edge off the hunger."

His eagerness was childlike and infectious.

"Permission to board, Captain Ansah?" she asked playfully, fighting the urge to kiss his cheek.

He waved his hand with a nod of his head.

Together they boarded. Alek introduced her to Chef Justice Brown, a Michelin-starred chef and winner of a James Beard Award, before Alessandra removed her heels. She already knew it was yacht etiquette not to wear street shoes on board and slipped on brand-new flip-flop sandals sitting in a basket. He led her up to the aft deck.

As he removed his suit jacket he stood in the helm station and began pushing buttons on the panel to start the engine. Alessandra moved to stand at the railing as a soft summer breeze blew in from the river again and fluttered a tendril of her hair that loosened from her topknot. "I would have gone home and changed or had my stylist bring me something if I knew you were planning all of this," she said, looking down at the marina's dockhands working fast to cast off the lines securing the vessel to the dock.

"Actually, I called Shiva myself and you have a change of clothes on board," he said with a mischievous glint in his eye as he slowly shifted into forward at idle speed.

"And?" she asked, just as the yacht began to pull away from the dock.

He focused on keeping the yacht clear of any other boats, looking handsome sans tie and jacket with the top buttons of his custom shirt undone. "*And* there's an outfit for tomorrow—"

"Tomorrow!" she exclaimed, her eyes widened by shock.

Alek cast her a charming smile that was all white teeth and bright eyes. "I thought we were celebrating our new alliance," he said.

"A night on a yacht is more about the pleasure you seek than the business, Alek," she said, hating that his charm softened her tone. "And we agreed it was just that one night, remember?"

He opened his mouth.

She shook her head. "Today in your office didn't change that for me, Alek," she insisted. "So why play with fire?"

As the boat entered free and clear water, Alek gradually increased the speed until soon the wind whipped across their bodies. "You have your own cabin and tomorrow I want to take us to my family's private island off East Hampton."

Alessandra was reluctant. "'I can resist everything except temptation,'" she reminded him.

"I promise to be on my best behavior," Alek said, watching her closely.

She smiled. "That's what I'm worried about," she mused.

They shared a laugh filled with the all-too-familiar sexual tension pulsing between them.

"To resisting temptation," he said.

She said nothing as she looked out at the moon's reflection on the water.

"Today was amazing, Alek. Thank you for sharing your island with me."

He glanced back at her from behind the aviator shades he wore to block some of the sun's rays. They were lounging on the bi-level deck that connected to the dock and enjoying the view of the river vista with the bright blue skies only broken up with clouds of varying thickness. She looked beautiful with her hair undone from her topknot, pulled back off her face and the bottom half loosened and floating down just past her shoulders in a white off-the-shoulder crochet cover she wore atop a white strapless bikini. "You're welcome," he said, forcing himself to look away as he sat on the dock with the legs of his white linen pants folded up to have his feet in the water.

As they had explored the abandoned camp in the midst of the towering pine trees, Alek told her of his plans to create a North American vacation spot for his family and the generations to come complete with a landing strip to enjoy entry to the island retreat by private airplane. He was going to clear it all except the surrounding acreage protected by a conservation easement and build a new dock close enough to the estate to walk out of the house and down one flight of steps to reach it.

He had enjoyed sharing his vision with her and loved the suggestions she made. She truly was smart and innovative, with a sharp wit that had him laughing several times throughout the day.

He looked back at her again, swatting away some flying insect that landed against his bare, sweat-soaked chest to find her eyes on him. She looked away as if caught doing something wrong. His eyes dipped to take in her long, shapely legs where she lay on a blanket he brought to enjoy their picnic lunch.

Last night, after he dropped anchor in the middle of the river, they'd enjoyed their dinner of roasted lamb shoulder in the main salon and successfully resisted that familiar buzz of awareness they created around each other. Afterward they sipped champagne and lounged on the deck stargazing. Neither said much, but the night air around them was bursting with tension and temptation.

Long after they retired to their separate staterooms, Alek had lain naked atop the covers on his king-size bed fighting his desire to go to her. Alessandra wanted him just as badly as he wanted her, that he knew. He was confident a knock at her door would lead to another explosive night.

But he refrained. It had been a true test of his will.

He took in the curves of her body with a regret-filled shake of his head.

That resolve was fading fast.

"I'm not blind, Alek," she said, sitting up with her arms braced against the desk. "Is that too much? Me and you being here…alone?"

He smiled and focused his eyes on the yacht sitting moored to the dock. "Honestly, it is," he admitted. "I want nothing more than to come over and give you what we *both* want, Alessandra."

She rose and came over to sit on the dock beside him. "What do you want from me, Alek?" she asked. "If I admit that I would surprise you with how wet I am from just looking at you, then what? Because I'm not looking for love or a relationship, and sex could complicate things with ADG, don't you think?"

He removed his shades and looked into her eyes, seeing the question, the concern and the hesitance. "I can't put what we shared behind me, and I don't want to, Alessandra," he confessed, heart pounding.

Her eyes warmed over and she brought her hand up to cup the back of his neck as she leaned in to touch her forehead to his. "I crave you," she admitted, her words softly whispering against his mouth.

"Just once more," he said, his body alive with hope and want.

"We said that the last time," she reminded him with a teasing smile before she brought her hand up to his chest and stroked the fine, flat hairs there as she tilted her chin up to taste his full mouth with her own.

He grunted in pleasure, pulling her pliant body over to straddle his lap as he removed the cover-up that did its job far too well.

They gave in to that craving yet again with nothing but surrounding flora to tell. They were witnesses to their passion. The rays of the sun and their slow, deliberate exertion caused sweat to coat their brown skin, slickening the primal movements against each other. And when they reached their climax together, their wild cries of release and fulfillment blended in the air above, echoing for miles.

Afterward, as they lay there seeking control of their bodies again, Alessandra breathlessly asked, "This wasn't the last time, was it?"

"Hell no," Alek swore.

Chapter 9

Three months later

It was only late October but the northeastern chill was present, the type of wintry air you feel in your bones. The type of cold to make you thankful for a warm body to press up against. To yearn to be close to.

Thank God it's Friday.

Alessandra stretched her arms wide across the smooth leather of the back of the Jaguar with a smile on her face almost as wide. The week was over and Passion Grove was her destination, but lately her weekends at home had found new meaning. She thought of that song "The Weekend" by R & B soulstress SZA.

As the lyric played in her head, she smiled and let her head fall back against the seat. Monday through Friday she and Alek were all business, but their weekends in her little guesthouse in Passion Grove were all about each other, their escape from hiding their liaisons from the world.

Alek had agreed to her request to not reveal their affair because of her fear she would lose her respect in the industry—something she worked so hard to attain and maintain. They even went so far as publicly dating other people at work functions—with the stipulation that the dates went no further than just that. Sex with anyone else was completely off the table.

She remembered the late-summer party they held on the terrace of their office building to celebrate the acquisition and ADG's shift into the airline industry with his brother Naim being named the president. She'd brought Hill and he had his standard model type floating beside him when he entered. All night they surreptitiously watched each other until the party was over. In the end, it was all foreplay because they both sent their dates home before hotly pleasing each other atop the conference table in their boardroom.

As Roje drove up to the guesthouse on her estate, her heart skipped a beat to see that the windows of her living room were bright with light. She hadn't left them on when she left on Monday and her cleaning staff wouldn't have done so. Quickly, she eased her underwear over her hips and down the length of her legs and her heels to shove inside her purse. "Enjoy your weekend, Roje," she said, climbing from the rear before he could exit.

"Yes, ma'am," he said,

Alessandra held the edges of her bright yellow Maki Oh robe coat closer as she hurried inside the house. She moaned in satisfaction at the feel of the heat as she pulled off her coat and eyed Alek sitting atop the plush rug before the fire, already naked and waiting. She dropped her handbag and briefcase on the sofa as she walked over to him and hitched the leather eyelet hem of her fitted black dress up around her waist as she stood over him.

"You beat me here," she said.

"That damn dress drove me crazy all day," he said, leaning in to lightly bite her plump mound before he pulled her down onto his lap and kissed her with every bit of the hunger he felt.

It was just what she needed.

Monday through Friday they were married to their business, but on Saturday and Sunday?

The weekend was all about getting lose in each other.

"Are you sure you want to do this?"

Alek dug his hands deeper into the pockets of his wool jacket and looked at the lengthy line of people waiting before he answered Alessandra's question. "Yeah," he said, his reluctance obvious.

She laughed as she tucked one of her hands in his pocket and entwined her cold fingers with his.

He looked down at her with her shades and a navy skullcap on over her now-waist-length hair in a long braid over one shoulder. *She's adorable*, he thought, loving the casual look of her navy peacoat, jeans and caramel riding boats as they shifted forward with the crowd awaiting entrance to the annual harvest festival held by Passion Grove's local orchard.

Nearly every resident of the small town had to be in attendance, plus those from neighboring cities. When she lightly hinted that she hadn't missed the annual festival celebrating the fall season since she was a kid, he had set aside his reluctance and offered to go.

Hayrides, apple bobbing and pumpkin carving were out of character for his jet-set lifestyle, but making Alessandra happy had become his favorite pastime. So they were both in skullies and shades—their idea of incognito—preparing to enjoy a day of fall frivolity.

Alek felt his iPhone vibrating against his buttocks in the back pocket of his distressed denims. He pulled it out and smiled at Chance's name, quickly answering. "What's up, Mr. Castillo?" he asked.

Alessandra gave him a wide stare and held a finger to her bare mouth. He nodded, assuring her that he wouldn't reveal his location to a man she'd discovered was his best friend and confidant.

"Well, hi, stranger. What do you have going on today?" Chance asked. "Helena needs a break from the cold and we're jetting to my place in Cabrera. You in?"

Alek thought about relaxing in the warmth on the terrace of his friend's palatial estate in the small and beautiful town in the Dominican Republic. "You won't believe where I am right now," he drawled, hardly believing it himself as the gates to the orchard opened and the small crowd swelled. Alessandra pulled him by the arm to a stand selling apple cider.

"Where's that, amigo?"

"A fall festival," he said, looking around at the line of booths and the elaborate fall decor that he had to admit was warm and inviting. Children were in line to have their faces painted by someone in a pumpkin costume. Booths offering different fall-centered treats were selling their goodies. In the distance, a band was playing upbeat music from a stage next to a line of food trucks and picnic tables. People were already picking pumpkins from the large crates on display.

Chance laughed. "No way."

Alek nodded as he accepted the cup Alessandra handed him before she tore off a piece of pastry and slid it into his mouth.

"Apple turnover. Good, right?" she asked, before enjoying a bite of the treat herself and then licking the sweet glaze from her fingertips.

"I assume a lady is involved," Chance mused.

Alek chewed and swallowed. "Good assumption," he said, brushing crumbs from his beard as he watched Alessandra walk over to a hand-painted sign announcing a cornfield maze before waving him over.

Her face was bright and alive with her eagerness. It tugged at his heart.

"She must be special, bro," Chance said.

"That she is," Alek admitted, before ending the call and walking over to join her.

Darkness reigned in Passion Grove and the illumination from the black steel lampposts was soft, breaking up the shadows cast by the trees lining the streets. Alek and Alessandra walked the few blocks from the orchard to her estate, and although the town was already relatively safe, she felt secure in his presence. Even the night chill of October wasn't quite as biting with him at her side and his strong arm resting across her shoulders.

"That wasn't so bad, was it?" she asked, breaking the comfortable silence as they walked past the wrought iron fences surrounding properties of sizable homes all set back from the street three hundred feet or more per local ordinance.

Alek shook his head. "No, it wasn't. I really liked sitting by the campfire after the hayride and listening to the music."

"Good," she said.

They fell into that easy silence again, eventually coming to the beginning of the private road leading to her estate. Her all-black golf cart was sitting where they left it that morning. Alessandra removed the key from her back pocket and handed it to Alek before climbing onto the passenger seat. She settled her hand on his thigh as he drove them down the length of the paved road lit with lampposts, as well.

The gate opened as they neared it and they both waved at the security camera as they passed.

"It really is a beautiful house," Alek said when the view of it came into sight.

"Thank you," she said.

The white up-lighting gave the expansive mansion a soft glow that illuminated it in the darkness surrounding it. It was grand but still welcoming.

"You wanna check on your fam?" he asked.

"Speed up, please," she said.

Alek chuckled as he accelerated past the house and under the stone carport. "Sometimes I want to give them all eviction notices in one hand and leases to their own homes in the other," she said. "I love them but they're a bit much, you know?"

"Well, I thought that the morning I saw your cousin Victor sneaking into the maid's quarters," he said as he pulled to a stop before the guesthouse.

"You what?" she shrieked, looking at him with wide eyes.

Alek looked surprised. "I never told you?" he asked. "Aw, man. It was unreal."

Alessandra turned on the seat of the golf cart to look up at the main house. "I knew he had a side piece across town, but to mess with one of the maids right here under his wife's nose?" she said, her top lip curling in disgust.

Alek leaned over to kiss the corner of her mouth before exiting the cart. "He's bold, that's for sure."

Alessandra was steaming with anger and frustration. "So, I'm paying someone to screw his old horny self?" she said, her tone exasperated. "I ought to go to his suite and pour ice water on his crotch."

Alek picked her up in his arms and kissed her to end her tirade.

She broke the kiss. "Which maid?" she asked as he carried her around the golf cart and into the house.

"Are you going to fire her?" he asked as he reached his foot back to push the door closed before continuing across the living room and down the hall to her master suite.

"Immediately," she spouted.

"Then I don't remember which one," Alek said, setting her on her feet in the bathroom before he removed her coat and began undressing her.

"Alek!"

"I know sometimes we forget because of our privilege, but there is a large segment of people who have to work to provide the basics," he said as he bent to lift each of her feet to remove her boots. "People are one check away from homeless, Alessandra."

"But—"

Alek rose and matched his gaze with hers. "*But* your uncle is in a position of power and it's possible she may feel she cannot tell his old horny self—as you call him—no," he explained.

His tone and manner made her feel like he felt he was talking to an imbecile. "Alek, she works for me, not Victor," she stressed.

"Alessandra, you live in the guesthouse," he exclaimed, as he bent to remove his dark brown ankle boots. "Perhaps she's confused as to just who runs what."

"Or?" she asked, arching a brow.

Alek bit back a smile and shrugged one shoulder as he removed his wool peacoat and tossed it onto the pile of her clothes on the floor. "Or she enjoys screwing the old fart," he said, making a comical face before pulling the light gray sweater and white shirt he wore over his head.

Alessandra eyed the hard definition of Alek's abdomen. "Do you work out?" she asked.

"Of course," he said, unbuttoning his denims and letting them and his boxers drop down his legs before kicking them free with his feet.

"So what do I do? Nothing?" she asked, unbuttoning and removing her snug jeans and panties with much more effort than he had.

Alek walked across the room to turn on the shower; he looked back over his shoulder. "About?" he asked, his face confused.

Alessandra removed her socks and balled them together to throw. It landed solidly against one hard butt cheek. "The horny fart and the maid," she said.

"Oh…um…stay out of it or deal with Victor, because you could fire her and he could just get it going with the new one—young or old, cute or not," he said. "Men talk a lot of ying-yang about a woman's looks but trust me, ugly women get the business, too, especially when the wrong head is making decisions."

Alessandra looked aghast. "That's terrible."

"But very true." He walked down the length of the bathroom with his penis swinging across the top of his thighs before he scooped her up into his arms again and carried her into the shower already filling with steam.

"Alek, but what—"

"No, enough about the horny old fart and the maid," he said, walking them under the spray of the rainfall showerhead as he set her on her feet. "It's time for the horny *young* fart and the billionaire heiress."

After a long day out in the elements, she had to admit that a shower was perfection. She tilted her face, leaning back with a sigh to let the water coat her body. She was startled at the feel something against her belly and opened her eyes to find Alek washing her with a lathered cloth. Her belly. Her back. Shoulders. Arms and then her breasts.

Their eyes locked at that and they shared a soft smile.

With obvious reluctance, he withdrew to rinse and lather the cloth again.

"I've never been bathed before," she whispered into the thick stream before turning to press her hands against the wall and arch her back as she offered him her buttocks.

Alek slapped one smooth brown cheek with the

back of his hand before he massaged the cloth over her intimacy and inner thighs before cleansing her buttocks.

She looked back over her shoulder, her mouth forming a circle as he raised the cloth high in the air to squeeze, sending the warm suds drizzling down her cheeks and the back of her thighs. He grabbed the base of his hard, curving length, propping one foot up on the bench running down the length of the massive shower, to slide his sudsy hardness over the smooth expanse of her cheeks. She raised up on her toes and reached back to push his hand away and ease his hardness inside her.

They both hissed in pleasure as she wiggled her hips back and forth until she was filled with him to the hilt. His hardness divided her. His thickness spread her. His heat infused her. "Yes," she said with a deep, guttural moan that was wild.

Alek bent his legs and began pumping inside her as he dug his fingers into her wet and shiny bottom as the water showered down on them, slickening each stroke. He bit his bottom lip as he looked down at the sight of his thick inches sliding in and out of her, its dark skin shiny from both the water and her juices.

Alessandra bent over to wrap her hands around her ankles.

He cried out as her walls tightened down on his hardness. "Damn, Alessandra!"

She bent her legs wide and arched her back, circling her hips and pulling downward on his hard length until she was able to kiss the smooth tip with the plump lips of her privates before sliding her core up again.

Alek's legs weakened as he shook his head and reached out to the wall for support.

He got harder inside her as she continued that up-and-down slide with a kiss on the tip over and over again.

Alek grabbed her cheeks to stop her as he felt his nut build up in a rush. "No," he begged, stepping back and removing his inches from inside her.

Alessandra stood up, wiping the water and her wet hair from her face as she turned to find him walking down the length of the shower away from her. "What's wrong, Alek?" she asked.

He turned, his hard-on still hard and curving away from his rock-hard body as he pressed his hands to his hips. "I tapped out. I was about to nut. I couldn't take it," he admitted, looking frustrated.

She smiled even as her clit and heart both pulsed with life and desire. Want. Need. She walked to him through the thick steam and pressed his back to the tiled wall. He slid down onto the bench and she strad-dled his hips, guiding her womanhood onto his hard-ness as she cupped his face. She smiled and pressed her knees on the wall on either side of his body as she lowered her head to suck his mouth into hers.

Alek moaned, bringing his trembling hands up to cup her breasts and stroke her hard nipples with his thumbs as she began to ride him with a small and tight rotation of her hips.

He felt all of her against him, gripping him and pleasing him. The way she made love to him with such slowness as she sucked gently at his tongue and looked into his eyes touched something deep inside him. There was a shift. His chest felt filled with lightness even as his heart continued to pound with the wildness of a racehorse. He brought one of his hands up to lightly grasp her chin and he slid the other around her body to press to her lower back.

Alessandra had never felt so connected to him before. She broke their kiss to sweetly suck his forehead as he lightly bit her chin, his hand pressing her body closer to him until her soft breasts cushioned his hard chest and the feel of his arm around her body made her feel cherished and protected.

They both gasped and she looked down at him just as he looked up at her. Their mouths gaped as they breathed in each other and the steam in that small space between them. They were connected. Lost in each other. Pleasure personified. Emotions on overload.

"Come with me," she whispered into the steam, leaning back in his embrace with a deep sigh as she worked in snakelike motion that thrust her breasts and hard nipples upward as her tight, wet, hot core eased up and down the length of him with a slowness that caused them both to ache.

Alek was mesmerized by the sight of her as she rode him with ease. He leaned forward to suck at the valley between her breasts as she tilted her head back and called his name.

Together their climax was stoked. Their pleasure was in sync. They knew their release would be so good. Their anticipation was intense.

Both cried out in pleasure as they reached their sizzling pinnacle.

Alek's hold on her supple body tightened as he

coated her walls with spasms of release that left him spent.

Alessandra worked her hips and the muscles of her walls to empty him as tiny explosions of pleasure burst inside her until she was lost to time and place. Nothing mattered but pushing herself over the edge until she felt like she was free-falling through space.

Both were speechless, shaken and moved far more than either wanted to admit.

Lazy Sunday mornings had become their thing, and the next morning was no exception. They didn't awaken until well after noon and even then, they remained in bed, lounging in pajamas or comfortable clothes, watching the Sunday morning news programs, reading the print papers, watching movies or sports, and nibbling off the tray of delicacies usually Alessandra retrieved from the kitchen of the main house.

Sundays were bittersweet because it signaled the end of their retreat and the return to the facade that they weren't deep into the throes of a sexy affair. They protected their weekends in Passion Grove, even agreeing to avoid talking business when they were alone together.

And when the night reigned, they both hated the call from her security requesting permission to admit Alek's driver to pick him up.

Alek would hitch his caramel leather duffel bag high on his shoulder and reach for Alessandra's hand to pull her into a tight embrace as he pressed kisses to her forehead and cheek. She said nothing, afraid that she would plead with him not to go because she wasn't sure that he wouldn't deny her request, so she just accepted his kisses, set aside her regrets and turned her back to keep from watching him walk out the house to climb into the rear of his car.

And she knew it was silly when they would see each other the next day, but there was just something about those weekends in Passion Grove.

Three days later

"Can I get you anything, sir?" Huntsman asked.

Alek took a sip of his cognac as his grip tightened on the glass, and he checked his Patek Philippe watch. He and Alessandra were supposed to be having dinner at his penthouse apartment in Tribeca, but she had yet to show and she was more than twenty minutes late. *Where is she?*

"No, I'm fine, Huntsman," he said, reaching in his pocket for iPhone.

He called her as he paced the length of the forty-four-foot great room of his loft-style apartment of nearly six thousand square feet. Her phone rang several times and went to voice mail. He didn't bother to leave a message.

He was beginning to get concerned. Alessandra was punctual to a fault.

Releasing a heavy breath, he strode across the modernly styled room, ignoring the polished bocote wood dining room table set for their dinner, and jogged up the wood and black steel staircase to the second level.

Bzzz.

He stopped on his path across the second foyer into the glass-enclosed sunroom to look down at his phone still in his hand. A text from Alessandra. *Thank you, God, she's okay.*

"'In a business dinner with Omar Freed. Have to cancel our plans. Will call as soon as we're done,'" he read, his face steadily becoming incredulous.

Cancel?

He frowned. *Have I been stood up?*

For dinner with Omar Freed. His frown deepened.

The politician was canvassing for donations and support for his senate campaign, but when both he and Alessandra met him last week at a fund-raiser it was clear his interest in her was personal. He envisioned her sitting across from the tall, handsome man with a smile in her eyes that he thought only he could give her.

His expression darkened and his entire body felt angry with hurt and disappointment that she had so easily forgotten their plans. Needing air, even if it was frigid, he stepped out of the sunroom and onto the spacious terrace running down the entire length of his apartment. He looked out at the industrial-age architecture, converted warehouses and cobblestoned streets that gave the trendy neighborhood its character and charm. As the cold night air whipped around him, he looked over the low-rise buildings at the waterfront of the Hudson River.

Usually the view gave him peace. It was the reason he'd purchased the apartment, but now the sight offered him no respite at all.

With his supple lips still turned downward, he walked back inside, passing the elevator as he strode across the space and down the stairs. "Huntsman," he called out.

His manservant came down the short hall leading from the eat-in chef's kitchen wiping his hands on a cloth. "Sir," he said, wearing a black apron over his signature black shirt and pants.

"You can serve dinner," he said, taking a seat at the dining room table flanked by a black slate focal fireplace wall that was lit, adding warmth and ambience to the room.

"Alone?" Huntsman asked.

"Yes," he stressed. "Unless a man can no longer have dinner at his table like a civilized human being, Huntsman."

Huntsman removed one of the place settings and used a matte black candle snuffer to put out the lit candles. "When dinner for two was planned?"

Alek stared at him when he saw humor in his eyes. "On second thought I'm not hungry," he said, tossing his black cotton napkin atop the table as he slumped down in the chair.

He wiped his bearded chin with his hand as he looked across the table into the fireplace. His stomach was lit with a flame that even it couldn't match. Jealousy had a way of burning the gut of the man it plagued.

Alek couldn't remember the last time a woman brought out the "green-eyed monster" in him. He could barely think straight.

I love her. I love Alessandra.

He swore, sitting up to press his elbows into the wood as he rubbed his hands together before placing them against his face.

This wasn't how things were supposed to go. Love was a complication he never expected, but as he sat there envisioning tossing whatever dinner Omar had ordered at him, Alek knew he had to face the truth. What did he do with his love when Alessandra made it clear that she wanted nothing more than sex?

Maybe she's moving on to Omar?

He shook his head. He didn't believe that. That was irrational.

Alessandra cared for him. That he knew. But love? That he didn't believe at all.

She was as driven about her career as he was and had never expressed a desire for love and family—things he always wanted in a wife. Things he was not willing to compromise on.

What do I do now?

He had played with fire and now he was getting burned.

Three days later

It was her first weekend alone in months.

When she got to Passion Grove last night she had thought Alek was there waiting on her and when that didn't happen, she waited up all night thinking he would make an appearance eventually. It took several glasses of wine to relax herself enough to fall asleep on the sofa while the television watched her.

Somewhere in the middle of the night she had awakened with a start, drool dried on her chin as she looked around at the darkness and it set in that Alek had never arrived. She picked up her iPhone to call him, but decided against it.

She had no right to question him or expect anything from him.

The next morning, she was lounging on her window seat swiping through news articles on her iPad when she spotted a photo of Alek and his date at a charity event from the night before. "What the what," she exclaimed softly, her heart pounding and her gut clenched as she enlarged the picture.

Her eyes missed not one detail.

The smile on his handsome face. His hand on her hip. Her beauty. How good they looked together.

Is she the reason he didn't come to Passion Grove?

An image of their bodies coupled in passion flashed and she shook her head as she pressed her eyes closed. She seethed with jealousy at the thought of Alek sharing his body with another woman. She knew she had no right. The rules had been clear. No strings. Just sex.

At the idea of Alek loving another woman, tears filled her eyes and a sadness swelled deep in her soul. She shifted the photo and zoomed in on his face. *He really is handsome.*

Her emotions were all over the place and she felt so confused by it all.

What's wrong with me?

She sat the tablet down beside her and pulled her knees to her chest, setting her chin in the groove between them. Memories of the lovemaking in the shower just last weekend stuck uppermost in her mind. The passion and emotion had been on overload. Far more than they should have been for a fling.

You deserve love, my beautiful niece.

Is that what this is? she wondered as a tear raced down her cheek. *Have I fallen for Alek Ansah?*

The kind of love your parents had for each other.

She snorted in derision. It definitely wasn't that.

Her father had adored her mother and even after her death he never remarried or had another committed relationship.

I want that for you. A lifetime without love—real love—is not easy.

But it wasn't safe and the idea of loving Alek scared her more than anything.

Tap-tap.

Alessandra jumped in surprise at her aunt Leonora standing at the window in a chinchilla fur coat with matching hat. She sat her tablet down and rushed over to open the door. "Aunt Leonora, what are you doing out there?" she asked, grabbing her arm and pulling her inside before she closed the door and blocked the November chill.

"I've been watching you moping in this window seat all morning," she said, removing her coat and hat to reveal she wore hot-pink satin pajamas.

Alessandra glanced at the seat and her eyes fell on the tablet. Pain radiated across her chest.

"No houseguest this weekend?" Aunt Leonora asked lightly.

Alessandra shook her head.

Leonora wrapped her arms around her and Alessandra was grateful to be held tightly.

"It's over," she decided, biting her bottom lip as tears welled in her eyes, because she knew it was time to end her physical relationship with Alek before she set herself up for even bigger heartache.

Chapter 10

Two weeks later

As Alessandra rode up in the elevator to LuLu's apartment on the Upper East Side, she pulled her compact from her clutch and checked her makeup. She had called in her glam squad. Shiva had delivered an off-the-shoulder brocade fit-and-flare dress by B Michael. Her hairstylist had pulled her hair back in a sleek ponytail that highlighted her diamond chandelier earrings, and her makeup artists had hopefully camouflaged the darkness and puffiness under her eyes from the tears she cried at night.

For the last two weeks Alek had been traveling overseas, personally checking up on some of their subsidiaries, and outside of business they rarely spoke. She'd put up her guard to protect her heart, but it was still broken. The time had long since passed for her to avoid loving Alek.

The elevator doors opened and she was stepping inside the foyer to LuLu's vibrant and colorful apartment filled with tastefully dressed people there for the surprise birthday party she was throwing Alek. As she handed her topper to the uniformed butler and picked up a flute of champagne from those on the table in the foyer, she wondered if she'd made the right choice to attend.

Alessandra greeted those she knew with a cheerful grin and press of her lips to their cheeks, recognizing ADG executives and board members in the mix. She spotted LuLu across the room and made her way toward her. She was hard to miss in a towering head wrap and flowing bejeweled caftan.

"You came, and look how beautiful you look, Alessandra," LuLu said with a stunning red-lipped smile.

They shared a warm hug.

"I didn't bring a gift," Alessandra said. "What do you get the man who has everything?"

LuLu waved her hand dismissively. "He won't mind. Let me tell you a little something about my sweet eldest son," she said, wrapping her arm around Alessandra's as they moved through the mingling crowd with ease. "Every year on his birthday he buys me a gift to thank me for bringing him into the world."

Alessandra took a sip of her champagne, imagining a showy expensive gift.

LuLu extended her arm. A delicate charm bracelet dangled around her wrist. "It arrived this morning. And every little charm has meaning. It was a very thoughtful gift," she said, stroking it with her fingertips.

Yes, it is.

LuLu came to a stop and faced Alessandra. "He appears hard and unreachable, Alessandra, but my son is a good man with a great heart and integrity," she said. "I'll admit he won't show it easily, but once he does he holds nothing back."

Alessandra tried in vain to pull from the tricks of the trade she'd relied on the last five years to present the right image, to be stoic, even cold. In that moment, she failed and knew she had to flee before her tears rose and fell. "You're very lucky, Ms. Ansah, to have such a good son," she said before walking away quickly, pressing her nails into the flesh of her palm to shock herself out of her feelings.

She stopped before a wall of Ghanaian artwork and artifacts that were vibrant against the stark white of the wall. She leaned in to study a picture of a beautiful little girl of about ten who was wet with her hair plastered to her scalp by the water. She didn't know whether to be drawn into figuring out the emotions in her brown eyes or deciding whether it was a digital photo or a painting. *Wow.*

"It's a painting by Ghanaian artist Jeremiah Quarshie."

Alessandra stepped back and smiled at Samira standing beside her looking radiant in a bright red strapless dress that glowed against her chocolate skin. "Hello, Samira," she said. "How have you been?"

Samira smiled at her. "Patiently waiting to hear from you," she said, her eyes twinkling with humor but still determined.

Alessandra flushed with guilt. The Jubilee celebration seemed so long ago. She had gotten so lost in Alek that she hadn't given Samira's request for help any further thought. "I did speak to Alek about it, but I admit I got distracted. Forgive me," she said, reaching out to squeeze the woman's hand.

Samira clasped hers back. "The birthday boy is a handful, right?" she said, nodding in understanding.

Alessandra's heart swelled with sadness. Even with her conflicting feelings on her relationship with Alek, she had missed him during the last two weeks. "Yes, he is."

Samira eyed her oddly.

"What?" Alessandra asked, looking down at herself.

Samira's eyes brightened with awareness before she smiled. "Alek, Alek, Alek," she said. "Good luck, love."

She turned and walked away.

Alessandra didn't stop her or bother to convince her otherwise of whatever she revealed in her face about her feelings for Alek. *I should go.*

LuLu clapped her hands. "Alek is on his way up," she said, motioning for the music playing softly in the background to end as Samira and Naim joined her by the elevator.

Alessandra felt so anxious she was light-headed.

"Where is Chance?" LuLu asked, turning to look about the crowd until she spotted him and waved urgently. "Come on."

Over the rim of her glass Alessandra eyed the tall, handsome man making his way through the crowd in a navy blazer, shirt and slacks. She'd never met Chance Castillo but she knew he was Alek's best friend. He reached LuLu and her children just a moment before the elevator doors opened.

Alek's eyes widened as he stood there in all black. "Surprise!"

Alek playfully stepped back onto the elevator, but Naim and Chance rushed behind him to pull him into the foyer before they each hugged him close and patted his back.

Alessandra felt left out as she stood there in the background watching his family and friends greet him. For months, they had created a world with no one but them. Being there in the crowd felt so achingly different from the intimate moments they shared.

When Alek began to look about the crowd she wondered for whom he was searching, until his eyes landed on hers. They locked. She couldn't hold back her smile when his face lit at the sight of her. As he made his way through the crowd, she was unable to resist doing the same. In that moment, she was willing to risk it all just to feel his lips on hers. Be damned who saw.

Alessandra's steps faltered before she came to a stop at the sight of a beautiful woman in a crimson-red strapless jumpsuit stepping in front of Alek, pressing her hands to the lapels of his blazer before she eased them up around his neck.

He lightly grabbed her wrists and lowered her arms to keep her from wrapping them around his neck as he cast Alessandra an apologetic look. She was thankful no one was aware of the little drama that just unfolded as she gave him a tight smile and raised her flute to him in a toast before she turned and walked away.

I knew I shouldn't have come.

Stiffening her back, she moved away from the crowd. "Restroom, please?" she asked a passing waiter.

"Last door at the end of this hall," he directed her.

Alessandra nodded and hurried down the hall, quickly entering and closing the door behind herself. She licked her lips and sat her flute on the marble counter as she studied her reflection. Her regret was palpable.

I never should have started this with Alek.

I never should have let him in my heart.

I never should have come here.

She swore in a harsh whisper, closing her eyes and tilting her head back as she fought so hard to maintain her composure.

She opened her eyes and was startled to see the woman in the red jumpsuit in the reflection behind her. *What the...*

"So, you're Alessandra," she said.

Alessandra turned, her eyes shifting to the door she forgot to lock and back to the woman. "And you are?" she asked.

"I'm Kenzay Ansah, Alek's wife."

"Ex-wife," Alessandra countered, feeling the woman's animosity radiate toward her. "And?"

Am I going to have to hurt her?

Kenzay smiled before she shifted her eyes past Alessandra to study her reflection and play with her hair. "*And...* I wanted to meet the little sucker Alek was so desperate to get rid of that he was willing to seduce her into submission...if his attempts to sway the board to vote you out failed," she taunted, locking her cold eyes on her again.

For a moment, Alessandra felt taken back to her time as Alex, the girl who was afraid of her own shadow, lacked confidence and just wanted to be forgotten.

But just for a moment.

That wasn't her any longer.

"Kenzay, I don't know you and you don't know me, but if you think coming in here brimming with insecurity and immaturity, hoping that I will dwell with you there, is a good look then you are not only desperate and attention-seeking but dead-ass wrong," she said, her voice stone-cold and her eyes brimming with her disdain. "Let me introduce you, little girl, to what you hope to be one day, which is a grown-ass woman. Go find someone else to play with."

Alessandra picked up her flute of champagne and her clutch before leaving the woman standing there with her mouth open in shock.

Where did she go? Where is Alessandra?

After he bypassed Kenzay, Alessandra turned away from him. He followed behind her but the party guests kept stopping him to wish him well and he lost sight of her.

Although he knew nothing of the party and hadn't invited his ex-wife, he felt an urgency to explain himself to Alessandra. Things were already so off between them.

He never reminded her that she'd stood him up but quietly clung to his anger and jealousy, pulling a deliberate stunt by taking another woman to an event he initially had no plans on attending to avoid going to Passion Grove. It was an irrational move and childish act that he regretted.

And so he fled under the premise of work out of the country, needing space to grapple with his feelings for her—his want of her.

Over the last couple of weeks, Alek had also noticed a shift in Alessandra. The warmth in her voice disappeared and their conversations outside of business were brief. He wondered if their time together was over. He hoped not.

He missed her.

He loved her.

And he decided that he loved her enough to lay it all on the line and risk disappointment and hurt so that he would never wonder "what if."

When he entered his mother's apartment he was surprised by the birthday party, but not pleased. His intention had been to spend a little time with his family, collect his gift, blow out candles and then head out to find Alessandra. His anxiousness about working the room for a little while before taking his leave evaporated when he spotted Alessandra standing out among the crowd with her eyes locked on him.

Nothing had mattered to him more than getting to her.

And then Kenzay swooped in.

Did she leave?

He turned and spotted her just as she came out of the guest bathroom. "Alessandra," he called out, heading toward her.

She met him halfway, surprising him when she grabbed his wrist and pulled him out onto the balcony.

"I missed you," he moaned, reaching for her hips and leaning in to finally kiss her.

Alessandra tilted her head back from him and scowled.

Uh-oh.

"Did you try to rally the board to vote me out?"

she asked, crossing her arms over her chest as she eyed him.

Damn.

Any ideas of sharing a passionate kiss with her quickly faded. He released a heavy breath and looked up to the dark skies.

"Wow, Alek," she said in disbelief. "Just…wow."

He looked at her. "That was in the beginning, Alessandra. That was before we even linked up to—"

"Screw?" she interjected angrily.

He frowned. "Don't do that, Alessandra. I was going to say before we linked up on the airline deal."

"Don't do that?" she asked with calm. "What you shouldn't have done, Alek Ansah, is seduce me just to weaken my interest in the business and then let your ex-wife—and God knows who else—know all about it."

Alek's face immediately filled with guilt. "That was a joke, Alessandra, I swear," he said, remembering the dinner party at Chance's apartment.

He reached for her, and she shook her head and held up her hand as she stepped back. His heart ached to see the tears brimming in her eyes as she fought so hard to maintain her calm.

"You'll do anything to get me out of the company," she said with a bitter laugh. "Just like you threatened to cut your sister off to keep her from entering the business. Right?"

Alek felt desperate, as if he were trying to contain sand that slipped through his open fingers.

"I love you, Alessandra," he said, praying she could see the sincerity in his eyes.

"No, you do not," she said plainly. "Don't go that far, Alek. Don't cross every line."

"I love you," he stressed, grasping her arm and trying to lock eyes with her. "Please believe me."

"Stay the hell away from me if it has nothing to do with ADG," she said, roughly jerking her arm from his grasp and entering the apartment through the balcony door before disappearing into the crowd.

"Damn," Alek swore, trying to follow behind her, but he was surrounded by his guests.

He lost sight of her and knew he couldn't catch up to her.

Curiosity was killing LuLu.

She eased away from the party, entered her master suite and crossed the room to step out onto the balcony. She shivered in the coldness but she still clutched the metal railing of her balcony and looked down at the row of chauffeured cars on the street below. It wasn't hard to spot Alessandra's vintage Jaguar, nor for her to pick out her driver among those chauffeurs braving the night chill to pass their time waiting together.

"Roje," she whispered, pressing a hand to her pounding heart.

"What you shouldn't have done, Alek Ansah, is seduce me just to weaken my interest in the business and then let your ex-wife—and God knows who else— know all about it."

First LuLu's eyes widened and then her mouth dropped at the sound of Alessandra's raised voice. They had to be on the balcony in the great room. *Alek did what?*

"That was a joke, Alessandra, I swear."

Oh, Alek.

LuLu was torn between rudeness at eavesdropping and a mother's innate curiosity about her children's lives. And she did listen on and she felt like weeping because it was clear they both were hurting.

"I love you. Please believe me."

LuLu heard the raw emotion in her son's voice and knew him well enough to know he spoke the truth of his heart. *Alek is in love.*

"Stay the hell away from me if it has nothing to do with ADG."

And Alessandra loved him, as well. That level of hurt and anger were the shadows to being deeply in love. That LuLu knew as she took off across her bedroom suite in her heels. She denied herself happiness and love. She did not want that for any of her children.

They already sneaked this past me.

LuLu made it down the hall and onto the elevator behind Alessandra just before the doors closed. She looked down to make sure her flowing caftan hadn't been caught. "Come, come, come, come, come," LuLu said, beckoning her with her fingers at seeing the young woman's emotions on overload.

They shared a brief look before LuLu closed the distance and embraced her. Moments later, Alessandra's body shook with her tears. "I know about you and Alek," she admitted as she stroked the woman's back and gently rocked their bodies. "I overheard your argument on the balcony."

"Oh no," Alessandra wailed. "Did everyone hear us?"

"No, just me," LuLu said, leaning back to look at

her as she wiped away the track of her tears with her thumb.

The elevator came to a stop and LuLu took Alessandra's hand in hers to lead her to a sitting area in the lobby. "I know you think I am saying this because he is my son, but I heard the love he has for you in my son's voice, Alessandra," she said. "Before I was his mother, I was a woman who lived and loved and lost."

Alessandra removed tissues from her clutch and pressed them to her cheeks. "I'm sorry but I don't believe that," she admitted.

"What do you believe?" LuLu asked.

"I believe that Alek betrayed me. I believe he would go to any lengths to oust me from the company," Alessandra said, releasing a heavy breath before she continued. "I believe I am so disappointed that I feel betrayed by my own heart."

LuLu's ached for her. "The only advice I have is to remember the time you shared and follow your gut if you really believe all of it was fake. I believe you're smarter than that, Alessandra. Don't you?"

"I thought I was smart enough not to risk everything I worked so hard to establish in business for a man, and well, I guess I wasn't that smart, after all," she said, rising to her feet. "I left my jacket."

"Would you like me to go up and get it?" LuLu asked.

"No, that's okay," she said, taking out her phone. "I'll just make sure my driver turns up the heat."

LuLu looked up at her. "Your parents loved each other and in time they were lost to each other, but I promise you neither one regretted the love. They would want that for you. I want that for my son."

Alessandra's lingering sadness was clear. "Thank you for your kindness," she said.

LuLu rose as well, walking her to the door.

The doorman held the door open for them.

"Thank you, William," LuLu told him before turning back to Alessandra. "I hope you think of what I've said."

Alessandra remained quiet.

Roje spotted them and came walking up to them, quietly standing beside Alessandra with his eyes resting on LuLu.

"Life is too short to deny yourself love," LuLu said, unable to look away from him.

Alessandra hugged her. "Seems like advice you could use as well, Ms. Ansah," she said before turning and walking away.

LuLu barely felt the cold as she stood there lost in the regret in Roje's eyes.

"Ms. Ansah." Roje greeted her with a nod before finally breaking their stare and following behind Alessandra.

She watched as he helped Alessandra into the rear of the Jaguar before looking back at her. With one last glance at him, she walked back inside determined to be okay with her decision to deny herself love.

Alek was on the chase.

He wasn't a violent man. He didn't want to lay hands on his ex-wife, but he would pay good money to lay eyes on hers.

He wiped his mouth with his hands as he flipped over his iPhone and called Kenzay's phone number for the third time. It went straight to voice mail. "Shit," he swore.

Alek looked up as Chance and his fiancée, Helena, came toward him where he stood away from the crowd by the entrance to the kitchen.

"You're missing the party," Chance said, handing Alek the extra glass of champagne he carried.

"Have either of you seen Kenzay?" he asked them.

Chance shook his head.

"She left," Helena said, the diamonds of her numerous bracelets and her engagement ring shining brightly as she tucked her blond hair behind her ear. "Something about a headache."

Alek gritted his teeth as he slid his phone into the inside pocket of his blazer. "She's the damn headache," he muttered.

Helena made a face. "That's not nice, Alek," she said before playfully pouting.

Chance and Alek shared a brief look.

"What isn't nice is her telling Alessandra that I was planning a hostile takeover of the business and—"

"Weren't you, though?" Helena said lightly with a wince.

Alek looked at Chance again.

"And that I planned to seduce her to get her to leave the business," he added, his ire rising.

Helena seemed oblivious to it. "You *did* say it. I was there," she said.

Alek frowned. "So, your moral compass says it's okay to be mean and spiteful to a woman you don't even know just because you're jealous?" he asked, his tone hostile. "Then what does that say about you?"

Chance eased in between them. "We're gonna head on out, Alek," he said.

Alek held up his hands. Helena irked his spirit but she still was his best friend's bride-to-be. "Nope. Y'all stay. I'm leaving," he said, turning and striding away.

He reached the foyer, happy that the partygoers didn't even notice him as he summoned the elevator. The doors opened and he was surprised to see his mother exiting. He noticed her sadness. "Ma, you okay?" he asked.

She forced a smile that didn't reach her eyes. "I wasn't happy to overhear that my son even joked about playing with a woman's heart for any reason," she said.

His broad shoulders slumped and he looked down at his feet. "It's all a misunderstanding," he explained.

She grasped his chin and tilted his head up. "Then go fix it," she said before patting his cheek and then gently nudging him onto the elevator. "We'll cut the cake and open presents tomorrow. Okay?"

"I will, but first it's time to get some clarity with Kenzay," he said.

"Make it clear that when she invites herself to a party she shouldn't upset invited guests, so she is no longer welcome in my home," LuLu said with a broad smile just before the elevator doors closed.

Alek couldn't get the look of hurt and betrayal in Alessandra's eyes out of his mind. He hurt because he knew she was hurt.

You'll do anything to get me out of the company.

There was a time he would have, but she had gained his respect.

The elevator doors opened and he quickly strode across the marble lobby out the door to the street. Before he reached the curb, Julius was pulling the black Bentley Mulsanne out of his parking spot down the street and easing to a stop in front of the building. "The Peninsula Hotel, Julius," he said as he soon as he slid onto the rear seat and closed the door.

The Peninsula was Kenzay's go-to spot when she was in town.

As Julius sped up the street, Alek thought he spotted a flash of red as they passed a parked SUV. "Pull over, Julius," he said, already reaching for the handle before the car came to a complete stop.

Alek jogged up the street and pulled open the door to the SUV. Kenzay looked at him before glancing away with a bored sigh.

"Hey," the driver yelled out, turning around in his seat.

"What was your purpose tonight, Kenzay?" he asked, his voice cold and unrelenting.

"Awww, did Kenzay make someone cry?" she asked, her voice petulant as she pulled a compact from her clutch. It lit her face when she opened it, exposing her smugness.

Alek paused as he looked at her and really saw her for the first time. "What did Alessandra ever do to you?" he asked.

She snapped her compact closed as looked at him. "She took your attention off of me," she said. "No other woman has ever made you reject me, *and* in public. That was a first for us, and if you ever want to have me again it best be the last."

This was about her ego and her belief that she controlled him.

"I love her, Kenzay," he said. "If I lose Alessandra because of you—"

"Because of *me*?" Kenzay retorted. "I shouldn't have that much power in your silly little relationship. If I'm able to make it crumble just like that...then it was already broken somewhere."

He hated that there was truth in her words. His relationship with Alessandra—if it could be called that—had not been perfect at all. The hesitance to be together. The secrecy of their dealings. The resistance to accepting her just as easily in the boardroom as the bedroom.

"We're done, Kenzay," he said, his anger with her dissipating. "It's time we both moved on for good."

She looked at him for a long time. Even the driver shifted uncomfortably in his seat. "She gets the love you never gave me?" she asked.

He shook his head. "I'm calling foul on that, Kenzay. Alessandra has nothing to do with the love we didn't have for each other," he stressed, stepping back and reaching for the door.

"You'll call me, but will I answer, that's the question," she said, her feigned hurt gone and replaced by her conceit again.

"Goodbye, Kenzay," Alek said, closing the car door firmly before he turned and walked away.

He didn't flinch or look back when Kenzay began screaming expletives out the window of the SUV detailing just what he could with both his head and his goodbyes. He was thankful when he climbed back in the Bentley and closed the door, shutting her tirade off as he called Alessandra's phone.

It rang just once.

She was sending his calls to voice mail.

He slumped down in the back of the car and covered his eyes with his fingers. He felt sick.

"Where to now?" Julius asked.

"Passion Grove," he said, sitting up to text Alessandra.

I LOVE YOU, ALESSANDRA. WE NEED TO TALK. PLEASE ANSWER. PLEASE CALL ME.

He had no shame. He wanted her back.

During the nearly one-hour drive Alek forced himself not to continue to text her like an obsessed stalker.

As they drove through the quiet streets of Passion Grove he thought back to all the time they shared there. An ache of loss radiated across his chest.

Julius pulled the car up to the gate of her estate and Alek jumped out of the car to walk up to the security video camera. "Hey, fellas," he said with a wave. "Is Alessandra home?"

"Good evening, Mr. Ansah," a voice said through the intercom. "I'm sorry, but Ms. Dalmount has alerted us not to allow you on the estate, sir."

He turned just as Julius respectfully rolled the driver's-side window up.

"Could you call her, please?" he asked.

"We've been instructed not to, sir."

Through the gate, Alek looked up the long drive as he paced. The irony of it all was not lost on him. He finally laid his feelings out for her and he could understand her inability to trust that the words were true.

He moved back over to the security camera. "Were

you instructed not to call anyone else on the property?" he asked, thinking quickly on his feet.

The pause was lengthy.

"No, sir," the male voice finally answered.

"Then please call her aunt Leonora for me," he said.

As he waited, Alek knew the sense of urgency he felt was brought on by his guilt. He had tried to orchestrate her removal from ADG and for that he had been wrong.

He turned as light suddenly radiated across his body. It gradually brightened. Soon he distinguished the golf cart coming down the drive. He slid his hands into his pockets as he stood facing the gate. It came to a stop and he watched as Leonora exited wearing a fur with a hood. She came to stand on the other side of the gate as she lit a cigarette.

"Hello, Alek," she said, the tip of her extra-long cigarette reddening as she inhaled. "The camera and intercoms are off."

He nodded as he stepped closer to the gate. "I need to speak with Alessandra," he said.

"Listen, I can see a lot from my bedroom balcony. I honestly don't think you spent every weekend for the last three months cooped up in that guesthouse with my niece just to get her away from ADG," she said firmly. "The vote could have done that. Okay?"

"Okay," he said, surprised that she knew of their relationship.

"She's gone, Alek," she said, pausing to take another draw. "Best advice I can give you is to allow her the time she needs. Okay?"

He felt gut-punched as he nodded and stepped back from the gate. She was gone. He remembered when he wanted that so badly. Now it broke his heart. With a final nod of understanding he walked back to the Bentley and got in the rear. As Julius reversed, the lights from the golf cart and the red flame of her cigarette eventually disappeared.

Chapter 11

One month later

Alessandra smiled as Roje drove her past the large bronze sign welcoming them back to Passion Grove, New Jersey. Snow covered the tops of buildings and the ground. Christmas decor was in abundance. It was the holiday season.

"Feel good to be back?" Roje asked, eyeing her in the rearview mirror.

"Yes," she admitted without hesitation.

"I'm very happy you're back," he said. "Driving Marisa around has been an…adventure."

Alessandra nodded, glancing out the window at the line of storefronts before glancing back at him. "Thank you for letting me know what's going on with her, Roje," she said. "I'm disappointed to hear her partying has advanced to drug use."

"She needs you," was all that he said.

Alessandra had been working out of the London offices for the last month, needing a break from Alek and her foolish feelings for him. That night she had fled home to Passion Grove, falling into a crying heap at her aunt's feet in her bedroom suite. When Alek came to the security gate she had been safely ensconced in a ball in the middle of her aunt's bed and Leonora had gone down to the gate to lie to him for her. Alessandra had never appreciated her more.

The next morning, she packed an overnight bag and headed out on the company jet for an early flight to London. There was an executive penthouse apartment in London, but Alek had resided there for five years and she knew it would be too much to take. She spent one night at the Four Seasons Hotel and the next day moved into a spacious four-bedroom, four-bathroom furnished home after a call to Harrods Estates. Shiva arrived for the day to shop for her wardrobe, organize her massive walk-in closet, and find a hairdresser/makeup artist to use while she was in London.

That Monday she was spit-shined and polished for her first day working out of the London office without a bit of notice to her team of her arrival. That had been fun to see them all scramble to accommodate one of their bosses.

Between exploring England and work, she had almost been able to forget him.

Almost.

Her hurt was still there. It still nagged at her, but time had dulled it to an ache and not a piercing pain that radiated. She felt better prepared to return to the offices Monday with her head held high and her dignity and poise intact.

As they drove past the frozen heart-shaped pond, she sat up to look at all the townspeople either ice-skating or figure skating, their faces filled with joy and happiness. *I'm home*, she thought, sitting back when the frivolity on the lake was no longer in sight.

Soon they were coasting up the long driveway to the house. "The main house, Roje," she said.

"Luggage, too?" he asked.

"Yes."

He nodded as he pulled to a stop before exiting to open her door and assist her out.

"Thank you, Roje," she said, giving his hand a gentle squeeze before releasing it.

As she walked up the steps she paused, turning to look at Roje removing her hard-side suitcase from the trunk. "Roje, how are you?" she asked.

Myriad emotions showed on his face ranging from surprise to understanding.

He knew she was asking of LuLu Ansah.

He smiled. "The same," he said.

She offered him a smile and left it at that. There was a line of privacy she was trying not to cross. She took it to the line and leaned against it, but she did not want to step over.

As soon as she opened one of the towering double doors to enter the foyer, the twins came running across her path with high-pitched squeals. "Harper and Parker!" she shouted.

They stopped and turned to look at her. Their eyes were wide and their little barrel chests heaved with their exertion.

"Walk where you're going," she said sternly. "You're *not* outside. Respect my house."

They looked at each other briefly before looking back at her.

"Do you understand me?" she asked, knowing they were confused by being disciplined by her. "Yes, ma'am or no, ma'am?"

"Yes, ma'am," they said in unison desolately.

"Shoo-shoo," she said.

They walked away holding hands but soon she heard their feet pounding the floors as they upped it back to a run. Memories of her time in the guest-house with Alek made it uninhabitable for Alessandra and she was moving back into the master suite in the main house. The twins would have to be reined in. In fact, everyone would. Aunt Leonora's drinking. Aunt Brunela's resentment for not being given the same opportunity as her niece. Victor's philandering with staff. His wife's lackluster discipline of the twins.

She walked to the side of the grand staircase to take the hall leading into the dining room. Aunt Leonora stood beside her aunt Brunela, who sat at the table with her head bent and her shoulders shaking with tears.

"I'm sure Marisa is okay, sis," Leonora said, picking up a half-filled glass tumbler of heavily diluted orange.

"Where is Marisa?" Alessandra asked, coming to stand behind one of the parson chairs.

They both looked to her in surprise before coming over to hug her and press a kiss to her cheek.

"Thank God you're back," Brunela said, wiping her tears with a satin handkerchief that was already damp from her weeping. "You're the only one Marisa listens to, Alessandra."

"What happened?" she asked, feeling alarmed.

"She's been partying pretty hard lately," Leonora said. "And didn't come home last night at all."

Brunela cried out in anguish and slumped back down onto her chair.

Driving Marisa around has been an...adventure. Roje.

She turned and quickly strode down the length of the hall.

"Alessandra, where are you going?" Leonora called behind her.

"Hopefully to find Marisa," Alessandra said over her shoulder before she flung the door open and raced down the steps.

Roje was just pulling off in the Jag.

Alessandra waved frantically to get his attention.

He stopped and lowered the window.

"Did you drive Marisa last night?" she asked as she rushed over to the car.

He shook his smooth bald head. "She drove one of the cars to a weekend party."

"You know where?" Alessandra asked, already climbing in the back of the car.

"She texted me the address when she wanted me to drive her at first."

"Take me there, please," she said, rotating her head on her neck to remove the tension steadily building.

"Right away," Roje said, accelerating down the drive.

As he drove through the streets of Passion Grove and then out toward Manhattan, Alessandra wrestled with whether to share with her aunts what Roje told her about Marisa using cocaine. She'd come home from London earlier than she planned to try to get her cousin in rehab.

Roje slowed the Jaguar to a stop in front of a modest brick home in a suburban neighborhood forty minutes outside of Midtown Manhattan. Alessandra looked around at the tree-lined streets filled with modest homes with cars and SUVs parked nearly bumper-to-bumper. "You sure this is the right address, Roje?" she asked.

His head bent as he looked down at his phone to double-check the address. "This is it," he said, looking through the driver's-side window.

"Okay, I don't see any parking, so you circle the block and come back to pick us up," she said, climbing from the back of the car and pulling the red wool coat she wore tighter around the white T-shirt and distressed jeans she wore with high-heeled boots.

Alessandra walked up the snow-covered path to the small stoop. She was admittedly nervous as she rang the doorbell. She looked up and down the stretch of homes as she waited.

The door opened and a tall, slender woman with bright red hair and freckles stood there. "Yes?" she said.

"I was looking for Marisa. Is she still here?" Alessandra said, looking past her at the living room. Her eyes widened to see her cousin stark naked and dancing atop a table.

She brushed past the redhead, already removing her coat, as she reached up to snatch Marisa down off the table. The crowd of people in the living room either laughed or complained. Alessandra ignored them all as she wrapped the coat around her cousin's nakedness.

"We're leaving now," she said as Marisa tried to resist her, but was too high to muster the strength to succeed.

Boom.

Alessandra froze as the front door flew wide open and the police in SWAT gear rushed inside the house as people scattered.

"Everybody down," several police officers roared.

"Uh-oh, we in trouble now, coz," Marisa whispered, before bursting into a fit of foolish giggles.

More than thirty days had passed and his love for Alessandra had not faded one bit. But she also had not returned from London or spoken to him outside of conference calls to deal with their business. He ached for her. Still.

With a sigh, he looked down at a photo he'd taken of her the night of the Jubilee Ball from across the room. He'd never told her about the picture, and over the last month he'd often turn to it when he missed her in his life, his bedroom and their boardroom. She wasn't at all the wife he envisioned over the years but he couldn't imagine loving anyone else the way he cared for Alessandra.

He put away his phone and looked over his shoulder from where he sat at the front of the church's sanctuary. Although Chance and Helena had planned their wedding in just a month, the church was filled with their guests and elaborately decorated with flowers and white satin. Through the clear glass panes at the top of the entry doors he spotted Chance and Helena in the vestibule talking emphatically. She was in her gown and veil, but it was clear Chance's face was lined with anger.

This ain't looking good.

When the wedding planner, Olivia Joy, quietly entered the sanctuary Alek rose and made his way to her.

He forced himself to keep his pace slow and leisurely as he made his way down the side aisle, ignoring the curious looks of his own family. "What's going on?" he asked Olivia when he reached her.

She leaned in close. "The wedding's off," she whispered to him.

Alek's eyes widened in surprise. "Okay, let me check on my boy," he said, opening the door when she eased from in front of it.

The front doors to the church were wide open and Chance stood in the doorway taking the brunt of the December chill that blew in. "You okay, Chance?" he asked, coming to stand beside him.

Chance shrugged one shoulder as he shook his head. *"Elegir una esposa más bien por su oído que su ojo,"* he said.

Choose a wife rather by your ear than your eye.
Alek remained quiet; he didn't know Helena very well and their relationship had been a whirlwind.

"She's gone. She was double-dipping with her ex and seems he didn't have a problem sharing the goodies as long as she wasn't a wife," he said, his voice cold.

Alek winced. He hadn't seen that coming.

"I'm sorry, Chance," he said, reaching over to give his shoulder a solid but comforting pat.

Chance clenched his jaw. *"Usted debe cumplir la aspereza con la aspereza,"* he said, the usual warmth in his eyes replaced with bristling anger.

You must meet roughness with roughness.

Alek dropped his hand, surprised by his friend's rage. In all the years of their friendship Chance was the lighthearted, fun-loving one. He rarely turned to fury. "Hey, you all right, man?" he asked.

Chance smiled but it didn't reach his eyes. "Let's go announce the wedding is off and turn the reception into a party, amigo," he said, turning to walk back into the church.

Olivia gave Alek a confused look as Chance strode past her and up the middle of the aisle.

"Take your team to the reception site and remove as much wedding stuff as you can and have the wedding cake completely sliced and put on plates," he said.

She unclipped a walkie-talkie from the waist of her skirt before she walked away.

As Chance spoke briefly with the minister at the front of the church, Alek turned and pulled his phone from the inner pocket of his tuxedo as it vibrated. "Google alert," he said. He had alert sets up for any mention of the Ansah Dalmount Group.

"'Billionaire heiress and ADG co-CEO Alessandra Dalmount arrested in drug bust,'" he read. "Wait. What?"

He read the headline again before opening the article and reading it in its entirety, his eyes widening and his heart pounding furiously. He was lost. *I thought Alessandra was still in London.*

In jail?
A drug bust?
This has to be a mistake, right?
What the hell?

The cold felt good.

Alessandra inhaled deeply of it, letting it fill her

lungs and invigorate her. Even one night of captivity had been too much, and freedom was sweet. Not enough to curb the anger that stewed overnight as she sat in a cell but enough where she didn't feel encaged.

"Alessandra—"

Sharply, she put up her hand to silence her cousin as they stood on the sidewalk outside the police station.

"You have a choice to make, Marisa," she said, staring down the street at the bustling traffic, unable to even look at her cousin. She did a double take when she thought she spotted Alek's Bugatti pulling out a parking spot down. She blinked and scrunched her face.

"About what?" Marisa asked.

Alessandra looked down at her, still dressed in her coat with her face puffy and reddish from her over-indulgence. "What?" she asked, glancing back down the street.

"You said I have a choice," Marisa said, using the sides of her hands to wipe her eyes.

Putting aside what she considered daydreams, Alessandra nodded as Roje pulled up in the Jaguar and climbed out to hand her a faux fur that was still luxuriously warm. "You okay?" he asked.

"No," she admitted before turning back to her charge. "Rehab or I'm done with you. I will love you always, but you are not coming back into my life or my home as an addict."

"Rehab!" Marisa shrieked, pushing back her wild array of curls that the wind blew in her face.

Alessandra glanced back at her personal attorney, Ngozi Johns, quietly standing off to the side in a brilliant red pantsuit and matching wool coat. "Ms. Johns's staff has located a long-term facility for you to get bet-

ter mentally and physically, Marisa," she said, pointing to an SUV that double-parked behind the Jaguar.
"Rehab with Ms. Johns or back to the estate with me
to pack your things and leave."

Marisa's eyes hardened and her mouth became a
straight line before she walked down the steps toward
the waiting SUV.

"I will call you when we arrive," Ngozi said.

"Thank you very much. I appreciate it—"

Marisa stopped in the middle of the street, causing
those passing by to quickly shift to avoid her. "You
can't just put me out. I have rights. You have to evict
me. Right? Doesn't she have to evict me?" Marisa
cried out, her desperation so abundantly clear.

"She's right," Ngozi said, her voice just for Alessandra's ears.

Alessandra came down the steps, brushing off Roje's
hand when he reached for her wrist. "Is that how you
want to do this? In this moment where you can choose
victory or defeat over your own damn life, is that the
level you want to sink to? Court? Eviction!" she snapped,
her eyes burning with hurt and anger. "Why is it every
damn time I try to help you, *you* make me suffer for it,
Marisa? Huh? Why is that? *Why?*"

Marisa lowered her head.

"Do you understand my career and everything I
worked hard for may be over? I have an arrest record. My *mug shot* is *all* over the news," Alessandra
stressed, pressing her hand to her chest as she eyed
her cousin. "But I didn't think of any of that because I
just wanted to help you. And that's how you want this
to go down? Because it can. Because I will. So you let
me know how we are doing this, Marisa."

"I'm sorry," she mouthed, a single tear racing down her cheek, before she turned and walked to the SUV and climbed inside without looking back.

Alessandra's shoulders dropped as she tucked her hands inside the deep pockets of her coat.

"The board wants to meet with you," Ngozi said, coming to stand beside her.

Alessandra felt like a vise grip closed down on her gut. She'd assumed they'd at least wait until Monday to call her on the carpet. She thought of Alek, something she rarely allowed herself to do, and she couldn't help but envision him with a smug expression as she was voted out of the company. *Just the way he always wanted.*

"Okay," Alessandra said, following Roje to the Jag to climb in the back as he held the door open.

She gave Ngozi a wave before she strode to the SUV and climbed into the rear beside Marisa.

"ADG, Roje," she said, crossing her legs in her distressed jeans as she sank down in the seat and closed her eyes.

As they made the drive to Manhattan, she felt her driver's eyes on her occasionally but she was thankful he respected her need for silence. She felt so embarrassed by having her life—her privacy—wrecked by the arrest. *And now I have to see Alek.*

A dull ache began to radiate across her nape, and by the time they reached the office and she made her way inside via her private entrance, it had not lessened. She entered the bathroom in her office and was thankful to remove every stitch of clothing she was sure still reeked of jail. As she showered and brushed her teeth, tears threatened to fall, but she refused to let them.

Dressed in a long-sleeved black lace dress with a wide skirt and her hair up in a tousled topknot, she felt more like herself as she paced her office waiting the five minutes before the meeting was to begin. She knew the procedure; the meeting had already begun. Decisions were being made. Votes cast. By the time she arrived her fate would be sealed.

Alek would have won.

Little sucker. Little sucker. Little sucker.

Alessandra covered her face with her hands, hating how foolish she felt. Still.

I love you, Alessandra. Please believe me.

She shook his deceiving words from her thoughts and checked her watch as she sat down, then quickly rose to her feet, leaving her iPhone on the sofa. She smoothed her hair up, straightened the skirt of her dress and stiffened her spine as she walked out of her office and made her way to the boardroom. Pretending she wasn't nervous. Pretending she wasn't embarrassed. Pretending she wasn't still heartbroken.

Her steps faltered at the sight of Ms. Kingsley sitting at the receptionist desk to the right. *Why is she here on a Saturday?*

"Good morning," Alessandra said, giving her a smile. More pretending.

Ms. Kingsley stood up, her face showing her unease. "Good morning, Ms. Dalmount. The board requested to be alerted when you arrived," she said, her face apologetic.

Alessandra arched a brow. "I think the board is confused as to who owns forty-nine percent of this building, and that's a fact no one can change, Ms.

Kingsley," she said, turning to open both doors to the boardroom at once.

Their vote could affect her position as CEO but not her ownership, and she refused to be disrespected regardless of anything.

All conversation ceased at the sight of her. Several of them looked at each other and shifted uncomfortably in their seats.

Her eyes fell on Alek. A kaleidoscope of emotions washed over her, mostly surprise that he had lost weight and wasn't quite as sharply groomed as usual. They shared a brief look before he focused his gaze out the window.

She took that for guilt and she hated that Alek Ansah could still hurt her.

Keep it together.

"Have a seat, Alessandra," Aldrich said, looking out of place in a polo shirt and sweatpants.

She crossed her hands in front of her and eyed each and every board member who would even look at her. "I prefer to stand," she said.

Aldrich shook his head as he patted his hand atop the table. "It's not like that," he said.

"Isn't it, though?" Alessandra returned.

Aldrich sighed. "As you know, an emergency board meeting was called in light of your arrest yesterday," he began. He then met her eyes, the bright blue of his unflinching. "It was an embarrassment to this company and the reputation both Kwame and Frances worked so hard to establish. As the CEO, it could immediately and detrimentally affect our standing, and certainly makes everyone including many in this room question your ability to effectively lead."

She briefly glanced at Alek's stoic profile. "I am not, nor have I ever been on drugs—"

Aldrich held up his hand. "That's good to hear, but it doesn't change the perception that you are," he said. "This was reckless and irresponsible, Alessandra, and made us wonder if you are truly fit to help run this company."

She knew he was right.

At the clearing of a throat, she looked toward Charlie Memminger, one of the few board members who had openly challenged Alessandra consistently.

"There is a little-known market out clause that was put in place by the original underwriters of ADG's initial public offering," he said, picking up a pair of spectacles from the table to slide on as he looked down at the piece of paper. "The clause—basically a morality clause—leaves the opportunity for one or both of the CEOs to be ousted if they do anything to the detriment of the company."

Alessandra was well aware of the clause but remained quiet. She knew with a majority vote by the board of the directors she would keep her stake in the company but be removed from her position and her seat on the board of directors. The arrest was scandalous and handed them a golden ticket to get rid of her.

She held up her hand. "I want a moment to speak because it is my character and my ability to lead that is in question, but it is in fact my leadership and my character that led to a very unfortunate event. My cousin was in need, my family was in crisis, and I am their leader. I wanted to fix it because I am a problem solver, but unfortunately, I was not fully aware of just what situation I got myself into when I simply went to pick up my cousin at the wrong place and definitely the wrong time."

"Alessandra, you do understand that a part of being a good leader is to avoid creating more problems to solve just one," Garrison Wyndham said, his face kind but still concerned.

"I agree, Garrison, I do," she said. "And it is a lesson to be learned for sure, but I think we all have to remember everything I have accomplished in the brief time since becoming cochief executive officer and have some foresight into what I can continue to do."

"And your family issues?" Aldrich asked.

"I have already entered her into a long-term rehabilitation facility," Alessandra said. "I do admit that it will take some good PR and spin to get control of it, and I will take on the cost of doing that, personally. Also, I have been advised by my personal attorney, Ngozi Johns, that the charges will be dropped. Listen, I apologize for the misstep and ensure you all that nothing remotely similar will ever happen again."

"I say we vote. A blind vote," Charlie said.

Alessandra's eyes went to Alek again. He remained stoic. "Without me in attendance?" she asked.

Aldrich motioned to the board's secretary and she quietly moved from her spot next to him to hand Alessandra a notepad with the ADG logo and a pen.

"As a board member, you do get a vote, as well," Aldrich said. "And once you cast yours we do ask you to step outside until we're done."

Ever defiant, she pushed the paper and pen aside. "Of course I vote that I retain my position as co-CEO and executive board member of the Ansah Dalmount

Group," she said, before turning to leave the board-room. She paced the length of the reception area.

"Ms. Kingsley, come in," Aldrich said into the in-tercom.

Alessandra gave her a soft smile as she rose to come around the desk and enter the boardroom, softly clos-ing the door.

Still pretending.

She had nothing to smile about.

Forgive me, Daddy.

"Alessandra."

She turned. Ms. Kingsley beckoned her in.

With a heavy breath, Alessandra strode back inside the boardroom. "And the vote is?" she asked.

"Do not let down those who voted for you to re-main, Alessandra," Aldrich said, rising to come around the table and offer her his hand.

She shook it with strength as relief flooded her. "Thank you. Thank you all. I will let not let *any* of you down again," she said.

Alek rose from his seat and stared at her. They shared a brief look before he left the room along with the rest of the board of directors.

Alessandra went to the window to look out at the New York cityscape as Ms. Kingsley walked to the door, as well. Alessandra felt like the weight of the world was on her shoulders, but she stiffened her back, straight-ened her shoulders and took a long, steadying breath.

"He voted for you to stay, Alessandra," Ms. Kings-ley said softly from behind her. "His vote broke the tie."

Alessandra turned from the window just as the

other woman left the boardroom and quietly closed
the door behind her, leaving her alone in total shock.

Alek saved me?

"Huh?" she said into the quiet of the room, her
heart racing. She was at a loss for words and clarity.
Her world felt topsy-turvy.

In just an instant everything she thought and assumed to be…wasn't.

Gathering herself quickly, she rushed from the
boardroom on her high heels to Alek's office only
to find it empty. Feeling an urgency to speak to him,
she went to his private elevator and rode it down to
the underground parking level, anxiously wringing
her hands.

Her heels beat against the concrete floor as she
looked at his designated parking spot. It was already
empty, and if he had his driver pick him up in the
front, she would never make it in time to catch him.
The breath she released was harsh as she placed a hand
on her hip and shook her head. Her adrenaline caused
her heart to pound and her pulse to race as she wondered just why Alek gave up his one surefire chance
to oust her from the company.

Alek was waiting in his car at the end of Dalmount
Lane in Passion Grove when her Jaguar turned the
corner. It pulled to a stop beside him and he climbed
from warmth and comfort just as the rear door opened,
and she did the same.

He felt like a bundle of pure nerves as the frigid
wind whipped around them.

Her surprise at seeing him was clear.

He was just as shaken by the sight of her as he was

earlier when she entered the boardroom. So much so that he couldn't stand to look at her and not rush across the room to embrace her. Kiss her. Love on her.

"Why did you vote for me to remain in my position at ADG?" she asked, her eyes on him.

That surprised him.

"I think you're qualified to do the job, Alessandra," he said. "I have come to value your intelligence, your insight and your vision for *our* company. I want you there to have my back the same way I will have yours."

She lightly chewed at her lips and leaned back against the Jag as she looked up the street and then back at him.

"Forgive me for the time I wasted trying to undermine you," he said, pulling the fitted wool cap he wore down over his ears.

Alessandra looked so unsure. "Thank you for the vote, Alek," she said, offering him a soft and hesitant smile. "But was it because of what we once shared?"

"I don't mix business with pleasure, Alessandra," he told her, his eyes locking on hers as he allowed himself to enjoy the sight of her before him. "Together, you and I are going to make ADG more successful."

They eyed each other, surrounded by winter and almost unaffected by the chill because that simmering chemistry they created was still there, pulsing and waiting to be acknowledged.

"In that second right after I found out you voted for me my mind went back to the night of the party," she admitted, digging her hand down deeper into the pockets of her fur. "And in that same second, I wondered if maybe—just maybe—you really did love me, Alek."

Her eyes were filled with her reluctance to believe in him. That pained him.

He stepped closer to her and reached in her pockets to take her cold hands into his own, rubbing them and warming them, just as he hoped he thawed her heart. "I will *always* love you, Alessandra."

He felt hopeful when her hands tightened around his.

The tears that filled her eyes tore at his soul, but he fought off his impulse to draw her into his arms. He understood that this was her choice, her opportunity to forgive. She had to come to him, not because of his ego but instead because of his acknowledgment of his wrongdoing.

"I stayed outside the police station all night in my car because I couldn't stand the thought of enjoying luxury while you sat in a jail cell," he confessed.

"So that was you I saw leaving this morning?" she asked.

Alek nodded. "I couldn't leave until I knew you were free."

"Wow," she said softly, looking down at their feet.

He freed one of her hands to lightly grab her chin and tilt her head up until their eyes locked once again. "That day on the island, I envisioned you there with me with our kids," he said. "I won't lie. I pushed aside that vision that came to me so easily because I thought I wanted something different, but now I know better, Alessandra."

"Oh, Alek."

"For the last month, I have dreamed of nothing more than you having my babies *and w*orking beside me to grow our business." He stepped back to drop down to his knee, thankful that the snow had been shoveled off the street.

She gasped at the sight of the five-carat engagement ring he held in his hand.

"I purchased this the day after you left for London and today I know I have to try. I have to ask, even if you say no. I have to tell you how much I love you and ask you to be my forever."

Alessandra came to him and pulled him up to his feet to kiss him softly. "I love you, too, Alek," she whispered in between kisses. "I love you so much."

"Yes, but will you marry me?" he asked, holding up the ring.

"I want it all and I deserve to have it all," she said, holding up her own hand and wiggling her ring finger. "Yes, I will be your forever."

He slid the ring on her finger.

"So the war is over?" she asked, leaning back in his embrace.

"Damn right. From now on it's nothing but love," he answered before he kissed her deeply with a moan of satisfaction.

Alessandra pulled the collar of his coat into her fists as she closed her eyes and kissed him back.

It felt good to be reconnected.

"Congratulations," Roje called out.

Alessandra and Alek broke their kiss to look on as he waved and drove toward the estate away from them.

"Let's go get heated," he said, moving around the car to open the passenger door for Alessandra to climb in.

He hurried to the driver's seat, driving with one hand to hold Alessandra's with the other.

"This is good," she said, smiling at him.

"This is damn good," he agreed.

Soon they were beyond the security gates.

"I live in the main house now," she said.

Alek shook his head. "Not tonight. No way. We have some catching up to do."

"Whatever you say, my love."

He pulled the Bugatti to a stop before the guest-house. When he left the car, he looked up and spotted her aunt Leonora on her balcony in the distance. She raised her glass of wine to him in tribute before disappearing inside her room and pulling the curtains on the patio doors closed.

Alek helped Alessandra out her car and picked her up to carry inside the cottage to make love to her.

Epilogue

Eight months later

Alessandra climbed the steps of the wrought iron staircase to reach the second level of their Georgian manor on the newly named Hope Island. The construction of the estate was complete and now their entire family and some close friends were there with them to celebrate the housewarming and their announcement of a new arrival to the Ansah-Dalmount clan. They were able to have up to thirty family members and friends there at one time.

Everything they envisioned that day as they explored the island had come to fruition.

She pressed a hand against her rounded stomach as she walked out onto the spacious balcony and took in the beautiful view of colorful gardens and extensive lawns.

At the sound of laughter, she looked down at their family enjoying the August weather on the hundred-foot terrace.

Nothing about love and life was perfection, but they were in a good place and happy.

Thank God.

Her plan to recover from the scandal of her arrest was effective, and eventually the news coverage of it died down and they were back to normal ADG business again. Plus, the announcement of their engagement had taken prominence anyway.

No one on the board saw that coming.

She smiled as her aunt Leonora and aunt Brunela both leaned against the whitewashed railings of the veranda, looking out as Marisa went running off the end of the deck to cannonball into the water with a huge splash. Her cousin had completed her rehabilitation program just a little under a month ago and so far, everyone could see the difference in her. The calm and reliability. She was different. But only time could truly tell. *I'm rooting for her.*

And so is Naim, she thought, noticing how his eyes kept going back to Marisa in her swim shirt and boy-cut bottoms, both accentuating her curvy, well-toned figure. After all the turmoil she and Alek put each other through, Alessandra didn't know if she could take another Dalmount-Ansah love match. Especially with Marisa finally in the right headspace to find her true self. *A relationship could be the wrong distraction.*

Samira sat on the middle of one of the thirty lounge chairs on the spacious terrace enjoying the sun beaming down on her bare shoulders in the strapless one-piece she wore, but still tapping away on her computer.

In the seven months since she began working at ADG, the young woman had been on a mission to prove herself. *She reminds me of myself.*

Victor went flying past on one of the Jet Skis.

Alessandra rolled her eyes. After one late night/ early morning stroll to the maid's quarters, his wife Elisabetta caught him with his pants down, literally, and reminded him they married without a prenuptial agreement. Once Alessandra made it clear she would not increase his allowance to cover the cost of alimony and child support, Victor curbed his doggish ways. *It seems the only thing Victor loves more than himself is his money.*

"You think they'll notice we sneaked off?" Alek asked as he walked into their massive master suite, already unbuttoning the white linen shirt he wore.

"Who cares?" Alessandra said, turning to lean back against the railing as she awaited her husband.

As the sun set, casting shadows in subtle shades of blues, Alek eased down the straps of her sundress and pressed kisses to her shoulder, clavicles and neck as he exposed her body for his eyes alone. She sighed in pleasure and pressed her hand to the back of his head as he knelt to press kisses to her belly.

"I love you," he said, looking up at her.

"More than I love you?" she asked, stroking his beard.

"Yes."

"Impossible."

* * * * *

LET'S TALK
Romance

For exclusive extracts, competitions
and special offers, find us online:

- **f** facebook.com/millsandboon
- 🐦 @MillsandBoon
- 📷 @MillsandBoonUK

Get in touch on 01413 063232

For all the latest titles coming soon, visit
millsandboon.co.uk/nextmonth